AN OPPORTUNITY TO EXPERIENCE TRULY
CONTEMPORARY THEATER—FROM THE
MASTERY OF SAMUEL BECKETT TO THE
NEW VOICE OF SUZAN-LORI PARKS

Ohio Impromptu by Samuel Beckett
In this 1983-84 Obie winner, the spare set and disturbing
exchange of two nearly identical characters convey Beckett's eloquent vision of the mystery, and the silence, at
the heart of existence.

The Danube by Maria Irene Fornes
Considered one of the nations's most gifted—but most
unrecognized—playwrights, Fornes creates a chilling play
about nuclear annihilation by transforming commonplace
conversation into unutterable anguish.

Edmond by David Mamet
The ''poetry of profanity'' remains the signature of the
creator of *Glengarry Glen Ross*, and the verisimilitude of
this tabloid odyssey of sex and violence is powerful and
provocative.

Imperceptible Mutabilities in the Third Kingdom
by Suzan-Lori Parks
All five sections of this surrealist, experimental work address
issues of black history and identity as each creates a disso-
nance between the words being spoken by the actors and the
visual imagery of projected slides above them.

AND FOUR MORE EXCITING WORKS THAT
WON THE COVETED OBIE . . .

Ross Wetzsteon, a senior editor at *The Village Voice*,
has served as Chairman of the Obie Awards Committee
since 1970. He is the editor of a previous collection of
plays, *The Obie Winners*.

MENTOR Books of Plays

☐ **EIGHT GREAT TRAGEDIES edited by Sylvan Barnet, Morton Berman and William Burto.** The great dramatic literature of the ages. Eight memorable tragedies by Aeschylus, Euripides, Sophocles, Shakespeare, Ibsen, Strindberg, Yeats and O'Neill. With essays on tragedy by Aristotle, Emerson and others. (626788—$5.99)

☐ **EIGHT GREAT COMEDIES edited by Sylvan Barnet, Morton Berman and William Burto.** Complete texts of eight masterpieces of comic drama by Aristophanes, Machiavelli, Shakespeare, Molière, John Gay, Wilde, Chekhov, and Shaw. Includes essays on comedy by four distinguished critics and scholars. (623649—$5.99)

☐ **THE GENIUS OF THE EARLY ENGLISH THEATRE edited by Sylvan Barnet, Morton Berman and William Burto.** Complete plays including three anonymous plays—"Abraham and Isaac," "The Second Shepherd's Play," and "Everyman," and Marlowe's "Doctor Faustus," Shakespeare's "Macbeth," Johnson's "Volpone," and Milton's "Samson Agonistes," with critical essays. (627490—$5.99)

☐ **SCENES AND MONOLOGUES FROM THE NEW AMERICAN THEATER Edited by Frank Pike and Thomas G. Dunn.** A collection of exciting, playable new scenes for two men, two women, or a man-woman team, plus 19 outstanding monologues. Fresh material from America's dynamic young playwrights. An essential book for every actor. (625471—$5.99)

Prices slightly higher in Canada.

Buy them at your local bookstore or use this convenient coupon for ordering.

PENGUIN USA
P.O. Box 999 – Dept. #17109
Bergenfield, New Jersey 07621

Please send me the books I have checked above.
I am enclosing $_____ (please add $2.00 to cover postage and handling). Send check or money order (no cash or C.O.D.'s) or charge by Mastercard or VISA (with a $15.00 minimum). Prices and numbers are subject to change without notice.

Card #_____ Exp. Date _____
Signature_____
Name_____
Address_____
City _____ State _____ Zip Code _____

For faster service when ordering by credit card call **1-800-253-6476**

Allow a minimum of 4-6 weeks for delivery. This offer is subject to change without notice.

THE BEST OF OFF-BROADWAY

Eight Contemporary Obie-Winning Plays

EDITED AND WITH
AN INTRODUCTION BY

Ross Wetzsteon

A MENTOR BOOK

MENTOR
Published by the Penguin Group
Penguin Books USA Inc., 375 Hudson Street,
New York, New York 10014, U.S.A.
Penguin Books Ltd, 27 Wrights Lane,
London W8 5TZ, England
Penguin Books Australia Ltd, Ringwood,
Victoria, Australia
Penguin Books Canada Ltd, 10 Alcorn Avenue,
Toronto, Ontario, Canada M4V 3B2
Penguin Books (N.Z.) Ltd, 182-190 Wairau Road,
Auckland 10, New Zealand

Penguin Books Ltd, Registered Offices:
Harmondsworth, Middlesex, England

First published by Mentor, an imprint of Dutton Signet,
a division of Penguin Books USA Inc.

First Printing, February, 1994
10 9 8 7 6 5 4 3 2 1

Library of Congress Cataloging Card Number: 93-079101

CAUTION: Professionals and amateurs are hereby warned that all the plays in
this volume are subject to a royalty. They are fully protected under the copyright laws of the United States of America, the British Commonwealth, including Canada, and all other countries of the Copyright Union. All rights, including
professional, amateur, motion pictures, recitation, lecturing, public reading,
radio broadcasting, television, and the rights of translation into foreign lan-
guages are strictly reserved.

PUBLISHER'S NOTE
These are works of fiction. Names, characters, places, and incidents either are the product of the authors' imagination or are used fictitiously, and any resemblance to actual
persons, living or dead, events, or locales is entirely coincidental.

To Laura—my companion
at the theater and in life

And to Rachel—my dd

Contents

Contents

Acknowledgments

I would like to thank my editor, Arnold Dolin, for his help in selecting the plays and for his careful attention to the manuscript, and Randy Gener, my intern at the *Village Voice*, for his energetic and always reliable assistance.

I am especially grateful to my fellow judges on the Obie committee, who have included, in the years covered by this anthology, the following:

Voice judges: Eileen Blumenthal, Cindy Carr, Michael Feingold, Terry Curtis Fox, Robert Massa, Erika Munk, Julius Novick, Gordon Rogoff, and Alisa Solomon.

Guest judges: Billie Allen, Rene Buch, Harold Clurman, Martha Coigney, Gautam Dasgupta, Clinton Turner Davis, Rosalyn Drexler, Gus Edwards, Max Ferra, Maria Irene Fornes, Richard Gilman, John Guare, Margo Jefferson, Woodie King, Norris Houghton, James Leverett, Margot Lewitin, Joan MacIntosh, Judith Malina, Edith Oliver, Lanford Wilson, and Linda Winer.

Introduction:
Forms of Celebration

"Let the games begin!" declared President Reagan to open the 1984 Olympics in Los Angeles, and in a sense his words were not merely a proclamation for the assembled athletes but the defining moment of the ebullient 1980s. "Let the games begin!"—what a stirring invitation to celebrate national pride, to reassert American hegemony abroad, to relax governmental restraints at home, to release economic expansiveness and exuberant acquisitiveness and the untrammeled pursuit of prosperity! "Let the games begin!"—what a symbolic signal for a nation at play!

Games indeed. For even before the decade came to an end, most Americans had become all too aware of the costs and consequences of our manic celebration—debilitating recession, Wall Street scandals, the savings and loan debacle, and a soaring national debt, to say nothing of the problems hardly even acknowledged, from recrudescent racism to revived assaults on women's rights, from the AIDS plague to the precipitous decline in social services, from the increasing gap between rich and poor to the ugly divisiveness of differing cultural values.

Many Americans refused to join in the games, of course—in addition to the millions the games ruthlessly excluded—and among those who attempted to warn their countrymen about the misery beneath the frivolity, the greed behind the exultation, the waste accompanying the prodigality, were many of the playwrights of Off-Broadway. As a character in David Mamet's *Edmond* put it, "The world seems to be crumbling around us," and as Eric Bogosian wrote in his introduction to *Sex, Drugs,*

Rock & Roll, "My brain is finally clearing up the morning after the big party."

Indeed, all the playwrights in this anthology, in one way or another, voice their unease at the excesses of the American spree, their concern at its fracturing of communal commitment, their rage at its debasement of the nation's principles. David Mamet, in *Edmond,* exposes the spiritual emptiness of the middle class the Reagan Revolution supposedly liberated. Christopher Durang, in *The Marriage of Bette and Boo,* reveals the hypocrisies of the "family values" championed by the religious right. Wallace Shawn, in *Aunt Dan and Lemon,* cautions against the complacency concealing a resurgence of fascist impulses. The ever-present threat of nuclear annihilation is the theme of Irene Fornes's *The Danube.* The inescapable persistence of racial stereotypes is forcefully reasserted in Suzan-Lori Parks's *Imperceptible Mutabilities in the Third Kingdom.* Samuel Beckett, in *Ohio Impromptu*—as his plays have been doing for decades—grimly reminds us of the grief that awaits us all. Eric Bogosian, in *Sex, Drugs, Rock & Roll,* hilariously but brutally depicts the moral corruption of our materialistic culture. And Craig Lucas, in *Prelude to a Kiss*—even while enchanting us with his fairy tale of the transforming power of love—painfully evokes the specter of AIDS.

Of course it could be said that these plays were chosen precisely to illustrate a predetermined point, but in fact this congruence of conviction only became clear to me after the selection had been completed. And it should be pointed out that nearly *all* of the fifty-some Obie-winning plays of the eighties can be characterized by the same attitudes of skepticism, disenchantment, or revulsion. To cite just a few examples: David Henry Hwang's *FOB* dealt with repellent racial imagery; Caryl Churchill's *Serious Money* with financial chicanery; Amlin Gray's *How I Got That Story* and Emily Mann's *Still Life* with the painfully lingering residue of Vietnam; Harvey Fierstein's *Torch Song Trilogy* with the brutalities of homophobia. And even playwrights who raised social concerns less directly, far from joining in the American parade, kept alive, and as noisily as possible, the sounds of different drums. Indeed, one of the marks of artistic vision, particularly in a society blind to its impulses, is political prescience.

In a sense, then, these plays are modern versions of the medieval *Mousetrap*—the text Hamlet asked the itinerant actors to perform for Claudius—plays meant not to comfort our evenings or confirm our values but to discomfort, to challenge, to disturb, to dismay, plays intended to send us reeling out of the theater examining our consciences.

But an adversarial stance is hardly the only quality shared by the playwrights in this anthology, for their aesthetic achievements are just as compelling. Mamet's Dantesque descent into the urban underworld constructs a contemporary epic from fragmentary vignettes, while Durang's deadpan naiveté disguises a sophisticated absurdism. Shawn forsakes the familiar polemics of political theater to make a devastating political statement, while Fornes renounces verbal flair to reveal the hidden expressiveness of language. Parks fractures linear narrative to expose the discontinuous narrative of racial imagery. Beckett finds the essence of drama by ruthlessly eliminating theatrical conventions. And while Bogosian makes use of one of our newest forms, the collage, and Lucas revitalizes one of our most ancient, the fairy tale, both give voice to pressing contemporary concerns.

So all the playwrights in this collection reject the slice-of-life naturalism, psychological realism, and lyric populism that have been the staples of twentieth-century American theater. The fact that movies and television have largely taken over these genres has impoverished our commercial stage, but has challenged our dramatic artists to liberate the unique potential of live theater, to move beyond the fourth-wall, well-made play in search of visionary expression. Oblique, imagistic, elliptical, nonlinear, nonrealistic, calling on new modes of acting, demanding new concepts of design—whatever route they have taken, the playwrights of Off-Broadway have explored the formal inventiveness, the dramaturgical daring so provocatively exemplified by these eight scripts.

* * *

If the most stimulating playwrights of the eighties were adversarial in content and adventurous in form, rejecting both mainstream political values and middlebrow aesthetic conventions, they naturally rebelled against the traditional institutions of the American theater as well, finding in the alternative theaters and audiences of Off-Broadway a community that could sustain their work.

Off-Broadway began, as its name implies, in opposition—to the commodity theater of Broadway, to its packaged products, to its role as part of the entertainment industry. In its place, playwrights, performers, directors, and designers hoped to establish a theater where success was measured not at the box office but on the stage, a theater regarded not as a money machine but as a means of personal expression. Freed from commercial pressures and audience expectations—and from "community standards" as well, for isn't that what art is called upon to challenge?—the playwrights of Off-Broadway were characterized not only by combative anarchism and aggressive iconoclasm but by an ardent affirmation of theater as an art form.

Off-Broadway may have been born with the legendary Circle-in-the-Square production of Eugene O'Neill's *The Iceman Cometh* in 1956, or with Joe Papp's Shakespeare on the back of a truck in Central Park in 1957, or with the Living Theater's landmark production of Jack Gelber's *The Connection* in 1959, but whatever the date, its initial function was twofold—to revive neglected American masterpieces and European classics, and to encourage native avant-garde and experimental writers hoping to build upon this unappreciated past. Off-Broadway, in short, began not as a place but as an atmosphere, an atmosphere where creativity could be nourished.

Ironically, however, the astonishing success of the Off-Broadway movement brought with it many of the problems and temptations its founders had hoped to escape. So when, in the sixties, Off-Broadway took on two additional functions—as a place to stage commercial shows on smaller budgets and as a cheap in-town replacement for the costly out-of-town Broadway tryout—Off-Off-Broadway emerged as a kind of revolution against the revolutionaries. If counterculture productions like *Hair* were going to be transformed into box-office bonanzas, if Off-Broadway was in danger of becoming nothing but a way station on the road to Broadway, perhaps theater artists needed to pick up and move even farther afield. And in the seventies they began to leave New York City altogether, moving into the nonprofit resident theaters across the country, recommitting themselves to artistic quality, so that today we no longer have merely two theaters, uptown business and downtown artistry, but many theaters, many Off-Broadways, from Boston to Los Angeles, from Seattle to Atlanta, from Minneapolis to New Haven.

The debate continues: Are these institutions alternative theaters or places for apprenticeship, artistic enclaves or breeding grounds for Broadway, movies, and television? But whatever the definition of "career," even those who've "graduated" into bigger and in most cases worse things often feel, when they return to Off-Broadway, that they're returning home. And one definition of home is the annual Obie awards ceremonies, an informal family reunion where the artists of Off-Broadway have gathered every spring since 1956 to celebrate their own.

Founded by *The Village Voice* "to honor creative achievement in the Off-Broadway theater," the Obies—selected by a committee composed of *Voice* critics and guest judges—are invariably the first recognition given to young, emerging talents. The list of winners reads like a roll call of the most gifted artists in the American theater—performers such as George C. Scott, Jason Robards, Colleen Dewhurst, Al Pacino, Meryl Streep, and Dustin Hoffman (who said, many years later, that he still regarded winning his Obie as the greatest thrill of his career), and playwrights such as Sam Shepard, Arthur Miller, Edward Albee, John Guare, Lanford Wilson, Jean Genet, and Robert Lowell.

There are many forms of celebration, of course, and this volume is an invitation to celebrate not games but visions, not the meretricious show-biz values of a commercialized culture but the enduring artistic values of a creative theater. Let the visions begin!

—*Ross Wetzsteon*

David Mamet

Edmond

To say that "a new voice" emerged in the American theater in the mid-seventies isn't to speak metaphorically but literally, for even more impressive than the moral ambiguities of David Mamet's *American Buffalo* or the erotic savageries of his *Sexual Perversity in Chicago* was the verbal virtuosity of his dialogue. As with Ernest Hemingway, another Chicago native, critics at first stressed the uncanny accuracy of Mamet's ear. This is *exactly* the way people speak, they marveled, as if he had secretly transcribed their conversation. Soon, however, again as with Hemingway, critics were stressing the subtle stylization of Mamet's prose—*no one* speaks that way, they concluded, as if he had skillfully invented every phrase. Both perceptions are true, of course, so how can this apparent contradiction between authenticity and artistry be resolved?

Mamet's characters alternate between the terse and the prolix, the everyday and the elevated, the pornographic and the grandiloquent. Indeed, the poetry of profanity has remained his signature, especially in his Pulitzer-Prize–winning *Glengarry Glen Ross*. But while his vocabulary and his rhythms are authentic transcriptions, their *interaction*, the way they're linked, the way they heighten one another, is an artistic stylization. Verisimilitude, in the theater in particular, is often a matter of "everyone" and "no one"—just as we know exactly what a "typical" person is like though we know no one exactly like that, so we instantly recognize the way Mamet's characters speak though we've never actually heard anyone speak the way they do.

And language is all the more crucial in a culture in which people fail to connect—especially in a society in which genders and races hardly seem able even to hear one another. Mamet's voice in *Edmond* is brutal, oblique, his rhythms halting, truncated, for as his protagonist descends into the underworld of New York City, he enters not only a realm whose rituals he can barely understand but a world whose emotions he can scarcely comprehend. In this tabloid odyssey of sex and violence, nearly every transaction is articulated in terms of money, and it sometimes seems the only way Edmond can communicate is to say, ''That's too much.''

We can place Edmond's adventure in a sociological context: the bitter resentment of a middle-class white man at the encroaching demands of the underclass—of blacks, of women, and of homosexuals in particular—and a man, moreover, named after the seminal British conservative. We can ''explain'' his encounters in psychological terms: as he is increasingly frustrated by his failure to achieve his goals, his inner turmoil at first expresses itself as malaise, then finally explodes in violence against those he considers beneath him. But Mamet's theatrical vision transcends these glibly reductive categories. The power of the play resides rather in its evocation of the inexplicable—language again, but language as the expression of what *can't* be said. ''It's something else,'' Edmond mutters near the end, but ''it'' has no antecedent, ''something'' has no referent. ''What do you think that is?'' his fellow prisoner asks. ''I think it's something *beyond* that,'' Edmond replies. ''*Beyond* those things that we can know.'' ''Well, *something's* going on,'' the prisoner concludes. ''I'll tell you that.''

There's a fierce dread woven into the texture of *Edmond* that finally reduces its characters, even its author, to silence, and the play ends not with a word but with a gesture, a gesture at once of hope and surrender—a kiss.

DAVID MAMET's first major play, *American Buffalo*, won an Obie in 1976. Subsequent works have included *A Life in the Theatre*, his Pulitzer-Prize–winning *Glengarry*

Glen Ross, *Speed-the-Plow*, and most recently, *Oleanna*. Mamet has also written several film scripts, among them *The Verdict* and *The Untouchables*, and has directed several films of his own, most notably *House of Games*.

Edmond opened at the Provincetown Playhouse on October 27, 1982, with the following cast:

A Mission Preacher, A Prisoner ....*Paul Butler*
The Manager, A Leafleteer, A Customer
....*Rick Cluchey*
 A Policeman, A Guard ....
A B-Girl, A Whore ....*Joyce Hazard*
A Peep-Show Girl, Glenna ....*Laura Innes*
A Man in a Bar, A Hotel Clerk ... *Bruce Tarchow*
 The Man in Back, A Chaplain.....................
Edmond's Wife .... *Linda Kimbrough*
The Fortune-teller, A Manager.. *Marge Kotlisky*
 A Woman in the Subway
A Shill, A Pimp.....................*Lionel Mark Smith*
A Cardsharp, A Guard....................*José Santana*
Edmond...*Colin Stinton*
A Bartender, A Bystander, ...*Jack Wallace*
 A Pawnshop Owner, An Interrogator............

This production was directed by Gregory Mosher; settings by Bill Bartelt; lighting by Kevin Rigdon; costumes by Marsha Kowal, fight choreography by David Woolley; stage managers, Tom Biscotto and Anne Clarke.

THE SCENES

THE CHARACTERS

FORTUNE-TELLER
EDMOND, *a man in his mid thirties*
HIS WIFE
A MAN IN A BAR
A B-GIRL
A BARTENDER
THE MANAGER
A PEEP-SHOW GIRL
THREE GAMBLERS
A CARDSHARP
A BYSTANDER
TWO SHILLS
A LEAFLETEER
A MANAGER (F)
A WHORE
A HOTEL CLERK
A PAWNSHOP OWNER
A CUSTOMER
THE MAN IN BACK
A WOMAN ON THE SUBWAY
A PIMP
GLENNA, *a waitress*
A TRAMP
A MISSION PREACHER
A POLICEMAN
AN INTERROGATOR
A PRISONER
A CHAPLAIN
A GUARD

THE SETTING

New York City.

Scene 1

The Fortune-teller

EDMOND *and the* FORTUNE-TELLER *seated across the table from each other.*

FORTUNE-TELLER. If things are predetermined surely they must manifest themselves.

When we look back—as we look back—we see that we could never have done otherwise than as we did. (*Pause.*) Surely, then, there must have been signs.

If only we could have read them.

We say, "I see now that I could not have done otherwise . . . my *diet* caused me. Or my stars . . . which caused me to eat what I ate . . . or my *genes,* or some other thing beyond my control forced me to act as I did . . ."

And those things which *forced* us, of course, must make their signs: our *diet,* or our *genes,* or our *stars.*

(*Pause.*)

And there *are* signs. (*Pause.*)

What we see reflects (more than what is) what is to be.

(*Pause.*)

Are you cold?

EDMOND. No. (*Pause.*)

FORTUNE-TELLER. Would you like me to close the window?

EDMOND. No, thank you.

FORTUNE-TELLER. Give me your palm.

(EDMOND *does so.*)

You are not where you belong. It is perhaps true none of us are, but in your case this is more true than in most. We all like to believe we are special. In your case this is true.

Listen to me. (*She continues talking as the lights dim.*)

The world seems to be crumbling around us. You look and you wonder if what you perceive is accurate. And you are unsure what your place is. To what extent you are cause and to what an effect. . . .

Scene 2

At Home

EDMOND *and his* WIFE *are sitting in the living room. A pause.*

WIFE. The girl broke the lamp. (*Pause.*)

EDMOND. Which lamp?

WIFE. The antique lamp.

EDMOND. In my room?

WIFE. Yes. (*Pause.*)

EDMOND. Huh.

WIFE. That lamp cost over two hundred and twenty dollars.

EDMOND. (*Pause.*) Maybe we can get it fixed.

WIFE. We're never going to get it fixed.

I think that that's the *point.* . . .

I think that's why she did it.

EDMOND. Yes. Alright—I'm going.

(*Pause. He gets up and starts out of the room.*)

WIFE. Will you bring me back some cigarettes. . . .

EDMOND. I'm not coming back.

WIFE. What?

EDMOND. I'm not coming back. (*Pause.*)

WIFE. What do you mean?

EDMOND. I'm going, and I'm not going to come back. (*Pause.*)

WIFE. You're not *ever* coming back?

EDMOND. No.

WIFE. Why not? (*Pause.*)

EDMOND. I don't want to live this kind of life.

WIFE. What does that mean?

EDMOND. That I can't live this life.

WIFE. "You can't live this life" so you're leaving me.

EDMOND. Yes.

WIFE. Ah. Ah. Ah.

And what about *ME*?

Don't you *love* me anymore?

EDMOND. No.

WIFE. You don't.

EDMOND. No.

WIFE. And why is that?

EDMOND. I don't know.

WIFE. And when did you find this out?

EDMOND. A long time ago.

WIFE. You did.

EDMOND. Yes.

WIFE. How long ago?

EDMOND. Years ago.

WIFE. You've known for years that you don't love me.

EDMOND. Yes. (*Pause*.)

WIFE. Oh. (*Pause*) Then why did you decide you're leaving *now*?

EDMOND. I've had enough.

WIFE. Yes. But why *now*?

EDMOND. (*Pause*) Because you don't interest me spiritually or sexually. (*Pause*.)

WIFE. Hadn't you known this for some time?

EDMOND. What do you think?

WIFE. I think you did.

EDMOND. Yes, I did.

WIFE. And why didn't you leave *then*?

Why didn't you leave *then*, you stupid *shit*!!!

All of these years you say that you've been living here? . . . (*Pause*.)

Eh? You idiot. . . .

I've had enough.

You idiot . . . to see you passing *judgment* on me all this time . . .

EDMOND. . . . I never judged you. . . .

WIFE. . . . and then you tell me. "You're leaving."

EDMOND. Yes.

WIFE. *Go*, then. . . .

EDMOND. I'll call you.

WIFE. Please. And we'll talk. What shall we do with the house? Cut it in half?

Go. Get out of here. Go.

EDMOND. You think that I'm fooling.

WIFE. I do *not*. Good-bye. Thank you. Good-bye. (*Pause.*) Good-bye. (*Pause.*)

Get *out*. Get *out* of here.

And don't you *ever* come back.

Do you hear me?

(WIFE *exits. Closing the door on him.*)

Scene 3

A Bar

EDMOND *is at the bar. A* MAN *is next to him. They sit for a while.*

MAN. . . . . I'll tell you who's got it *easy*. . . .

EDMOND. Who?

MAN. The niggers. (*Pause.*) Sometimes I wish I was a nigger.

EDMOND. Sometimes I do, too.

MAN. I'd rob a store. I don't blame them.

I swear to God. Because I want to tell you: we're *bred* to do the things that we do.

EDMOND. Mm.

MAN. Northern races *one* thing, and the southern races something else. And what *they* want to do is sit beneath the tree and watch the elephant. (*Pause.*) And I don't blame them one small bit. Because there's too much *pressure* on us.

EDMOND. Yes.

MAN. And that's no joke, and that's not *poetry*, it's just too much.

EDMOND. It is. It absolutely is.

MAN. A man's got to get *out*. . . .

EDMOND: What do you mean?

MAN. A man's got to get *away* from himself. . . .

EDMOND. . . . that's true . . .

MAN. . . . because the pressure is too much.

EDMOND. What do you do?

MAN. What do you mean?

EDMOND. What do you do to get out?

MAN. What do I do?

EDMOND. Yes.

MAN. What are the things to do? What are the things *anyone* does? . . . (*Pause.*)

Pussy . . . I don't know. . . . *Pussy* . . . *Power* . . . *Money* . . . uh . . . *adventure* . . . (*Pause.*)

I think that's it . . . uh, self-*destruction* . . .

I think that that's it . . . don't you? . . .

EDMOND. Yes.

MAN. . . . uh, *religion* . . . I suppose that's it, uh, *release*, uh, ratification. (*Pause.*)

You have to get *out*, you have to get something opens your *nose*, life is too short.

EDMOND. My wife and I are incompatible.

MAN. I'm sorry to hear that. (*Pause.*)

In what way?

EDMOND. I don't find her attractive.

MAN. Mm.

EDMOND. It's a boring thing to talk about. But that's what's on my mind.

MAN. I understand.

EDMOND. You do?

MAN. Yes. (*Pause.*)

EDMOND. Thank you.

MAN. Believe me, that's alright. I know that we all *need* it, and we don't know where to *get* it, and I know what it *means*, and I understand.

EDMOND. . . . I feel . . .

MAN. I know. Like your balls were cut off.

EDMOND. Yes. A long, long time ago.

MAN. Mm-hm.

EDMOND. And I don't feel like a man.

MAN. Do you know what you need?

EDMOND. No.

MAN. You need to get laid.

EDMOND. I do. I know I do.

MAN. That's why the niggers have it easy.

EDMOND. Why?

MAN. I'll tell you why: there are responsibilities they never have accepted. (*Pause.*)

Try the Allegro.

EDMOND. What is that?

MAN. A bar on Forty-seventh Street.

EDMOND. Thank you.

(*The* MAN *gets up, pays for drinks.*)

MAN. I want this to be on me. I want you to *remember* there was someone who listened. (*Pause.*)

You'd do the same for me.

(*The* MAN *exits.*)

Scene 4

The Allegro

EDMOND *sits by himself for a minute. A* B-GIRL *comes by.*

B-GIRL. You want to buy me a drink?

EDMOND. Yes. (*Pause.*)

I'm putting myself at your *mercy* . . . this is my first time in a place like this. I don't want to be taken advantage of.

(*Pause.*)

You understand?

B-GIRL. Buy me a drink and we'll go in the back.

EDMOND. And do what?

B-GIRL. Whatever you want.

(EDMOND *leans over and whispers to* B-GIRL.)

B-GIRL. Ten dollars.

EDMOND. Alright.

B-GIRL. Buy me a drink.

EDMOND. You get a commission on the drinks?

B-GIRL. Yes.

(*She gestures to* BARTENDER, *who brings drinks.*)

EDMOND. How much commission do you get?

B-GIRL. Fifty percent.

BARTENDER. (*Bringing drinks.*) That's twenty bucks.

EDMOND. (*Getting up.*) It's too much.

BARTENDER. What?

EDMOND. Too much. Thank you.

B-GIRL. Ten!

EDMOND. No, thank you.

B-GIRL. Ten!

EDMOND. I'll give you five. I'll give you the five you'd get for the drink if I gave them ten.

But I'm not going to give them ten.

B-GIRL. But you have to buy me a drink.

EDMOND. I'm sorry. No.

B-GIRL. Alright. (*Pause.*) Give me ten.

EDMOND. On top of the ten?

B-GIRL. Yeah. You give me twenty.

EDMOND. I should give you twenty.

B-GIRL. Yes.

EDMOND. To *you*.

B-GIRL. Yes.

EDMOND. And then you give him the five?

B-GIRL. Yes. I got to give him the five.

EDMOND. No.

B-GIRL. For the *drink*.

EDMOND. No. You don't have to pay him for the drink. It's *tea* . . .

B-GIRL. It's not tea.

EDMOND. It's not tea!? . . .

(*He drinks.*)

If it's not *tea* what *is* it, then? . . .

I came here to be *straight* with you, why do we have to go *through* this? . . .

MANAGER. Get in or get out. (*Pause.*)

Don't mill around.

Get in or get out . . . (*Pause.*)

Alright.

(MANAGER *escorts* EDMOND *out of the bar.*)

Scene 5

A Peep Show

Booths with closed doors all around. A GIRL *in a spangled leotard sees* EDMOND *and motions him to a booth whose door she is opening.*

GIRL. Seven. Go in Seven.

(*He starts to Booth Seven.*)

No. Six! I mean Six. Go in Six.

(*He goes into Booth Six. She disappears behind the row of booths, and appears behind a Plexiglas partition in Booth Six.*)

Take your dick out. (*Pause.*)
Take your dick out. (*Pause.*)
Come on. Take your dick out.
EDMOND. I'm not a cop.
GIRL. I know you're not a cop. Take your dick out.
I'm gonna give you a good time.
EDMOND. How can we get this barrier to come down?
GIRL. It doesn't come down.
EDMOND. Then how are you going to give me a good time?
GIRL. Come here.

(*He leans close. She whispers.*)

Give me ten bucks. (*Pause.*)
Give me ten bucks. (*Pause.*).
Put it through the thing.

(She indicates a small ventilator hole in the Plexiglas. Pause.)

Put it through the thing.

EDMOND. *(Checking his wallet.)* I haven't got ten bucks.

GIRL. Okay . . . just . . . yes.

Okay. Give me the twenty.

EDMOND. Are you going to give me change?

GIRL. Yes. Just give me the twenty. Give it to me. Good. Now take your dick out.

EDMOND. Can I have my ten?

GIRL. Look. Let me hold the ten.

EDMOND. Give me my ten back. *(Pause.)*

Come on. Give me my ten back.

GIRL. Let me hold the ten. . . .

EDMOND. Give me my ten back and I'll give you a tip when you're done.

(Pause. She does so.)

Thank you.

GIRL. Okay. Take your dick out.

EDMOND. *(Of the Plexiglas.)* How does this thing come down?

GIRL. It doesn't come down.

EDMOND. It doesn't come down?

GIRL. No.

EDMOND. Then what the fuck am I giving you ten bucks for?

GIRL. Look: You can touch me. Stick your finger in this you can touch me.

EDMOND. I don't want to touch *you*. . . .

I want *you* to touch *me*. . . .

GIRL. I can't. *(Pause.)* I would, but I can't. We'd have the cops in here. We would.

Honestly. *(Pause.)*

Look: Put your finger in here . . . come on.

(Pause.) Come on.

(*He zips his pants up and leaves the booth.*)

You're only cheating your*self*. . . .

Scene 6

On the Street, Three-Card Monte

EDMOND, A CARDSHARP, *a* BYSTANDER *and* TWO SHILLS.

SHARPER. You pick the red you win, and twenty get you forty. Put your money up.

The *black* gets *back,* the *red* you go ahead. . . .

Who saw the red? . . . Who saw the red?

Who saw her? . . .

BYSTANDER. (*To* EDMOND.) The fellow over there is a shill . . .

EDMOND. Who is? . . .

BYSTANDER. (*Points.*) You want to know how to beat the game?

EDMOND. How?

BYSTANDER. You figure out which card has *got* to win. . . .

EDMOND. . . . Uh-huh . . .

BYSTANDER. . . . and bet the *other* one.

SHARPER. Who saw the Red? . . .

BYSTANDER. They're all shills, they're all part of an act.

SHARPER. Who saw her? Five will get you ten. . . .

SHILL. (*Playing lookout*): Cops . . . cops . . . cops . . . don't run . . . don't run. . . .

(*Everyone scatters.* EDMOND *moves down the street.*)

Scene 7

Passing Out Leaflets

EDMOND *moves down the street. A man is passing out leaflets.*

LEAFLETEER. Check it out . . . check it out. . . .
This is what you looking for. . . . Take it . . .
I'm *giving* you something. . . . *Take* it. . . .

(EDMOND *takes the leaflet.*)

Now. Is that what you looking for or not? . . .
EDMOND. (*Reading the leaflet.*) Is this true? . . .
LEAFLETEER. Would I give it to you if it wasn't? . . .
(EDMOND *walks off reading the leaflet. The* LEAFLETEER *continues with his spiel.*)

Check it out. . . .

Scene 8

The Whorehouse

EDMOND *shows up with the leaflet. He talks to the* MAN-AGER, *a woman.*

MANAGER. Hello.

EDMOND. Hello.

MANAGER. Have you been here before?

EDMOND. No.

MANAGER. How'd you hear about us? (EDMOND *shows her the leaflet.*) You from out of town?

EDMOND. Yes. What's the deal here?

MANAGER. This is a *health* club.

EDMOND. . . . I know.

MANAGER. And our rates are by the hour. (*Pause.*)

EDMOND. Yes?

MANAGER. Sixty-eight dollars for the first hour, sauna, free bar, showers . . . (*Pause.*)

The hour doesn't start until you and the masseuse are in the room.

EDMOND. Alright.

MANAGER. Whatever happens in the room, of course, is between you.

EDMOND. I understand.

MANAGER. You understand?

EDMOND. Yes.

MANAGER. . . . Or, for two hours it's one hundred fifty dollars. If you want two hostesses that is two hundred dollars for one hour. (*Pause.*) Whatever arrangement that you choose to make with *them* is between *you.*

EDMOND. Good. (*Pause.*)

MANAGER. What would you like?

EDMOND. One hour.

MANAGER. You pay that now. How would you like to pay?

EDMOND. How can I pay?

MANAGER. With cash or credit card. The billing for the card will read "Atlantic Ski and Tennis."

EDMOND. I'll pay you with cash.

Scene 9

Upstairs at the Whorehouse

EDMOND *and the* WHORE *are in a cubicle.*
    WHORE. How are you?
    EDMOND. Fine. I've never done this before.
    WHORE. No?

(*She starts rubbing his neck.*)

    EDMOND. No. That feels very good. (*Pause.*)
    WHORE. You've got a good body.
    EDMOND. Thank you.
    WHORE. Do you work out? (*Pause.*)
    EDMOND. I jog.
    WHORE. Mmm. (*Pause.*)
    EDMOND. And I used to play football in high school.
    WHORE. You've kept yourself in good shape.
    EDMOND. Thank you.
    WHORE. (*Pause.*) What shall we do?
    EDMOND. I'd like to have intercourse with you.
    WHORE. That sounds very nice. I'd like that, too.
    EDMOND. You would?
    WHORE. Yes.
    EDMOND. How much would that be?
    WHORE. For a straight fuck, that would be a hundred fifty.
    EDMOND. That's too much.
    WHORE. You know that I'm giving you a break. . . .
    EDMOND. . . . no . . .
    WHORE. . . . Because this is your first time here. . . .
    EDMOND. No. It's too much, on top of the sixty-eight at the door. . . .
    WHORE. . . . I know, I know, but you know, I don't

get to keep it all. I *split* it with them. Yes. They don't pay me, I pay *them*.

EDMOND. It's too much. (*Pause. The* WHORE *sighs*.)

WHORE. How much do you have?

EDMOND. All I had was one hundred for the whole thing.

WHORE. You mean a hundred for it all.

EDMOND. That only left me thirty.

WHORE. Noooo, honey, you couldn't get a *thing* for that.

EDMOND. Well, how much do you want?

WHORE. (*Sighs*.) Alright, for a straight fuck, one hundred twenty.

EDMOND. I couldn't pay that.

WHORE. I'm sorry, then. It would have been nice.

EDMOND. I'll give you eighty.

WHORE. No.

EDMOND. One hundred.

WHORE. Alright, but only, you know, 'cause this is your first time.

EDMOND. I know.

WHORE. . . . 'cause we *split* with them, you understand. . . .

EDMOND. I understand.

WHORE. Alright. One hundred.

EDMOND. Thank you. I appreciate this. (*Pause*.) Would it offend you if I wore a rubber? . . .

WHORE. Not at all. (*Pause*.)

EDMOND. Do you have one? . . .

WHORE. Yes. (*Pause*.) You want to pay me now? . . .

EDMOND. Yes. Certainly.

(*He takes out his wallet, hands her a credit card*.)

WHORE. I need cash, honey.

EDMOND. They said at the door I could pay with my . . .

WHORE. . . . That was at the door . . .

you have to pay *me* with *cash*. . . .

EDMOND. I don't think I *have* it. . . . (*He checks through his wallet*.)

I don't *have* it. . . .

WHORE. How much do you have? . . .

EDMOND. I, uh, only have *sixty*.

WHORE. Jeez, I'm *sorry,* honey, but I can't *do* it. . . .

EDMOND. Well, wait, wait, wait, wait, maybe we could . . . wait. . . .

WHORE. Why don't you *get* it, and come *back* here. . . .

EDMOND. Well, where could I *get* it? . . .

WHORE. Go to a restaurant and cash a check. I'll be here till *four*. . . .

EDMOND. I'll. I'll . . . um, um, . . . *yes. Thank* you . . . .

WHORE. Not at all.

(EDMOND *leaves the whorehouse.*)

Scene 10

Three-Card Monte

EDMOND *out on the street, passes by the three-card-monte men, who have assembled again.*

SHARPER. You can't win if you don't play. . . . (*To* EDMOND) *You*, sir . . .

EDMOND. Me? . . .

SHARPER. You going to try me again? . . .

EDMOND. Again? . . .

SHARPER. I remember you beat me out of that *fifty* that time with your girlfriend. . . .

EDMOND. . . . When was this?

SHARPER. On four*teenff* street. . . .

You going to try me one more time? . . .

EDMOND. Uh . . .

SHARPER. . . . Play you for that fifty. . . . Fifty get you one hundred, we see you as fast as you was. . . .

Pay on the red, pass on the black. . . .

Where is the queen? . . . You pick the queen you win. . . .

Where is the queen? . . . Who saw the queen? . . .

You put up fifty, win a hundred. . . . Now: Who saw the queen? . . .

SHILL. I got her!

SHARPER. How much? Put your money up. How much?

SHILL. I bet you fifty dollars.

SHARPER. Put it up.

(*The* SHILL *does so. The* SHILL *turns a card.*)

SHILL. There!

SHARPER. My man, I'm jus' too quick for you today. *Who* saw the queen? We got two cards left.

Pay on the *red* queen, who saw her?

EDMOND. I saw her.

SHARPER. Ah, *shit,* man, you too fass for me.

EDMOND. . . . For fifty dollars . . .

SHARPER. All right—all right.

Put it up. (*Pause.*)

EDMOND. Will you pay me if I win?

SHARPER. Yes, I will. If you win. But you got to win first. . . .

EDMOND. All that I've got to do is turn the queen.

SHARPER. Thass all you got to do.

EDMOND. I'll bet you fifty.

SHARPER. You sure?

EDMOND. Yes. I'm sure.

SHARPER. Put it up. (EDMOND *does so.*) Now: Which one you like?

EDMOND. (*Turning card.*) There!

SHARPER. (*Taking money.*). I'm *sorry,* my man. This time you lose—

now we even. Take another shot. You pick the queen you win . . . bet you another fifty. . . .

EDMOND. Let me see those cards.

SHARPER. These cards are fine, it's you thass slow.

EDMOND. I want to see the cards.

SHARPER. These cards are good my man, you *lost.*

EDMOND. You let me see those cards.

SHARPER. You ain't goin' *see* no motherfuckin' cards, man, we playin' a *game* here. . . .

SHILL. . . . You lost, *get* lost.

EDMOND. Give me those cards, fella.

SHARPER. You want to see the cards? You want to see the cards? . . . *Here* is the motherfuckin' cards. . . .

(*He hits* EDMOND *in the face. He and the* SHILL *beat* EDMOND *for several seconds.* EDMOND *falls to the ground.*)

Scene 11

A Hotel

EDMOND, *torn and battered, comes up to the* DESK CLERK.

EDMOND. I want a room.

CLERK. Twenty-two dollars. (*Pause.*)

EDMOND. I lost my wallet.

CLERK. Go to the police.

EDMOND. You can call up American Express.

CLERK. Go to the police. (*Pause.*)

I don't want to hear it.

EDMOND. You can call the credit-card people. I have insurance.

CLERK. Call them yourself. Right across the hall.

EDMOND. I have no money.

CLERK. I'm sure it's a free call.

EDMOND. Do those phones require a dime?

CLERK. (*Pause*). I'm sure I don't know.

EDMOND. You know if they need a *dime* or not.

To get a *dial* tone . . . You know if they need a *dime,* for chrissake. Do you want to live in this kind of world? Do you want to live in a *world* like that? I've been *hurt*! Are you *blind*? Would you appreciate it if I acted this way to *you*? (*Pause.*)

I asked you one simple thing.

Do they need a *dime*?

CLERK. No. They don't need a dime. Now, you make your call, and you go somewhere else.

Scene 12

The Pawnshop

The OWNER *waiting on a customer who is perusing objects in the display counter.*

CUSTOMER. Whaddaya get for that? What is that? Fourteen or eighteen karat?

OWNER. Fourteen.

CUSTOMER. Yeah? Lemme see that. How much is that?

OWNER. Six hundred eighty-five.

CUSTOMER. Why is that? How old is that? Is that *old*?

OWNER. You know how much *gold* that you got in there?

Feel. That. Just feel that.

CUSTOMER. Where is it marked?

OWNER. Right there. You want that loupe?

CUSTOMER. No. I can see it.

(EDMOND comes into the store and stands by the two.)

OWNER. (*To* EDMOND.) What?

EDMOND. I want to pawn something.

OWNER. Talk to the man in back.

CUSTOMER. What else you got like this?

OWNER. I don't know *what* I got. You're *looking* at it.

CUSTOMER. (*Pointing to item in display case.*) Lemme see that.

EDMOND. (*Goes to* MAN IN BACK *behind grate.*) I want to pawn something.

MAN. What?

EDMOND. My ring.

(Holds up hand.)

MAN. Take it off.
EDMOND. It's difficult to take it off.
MAN. Spit on it.

(EDMOND *does so*.)

CUSTOMER. How much is that?
OWNER. Two hundred twenty.
EDMOND. (*Happily.*) I got it off.

(EDMOND *hands the ring to the* MAN.)

MAN. What do you want to do with this?
You want to pawn it.
EDMOND. Yes. How does that work?
MAN. Is that what you want to do?
EDMOND. Yes. Are there other things to do?
MAN. . . . What you can *do*, no, I mean, if you wanted
it *appraised* . . .
EDMOND. . . . Uh-huh . . .
MAN. . . . or want to *sell* it . . .
EDMOND. . . . Uh-huh . . .
MAN. . . . or you wanted it to *pawn*. . . .
EDMOND. I understand.
MAN. Alright?
EDMOND. How much is getting it appraised?
MAN. Five dollars.
CUSTOMER. Lemme see something in black.
EDMOND. What would you give me if I pawned it?
MAN. What do you want for it?
EDMOND. What is it worth?
MAN. You pawn it all you're gonna get's approximately . . .
You know how this works?
CUSTOMER. Yes. Let me see that. . . .
EDMOND. No.
MAN. What you get, a quarter of the value.
EDMOND. Mm.
MAN. Approximately. For a year. You're paying twelve
percent. You can redeem your pledge with the year you

pay your twelve percent. To that time. Plus the amount of the loan.

EDMOND. What is my pledge?

MAN. Well, that depends on what it *is*.

EDMOND. What do you mean?

MAN. What it *is*. Do you understand?

EDMOND. No.

MAN. Whatever the amount *is*, that is your pledge.

EDMOND. The amount of the loan.

MAN. That's right.

EDMOND. I understand.

MAN. Alright. What are you looking for, the ring?

CUSTOMER. Nope. Not today. I'll catch you next time. Lemme see that knife.

EDMOND. What is it worth?

MAN. The most I can give you, hundred and twenty bucks.

CUSTOMER. This is nice.

EDMOND. I'll take it.

MAN. Good. I'll be right back. Give me the ring.

(EDMOND *does so.* EDMOND *wanders over to watch the other transaction.*)

CUSTOMER. (*Holding up knife.*) What are you asking for this?

OWNER. Twenty-three bucks. Say, twenty bucks.

CUSTOMER. (*To himself.*) Twenty bucks . . .

EDMOND. Why is it so expensive?

OWNER. Why is it so expensive?

CUSTOMER. No. I'm going to pass. (*He hands knife back, exiting.*) I'll catch you later.

OWNER. Right.

EDMOND. Why is the knife so expensive?

OWNER. This is a *survival* knife. GI Issue. World War Two. And that is why.

EDMOND. Survival knife.

OWNER. That is correct.

EDMOND. Is it a good knife?

OWNER. It is the best knife that money can buy.

(*He starts to put knife away. As an afterthought.*) You want it?

EDMOND. Let me think about it for a moment.

Scene 13

The Subway

EDMOND *is in the subway. Waiting with him is a* WOMAN *in a hat.*

EDMOND. (*Pause.*) My mother had a hat like that. (*Pause.*) My mother had a hat like that. (*Pause.*) I . . . I'm not making conversation. She wore it for years. She had it when I was a child.

(*The* WOMAN *starts to walk away.* EDMOND *grabs her.*)

I wasn't just making it "up." It *happened*. . . .

WOMAN. (*Detaching herself from his grip.*) Excuse me. . . .

EDMOND. . . . who the fuck do you think you *are*? . . . I'm *talking* to you . . . What am I? A *stone*? . . . Did I say, "I want to lick your pussy? . . ." I said, "My mother had that same hat. . . ." You *cunt* . . . What am I? A *dog*? I'd like to slash your fucking *face* . . . I'd like to slash your motherfucking *face* apart. . . .

WOMAN. . . . WILL SOMEBODY *HELP* ME. . . .

EDMOND. *You* don't know who I am. . . . (*She breaks free.*)

Is everybody in this town *insane*? . . . Fuck you . . . fuck you . . . fuck you . . . fuck the *lot* of you . . . fuck you *all* . . . I don't *need* you . . . I worked all of my life!

Scene 14

On the Street, Outside the Peep Show

PIMP. What are you looking for?

EDMOND. What?

PIMP. What are you looking for?

EDMOND. I'm not looking for a goddamn thing.

PIMP. You looking for that *joint*, it's *closed*.

EDMOND. What joint?

PIMP. That *joint* that you was looking for.

EDMOND. Thank you, no. I'm not looking for that joint.

PIMP. You looking for *something,* and I think that I know what you looking for.

EDMOND. You do?

PIMP. You come with me, I get you what you want.

EDMOND. What do I want?

PIMP. *I* know. We get you some *action,* my friend. We get you something sweet to shoot on. (*Pause.*)

I know. Thass what I'm doing here.

EDMOND. What are you saying?

PIMP. I'm saying that we going to find you something nice.

EDMOND. You're saying that you're going to find me a woman.

PIMP. Thass what I'm *doing* out here, friend.

EDMOND. How much?

PIMP. Well, how much do you want?

EDMOND. I want somebody clean.

PIMP. Thass right.

EDMOND. I want a blow-job.

PIMP. Alright.

EDMOND. How much?

PIMP. Thirty bucks.

EDMOND. That's too much.

PIMP. How much do you want to *spen'*? . . .

EDMOND. Say fifteen dollars.

PIMP. Twenny-five.

EDMOND. No. Twenty.

PIMP. Yes.

EDMOND. Is that alright?

PIMP. Give me the twenty.

EDMOND. I'll give it to you when we see the girl.

PIMP. Hey, I'm not going to *leave* you, man, you *coming* with me. We *goin'* to see the girl.

EDMOND. Good. I'll give it to you then.

PIMP. You give it to me *now*, unnerstan'? Huh? (*Pause.*) Thass the transaction. (*Pause.*) You see? Unless you were a *cop*. (*Pause.*) You give me the *money*, and then thass en*trap*ment. (*Pause.*) You understand?

EDMOND. Yes. I'm not a cop.

PIMP. Alright. Do you *see* what I'm saying?

EDMOND. I'm sorry.

PIMP. Thass alright. (EDMOND *takes out wallet. Exchange of money.*) You come with me. Now we'll just walk here like we're talking.

EDMOND. Is she going to be clean?

PIMP. Yes, she is. I understand you, man.

(*Pause. They walk.*)

I understand what you want. (*Pause.*) Believe me. (*Pause.*)

EDMOND. Is there any money in this?

PIMP. Well, you know, man, there's *some* . . . you get done piecing off the *police*, this man *here* . . . the *medical*, the *bills*, you know.

EDMOND. How much does the girl get?

PIMP. Sixty percent.

EDMOND. Mm.

PIMP. *Oh* yeah. (*He indicates a spot.*) Up here.

(*They walk to the spot. The* PIMP *takes out a knife and holds it to* EDMOND'S *neck.*)

* * *

Now give me all you' money mothafucka! *Now!*
EDMOND. Alright.
PIMP. *All* of it. Don't turn aroun' . . . don't turn aroun'
. . . just put it in my hand.
EDMOND. Alright.
PIMP. . . . And don't you make a motherfuckin'
sound. . . .
EDMOND. I'm going to do everything that you say. . . .
PIMP. Now you just han' me all you got.
(EDMOND *turns, strikes the* PIMP *in the face.*)
EDMOND. YOU MOTHERFUCKING NIGGER!
PIMP. Hold on. . . .
EDMOND. You motherfucking *shit* . . . you *jungle*
bunny . . . (*He strikes the* PIMP *again. He drops his
knife.*)
PIMP. I . . .
EDMOND. You *coon,* you *cunt,* you *cock*sucker . . .
PIMP. I . . .
EDMOND. "Take me upstairs? . . ."
PIMP. Oh, my God . . . (*The* PIMP *has fallen to the
sidewalk and* EDMOND *is kicking him.*)
EDMOND. You *fuck.* You *nigger.* You dumb cunt . . .
You *shit* . . . You shit. (*Pause.*)
You fucking *nigger.* (*Pause.*) Don't fuck with me, you
coon. . . .

(*Pause.* EDMOND spits on him.)

I hope you're *dead.*
(*Pause.*)
Don't fuck with *me,* you *coon* . . .
(*Pause.* EDMOND spits on him.)

Scene 15

The Coffeehouse

Edmond, *seated in the coffeehouse, addresses the waitress,* GLENNA.

EDMOND. I want a cup of coffee. No. A beer. Beer chaser. Irish whiskey.

GLENNA. Irish whiskey.

EDMOND. Yes. A double. Huh.

GLENNA. You're in a peppy mood today.

EDMOND. You're goddamn right I am, and you want me to tell you *why*? Because I am *alive*. You know how much of our life we're alive, you and me? *Nothing*. Two minutes out of the year. You know, you know, we're *sheltered*. . . .

GLENNA. Who is?

EDMOND. You and I. White people. All of us. All of us. We're doomed. The white race is doomed. And do you know *why*? . . . Sit down. . . .

GLENNA. I can't. I'm working.

EDMOND. And do you know *why*—you can do anything you *want* to do, you don't sit down because you're "*working*," the reason you don't sit down is you don't *want* to sit down, because it's more comfortable to *accept* a law than question it and live your life. All of us. *All* of us. We've bred the life out of ourselves. And we live in a fog. We live in a dream. Our life is a *school*house, and we're dead.

(*Pause.*)

How old are you?

GLENNA. Twenty-eight.

EDMOND. I've lived in a fog for thirty-four years. Most of the life I have to live. It's gone.

It's gone. I wasted it. Because I didn't know. And you know what the answer is? To *live*. (*Pause.*)

I want to go home with you tonight.

GLENNA. Why?

EDMOND. Why do you think? I want to fuck you. (*Pause.*) It's as simple as that.

What's your name?

GLENNA. Glenna. (*Pause.*) What's yours?

EDMOND. Edmond.

Scene 16

Glenna's Apartment

EDMOND *and* GLENNA *are lounging around semiclothed.*
EDMOND *shows* GLENNA *the survival knife.*
EDMOND. You see this?
GLENNA. Yes.
EDMOND. That fucking nigger comes up to me, what am I fitted to do. He comes up, "Give me all your money." Thirty-four years fits me to sweat and say he's *underpaid*, and he can't get a *job*, he's *bigger* than me . . . he's a *killer*, he don't care about his *life*, you understand, so he'd do *anything*. . . .
Eh? That's what I'm fitted to do. In a mess of intellectuality to wet my *pants* while this *coon* cuts my *dick* off . . . eh? Because I'm taught to *hate*.
I want to tell you something. Something *spoke* to me, I got a *shock* (I don't know, I got mad . . .), I got a *shock*, and I spoke *back* to him. "Up your *ass*, you *coon* . . . you want to fight, *I'll* fight you, I'll cut out your fuckin' *heart*, eh, *I* don't give a fuck. . . ."
GLENNA. Yes.
EDMOND. Eh? I'm saying, "*I* don't give a fuck, *I* got some warlike blood in *my* veins, too, you fucking *spade*, you coon. . . ." The *blood* ran down his neck. . . .
GLENNA. (*Looking at knife.*) With *that*?
EDMOND. You bet your ass. . . .
GLENNA. Did you kill him?
EDMOND. Did I kill him?
GLENNA. Yes.
EDMOND. I don't care. (*Pause.*)
GLENNA. That's wonderful.
EDMOND. And in that *moment* . . .
when I *spoke*, you understand, 'cause that was more im-

portant than the *knife* when I spoke *back* to him, I
DIDN'T FUCKING WANT TO *UNDERSTAND* . . . let
him understand *me* . . .

I wanted to KILL him. (*Pause.*) In that *moment* thirty
years of prejudice came out of me. (*Pause.*) Thirty *years*.
Of all those um um um of all those *cleaning* ladies . . .

GLENNA. . . . Uh-huh . . .

EDMOND. . . . uh? . . . who *might* have broke the lamp.
SO WHAT? You understand? For the first *time,* I swear
to god, for the first *time* I saw: THEY'RE PEOPLE,
TOO.

GLENNA. (*Pause.*) Do you know who I hate?

EDMOND. Who is that?

GLENNA. Faggots.

EDMOND. Yes. I hate them, too. And you know *why*?

GLENNA. Why?

EDMOND. They suck cock. (*Pause.*) And that's the truest thing you'll ever hear.

GLENNA. I hate them 'cause they don't like women.

EDMOND. They *hate* women.

GLENNA. I know that they do.

EDMOND. It makes you feel good to *say* it. Doesn't it?

GLENNA. Yes.

EDMOND. Then *say* it. If it makes you whole. *Always*
say it. *Always* for your*self* . . .

GLENNA. It's hard.

EDMOND. *Yes.*

GLENNA. Sometimes it's hard.

EDMOND. You're goddamn right it's hard. And there's
a *reason* why it's hard.

GLENNA. Why?

EDMOND. So that we will stand up. So that we'll be
our*selves.* Glenna: (*Pause.*) Glenna: This world is a piece
of shit. (*Pause.*) It is a shit house. (*Pause.*) . . . There is
NO *LAW* . . . there is no *history* . . . there is just *now*
. . . and if there is a *god* he may love the weak, Glenna.
(*Pause.*) But he respects the strong. (*Pause.*) And if you
are a *man* you should be feared. (*Pause.*) You should be
feared . . . (*Pause.*)

You just know you command respect.

GLENNA. That's why I love the Theater. . . . (*Pause.*)
Because what you must ask respect for is yourself. . . .

EDMOND. What do you mean?

GLENNA. When you're on stage.

EDMOND. Yes.

GLENNA. For *your* feelings.

EDMOND. Absolutely. Absolutely, yes . . .

GLENNA. And, and, and *not* be someone else.

EDMOND. Why should you? . . .

GLENNA. . . . That's why, and I'm so proud to *be* in
this profession . . .

EDMOND. . . . I don't blame you . . .

GLENNA. . . . because your aspirations . . .

EDMOND. . . . and I'll bet that you're good at it. . . .

GLENNA. . . . they . . .

EDMOND. . . . They have no bounds.

GLENNA. There's nothing . . .

EDMOND. . . . Yes. I understand. . . .

GLENNA. . . . to *bound* you but your soul.

EDMOND. (*Pause.*) Do something for me.

GLENNA. . . . Uh . . .

EDMOND. *Act* something for me. Would you act something for me? . . .

GLENNA. *Now?*

EDMOND. Yes.

GLENNA. Sitting right here? . . .

EDMOND. Yes. (*Pause.*)

GLENNA. Would you really like me to?

EDMOND. You know I would. You see me sitting here,
and you know that I would. I'd *love* it.

Just because we both *want* to. I'd *love* you to.

(*Pause.*)

GLENNA. What would you like me to do?

EDMOND. Whatever you'd like. What plays have you
done?

GLENNA. Well, we've only done scenes.

EDMOND. You've only done scenes.

GLENNA. I shouldn't say "only." They contain the
kernel of the play.

EDMOND. Uh-huh.

(*Pause.*)

What *plays* have you done?

GLENNA. In college I played Juliet.

EDMOND. In Shakespeare?

GLENNA. Yes. In Shakespeare. What do you think?

EDMOND. Well, I meant, there's *plays* named Juliet.

GLENNA. There are?

EDMOND. Yes.

GLENNA. I don't think so.

EDMOND. Well, there are. —Don't. Don't. Don't.

Don't be so *limited* . . . . And don't assume I'm dumb because I wear a suit and tie.

GLENNA. I don't assume that.

EDMOND. Because what we've *done* tonight. Since you met me, it didn't make a difference then. Forget it. All I meant, you say you are an *actress*. . . .

GLENNA. I am an actress. . . .

EDMOND. Yes. I say that's what you *say*. So *I* say what *plays* have you done. That's all.

GLENNA. The work I've done I have done for my peers.

EDMOND. What does that mean?

GLENNA. In class.

EDMOND. In class.

GLENNA. In class or workshop.

EDMOND. Not, not for a paying group.

GLENNA. No, absolutely not.

EDMOND. Then you are not an actress. Face it.

Let's start right. The two of us. I'm not lying to *you*, don't lie to *me*.

And don't lie to yourself.

Face it. You're a beautiful woman. You have *worlds* before you. I do, too.

Things to do. Things you can discover.

What I'm saying, start *now*, start *tonight*. With *me*. *Be* with me. Be what you *are*. . . .

GLENNA. I am what I am.

EDMOND. That's absolutely right. And that's what I loved when I saw you tonight. What I *loved*.

I use that word. (*Pause.*) I used that word.

I loved a *woman*. Standing there. A working woman. Who brought life to what she did. Who took a moment to *joke* with me. That's . . . that's . . . that's . . . god *bless* you what you are. Say it: I am a waitress.

(*Pause.*)

Say it.

GLENNA. What does it mean if I say something?

EDMOND. Say it with me. (*Pause.*)

GLENNA. What?

EDMOND. "I am a waitress."

GLENNA. I think that you better go.

EDMOND. If you want me to go I'll go. Say it with me. Say what you are. And I'll say what *I* am.

GLENNA. . . . What *you* are . . .

EDMOND. I've *made* that discovery. Now I want you to change your life with me. *Right* now, for what*ever* that we can be. *I* don't know what that is, *you* don't know. Speak with me. Right now. Say it.

GLENNA. I don't know what you're talking about.

EDMOND. Oh, by the Lord, yes, you do. Say it with me. (*She takes out a vial of pills.*) What are those?

GLENNA. Pills.

EDMOND. For what? Don't take them.

GLENNA. I have this tendency to get anxious.

EDMOND. (*Knocks them from her hand.*) Don't take them. Go *through* it. Go *through* with me.

GLENNA. You're scaring me.

EDMOND. I am not. I know when I'm scaring you. *Be*lieve me. (*Pause.*)

GLENNA. Get out. (*Pause.*)

EDMOND. Glenna. (*Pause.*)

GLENNA. Get out! GET OUT GET OUT! LEAVE ME THE FUCK ALONE!!! WHAT DID I DO, PLEDGE MY LIFE TO YOU? I LET YOU FUCK ME. GO AWAY.

EDMOND. Listen to me: You know what madness is?

GLENNA. I told you go away. (*Goes to phone. Dials.*)

EDMOND. I'm lonely, too. I know what it is, too. Believe me. Do you know what madness is?

GLENNA. (*Into phone.*) Susie? . . .

EDMOND. It's self-indulgence.

GLENNA. Suse, can you come over here? . . .

EDMOND. Will you please put that *down*? You know how *rare* this is? . . .

(*He knocks the phone out of her hands.* GLENNA *cowers.*)

GLENNA. Oh fuck . . .

EDMOND. Don't be ridiculous. I'm *talking* to you.

GLENNA. Don't hurt me. No. No. I can't deal with this.

EDMOND. Don't be ridic . . .

GLENNA. I . . . No. Help! Help.

EDMOND. . . . You're being . . .

GLENNA. . . . HELP!

EDMOND. . . . are you *insane*? What the fuck are you trying to *do,* for godsake?

GLENNA. HELP!

EDMOND. You want to wake the *neighbors*?

GLENNA. WILL SOMEBODY HELP ME? . . .

EDMOND. Shut up shut up!

GLENNA. Will somebody help you are the get *away* from me! You are the *devil.* I know who you are. I know what you want me to do. Get *away* from me I curse *you,* you can't kill me, get away from me I'm *good*.

EDMOND. *WILL YOU SHUT THE FUCK UP?* You fucking *bitch.*

You're *nuts.* . . .

(*He stabs her with the knife.*)

Are you *insane*? Are you *insane,* you fucking *idiot*? . . .
You stupid fucking *bitch* . . .
You stupid fucking . . . *now* look what you've done.
(*Pause.*)
Now look what you've blood fucking done.

Scene 17

The Mission

EDMOND *is attracted by the speech of a* MISSION PREACHER. *He walks to the front of the mission and listens outside the mission doors.*

PREACHER. "Oh no, not me!" You say, "Oh no, not me. Not *me*, Lord, to whom you hold out your hand. Not *me* to whom you offer your eternal grace. Not *me* who can be saved. . . ."

But *who* but you, I ask you? *Who* but you.

You say you are a grievous sinner? He *knows* that you are. You say he does not know the *depth* of my iniquity. *Believe* me, friends, he does. And still you say, he does not know—you say this in your secret soul—he does not know the terrible depth of my unbelief.

Believe me friends, he knows that too.

To *all* of you who say his grace is not meant to extend to one as black as you I say to WHO but you? To you *alone*. Not to the blessed. You think that Christ died for the blessed? That he died for the heavenly hosts? That did not make him God, my friends, it does not need a God to sacrifice for angels. It required a God to sacrifice for MAN. You hear me? For *you* . . . there is *none* so black but that he died for you. He died *especially* for you. Upon my life. On the graves of my family, and by the surety I have of his Eternal Bliss HE DIED FOR YOU AND YOU ARE SAVED. Praise *God*, my friends. Praise God and testify. Who will come up and testify with me, my friends? (*Pause.*)

WOMAN *from subway walks by. She sees* EDMOND *and stares at him.*

EDMOND. (*Speaks up.*) I will testify.

PREACHER. *Who* is that?

EDMOND. I will testify.

PREACHER. Sweet *God*, let that man come up here!

(EDMOND *starts into the church.*)

WOMAN. (*Shouts.*) That's the man! Someone! Call a policeman! That's the man!

PREACHER. . . . Who will come open up his soul? Alleluia, my friends. *Be* with me.

WOMAN. That's the man. *Stop* him!

(EDMOND *stops and turns. He looks wonderingly at the* WOMAN, *then starts inside.*)

POLICEMAN. Just a moment, sir.

EDMOND. I . . . I . . . I . . . I . . . I'm on my way to church.

PREACHER. Sweet *Jesus*, let that man come forth. . . .

WOMAN. That's the man tried to rape me on the train. He had a knife. . . .

EDMOND. . . . There must be some mistake. . . .

WOMAN. He tried to rape me on the train.

EDMOND. . . . There's some mistake, I'm on my way to church. . . .

POLICEMAN. What's the trouble here?

EDMOND. No trouble, I'm on my way into the mission.

WOMAN. This man tried to rape me on the train yesterday.

EDMOND. Obviously this woman's mad.

PREACHER. Will no one come forth?

EDMOND. I . . . I . . . I . . . have to go into the church.

POLICEMAN. Could I see some identification please?

EDMOND. Please, officer, I haven't time. I . . . I . . . it's been a long . . . I don't have my *wallet* on me. My name's Gregory Brock. I live at 428 Twenty-second Street, I own the building. I . . . I have to go inside the church.

POLICEMAN. You want to show me some ID?

EDMOND. I don't have any. I told you.

POLICEMAN. You're going to have to come with me.

EDMOND. I . . . please . . . Yes. In one minute. Not . . . not now, I have to *preach*. . . .

POLICEMAN. Come on.

EDMOND. You're, you're, you're making a . . .

Please. Let me go. And I'll come with you afterward. I swear that I will. I swear it on my life.

There's been a mistake. I'm an elder in this church. Come *with* me if you will.

I have to go and speak.

POLICEMAN. Look. (*Conciliatorily, he puts an arm on* EDMOND. *He feels something. He pulls back.*) What's that?

EDMOND. It's nothing. (*The* POLICEMAN *pulls out the survival knife.*) It's a knife. It's there for self-protection.

(*The* POLICEMAN *throws* EDMOND *to the ground and handcuffs him.*)

Scene 18

The Interrogation

EDMOND *and an* INTERROGATOR *at the police station.*

INTERROGATOR. What was the knife for?

EDMOND. For protection.

INTERROGATOR. From whom?

EDMOND. Everyone.

INTERROGATOR. You know that it's illegal?

EDMOND. No.

INTERROGATOR. It is.

EDMOND. (*Pause.*) I'm sorry.

INTERROGATOR. Speaking to that woman in the way you did is construed as assault.

EDMOND. I never spoke to her.

INTERROGATOR. She identified you as the man who accosted her last evening on the subway.

EDMOND. She is seriously mistaken.

INTERROGATOR. If she presses charges you'll be arraigned for assault.

EDMOND. For *speaking* to her?

INTERROGATOR. You admit that you were speaking to her?

EDMOND. (*Pause.*) I want to ask you something. (*Pause.*)

INTERROGATOR. Alright.

EDMOND. Did you ever kick a dog?

(*Pause.*)

Well, that's what I did. Man to man. That's what I did. I made a simple, harmless comment to her, she responded like a fucking bitch.

INTERROGATOR. You trying to pick her up?

EDMOND. Why should I try to pick her up?

INTERROGATOR. She was an attractive woman.

EDMOND. She was *not* an attractive woman.

INTERROGATOR. You gay?

EDMOND. What business is that of yours?

INTERROGATOR. Are you?

EDMOND. No.

INTERROGATOR. You married?

EDMOND. Yes. In fact. I was going back to my wife.

INTERROGATOR. You were going back to your wife?

EDMOND. I was going home to her.

INTERROGATOR. You said you were going back to her, what did you mean?

EDMOND. I'd left my wife, alright?

INTERROGATOR. You left your wife.

EDMOND. Yes.

INTERROGATOR. Why?

EDMOND. I was *bored*. Didn't that ever happen to *you*?

INTERROGATOR. And why did you lie to the officer?

EDMOND. What officer?

INTERROGATOR. Who picked you up. There's no Gregory Brock at the address you gave. You didn't give him your right name.

EDMOND. I was embarrassed.

INTERROGATOR. Why?

EDMOND. I didn't have my wallet.

INTERROGATOR. Why?

EDMOND. I'd left it at home.

INTERROGATOR. And why did that embarrass you?

EDMOND. I don't know. I have had no *sleep*. I just want to go *home*. I am a *solid* . . . look: My name is Edmond Burke, I live at 485 West Seventy-ninth Street. I work at Stearns and Harrington. I had a tiff with my wife. I went out on the town. I've learned my lesson. *Believe* me. I just want to go home. Whatever I've done I'll make right. (*Pause.*) Alright? (*Pause.*) Alright? These things happen and then they're done. When he *stopped* me I was going to church. I've been unwell. I'll confess to you that I've been confused, but, but . . . I've learned my lesson and I'm ready to go home.

INTERROGATOR. Why did you kill that girl?

EDMOND. What girl?

INTERROGATOR. That girl you killed.

Scene 19

Jail

EDMOND's WIFE *is visiting him. They sit across from each other in silence for a while.*

EDMOND. How's everything?

WIFE. Fine. (*Pause.*)

EDMOND. I'm alright, too.

WIFE. Good. (*Pause.*)

EDMOND. You want to tell me you're *mad* at me or something?

WIFE. Did you kill that girl in her apartment?

EDMOND. Yes, but I want to tell you something. . . . I didn't mean to. But do you want to hear something *funny*? . . . (Now, don't laugh. . . .) I think I'd just had too much coffee. (*Pause.*)

I'll tell you something else: I think there are just too many people in the world. I think that's why we kill each other. (*Pause.*) I . . . I . . . I suppose you're mad at me for leaving you. (*Pause.*) I don't suppose you're, uh, inclined (or, nor do I think you should be) to stand by me. I understand that. (*Pause.*) I'm sure that there are marriages where the wife would. Or the husband if it would go that way. (*Pause.*) But I know ours is not one of that type.

(*Pause.*). I know that you *wished* at one point it would be. I wished that too.

At one point. (*Pause.*)

I know at certain times we wished we could be . . . closer to each other. I can say that now. I'm sure this is the way you feel when someone near you dies. You never said the things you wanted desperately to say.

It would have been so simple to say them. (*Pause.*) But you never did.

WIFE. You got the papers?
EDMOND. Yes.
WIFE. Good.
EDMOND. Oh, yes. I got them.
WIFE. Anything you need?
EDMOND. No. Can't think of a thing.

(*The* WIFE *stands up, starts gathering her things together.*)

You take care, now!

Scene 20

The New Cell

EDMOND *is put in his new cell. His cellmate is a large black* PRISONER. EDMOND *sits on his new bunk in silence awhile.*

EDMOND. You know, you know, you know, you know we can't distinguish between *anxiety* and *fear*. Do you know what I mean? I don't mean fear. I mean, I *do* mean "fear," I, I don't mean *anxiety*. (*Pause.*)

We . . . when we *fear* things I think that we *wish* for them. (*Pause.*) *Death.* Or "burglars." (*Pause.*) Don't you think? We mean we *wish* they would come. Every fear hides a wish. Don't you think?

(*A pause.*)

I always knew that I would end up here. (*Pause.*)

(*To himself*) Every fear hides a wish.

I think I'm going to like it here.

PRISONER. You do?

EDMOND. Yes, I do. Do you know why? It's simple. That's why I think that I am. You know, I always thought that *white* people should be in prison. I know it's the black race we keep there. But I thought *we* should be there. You know why?

PRISONER. Why?

EDMOND. To be with black people. (*Pause.*) Does that sound too *simple* to you? (*Pause.*)

PRISONER. No.

EDMOND. Because we're *lonely*. (*Pause.*)

But what I *know* . . . (*Pause.*) What I *know* I think that all this *fear,* this fucking *fear* we feel must hide a wish. 'Cause I don't feel it since I'm here. I *don't*. I think the first time in my life. (*Pause.*) In my whole adult life I don't feel fearful since I came in here.

I think we are like birds. I think that humans are like birds. We suspect when there's going to be an *earthquake*. Birds know. They leave three days earlier. Something in their soul responds.

PRISONER. The birds leave when there's going to be an earthquake?

EDMOND. Yes. And I think, in our soul, *we, we* feel, we sense there is going to be . . .

PRISONER. . . . uh-huh . . .

EDMOND. . . . a catacylsm. But we cannot flee. We're fearful. All the time. Because we can't trust what we know. That ringing. (*Pause.*)

I think we feel. Something tells us, "Get *out* of here." (*Pause.*)

White people feel that. Do you feel that? (*Pause.*) Well. But I don't feel it since I'm here. (*Pause.*) I don't feel it since I'm here. I think I've settled. So, so, so I must be somewhere safe. Isn't that funny?

PRISONER. No.

EDMOND. You think it's not?

PRISONER. Yes.

EDMOND. Thank you.

PRISONER. Thass alright.

EDMOND. Huh. (*Pause.*)

PRISONER. You want a cigarette?

EDMOND. No, thank you. Not just now.

PRISONER. Thass alright.

EDMOND. Maybe later.

PRISONER. Sure. Now you know what?

EDMOND. What?

PRISONER. I think you should just get on my body.

EDMOND. I, yes. What do you mean?

PRISONER. You should get on my body now.

EDMOND. I don't know what that means.

PRISONER. It means to suck my dick. (*Pause.*) Now don't you want to do that?

EDMOND. No.

PRISONER. Well, you jes' do it anyway.

EDMOND. You're joking.

PRISONER. Not at all.

EDMOND. I don't think I could do that.

PRISONER. Well, you going to try or you going to die.
Les' get this out the way. (*Pause.*)

I'm not no going to repeat myself.

EDMOND. I'll scream.

PRISONER. You *scream*, and you offend me. You are
going to die. Look at me now and say I'm foolin'.
(*Pause.*)

EDMOND. I . . . I . . . I . . . I . . . I can't, I can't do,
I . . . I . . .

PRISONER. The mother*fuck* you can't. *Right* now,
missy.

(*The* PRISONER *slaps* EDMOND *viciously several times.*)

Right now, Jim. An' you bes' be nice.

Scene 21

The Chaplain

EDMOND *is sitting across from the* PRISON CHAPLAIN.

CHAPLAIN. You don't have to talk.

EDMOND. I don't want to talk. (*Pause.*)

CHAPLAIN. Are you getting accustomed to life here?

EDMOND. Do you know what happened to me?

CHAPLAIN. No. (*Pause.*)

EDMOND. I was sodomized.

CHAPLAIN. Did you report it?

EDMOND. Yes.

CHAPLAIN. What did they say?

EDMOND. ''That happens.'' (*Pause.*)

CHAPLAIN. I'm sorry it happened to you. (*Pause.*)

EDMOND. Thank you.

CHAPLAIN. (*Pause.*) Are you lonely?

EDMOND. Yes. (*Pause.*) Yes. (*Pause.*) I feel so *alone*. . . .

CHAPLAIN. Shhhhh . . .

EDMOND. I'm so *empty*. . . .

CHAPLAIN. Maybe you are ready to be *filled*.

EDMOND. That's *bullshit*, that's *bullshit*. That's pious *bullshit*.

CHAPLAIN. Is it?

EDMOND. Yes.

CHAPLAIN. That you are ready to be filled? Is it impossible?

EDMOND. Yes. Yes. I don't know what's impossible.

CHAPLAIN. Nothing is impossible.

EDMOND. Oh. Nothing is impossible. Not to ''God,'' is that what you're saying?

CHAPLAIN. Yes.

EDMOND. Well, then, you're full of *shit*. You under-

stand that. If nothing's impossible to God, then let him
let me walk *out* of here and be *free*. Let him cause a new
day. In a perfect land full of *life*. And *air*. Where people
are *kind* to each other, and there's *work* to do. Where we
grow up in *love*, and in security we're *wanted*. (*Pause.*)
Let him do that.

Let him.

Tell him to do that. (*Pause.*) You *ass*hole—if nothing's
impossible . . . I think *that* must be *easy*. . . . Not: "Let
me *fly*," or, "If there is a God make him to make the
sun come out at night." Go on. Please. Please. Please.
I'm *begging* you. If you're so smart. Let him do that: Let
him do that. (*Pause.*) Please. (*Pause.*) Please. I'm begging you.

CHAPLAIN. Are you sorry that you killed that girl?
(*Pause.*)

Edmond?

EDMOND. Yes. (*Pause.*)

CHAPLAIN. Are you sorry that you killed that girl?

EDMOND. I'm sorry about everything.

CHAPLAIN. But are you sorry that you killed? (*Pause.*)

EDMOND. Yes. (*Pause.*) Yes, I am. (*Pause.*) Yes.

CHAPLAIN. Why did you kill that girl?

EDMOND. I . . . (*Pause.*) I . . . (*Pause.*) *I don't* . . .
I . . . I don't . . . (*Pause.*) I . . . (*Pause.*) I don't . . .
(*Pause.*) *I don't* . . . (*Pause.*) I don't think . . . (*Pause.*)
I . . . (*Pause.*) (*The* CHAPLAIN *helps* EDMOND *up and
leads him to the door.*)

Scene 22

Alone in the Cell

EDMOND, *alone in his cell, writes:*

EDMOND. Dear Mrs. Brown. You don't remember me. Perhaps you do. Do you remember Eddie Burke who lived on Euclid? Maybe you do. I took Debbie to the prom. I know that she never found me attractive, and I think, perhaps she was coerced in some way to go with me—though I can't think in what way. It also strikes me as I write that maybe she went of her own free will and I found it important to *think* that she went unwillingly. (*Pause.*) I don't think, however, this is true. (*Pause.*) She was a lovely girl. I'm sure if you remember me you will recall how taken I was with her then.

(*A* GUARD *enters* EDMOND's *cell.*)

GUARD. You have a visitor.

EDMOND. Please tell them that I'm ill.

(GUARD *exits.* EDMOND *gets up. Stretches. Goes to the window. Looks out.*)

(*To himself.*) What a day!

(*He goes back to his table. Sits down. Yawns. Picks up the paper.*)

Scene 23

In the Prison Cell

EDMOND *and the* PRISONER are each lying on their bunks.

EDMOND. You can't control what you make of your life.

PRISONER. Now, thass for *damn* sure.

EDMOND. There is a destiny that shapes our ends. . . .

PRISONER. . . . Uh-huh . . .

EDMOND. Rough-hew them how we may.

PRISONER. How *e'er* we motherfucking may.

EDMOND. And that's the truth.

PRISONER. You *know* that is the truth.

EDMOND. . . . And people say it's *heredity,* or it's environment . . . but, but I think it's something else.

PRISONER. What you think that it is?

EDMOND. I think it's something *beyond* that.

PRISONER. Uh-huh . . .

EDMOND. *Beyond* those things that we can know. (*Pause.*)

I think maybe in dreams we see what it is. (*Pause.*) What do you think? (*Pause.*)

PRISONER. I don't know.

EDMOND. I don't think we *can* know. I think that if we *knew* it, we'd be dead.

PRISONER. We would be *God.*

EDMOND. We would be God. That's absolutely right.

PRISONER. Or, or some *genius.*

EDMOND. No, I don't think even *genius* could know what it is.

PRISONER. No, some great *genius,* (*Pause.*) or some *philosopher* . . .

EDMOND. I don't think even a *genius* can see what we are.

PRISONER. You don't . . . *think* that . . . (*Pause.*)

EDMOND. I think that we can't perceive it.

PRISONER. Well, *something*'s going on, I'll tell you *that*. I'm saying, *somewhere some* poor sucker knows what's happening.

EDMOND. Do you think?

PRISONER. *Shit* yes. Some whacked-out sucker. Somewhere. In the Ozarks? (*Pause.*) *Shit* yes. Some guy. (*Pause.*) Some *inbred* sucker, walks around all day . . .

(*Pause.*)

EDMOND. You think?

PRISONER. Yeah. Maybe not *him* . . . but someone. (*Pause.*) Some fuck locked up, he's got time for reflection. . . .

(*Pause.*)

Or some fuckin' . . . *I* don't know, some *kid,* who's just been *born.* (*Pause.*)

EDMOND. Some kid that's just been born . . .

PRISONER. Yes. And you know, he's got no precon*ceptions* . . .

EDMOND. Yes.

PRISONER. All he's got . . .

EDMOND. . . . That's absolutely right. . . .

PRISONER. *Huh?* . . .

EDMOND. Yes.

PRISONER. Is . . .

EDMOND. Maybe it's *memory.* . . .

PRISONER. That's what I'm *saying.* That it just may *be.* . . .

EDMOND. It could be.

PRISONER. Or . . .

EDMOND. . . . or some . . .

PRISONER. . . . some . . .

EDMOND. . . . *knowledge* . . .

PRISONER. . . . some . . .

EDMOND. . . . some *intuition.* . . .

PRISONER. Yes.

EDMOND. I don't *even* mean "intuition." . . . Something . . . something . . .

PRISONER. Or some *animal* . . .

EDMOND. Why not? . . .

PRISONER. That all the time we're saying we'll wait for the men from *space*, maybe they're *here*. . . .

EDMOND. . . . Maybe they are. . . .

PRISONER. . . . Maybe they're *animals*. . . .

EDMOND. Yes.

PRISONER. That were *left* here . . .

EDMOND. *Aeons* ago.

PRISONER. *Long* ago . . .

EDMOND. . . . and have *bred* here . . .

PRISONER. Or maybe *we're* the animals. . . .

EDMOND. . . . Maybe we are. . . .

PRISONER. *You* know, how they, *they* are supreme on their . . .

EDMOND. . . . Yes.

PRISONER. On their *native* world . . .

EDMOND. But when you put them here.

PRISONER. *We* say they're only *dogs*, or *animals*, and *scorn* them. . . .

EDMOND. . . . Yes.

PRISONER. We scorn them in our fear. But . . . don't you think? . . .

EDMOND. . . . It very well could be. . . .

PRISONER. But on their native world . . .

EDMOND. . . . Uh-huh . . .

PRISONER. . . . they are *supreme*. . . .

EDMOND. I think that's very . . .

PRISONER. And what *we* have done is to disgrace ourselves.

EDMOND. We have.

PRISONER. Because we did not treat them with respeck.

EDMOND. (*Pause.*) Maybe *we* were the animals.

PRISONER. Well, thass what I'm saying.

EDMOND. Maybe they're here to watch over us. Maybe that's why they're here. Or to observe us. Maybe we're here to be punished.

(*Pause.*)

Do you think there's a Hell?

PRISONER. I don't know. (*Pause.*)

EDMOND. Do you think that we are there?

PRISONER. I don't know, man. (*Pause.*)

EDMOND. Do you think that we go somewhere when we die?

PRISONER. I don't know, man. I *like* to think so.

EDMOND. I would, too.

PRISONER. I sure would like to think so. (*Pause.*)

EDMOND. Perhaps it's Heaven.

PRISONER. (*Pause.*) I don't know.

EDMOND. I don't know either but perhaps it is. (*Pause.*)

PRISONER. I would like to think so.

EDMOND. I would, too.

(*Pause.*)

Good night. (*Pause.*)

PRISONER. Good night.

(EDMOND *gets up, goes over and exchanges a good-night kiss with the* PRISONER. *He then returns to his bed and lies down.*)

Christopher Durang

The Marriage of Bette and Boo

One definition of comedy might be that it defines what's serious. On the surface, Christopher Durang's *The Marriage of Bette and Boo* is the silliest play imaginable, but beneath its inane chatter and deadpan non sequiturs is one of the bleakest visions of the decade. As the characters sing "Ninety-nine bottles of beer on the wall," a priest off-handedly confesses the failure of faith. Bette's father farcically chokes on a piece of birthday cake, and his dead body stays on the stage, a sheet over its head, for the remainder of the play. And Bette herself, after a series of remorselessly comic pregnancies, watches bemusedly as her lifeless babies are casually dropped onto the floor. Durang has written perhaps the funniest play of his generation, yet he has also asked one of the most solemn questions of every generation, a question writers have asked as far back as the Book of Job—why, wonders Bette, "do I have to go through all this suffering"?

A "memory play" about "family life"—the staple of American drama since Eugene O'Neill—*The Marriage of Bette and Boo* takes every domestic cliché from birth to the grave and submits it to satire at once enraged and pitying, resentful and gentle, acidulous and compassionate, a kind of "Ozzie and Harriet's Journey into Night." Look at the snapshots in Bette and Boo's album—pelted with rice at their wedding, planning insurance deals on their honeymoon, bringing up their son Matt as if counseled by a berserk Dr. Spock. Miscarriages, alcoholism, and divorce follow, but the characters relentlessly refuse to address their problems. "Don't anybody argue," beseeches Bette's sister in the familiar family litany; a "man-to-man talk" founders when it becomes clear that Matt's father doesn't even know what college his son is attending; and the best way to deal with anything remotely "disagreeable," as in living rooms all across the land, is to change the subject. Only Karl, Boo's father, speaks his mind: "I never expected much from life," he says. "I wanted to get my way in everything, and that's about all."

The narrator—played by the author in the play's premier production—begins by saying, "If one looks hard enough one can usually see the order that lies beneath the surface," but having looked hard into the anguish behind the "everything's fine" facade he can only conclude, "I can't make sense out of these things anymore." Nor is religion any consolation, for after the family priest's futile efforts at cheery uplift he throws up his hands in nonchalant befuddlement and reveals that his true calling is for imitating a slab of frying bacon.

A caustic, scathing, even malevolent vision of the American family? Of course. Yet as in everything Durang writes, there's also an undeniable undertone of sadness, of poignancy, of heartbreaking vulnerability. His devastating humor is characterized not so much by embittered savagery as by a kind of amiable innocence, as if he were saying, "the clothes have no emperor." The result, Durang's unique signature, is a tender mockery, an affectionate derision, that's at once hilarious and forgiving.

This isn't merely to say that Durang falls back on that commonplace of conventional comedy, "the healing power of laughter," for he recognizes that reconciliation can help us transcend our pain only if we first acknowledge its potency. After all, the song Emily can't remember at Bette and Boo's wedding is *"Lachen und Weinen"*—"Laughing and Crying."

One of many extraordinary talents to emerge from the Yale School of Drama in the 1970s—along with a young actress named Meryl Streep, who appeared in many of his school productions, and his longtime cabaret partner

Sigourney Weaver—CHRISTOPHER DURANG first won ac-
claim for *Sister Mary Ignatius Explains It All for You* in
1980. Other outstanding plays include *History of the
American Film, Beyond Therapy,* and *Dentity Crisis.*

The Marriage of Bette and Boo was first presented by the New York Shakespeare Festival (Joseph Papp, President) at the Public/Newman Theater in New York City on May 16, 1985. It was directed by Jerry Zaks; the scenery was by Loren Sherman; the costumes were by William Ivey Long; the lighting was by Paul Gallo; the original music was by Richard Peaslee; the hair was designed by Ron Frederick; the associate producer was Jason Steven Cohen; the production stage manager was James Harker; the stage manager was Pamela Singer. The cast was as follows:

BETTE BRENNAN ....*Joan Allen*
MARGARET BRENNAN, her mother *Patricia Falkenhain*
PAUL BRENNAN, her father .... *Bill McCutcheon*
JOAN BRENNAN, her sister............. *Mercedes Ruehl*
EMILY BRENNAN, her sister............ *Kathryn Grody*
BOO HUDLOCKE .... *Graham Beckel*
KARL HUDLOCKE, his father .... *Bill Moor*
SOOT HUDLOCKE, his mother........*Olympia Dukakis*
FATHER DONNALLY/DOCTOR.......... *Richard B. Shull*
MATT .... *Christopher Durang*

CHARACTERS

BETTE BRENNAN
MARGARET BRENNAN, *her mother*
PAUL BRENNAN, *her father*
JOAN BRENNAN, *her sister*

EMILY BRENNAN, *her sister*
BOO HUDLOCKE
KARL HUDLOCKE, *his father*
SOOT HUDLOCKE, *his mother*
FATHER DONNALLY
DOCTOR
MATT

SCENES

ACT I

Scene 1

All the characters, in various wedding apparel, stand to-gether to sing: the BRENNAN *family, the* HUDLOCKE *family.* MATTHEW *stands apart from them.*
ALL. (*Sing.*)

> God bless Bette and Boo and Skippy,
> Emily and Boo,
> Margaret, Matt, and Betsy Booey,
> Mommy, Tommy too,
>
> Betty Betsy Booey Boozey,
> Soot, Karl, Matt, and Paul,
> Margaret Booey, Joanie Phooey,
> God bless us one and all.

(*The characters now call out to one another.*)
BETTE. Booey? Booey? Skippy?
BOO. Pop?
MARGARET. Emily, dear?
BETTE. Booey?
BOO. Bette?
KARL. Is that Bore?
SOOT. Karl? Are you there?
JOAN. Nikkos!
BETTE. Skippy! Skippy!
EMILY. Are you all right, Mom?
BETTE. Booey, I'm calling you!
MARGARET. Paul? Where are you?
JOAN. Nikkos!
BOO. Bette? Betsy?

BETTE. Boo? Boo?

(*Flash of light on the characters, as if their picture is being taken. Lights off the* BRENNANS *and* HUDLOCKES. *Light on* MATT, *late twenties or so. He speaks to the audience.*)

MATT. If one looks hard enough, one can usually see the order that lies beneath the surface. Just as dreams must be put in order and perspective in order to understand them, so must the endless details of waking life be ordered and then carefully considered. Once these details have been considered, generalizations about them must be made. These generalizations should be written down legibly, and studied. *The Marriage of Bette and Boo.*

(MATT *exits. Characters assume their places for photographs before the wedding.* BOO *stands to the side with his parents,* KARL *and* SOOT. BETTE, *in a wedding gown, poses for pictures with her family:* MARGARET, *her mother;* EMILY, *her sister, holding a cello;* JOAN, *another sister, who is pregnant and is using nose spray, and* PAUL, *her father.* BETTE, MARGARET, EMILY *smile, looking out.* PAUL *looks serious, fatherly.* JOAN *looks sort of grouchy. Lights flash. They change positions.*)

MARGARET. You look lovely, Bette.

EMILY. You do. Lovely.

MARGARET. A lovely bride. Smile for the camera, girls. (*Speaking out either to audience or to unseen photographer.*) Bette was always the most beautiful of my children. We used to say that Joanie was the most striking, but Bette was the one who looked beautiful all the time. And about Emily we used to say her health wasn't good.

EMILY. That's kind of you to worry, Mom, but I'm feeling much better. My asthma is hardly bothering me at all today. (*Coughs lightly.*)

MARGARET. Boo seems a lovely boy. Betsy, dear, why do they call him Boo?

BETTE. It's a nickname.

MARGARET. Don't you think Bette looks lovely, Joanie?

JOAN. (*Without enthusiasm.*) She does. You look lovely, Bette.

MARGARET. Where is Nikkos, dear?

JOAN. He's not feeling well. He's in the bathroom.

EMILY. Do you think we should ask Nikkos to play his saxophone with us, Joan dear?

JOAN. A saxophone would sound ridiculous with your cello, Emily.

EMILY. But Nikkos might feel left out.

JOAN. He'll probably stay in the bathroom anyway.

BETTE. Nikkos seems crazy. (JOAN *glares at her.*) I wish you and Nikkos could've had a big wedding, Joanie.

MARGARET. Well, your father didn't much like Nikkos. It just didn't seem appropriate. (EMILY *coughs softly.*) Are you all right, Emily?

EMILY. It's nothing, Mom.

JOAN. You're not going to get sick, are you?

EMILY. No. I'm sure I won't.

MARGARET. Emily, dear, please put away your cello. It's too large.

EMILY. I can't find the case.

(JOAN *uses her nose spray.*)

BETTE. I can't wait to have a baby, Joanie.

JOAN. Oh yes?

MARGARET. (*Out to front again.*) Betsy was always the mother of the family, we'd say. She and her brother Tom. Played with dolls all day long, they did. Now Joanie hated dolls. If you gave Joanie a doll, she put it in the oven.

JOAN. I don't remember that, Mom.

BETTE. I love dolls.

EMILY. Best of luck, Bette. (*Kisses her; to* JOAN:) Do you think Nikkos will be offended if we don't ask him to play with us?

JOAN. Emily, don't go on about it.

EMILY. Nikkos is a wonderful musician.

BETTE. So are you, Emily.

MARGARET. I just hope he's a good husband. Booey seems very nice, Betsy.

BETTE. I think I'll have a large family.

(*Lights flash, taking a photo of the* BRENNANS. *Lights dim on them. Lights now pick up* BOO, KARL, *and* SOOT, *who now pose for pictures.*)

KARL. It's almost time, Bore.

BOO. Almost, Pop.

SOOT. Betsy's very pretty, Booey. Don't you think Betsy's pretty, Karl?

KARL. She's pretty. You're mighty old to be getting married, Bore. How old are you?

BOO. Thirty-two, Pop.

SOOT. That's not old, Karl.

KARL. Nearly over the hill, Bore.

SOOT. Don't call Booey ''Bore'' today, Karl. Someone might misunderstand.

KARL. Nobody will misunderstand.

(*Photo flash. Enter* FATHER DONNALLY. *The families take their place on either side of him.* BETTE *and* BOO *come together, and stand before him.*)

FATHER DONNALLY. We are gathered here in the sight of God to join this man and this woman in the sacrament of holy matrimony. Do you, Bette . . . ?

BETTE. (*To* BOO.) I do.

FATHER DONNALLY. And do you, Boo . . . ?

BOO. (*To* BETTE.) I do.

FATHER DONNALLY. (*Sort of to himself.*) Take this woman to be your lawfully wedded . . . I do, I do. (*Back to formal sounding.*) I pronounce you man and wife.

(BETTE *and* BOO *kiss.* KARL *throws a handful of rice at them, somewhat hostilely. This bothers no one.*)

JOAN. Come on, Emily.

(EMILY *and* JOAN *step forward.* PAUL *gets* EMILY *a chair to sit in when she plays her cello. He carries a flute.*)

EMILY. And now, in honor of our dear Bette's wedding, I will play the cello and my father will play the flute, and my wonderful sister Joanie will sing the Schubert Lied *Lachen und Weinen*, which translates as ''Laughing and Crying.'' (JOAN *gets in position to sing.* PAUL *holds his flute to his mouth.* EMILY *sits in her chair, puts the cello between her legs, and raises her bow. Long pause.*) I can't remember it.

JOAN. (*Very annoyed.*) It starts on A, Emily.

EMILY. (*Tries again; stops.*) I'm sorry. I'm sorry, Bette. I can't remember it.

(*Everyone looks a little disappointed and disgruntled with* EMILY. *Photo flash. Lights change. Spot on* MATT.)

Scene 2

MATT *addresses the audience.*

MATT. When ordering reality, it is necessary to accumulate all the facts pertaining to the matter at hand. When all the facts are not immediately available, one must try to reconstruct them by considering oral history—hearsay, gossip, and apocryphal stories. And then with perseverance and intelligence, the analysis of these facts should bring about understanding. The honeymoon of Bette and Boo.

(MATT *exits. Enter* BETTE, *still in her wedding dress. In the following speech, and much of the time,* BETTE *talks cheerfully and quickly, making no visible connections between her statements.*)

BETTE. Hurry up, Boo. I want to use the shower. (*Speaks to audience, who seem to her a great friend.*) First I was a tomboy. I used to climb trees and beat up my brother Tom. Then I used to try to break my sister Joanie's voice box because she liked to sing. She always scratched me though, so instead I tried to play Emily's cello. Except I don't have a lot of musical talent, but I'm very popular. And I know more about the cello than people who don't know anything. I don't like the cello, it's too much work and besides, keeping my legs open that way made me feel funny. I asked Emily if it made her feel funny and she didn't know what I meant; and then when I told her she cried for two whole hours and then went to confession twice, just in case the priest didn't understand her the first time. Dopey Emily. She means well. (*Calls offstage.*) Booey! I'm pregnant! (*To audience.*) Actually I couldn't be, because I'm a virgin. A married man tried to have an affair with me, but he was married and so it would have been pointless. I didn't know he was married until two months ago. Then I met Booey, sort of on the rebound. He seems fine, though. (*Calls out.*) Booey! (*To audience.*) I went to confession about the cello practicing, but I don't think the priest heard me. He didn't say anything. He didn't even give me a penance. I wonder if nobody was in there. But as long as your conscience is all right, then so is your soul. (*Calls, giddy, happy.*) Booey, come on!

(BETTE *runs off. Lights change. Spot on* MATT.)

Scene 3

MATT *addresses the audience.*

MATT. Margaret gives Emily advice.

(MATT *exits. Enter* MARGARET, EMILY, *holding her cello.*)

EMILY. Mom, I'm so upset that I forgot the piece at the wedding. Bette looked angry. When I write an apology, should I send it to Bette, or to Bette *and* Boo?

MARGARET. Emily, dear, don't go on about it.

(*Lights change. Spot on* MATT.)

Scene 4

MATT *addresses the audience.*

MATT. The honeymoon of Bette and Boo, continued.

(MATT *exits. Enter* BETTE *and* BOO, *wrapped in a large sheet and looking happy. They stand smiling for a moment. They should still be in their wedding clothes—* BETTE *minus her veil,* BOO *minus his tie and jacket.*)

BETTE. That was better than a cello, Boo.

BOO. You're mighty good-looking, gorgeous.

BETTE. Do you think I'm prettier than Polly Lydstone?

BOO. Who?

BETTE. I guess you don't know her. I want to have lots of children, Boo. Eight. Twelve. Did you read *Cheaper by the Dozen*?

BOO. I have to call my father about a new insurance deal we're handling. (*Takes phone from beneath the sheets; talks quietly into it.*) Hello, Pop . . .

BETTE. (*To audience.*) Lots and lots of children. I loved the movie *Skippy* with Jackie Cooper. I cried and cried. I always loved little boys. Where is my pocketbook? Find it for me, Boo.

(*The pocketbook is in full sight, but* BETTE *doesn't seem to notice it.*)

BOO. I'm talking to Pop, Bette. What is it, Pop?

BETTE. (*To audience.*) When I was a little girl, I used to love to mind Jimmy Winkler. "Do you want me to watch Jimmy?" I'd say to Mrs. Winkler. He was five years old and had short stubby legs. I used to dress him up as a lamp shade and walk him to town. I put tassels on his toes and taped doilies on his knees, and he'd scream and scream. My mother said, "Betsy, why are you crying about *Skippy*, it's only a movie, it's not real." But I didn't believe her. Bonnie Wilson was my best friend and she got tar all over her feet. Boo, where are you?

BOO. I'm here, angel. No, not you, Pop. No, I was talking to Bette. Here, why don't you speak to her? (*Hands* BETTE *the phone.*) Here, Bette, it's Pop.

BETTE. Hello there, Mr. Hudlocke. How are you? And Mrs. Hudlocke? I cried and cried at the movie *Skippy* because I thought it was real. Bonnie Wilson and I were the two stupidest in the class. Mrs. Sullivan used to say, "The two stupidest in math are Bonnie and Betsy. Bonnie, your grade is eight, and Betsy, your grade is five." Hello? Hello? (*To* BOO.) We must have been cut off, Boo. Where is my pocketbook?

BOO. Here it is, beautiful.

(BOO *gives her the pocketbook that has been in full sight all along.*)

BETTE. I love you, Boo.

Scene 5

EMILY *sits at her cello.*

EMILY. I can't remember it. (*She gets up and addresses her chair.*) It starts on A, Emily. (*She sits down, tries to play.*) I'm sorry. I'm sorry, Bette. I can't remember it.

(*Enter* JOAN *with scissors.*)

JOAN. It may start on A, Emily. But it ends now.

(JOAN *raises scissors up. Freeze and/or lights change.*)

Scene 6

MATT *addresses the audience.*

MATT. At the suggestion of *Redbook*, Bette refashions her wedding gown into a cocktail dress. Then she and Boo visit their in-laws. Bette is pregnant for the first time.

(MATT *exits.* BETTE, BOO, KARL, SOOT. BETTE *is in a shortened, simplified version of her wedding dress.*)

SOOT. How nice that you're going to have a baby.

KARL. Have another drink, Bore.

BETTE. (*To* SOOT.) I think Booey drinks too much. Does Mr. Hudlocke drink too much?

SOOT. I never think about it.

KARL. Soot, get me and Bore another drink.

(BOO *and* KARL *are looking over papers, presumably insurance.*)

BETTE. Don't have another one, Boo.

SOOT. (*Smiles, whispers.*) I think Karl drinks too much, but when he's sober he's really very nice.

BETTE. I don't think Boo should drink if I'm going to have a baby.

SOOT. If it's a boy, you can name him Boo, and if it's a girl you can call her Soot after me.

BETTE. How did you get the name "Soot"?

SOOT. Oh, you know. The old saying "She fell down the chimney and got covered with soot."

BETTE. What saying?

SOOT. Something about that. Karl might remember. Karl, how did I get the name "Soot"?

KARL. Get the drinks, Soot.

SOOT. All right.

KARL. (*To* BETTE.) Soot is the dumbest white woman alive.

SOOT. Oh, Karl. (*Laughs, exits.*)

BETTE. I don't want you to get drunk again, Boo. Joanie's husband Nikkos may lock himself in the bathroom, but he doesn't drink.

BOO. Bette, Pop and I are looking over these papers.

BETTE. I'm your wife.

BOO. Bette, you're making a scene.

KARL. Your baby's going to be all mouth if you keep talking so much. You want to give birth to a mouth, Bette?

BETTE. All right. I'm leaving.

BOO. Bette. Can't you take a joke?

BETTE. It's not funny.

KARL. I can tell another one. There was this drunken airline stewardess who got caught in the propeller . . .

BETTE. I'm leaving now, Boo. (*Exits.*)

BOO. Bette. I better go after her. (*Starts to exit.*)

KARL. Where are you going, Bore?

BOO. Bette's a little upset, Pop. I'll see you later. (BOO *exits. Enter* SOOT *with drinks.*)

SOOT. Where's Booey, Karl?

KARL. He isn't here.

SOOT. I know. Where did he go?

KARL. Out the door.

SOOT. Did you say something to Bette, Karl?

KARL. Let's have the drinks, Soot.

SOOT. You know, I really can't remember how everyone started calling me Soot. Can you, Karl?

KARL. Go into your dance, Soot.

SOOT. Oh, Karl. (*Laughs.*)

KARL. Go get the veils and start in. The shades are down.

SOOT. Karl, I don't know what you're talking about.

KARL. You're the dumbest white woman alive. I rest my case.

(SOOT *laughs. Lights change.*)

Scene 7

MATT *addresses the audience.*

MATT. Bette goes to Margaret, her mother, for advice.

(MATT *exits.* BETTE, MARGARET, EMILY *on the floor, writing a note.* PAUL, *the father, is also present.*)

BETTE. Mom, Boo drinks. And his father insulted me.

MARGARET. Betsy, dear, marriage is no bed of roses.

EMILY. Mom, is the phrase "my own stupidity" hyphenated?

MARGARET. No, Emily. She's apologizing to Joanie again about forgetting the piece at the wedding. Joanie *was* very embarrassed.

BETTE. How can I make Boo stop drinking?

MARGARET. I'm sure it's not a serious problem, Betsy.

BETTE. Poppa, what should I do?

PAUL. W##hh, ah%#% enntgh oo sh#$w auns$$dr ehvg###ing%%#s ahm.

(NOTE TO READER AND/OR ACTOR: *Paul is meant to be the victim of a stroke. His mind is still functioning well, but his ability to speak is greatly impaired. Along these lines, I give him specific lines to say and be motivated by, but the audience and the other characters in the play should genuinely be unable to make out almost anything that he says—though they can certainly follow any emotional colorings he gives. I have found it useful for actors who read the part of Paul to say the lines written in the brackets, but to drop almost all of the consonants and to make the tongue go slack, so that poor Paul's speech is almost all vowels, mixed in with an occasional inexplicable group of consonants. Paul's first line up above—emphasizing that no one should be able to make out almost any of it—would be: "Well, I think you should consider giving things time."*)

BETTE. What should I do?

PAUL. (*Angry that he can't be understood.*) On ####%t ump oo%#% onoosns#$s. Eggh ing ahm#$. [Don't jump to conclusions. Give things time.]

MARGARET. Paul, I've asked you not to speak. We can't understand you.

EMILY. Mom, how do you spell "mea culpa"?

MARGARET. Emily, Latin is pretentious in an informal letter. Joanie will think you're silly.

EMILY. This one is to Father Donnally.

MARGARET. M-E-A C-U-L-P-A.

BETTE. Boo's father has given him a very bad example. (*Enter* JOAN, *carrying a piece of paper.*) Oh, Joan, quick—do you think when I have my baby, it will make Boo stop . . .

JOAN. Wait a minute. (*To* EMILY.) Emily, I got your note. Now listen to me closely. (*With vehemence.*) I *forgive* you, I *forgive* you, I *forgive* you.

EMILY. (*A bit startled.*) Oh. Thank you.

JOAN. (*To* BETTE.) Now, what did you want?

BETTE. Do you think when I have my baby, it will make Boo stop drinking and bring him and me closer together?

JOAN. I have no idea.

BETTE. Well, but hasn't your having little Mary Frances made things better between you and Nikkos? He isn't still disappearing for days, is he?

JOAN. Are you trying to make me feel bad about my marriage?

EMILY. I'm sorry, Joanie.

JOAN. What?

EMILY. If I made you feel bad about your marriage.

JOAN. Oh, shut up. (*Exits.*)

BETTE. (*To* MARGARET.) She's so nasty. Did you punish her enough when she was little?

MARGARET. She's just tired because little Mary Frances cries all the time. She really is a dreadful child.

BETTE. I love babies. Poppa, don't you think my baby will bring Boo and me closer together?

PAUL. Aszzs&* ot uh er#ry owowd#@ eeah oo ah uh ayee, ehtte. [That's not a very good reason to have a baby, Bette.]

(BETTE *looks at* PAUL *blankly. Lights change.*)

Scene 8

MATT *addresses the audience.*

MATT. Twenty years later, Boo has dinner with his son.

(BOO *and* MATT *sit at a table.*)

BOO. Well, how are things up at Dartmouth, Skip? People in the office ask me how my Ivy League son is doing.

MATT. It's all right.

BOO. Are there any pretty girls up there?

MATT. Uh huh.

BOO. So what are you learning up there?

MATT. Tess of the d'Urbervilles is a masochist.

BOO. What?

MATT. It's a novel we're reading. (*Mumbles.*) *Tess of the d'Urbervilles*.

BOO (*Laughs.*) A man needs a woman, son. I miss your mother. I'd go back with her in a minute if she wanted. She's not in love with her family anymore, and I think she knows that drinking wasn't that much of a problem. I think your old man's going to get teary for a second. I'm just an old softie. (BOO *blinks his eyes, wipes them.* MATT *exits, embarrassed.* BOO *doesn't notice but addresses the chair as if* MATT *were still there.*) I miss your mother, Skip. Nobody should be alone. Do you have any problems, son, you want to talk over? Your old man could help you out.

(BOO *waits for an answer. Lights change.*)

Scene 9

MATT *addresses the audience.*

MATT. The first child of Bette and Boo.

(MATT *exits. Enter* BOO, KARL, SOOT, MARGARET, EMILY *with her cello,* JOAN, PAUL. *They all stand in a line and wait expectantly. Enter the* DOCTOR, *who is played by the same actor who plays Father Donnally.*)

DOCTOR. She's doing well. Just a few more minutes. (*Exits.*)

EMILY. Oh God, make her pain small. Give me the pain rather than her. (*Winces in pain.*)

MARGARET. Emily, behave, this is a hospital.

BOO. Pop, I hope it's a son.

KARL. This calls for a drink. Soot, get Bore and me a drink.

SOOT. Where would I go?

KARL. A drink, Soot.

SOOT. Karl, you're teasing me again.

KARL. All right, I won't talk to you.

SOOT. Oh, please. Please talk to me. Booey, talk to your father.

BOO. Come on, Pop. We'll have a drink afterwards.

SOOT. Karl, I'll get you a drink. (*To* MARGARET.) Where would I go? (*To* KARL.) Karl?

KARL. This doctor know what he's doing, Bore?

SOOT. Karl? Wouldn't you like a drink?

EMILY. It's almost here. (*Having an experience of some sort.*) Oh no, no, no no no no.

MARGARET. Emily!

KARL. This Betsy's sister, Bore?

BOO. Pop, I hope it's a boy.

KARL. You were a boy, Bore. (*Enter the* DOCTOR, *holding the baby in a blue blanket.*) This is it, Bore.

EMILY. In the name of the Father, and of the Son, and of the Holy Ghost.

DOCTOR. It's dead. The baby's dead. (*He drops it on the floor.*)

EMILY. (*Near collapse.*) Oh no!

JOAN. I win the bet.

MARGARET. I'm here, Betsy, it's all right. (PAUL *picks up the baby.*) Paul, put the baby down. That's disrespectful.

PAUL. Buh uh ayee ah#$# ehh#! [But the baby's not dead.]

MARGARET. Don't shout. I can understand you.

PAUL. (*To* DOCTOR.) Uh ayee ah#$# ehh#! Yrr uh ahherr, ann## oo ee, uh ayee ah#$# ehh#! [The baby's not dead. You're a doctor, can't you see, the baby's not dead.]

DOCTOR. (*Takes the baby.*) Oh, you're right. It's not dead. Mr. Hudlocke, you have a son.

KARL. Congratulations, Bore.

EMILY. Thank you, God. (*Enter* BETTE, *radiant. She takes the baby.*)

BETTE. (*To audience.*) We'll call the baby Skippy.

EMILY. It has to be a saint's name, Bette.

BETTE. Mind your business, Emily.

MARGARET. Betsy, dear, Emily's right. Catholics have to be named after saints. Otherwise they can't be baptized.

BOO. Boo.

MARGARET. There is no Saint Boo.

EMILY. We should call it Margaret in honor of Mom.

BETTE. It's a boy.

EMILY. We should call him Paul in honor of Dad.

MARGARET. Too common.

SOOT. I always liked Clarence.

JOAN. I vote for Boo.

MARGARET. (*Telling her to behave.*) Joanie.

KARL. Why not name it after a household appliance?

SOOT. Karl. (*Laughs.*)

KARL. Egg beater. Waffle iron. Bath mat.

BETTE. (*To audience.*) Matt. I remember a little boy named Matt who looked just like a wind-up toy. We'll call him Matt.

BOO. It's a boy, Pop.

EMILY. Is Matt a saint's name, Bette?

BETTE. Matt*hew*, Emily. Maybe if you'd finally join the convent, you'd learn the apostles' names.

EMILY. Do you think I should join a convent?

BETTE. (*To audience.*) But his nickname's going to be Skippy. My very favorite movie.

(*Lights change.*)

Scene 10

MATT *addresses the audience.*

MATT. *My Very Favorite Movie,* an essay by Matthew Hudlocke. My very favorite movie . . . are . . . *Nights of Cabiria, 8½, Citizen Kane, L'Avventura, The Seventh Seal, Persona, The Parent Trap, The Song of Bernadette, Potemkin, The Fire Within, The Bells of St. Mary's, The Singing Nun, The Dancing Nun, The Nun on the Fire Escape Outside My Window, The Nun That Caused the Chicago Fire, The Nun Also Rises, The Nun Who Came to Dinner, The Caucasian Chalk Nun, Long Day's Journey into Nun, None But the Lonely Heart,* and *The Nun Who Shot Liberty Valance.*

Page two. In the novels of Thomas Hardy, we find a deep

and unrelieved pessimism. Hardy's novels, set in his home town of Wessex, contrast nature outside of man with the human nature inside of man, coming together inexorably to cause human catastrophe. The sadness in Hardy—his lack of belief that a benevolent God watches over human destiny, his sense of the waste and frustration of the average human life, his forceful irony in the face of moral and metaphysical questions—is part of the late Victorian mood. We can see something like it in A. E. Housman, or in Emily's life. Shortly after Skippy's birth, Emily enters a convent, but then leaves the convent due to nerves. Bette becomes pregnant for the second time. Boo continues to drink. If psychiatrists had existed in nineteenth century Wessex, Hardy might suggest Bette and Boo seek counseling. Instead he has no advice to give them, and in 1886 he writes *The Mayor of Caster-bridge*. This novel is one of Hardy's greatest successes, and Skippy studies it in college. When he is little, he studies *The Wind in the Willows* with Emily. And when he is very little, he studies drawing with Emily.

(EMILY, MATT. EMILY *has brightly colored construction paper and crayons.*)

EMILY. Hello, Skippy, dear. I thought we could do some nice arts and crafts today. Do you want to draw a cat or a dog?

MATT. A dog.

EMILY. All right, then I'll do a cat. (*They begin to draw.*) Here's the head, and here's the whiskers. Oh dear, it looks more like a clock. Oh, Skippy, yours is very good. I can tell it's a dog. Those are the ears, and that's the tail, right?

MATT. Yes.

EMILY. That's very good. And you draw much better than Mary Frances. I tried to interest her in drawing Babar the elephant the other day, but she doesn't like arts and crafts, and she scribbled all over the paper, and then she had a crying fit. (*Sits back.*) Oh dear. I shouldn't say she doesn't draw well, it sounds like a criticism of Joanie.

MATT. I won't tell.

EMILY. Yes, but it would be on my conscience. I better write Joanie a note apologizing. And really, Mary Frances draws *very* well, I didn't mean it when I said she didn't. She probably had a headache. I think I'll use this nice pink piece of construction paper to apologize to Joanie, and I'll apologize about forgetting the piece at your mother's wedding too. I've never been sure Joanie's forgiven me, even though she says she has. I don't know what else I can do except apologize. I don't have any money.

MATT. Your cat looks very good. It doesn't look like a clock.

EMILY. You're such a comfort, Skippy. I'll be right back. Why don't you pretend your dog is real, and you can teach it tricks while I'm gone.

(EMILY *exits.* MATT *makes "roll over" gesture to drawing, waits for response. Lights change,* MATT *exits.*)

Scene 11

BETTE *enters, carrying a chair. She sits on the chair.*
BETTE. (*To audience and/or herself.*) I'm going to pretend that I'm sitting in this chair. Then I'm going to pretend that I'm going to have another baby. And then I'm going to have another, and another and another. I'm going to pretend to have a big family. There'll be Skippy. And then all the A. A. Milne characters. Boo should join AA. There'll be Eeyore and Pooh Bear and Christopher Robin and Tigger . . . My family is going to be like an enormous orphanage. I'll be their mother. Kanga and six hundred Baby Roos. Baby Roo is Kanga's baby, but she's a mother to them all. Roo and Tigger and Pooh and Christopher Robin and Eeyore and Owl, owl, ow, ow, ow, ow, ow, ow, ow, ow, ow! I'm giving birth, Mom. Roo and Tigger and Boo and Pooh and Soot and Eeyore and Karl and Betsy and Owl . . .

(*Enter quickly:* BOO, KARL, SOOT, MARGARET, PAUL, EMILY, JOAN. *They stand in their same hospital positions. Enter the* DOCTOR *with the baby in a blue blanket.*)
DOCTOR. The baby's dead. (*Drops it on the floor.*)

MARGARET. Nonsense. That's what he said about the last one, didn't he, Paul?

DOCTOR. This time it's true. It *is* dead.

BETTE. Why?

DOCTOR. The reason the baby is dead is this: Mr. Hudlocke has Rh positive blood.

KARL. Good for you, Bore!

DOCTOR. Mrs. Hudlocke has Rh negative blood.

BETTE. Like Kanga.

DOCTOR. And so the mother's Rh negative blood fights the baby's Rh positive blood and so: the mother kills the baby.

EMILY. (*Rather horrified.*) Who did this??? The mother did this???

KARL. You married a winner, Bore.

BOO. The baby came. And it was dead. (*Picks up baby.*)

SOOT. Poor Booey.

BETTE. But I'll have other babies.

DOCTOR. The danger for your health if you do and the likelihood of stillbirth are overwhelming considerations.

BOO. The baby came. And it was dead.

BETTE. Mama, tell him to go away.

MARGARET. There, there. Say something to her, Paul. (PAUL *says nothing. Lights change.*)

Scene 12

MATT *addresses the audience.*

MATT. Bette and Margaret visit Emily, who is in a rest home due to nerves.

(MATT *exits.* EMILY *with her cello.* BETTE, MARGARET. BETTE *seems very depressed, and keeps looking at the floor or looking off.*)

EMILY. Oh, Mom, Bette. It's so good to see you. How are you feeling, Bette, after your tragedy?

MARGARET. Emily, don't talk about it. Change the subject.

EMILY. (*Trying desperately to oblige.*) Um . . . um . . . uh . . .

MARGARET. (*Looking around slightly.*) This is a very nice room for an institution. Bette, look up. Do you like the doctors, Emily?

EMILY. Yes, they're very good to me.

MARGARET. They should be. They're very expensive. I was going to ask your brother Tom for some money for your stay here, but he's really not . . . Oh, I didn't mean to mention Tom. Forget I said anything.

EMILY. Oh, what is it? Is he all right?

MARGARET. I shouldn't have mentioned it. Forget it, Emily.

EMILY. But what's the matter with him? Is he ill? Oh, Mom . . .

MARGARET. Now, Emily, don't go on about it. That's a fault of yours. If you had stayed in the convent, maybe you could have corrected that fault. Oh, I'm sorry. I didn't mean to bring up the convent.

EMILY. That's all right, Mom. (*Silence.*)

MARGARET. Besides, whatever happens, happens. Don't look that way, Emily. Change the subject!

EMILY. Um . . . uh . . .

MARGARET. There are many pleasant things in the world, think of them.

EMILY. (*Trying hard to think of something; then:*) How is Skippy, Bette?

BETTE. Who?

EMILY. Skippy.

BETTE. (*To* MARGARET.) Who?

MARGARET. She means Baby Roo, dear.

BETTE. Oh, Roo. Yes. (*Stares off in distance blankly.*)

EMILY. Is he well?

MARGARET. (*Telling* EMILY *to stop.*) He's fine, dear. Looks just like his mother.

EMILY. He's a lovely child. I look forward to seeing him when I finally leave here and get to go . . . (*Gets teary.*)

MARGARET. Emily, the doctors told me they're sure you're not here for life. Isn't that right, Bette. (*Whispers to* EMILY.) The doctors say Bette shouldn't have any more babies.

EMILY. Oh dear. And Bette's a wonderful mother. Bette, dear, don't feel bad, you have the one wonderful child, and maybe someday God will make a miracle so you can have more children.

BETTE. (*The first sentence she's heard.*) I can have more children.

EMILY. Well, maybe God will make a *miracle* so you can.

BETTE. I can have a miracle?

EMILY. Well, you pray and ask for one.

MARGARET. Emily, miracles are very fine . . .

EMILY. Oh, I didn't think, I shouldn't have . . .

MARGARET. But now you've raised Betsy's hopes . . .

EMILY. Oh, Bette, listen to Mom . . . I'm so sorry . . .

BETTE. I CAN HAVE MORE CHILDREN!

MARGARET. That's right, Betsy. Emily, I know you didn't mean to bring this up . . .

EMILY. I'm so stupid . . .

MARGARET. But first you start on your brother Tom who has a spastic colon and is drinking too much . . .

EMILY. Oh no!

BETTE (*Very excited, overlapping with* MARGARET.) I CAN HAVE MORE CHILDREN, I CAN HAVE MORE CHILDREN, I CAN HAVE MORE CHILDREN . . . (*etc.*)

MARGARET. (*Overlapping with* BETTE.) . . . and has been fired and there's some crazy talk about him and some boy in high school, which I'm sure isn't true, and even if it is . . .

EMILY. Tom's all right, isn't he, it isn't true . . .

BETTE. . . . I CAN HAVE MORE CHILDREN! . . . (*etc.*)

MARGARET. I didn't mean to tell you, Emily, but you talk and talk . . .

BETTE. . . . I CAN HAVE MORE CHILDREN, I CAN HAVE MORE CHILDREN . . .

EMILY. Oh, Mom, I'm so sorry, I . . .

MARGARET. . . . and *talk* about a thing until you think your head is going to explode . . .

EMILY. (*Overlapping still.*) I'm so sorry, I . . . WAIT! (*Silence.* EMILY *sits at her cello with great concentration, picks up the bow.*) I think I remember it. (*Listens, tries to remember the piece from the wedding, keeps trying out different notes.* MARGARET *looks between the two girls.*)

MARGARET. I wish you two could see yourselves. (*Laughs merrily.*) You're both acting very funny. (*Laughs again.*) Come on, Betsy.

(MARGARET *and* BETTE *exit, cheerful.* EMILY *keeps trying to remember. Lights change.*)

Scene 13

MATT *addresses the audience.*

MATT. Bette seeks definition of the word "miracle" from Father Donnally.

(MATT *exits.* BETTE, FATHER DONNALLY. *She kneels to him in the confessional, blesses herself.*)

FATHER DONNALLY. Hello, Bette, how are you?

BETTE. I'm feeling much better after my tragedy.

FATHER DONNALLY. It's a cross to bear.

BETTE. Have you ever read *Winnie the Pooh*, Father? Most people think it's for children, but I never read it until I was an adult. The humor is very sophisticated.

FATHER DONNALLY. I'll have to read it sometime.

BETTE. Do you believe in miracles, Father?

FATHER DONNALLY. Miracles rarely happen, Bette.

BETTE. I do too! Thank you, Father. You've helped me make a decision.

(*Lights change.*)

Scene 14

MATT *addresses the audience.*

MATT. Soot gives Bette some advice.

(MATT *exits.* BETTE, *pregnant,* BOO, SOOT, KARL.)

BETTE. And then Father Donnally said that I should

just keep trying and that even if this baby died, there would be at least one more baby that would live, and then I would be a mother as God meant me to be. Do you agree, Soot?

SOOT. I've never met this Father Donnally. Karl, Pauline has a retarded daughter, doesn't she? LaLa is retarded, isn't she? I mean, she isn't just slow, is she?

BETTE. I don't care if the child's retarded. Then that's God's will. I love retarded children. I like children more than I like people. Boo, you're drinking too much, it's not fair to me. If this baby dies, it's going to be your fault.

BOO. I don't think Father Donnally should have encouraged you about this. That's what I think.

BETTE. He's a priest. (*To* SOOT.) Did you ever see Jackie Cooper as a child? I thought he was much cuter than Shirley Temple, what do you think, Soot?

KARL. Bore, my wife Soot hasn't said one sensible thing in thirty years of marriage . . .

SOOT. Oh, Karl . . . (*Laughs, flattered.*)

KARL. But your little wife has just said more senseless things in one ten-minute period than Soot here has said in thirty years of bondage.

SOOT. Oh, Karl. I never was one for talking.

BETTE. (*To* KARL.) Look here, you. I'm not afraid of you. I'm not going to let Boo push me to a breakdown the way you've pushed Soot. I'm stronger than that.

SOOT. Oh my. (*Laughs.*) Sit down, dear.

KARL. Tell the baby-maker to turn it down, Bore.

BOO. Bette, sit down.

BETTE. I want a marriage and a family and a home, and I'm going to have them, and if you won't help me, Boo, I'll have them without you. (*Exits.*)

KARL. Well, Bore, I don't know about you and your wife. Whatever one can say against your mother, and it's most everything (*Soot laughs*), at least she didn't go around dropping dead children at every step of the way like some goddamned giddy farm animal.

SOOT. Karl, you shouldn't tease everyone so.

KARL. I don't like the way you're behaving today, Soot. (*Exits.*)

SOOT. (*Looks back to where* BETTE *was.*) Bette, dear, let me give you some advice. Oh, that's right. She left. (*A moment of disorientation; looks at* BOO.) Boo, Karl's a lovely man most of the time, and I've had a very happy life with him, but I hope you'll be a little kinder than he was. Just a little. Anything is an improvement. I wish I had dead children. I wish I had two hundred dead children. I'd stuff them down Karl's throat. (*Laughs.*) Of course, I'm only kidding. (*Laughs some more.*)

(*Lights change.*)

Scene 15

MATT *addresses the audience.*

MATT. Now the Mayor of Casterbridge, when drunk, sells his wife and child to someone he meets in a bar. Now Boo is considerably better behaved than this. Now the fact of the matter is that Boo isn't really an alcoholic at all, but drinks simply because Bette is such a terrible, unending nag. Or perhaps Boo *is* an alcoholic, and Bette is a terrible, unending nag in *reaction* to his drinking so much, and also because he just isn't "there" for her, any more than Clym Yeobright is really there for Eustacia Vye in *The Return of the Native,* although admittedly Eustacia Vye is very neurotic, but then so is Bette also.

Or perhaps it's the fault of the past history of stillbirths and the pressures that that history puts on their physical relationship. Perhaps blame can be assigned totally to the Catholic Church. Certainly Emily's guilt about leaving the convent and about everything else in the world can be blamed largely on the Catholic Church. (*Pleased.*) James Joyce can be blamed on the Catholic Church; but not really Thomas Hardy. And then in 1896 Hardy writes *Jude the Obscure.* And when Skippy is nine, Bette goes to the hospital for the third time. The third child of Bette and Boo.

(MATT *exits. Lights change.*)

Scene 16

Everyone assembles, except for BETTE. BOO, KARL, SOOT, MARGARET, PAUL, JOAN, EMILY. *They wait. Enter the* DOCTOR. *He drops the baby on the floor, exits. Pause. Lights change.*

Scene 17

BETTE *on the telephone, late at night.*

BETTE. Hello, Bonnie? This is Betsy. Betsy. (*To remind her.*) "Bonnie, your grade is eight, and Betsy, your grade is five." Yes, it's me. How are you? Oh, I'm sorry, I woke you? Well, what time is it? Oh, I'm sorry. But isn't Florida in a different time zone than we are? Oh. I thought it was. Oh well.

Bonnie, are you married? How many children do you have? Two. That's nice. Are you going to have any more? Oh, I think you should. Yes, I'm married. To Boo. I wrote you. Oh, I never wrote you? How many years since we've spoken? Since we were fifteen. Well, I'm not a very good correspondent. Oh dear, you're yawning, I guess it's too late to have called. Bonnie, do you remember the beach and little Jimmy Winkler? I used to dress him up as a lamp shade, it was so cute. Oh. Well, do you remember when Miss Willis had me stand in the corner, and you stand in the wastebasket, and then your grandmother came to class that day? I thought you'd remember that. Oh, you want to go back to sleep?

Oh, I'm sorry. Bonnie, before you hang up, I've lost two babies. No, I don't mean misplaced, stupid, they died. I go through the whole nine-month period of carrying them, and then when it's over, they just take them away. I don't even see the bodies. Hello? Oh, I thought you weren't there. I'm sorry, I didn't realize it was so late. I thought Florida was Central Time or something. Yes, I got twelve in geography or something you remember? "Betsy, your grade is twelve and Bonnie, your grade is . . ." What did you get in geography? Well, it's not important anyway. What? No, Boo's not home. Well, sometimes he just goes to a bar and then he doesn't come home until the bar closes, and some of them don't close at all and so he gets confused what time it is. Does your husband drink? Oh, that's good. What's his name? Scooter? Like bicycle? I like the name Scooter. I love cute things. Do you remember Jackie Cooper in *Skippy* and his best friend Sukey? I cried and cried. Hello, are you still there? I'm sorry, I guess I better let you go back to sleep. Goodbye, Bonnie, it was good to hear your voice. (*Hangs up.*)

(*Lights change.*)

Scene 18

MATT *addresses the audience.*

MATT. Several months later, Bette and Boo have the two families over to celebrate Thanksgiving.

(BETTE, MATT. BETTE *is on the warpath.*)

BETTE. (*Calling off, nasty.*) Come *up* from the cellar, Boo. I'm not going to say it again. They're going to be here. (*To* MATT.) He's hidden a bottle behind the furnace.

MATT. Please stop shouting.

BETTE. Do you smell something on his breath?

MATT. I don't know. I didn't get that close.

BETTE. Can't you go up and kiss him?

MATT. I can't go up and kiss him for no reason.

BETTE. You're so unaffectionate. There's nothing wrong with a ten-year-old boy kissing his father.

MATT. I don't want to kiss him.

BETTE. Well, I think I smelled something. (*Enter* BOO.)

BOO. What are you talking about?

BETTE. You're always picking on me. I wasn't talking about anything. Set the table, Skippy. (MATT *exits.*)

BOO. When are they all coming?

BETTE. When do you think they're coming? Let me smell your breath.

BOO. Leave my breath alone.

BETTE. You've been drinking. You've got a funny look in your eye.

(*Enter* MATT, *holding some silverware.*)

MATT. Something's burning in the oven.

BETTE. Why can't you stop drinking? You don't care enough about me and Skippy to stop drinking, do you?

MATT. It's going to burn.

BETTE. You don't give me anything to be grateful for. You're just like your father. You're a terrible example to Skippy. He's going to grow up neurotic because of you.

MATT. I'll turn the oven off. (*Exits.*)

BOO. Why don't you go live with your mother, you're both so perfect.

BETTE. Don't criticize my mother.

(*Enter* JOAN *and* EMILY. JOAN *has a serving dish with candied sweet potatoes.* EMILY *has a large gravy boat dish.*)

EMILY. Happy Thanksgiving, Bette.

BETTE. Hush, Emily. You're weak, Boo. It's probably just as well the other babies have died.

EMILY. I brought the gravy.

BETTE. We don't care about the gravy, Emily. I want you to see a priest, Boo.

BOO. Stop talking. I want you to stop talking.

(*Enter* MARGARET *and* PAUL. PAUL *is holding a large cake.*)

MARGARET. Hello, Betsy dear.

BETTE. He's been drinking.

MARGARET. Let's not talk about it. Hello, Boo, Happy Thanksgiving.

BOO. Hello.

(*Enter* SOOT *and* KARL. SOOT *is carrying a candelabra.*)

SOOT. Hello, Margaret.

MARGARET. How nice to see you. Paul, you remember Mrs. Hudlocke?

PAUL. Icse oo ee oo, issizzse uhoch##. Iht oo ab uhull ineing uh arreeng ace####? [Nice to see you, Mrs. Hudlocke. Did you have trouble finding a parking place?]

Soot. I guess so. (*To everybody.*) I brought a candelabra.

Bette. (*To* Soot.) You're his mother, I want you to smell his breath.

Boo. SHUT UP ABOUT MY BREATH!

(Boo *accidentally knocks into* Emily, *who drops the gravy on the floor.*)

Bette. You've spilled the gravy all over the rug!

Emily. I'm sorry.

Bette. Boo did it!

Boo. I'll clean it up, I'll clean it up. (*Exits.*)

Bette. I think he's hidden a bottle in the cellar.

Emily. Joanie didn't drop the sweet potatoes.

Soot. Are we early? (*Laughs.*)

Karl. Pipe down, Soot.

(Boo *enters with a vacuum cleaner. All watch him as he starts to vacuum up the gravy.*)

Bette. What are you doing? Boo!

Boo. I can do it!

Bette. You don't vacuum gravy!

Boo. I can do it!

Bette. Stop it! You're ruining the vacuum!

Soot. Oh dear. Let's go. (*Laughs.*) Good-bye, Booey. (Karl *and* Soot *exit.*)

Joan. I knew we shouldn't have had it here.

Margaret. Come on, Betsy. Why don't you and Skippy stay with us tonight?

Bette. YOU DON'T VACUUM GRAVY!

Margaret. Let it alone, Betsy.

Bette. You don't vacuum gravy. You don't vacuum gravy. You don't vacuum gravy!

Boo. (*Hysterical.*) WHAT DO YOU DO WITH IT THEN? TELL ME! WHAT DO YOU DO WITH IT?

Bette. (*Quieter, but very upset.*) You get warm water, and a sponge, and you sponge it up.

(Bette *and* Boo *stare at one another, spent.*)

Emily. Should we put the sweet potatoes in the oven? (Matt *exits.*)

Joan. Come on, Emily. Let's go home.

Margaret. Betsy, if you and Skippy want to stay at our house tonight, just come over. Good-bye, Boo.

EMILY. (*Calls.*) Good-bye, Skippy.

(MARGARET, JOAN, EMILY, *and* PAUL *exit. Enter* MATT *with a pan of water and two sponges. He hands them to* BETTE. BETTE *and* BOO *methodically sponge up the gravy. Music to the "Bette and Boo" theme in the background.*)

BOO. (*Quietly.*) Okay, we'll soak it up with the sponge. That's what we're doing. We're soaking it up. (*They more or less finish with it.*) I'm going to take a nap.

(BOO *lies down where he is, and falls asleep.*)

BETTE. Boo? Boo? Booey? Boo?

(*Enter* SOOT.)

SOOT. Did I lose an earring in here? Oh dear. He's just asleep, isn't he?

BETTE. Boo? Boo.

SOOT. He must have gotten tired. (*Holds up earring, to* MATT.) If you should see it, it looks like this one. (*Laughs.*) Booey? (*Laughs.*) I think he's asleep. Good-bye, Booey. (*Exits.*)

BETTE. Boo? Booey?

MATT. Please don't try to wake him up. You'll just argue.

BETTE. All right. I won't try to wake him. (*Pause.*) Boo. Booey. (*She pushes his shoulder slightly.*) Boo. (*To* MATT.) I just want to get through to him about the gravy. (*To* BOO.) Boo. You don't vacuum gravy. Are you awake, Boo? Boo? I wonder if he's going to sleep through the night. I can wait. Boo. Booey.

(BETTE *looks at* MATT, *then back at* BOO. MATT *looks at both of them, then out to audience, exhausted and trapped, but with little actual expression on his face. Lights dim. End Act I.*)

ACT II

Scene 19

BETTE, BOO, FATHER DONNALLY *down center.* MATT *to the side. All the others stand together as they did in the beginning to sing the ''Bette and Boo'' theme. Music introduction to the theme is heard.*

ALL. (*Except* BETTE, BOO, FATHER DONNALLY, MATT; *sing.*)

> Ninety-nine bottles of beer on the wall,
> Ninety-nine bottles of beer,
> Take one down, pass it around,
> Ninety-eight bottles of beer on the wall.
>
> Ninety-eight bottles of beer on the wall,
> Ninety-eight bottles of beer . . . (*etc.*)

(*They keep singing this softly under the following scene.*)

BOO. (*Holding up a piece of paper.*) I pledge, in front of Father Donnally, to give up drinking in order to save my marriage and to make my wife and son happy.

FATHER DONNALLY. Now sign it, Boo.

(BOO *signs it.*)

BETTE. (*Happy.*) Thank you, Boo. (*Kisses him; to* FATHER DONNALLY.) Should you bless him or something?

FATHER DONNALLY. Oh, I don't know. Sure. (*Blesses them.*) In the name of the Father, Son, and Holy Ghost. Amen.

BETTE. Thank you, Father.

FATHER DONNALLY. All problems can be worked out, can't they?

BETTE. Yes, they can.

FATHER DONNALLY. Through faith.

BETTE. And willpower. Boo, let's have another baby.

THOSE SINGING. (*Finishing.*)

Take one down, pass it around,
God bless us one and all!

(*Lights change.*)

Scene 20

BETTE *and* BOO *dance. Perhaps no music in the background.*

BETTE. This is fun to go dancing, Boo. We haven't gone since before our honeymoon.

BOO. You're mighty pretty tonight, gorgeous.

BETTE. I wonder if Bonnie Wilson grew up to be pretty. We were the two stupidest in the class. I don't think Joanie's marriage is working out. Nikkos is a louse.

BOO. I think the waiter thought I was odd just ordering ginger ale.

BETTE. The waiter didn't think anything about it. You think everyone's looking at you. They're not. Emily said she's going to pray every day that this baby lives. I wonder what's the matter with Emily.

BOO. Your family's crazy.

BETTE. Don't criticize my family, Boo. I'll get angry. Do you think I'm prettier than Polly Lydstone?

BOO. Who?

BETTE. You're going to have to make more money when this baby comes. I think Father Donnally is very nice, don't you? Your father is terrible to your mother. My father was always sweet to my mother.

BOO. I think the waiter thinks I'm odd.

BETTE. What is it with you and the waiter? Stop talking about the waiter. Let's just have a nice time. (*They dance in silence.*) Are you having a nice time?

BOO. You're lookin' mighty pretty tonight, Bette.

BETTE. Me too, Boo.
(*They dance, cheered up. Lights change.*)

Scene 21

MATT *addresses the audience.*

MATT. *Holidays,* an essay by Matthew Hudlocke. Holidays were invented in 1203 by Sir Ethelbert Holiday, a sadistic Englishman. It was Sir Ethelbert's hope that by setting aside specific days on which to celebrate things— the birth of Christ, the death of Christ, Beowulf's defeat over Grendel—that the population at large would fall into a collective *deep* depression. Holidays would regulate joy so that anyone who didn't feel joyful on those days would feel bad. Single people would be sad they were single. Married people would be sad they were married. Everyone would feel disappointment that their lives had fallen so far short of their expectations.

A small percentage of people, sensing the sadism in Sir Ethelbert's plan, did indeed pretend to be joyful at these appointed times; everyone else felt intimidated by this small group's excessive delight, and so never owned up to being miserable. And so, as time went on, the habit of celebrating holidays became more and more ingrained into society.

Eventually humorists like Robert Benchley wrote mildly amusing essays poking fun at the impossibility of enjoying holidays, but no one actually spoke up and attempted to abolish them.

And so, at this time, the Thanksgiving with the gravy having been such fun, Bette and Boo decided to celebrate the holiday of Christmas by visiting the Hudlockes.

(*Maybe a bit of Christmas music.* EMILY *sits near* KARL *and* SOOT. BOO *is off to one side, drinking something.* BETTE *is off to another side, looking grim; she is also looking pregnant.* MATT *sits on floor near* EMILY *or* SOOT.)

EMILY. I think Christmas is becoming too commercial.

We should never forget whose birthday we are celebrating.

SOOT. That's right. Whose birthday are we celebrating?

EMILY. Our Lord Savior.

SOOT. Oh yes, of course. I thought she meant some relative.

EMILY. Jesus.

SOOT. It's so nice of you to visit us today, Emily. I don't think I've seen you since you were away at that . . . well . . . away. (*Laughs.*)

EMILY. Skippy asked me to come along, but I'm enjoying it.

KARL. Soot, get Bore and me another drink.

BETTE. IF BOO HAS ANOTHER DRINK, I AM GOING TO SCREAM AND SCREAM UNTIL THE WINDOWS BREAK! I WARN YOU! (*Pause.*)

KARL. (*Looks at Bette.*) You're having another baby, woman?

BOO. I told you, Pop. Besty has a lot of courage.

KARL. You're trying to kill Betsy, Bore?

BETTE. I'm going to lie down in the other room. (*To Boo.*) Skippy will tell me if you have another drink. (*Exits.*)

KARL. You sound like quite a scout, Skip. Is Skip a scout, Bore?

BOO. What, Pop?

KARL. Is Skip a scout, Bore?

SOOT. I was a Brownie.

(*Re-enter* BETTE.)

BETTE. Boo upsets Skippy's stomach. (*Sits down.*) I'm not leaving the room. (*Pause.*)

SOOT. (*To* EMILY.) My friend Lottie always comes out to visit at Christmas time . . .

KARL. Her friend Lottie looks like an onion.

SOOT. Karl always says she looks like an onion. (*Doing her best.*) But this year Lottie won't be out till after New Year's.

KARL. She may look like an onion, but she smells like a garbage disposal.

SOOT. Oh, Karl. Because this year Lottie slipped on her driveway and broke her hip because of all the ice.

KARL. And she tastes like a septic tank.

SOOT. So when Lottie gets here she's going to have a cast on her . . . Karl, where would they put the cast if you broke your hip?

KARL. Lottie doesn't have hips. She has pieces of raw whale skin wrapped around a septic tank in the middle.

SOOT. Karl doesn't like Lottie.

KARL. That's right.

SOOT. Karl thinks Lottie smells, but I think he's just kidding.

BETTE. HOW CAN YOU SMELL HER WITH ALCOHOL ON YOUR BREATH?

BOO. Oh God.

KARL. What did you say, woman?

BETTE. You're too drunk to smell anything.

BOO. Will you lay off all this drinking talk?

KARL. (*Holds up his drink.*) I think it's time your next stillborn was baptized, don't you, Soot?

SOOT. Karl . . .

(KARL *pours his drink on Bette's lap.* BETTE *has hysterics. Lights change.*)

Scene 22

MATT *addresses the audience.*

MATT. Twenty years later, Boo has dinner with his son.

(BOO, MATT.)

BOO. Well, how are things up at Dartmouth, Skip? People in the office ask me how my Ivy League son is doing.

MATT. It's all right.

BOO. Are there any pretty girls up there?

MATT. Uh huh.

BOO. So what are you learning up there?

MATT. Tess of the d'Urbervilles is a . . . I'm not up

at Dartmouth anymore. I'm at Columbia in graduate school.

Boo. I know that. I meant Columbia. How is it?

MATT. Fine.

Boo. Why are you still going to school?

MATT. I don't know. What do you want me to do?

Boo. I don't know. Your mother and I got divorced, you know.

MATT. Yes, I know. We have discussed this, you know.

Boo. I don't understand why she wanted a divorce. I mean, we'd been separated for several years, why not just leave it at that?

MATT. She wants to feel independent, I guess.

Boo. I thought we might get back together. You know, I always found your mother very charming when she wasn't shouting. A man needs a woman, son. I think your old man's going to get teary for a second. Do you have any problems you want to talk over? (*Blinks his eyes.*) I'm just an old softie.

(MATT *steps out of the scene.* Boo *stays in place.*)

MATT. (*To audience.*) At about the same time, Bette also has dinner with her son.

(BETTE, MATT.)

BETTE. Hello, Skippy, dear. I made steak for you, and mashed potatoes and peas and cake. How many days can you stay?

MATT. I have to get back tomorrow.

BETTE. Can't you stay longer?

MATT. I really have to get back.

BETTE. You never stay long. I don't have much company, you know. And Polly Lydstone's son goes to her house for dinner twice a week, and her daughter Mary gave up her apartment and lives at home. And Judith Rankle's son moved home after college and commutes forty minutes to work.

MATT. And some boy from Pingry School came home after class and shot both his parents. So what?

BETTE. There's no need to get nasty.

MATT. I just don't want to hear about Polly Lydstone and Judith Rankle.

BETTE. You're the only one of my children that lived. You should see me more often.

(MATT *looks aghast.*)

MATT. That's not a fair thing to say.

BETTE. You're right. It's not fair of me to bring up the children that died; that's beside the point. I realize Boo and I must take responsibility for our own actions. Of course, the Church wasn't very helpful at the time, but nonetheless we had brains of our own, so there's no point in assigning blame. I must take responsibility for wanting children so badly that I foolishly kept trying over and over, hoping for miracles. Did you see the article in the paper, by the way, about how they've discovered a serum for people with the Rh problem that would have allowed me to have more babies if it had existed back then?

MATT. Yes, I did. I wondered if you had read about that.

BETTE. Yes, I did. It made me feel terribly sad for a little while; but then I thought, "What's past is past. One has no choice but to accept facts." And I realized that you must live your own life, and I must live mine. My life may not have worked out as I wished, but still I feel a deep and inner serenity, and so you mustn't feel bad about me because I am totally happy and self-sufficient in my pretty sunlit apartment. And now I'm going to close my eyes, and I want you to go out into the world and live your life. Good-bye. God bless you. (*Closes her eyes.*)

MATT. (*To audience.*) I'm afraid I've made that conversation up totally.

(*They start the scene over.*)

BETTE. Hello, Skippy, dear. I made steak for you, and mashed potatoes and peas and cake. You know, you're the only one of my children that lived. How long can you stay?

MATT. Gee, I don't know. Uh, a couple of days. Three years. Only ten minutes, my car's double-parked. I could stay eight years if I can go away during the summer. Gee, I don't know.

(*Lights change.*)

Scene 23

MATT *addresses the audience.*

MATT. Back in chronology, shortly after the unpleasant Christmas with the Hudlockes, Bette brings Boo back to Father Donnally.

(MATT *exits.* BETTE, BOO, FATHER DONNALLY. BETTE *in a foul temper.*)

BOO. (*Reading.*) I pledge in front of Father Donnally to give up drinking in order to save my marriage and to make my wife and son happy, and this time I mean it.

BETTE. Read the other part.

BOO. (*Reading.*) And I promise to tell my father to go to hell.

FATHER DONNALLY. Oh, I didn't see that part.

BETTE. Now sign it. (BOO *signs it. Crossly, to* FATHER DONNALLY.) Now bless us.

FATHER DONNALLY. Oh, all right. In the name of the Father, Son, and Holy Ghost. Amen.

BETTE. Now let's go home. (BETTE *and* BOO *cross to another part of the stage;* FATHER DONNALLY *exits.*) Now if you give up drinking for good this time, maybe God will let this next baby live, Boo.

BOO. Uh huh.

BETTE. And I'm going to go to Mass daily. And Emily is praying.

BOO. Uh huh.

BETTE. You're not very talkative, Boo.

BOO. I don't have anything to say.

BETTE. Well, you should have something to say. Marriage is a fifty-fifty proposition.

BOO. Where do you pick up these sayings? On the back of matchpacks?

BETTE. Why are you being nasty? Have you had a drink already?

BOO. No, I haven't had a drink already. I just find it very humiliating to be constantly dragged in front of that priest all the time so he can hear your complaints about me.

BETTE. You have an idiotic sense of pride. Do you

think he cares what you do? And if you don't want people to know you drink, then you shouldn't drink.

Boo. You are obsessed with drinking. Were you frightened at an early age by a drunk? What is the matter with you?

BETTE. What is the matter with *you*?

Boo. What is the matter with *you*?

BETTE. What is the matter with you?

Boo. What is the matter with you?

(*This argument strikes them both funny, and they laugh. Lights change.*)

Scene 24

MATT *addresses the audience.*

MATT. Shortly after the second pledge, Bette and Skippy visit the Brennans to celebrate Joanie's birthday. Boo stays home, drunk or sulking, it's not clear.

(MARGARET, PAUL, BETTE, EMILY, JOAN, *and* MATT. JOAN *looks pregnant;* BETTE *also looks pregnant.* MARGARET *comes downstage and addresses the audience.*)

MARGARET. All my children live home, it's so nice. Emily's here, back from the rest home. And Joanie's here because her marriage hasn't worked out and somebody has to watch all those children for her while she's working, poor thing. And Tom's here sometimes, when he gets fired or when his spastic colon is acting up really badly. Then he always goes off again, but I bet he ends up here for good eventually! (*Chuckles, pleased.*) The only one who hasn't moved back home is Betsy, because she's so stubborn, but maybe she'll end up here too someday. I just love having the children home, otherwise there'd be no one to talk to—unless I wanted to learn sign language with Paul. (*Laughs.*) Sometimes I'm afraid if I had to choose between having my children succeed in the world and live away from home, or having them fail and live home, that I'd choose the latter. But luckily, I haven't had to choose! (*Smiles, returns to the scene.*) Come on, everybody, let's celebrate Joanie's birthday, and don't anybody mention that she's pregnant with yet another baby.

BETTE. Every time I look at you, you're using nose spray.

JOAN. You just got here.

BETTE. But the last time I was here. You're going to give yourself a sinus infection.

JOAN. I already have a sinus infection.

MARGARET. The girls always fight. It's so cute. Now, girls.

BETTE. Well, you use too much nose spray. You might hurt the baby inside you.

JOAN. Let's drop the subject of babies, shall we?

BETTE. I can't imagine why you're pregnant again.

EMILY. Happy birthday, Joan! (*Everyone looks at her.*) I made the cake. I better go get it. (*Exits.*)

MARGARET. Where's Booey, Bette?

BETTE. He's home, drunk or sulking, Skippy and I can't decide which. Where's Nikkos, Joan?

JOAN. Under a truck, I hope.

BETTE. Well, you married him. Everyone told you not to.

MARGARET. Let's change the subject. How are you doing in school, Skippy?

MATT. (*Glum.*) Fine.

MARGARET. Isn't that nice?

BETTE. Skippy always gets A's. Is little Mary Frances still getting F's? Maybe if you were home more, she'd do better.

JOAN. I can't afford to be home more. I don't have a life of leisure like you do.

(*Enter* EMILY *with the cake.*)

EMILY. Happy birthday, Joan.

BETTE. Hush, Emily. If I had several children, I'd *make* time to spend with them.

JOAN. You have a home and a husband, and I don't have either.

BETTE. Well, it's your own fault.

EMILY. Please don't argue, Bette.

BETTE. Why do you say "Bette"? Why not "Joanie"? She's the one arguing.

EMILY. Don't anybody argue.

MARGARET. Don't excite yourself, Emily.

JOAN. You see what your talking has done? You're going to give Emily another breakdown.

EMILY. That's sweet of you to worry, Joanie, but I'm all right.

BETTE. (*To Joan.*) You're just a neurotic mess. You're going to ruin your children.

JOAN. Well, it's lucky you only have one to ruin, or else the mental ward wouldn't have just Emily in it.

(EMILY *has an asthma attack.*)

MARGARET. This cake looks very nice, Emily. Why don't we all have some. I bet Skippy would like a piece.

(MARGARET *cuts the cake and passes it around.*)

EMILY. We forgot to have Joanie blow out the candles.

JOAN. There aren't any candles on the cake.

EMILY. Oh, I forgot them. I'm sorry, Joanie.

JOAN. Why should I have candles? I don't have anything else.

MARGARET. Poor Joanie.

BETTE. The dough's wet. Don't eat it, Skippy, it'll make you sick.

EMILY. It isn't cooked right?

BETTE. It's wet, it's wet. You didn't cook it enough.

JOAN. I don't like cake anyway.

MARGARET. Poor Joanie.

BETTE. Everything's always "poor Joanie." But her baby's going to live.

EMILY. Oh, Bette.

JOAN. Well, maybe we'll both have a miracle. Maybe yours'll live and mine'll die.

EMILY. Oh, Joanie.

BETTE. Stop saying that, Emily.

MARGARET. Girls, girls. This isn't conversation for the living room. Or for young ears.

PAUL. (*Choking on cake.*) #%#%#%GHGHR#%#%#**-***** **#@#@#********

MARGARET. Paul, stop it. Stop it.

(PAUL *falls over dead. Lights change.*)

Scene 25

MATT *puts a sheet over* PAUL *and addresses the audience.*

MATT. The funeral of Paul Brennan.

(PAUL *in a chair with a sheet over him. Present are* MATT, BETTE, BOO, MARGARET, EMILY, JOAN.)

MARGARET. Paul was a fine husband. Good-bye, Paul. (*Teary.*)

BETTE. Boo, thank you for being sober today. (*Kisses him.*) Look how happy it makes Skippy.

BOO. Skippy's drunk.

BETTE. That's not funny.

(*Enter* FATHER DONNALLY.)

FATHER DONNALLY. Dearly bereaved, Paul Brennan was a fine man, and now he's dead. I didn't know Paul very well, but I imagine he was a very nice man and everyone spoke well of him. Though he wasn't able to speak well of them. (*Laughs; everyone looks faintly appalled.*)

It's going to be hard not to miss him, but God put his children on this earth to adapt to circumstances, to do His will.

I was reminded of this fact the other morning, when I saw my colored garbage man collecting the refuse as I was on my way to say Mass. "Good morning, Father," he said. "Nice day." "And what's your name?" I said. "Percival Pretty, Father," he said. I smiled a little more and then I said, "And how are you—Percival?" And he said, "I'm doing the will of God, Father. God saw fit to take my little Buttermilk to Him, and now I'm emptying the garbage." "And who is little Buttermilk?" I said, and he said, "Why, Buttermilk was my daughter who broke her neck playing on the swings." And then he smiled. Colored folk have funny ideas for names. I knew one colored woman who named her daughter "January 22nd." It wasn't easy to forget *her* birthday! (*Everyone looks appalled again.*)

But I think Percival Pretty's smile is a lesson for us all, and so now when I think of Paul Brennan, I'm going to smile. (*Smiles.*) And then nothing can touch you. (*Shakes hands with* MARGARET.) Be strong, dear.

EMILY. Thank you, Father, for your talk.

JOAN. (*To* PAUL'*s dead body.*) I've turned against Greeks after Nikkos. You were right, Dad, you were right!

MARGARET. Thank you, Joanie. That was a nice gesture.

FATHER DONNALLY. Hello, Bette. Hello, Boo. You're putting on weight, Bette.

BETTE. It's nothing. (*Sadly.*) I mean, it will be nothing.

(*Lights change.*)

Scene 26

MATT *addresses the audience.*

MATT. Bette goes to the hospital for the fourth time, et cetera, et cetera.

(MATT *exits.* KARL, SOOT, BOO *in their hospital "waiting" positions.*)

BOO. Pop. Eventually there's menopause, right? I mean, something happens, and then it stops, and . . .

KARL. Where are the Brennans? Have they lost the playing spirit?

BOO. Bette wasn't that way when I married her, was she?

SOOT. Karl, is there still a space between my eyes?

KARL. What did you say, Soot?

SOOT. Nothing. I'll wait till I get home. (*Smiles, feels between her eyebrows.*) Lottie always said when your eyebrows start to kiss, you better watch it.

KARL. Your mother's eyebrows are kissing, Bore.

SOOT. You make everything sound so dirty, Karl. I wish I hadn't said that.

KARL. You want to hear a dirty story? Bore, are you listening? Once there was a traveling salesman, Soot, who met a girl in a barn who was more stupid than you.

SOOT. I don't know this one.

KARL. The girl was an albino. Bore, you listening? She was an albino humpback with a harelip.

BOO. I'm going to get a drink. (*Exits.*)

KARL. And this albino humpback saw the traveling salesman with his dickey hanging out . . .

SOOT. Karl, I have heard this one.

KARL. And she saw his dickey, and she said, "What's that?" and he said, "That's my dickey."

SOOT. Karl, you told this story to Lottie, and she didn't like it.

KARL. And she said, "Why does it swing around like that?" and he said . . . Soot, what's the end of the story?

SOOT. Karl, I never listen to your stories.

KARL. WHAT'S THE ANSWER TO THE JOKE?

SOOT. (*Cries.*) Karl, I don't know. Something about a dickey. Maybe Bore knows. Booey? I have to go home and take a bath. I feel awful. (*Enter the* DOCTOR. *He drops the baby on the floor, exits.* KARL *and* SOOT *stare at it a moment.*) Catholics can't use birth control, can they? (*Laughs.*) That's a joke on someone. (*Enter* BOO.)

KARL. You missed it, Boo.

BOO. Did it live?

KARL. Not unless they redefined the term.

SOOT. Don't tease Booey, Karl. Let's distract him, see if he remembers the joke.

KARL. You tell it, Soot.

SOOT. No, I don't like the joke. I just thought maybe he'd remember it.

BOO. It didn't live.

KARL. Tell the joke, Soot.

BOO. Pop, I don't feel like hearing a joke.

SOOT. Poor Booey.

BOO. I should probably see Bette, but I don't think I can face her.

SOOT. Why don't you go get a drink, Booey, you look awful. I've got to go home and check my forehead.

KARL. Tell the damn joke, Soot.

BOO. Pop, I don't want to hear a joke.

SOOT. It's all right, Booey. I'll tell it. Your father seems obsessed with it.

KARL. (*Rams his cigar in her mouth.*) Here, you'll need this.

SOOT. Oh, Karl. (*Laughs.*) All right, Booey, you ready?

BOO. I don't want to hear a joke.

KARL. You'll like it, Bore.

SOOT. Now, Booey . . . (BOO *starts to exit; they follow.*) . . . it seems there was this poor unfortunate, stupid crippled girl, and she met this salesman . . .

BOO. Will you two shut up? I don't want to hear a joke. (*Exits.*)

SOOT. He doesn't want to hear the joke.

KARL. You told it wrong, Soot.

SOOT. I'm sorry, Karl. I'm really not myself today. (*Touches between her eyes.*) I'm sorry, Booey. Booey!
(*They exit.*)

Scene 27

BETTE, *playing rope or some such thing.*
BETTE.
What is the matter with Mary Jane?
It isn't a cramp, and it isn't a pain,
And lovely rice pudding's for dinner again,
What is the *matter* with Mary Jane?

Christopher Robin had weasles and sneezles,
They bundled him into his bed.
(*Kneels, looks at imaginary gravestones; then to audience, sadly.*) The names of the children are: Patrick Michael, February twenty-sixth; Christopher Tigger, March eighth; and Pooh Bear Eeyore, March twenty-fifth. Bonnie Wilson and I were, were . . . (*Calls.*) Father Donnally! Father Donnally . . . (FATHER DONNALLY *enters into* BETTE's *space.*) Father Donnally, can you help me?

FATHER DONNALLY. I'll try. What's on your mind, Bette?

BETTE. I know sometimes one can misunderstand the

will of God. But sex is for having babies, right? I mean, it's not just for marriage. Well, even if it is somewhat, I feel that I should be a mother; and I think it would be a sin for me not to try again. But I don't think Boo wants me to get pregnant again.

FATHER DONNALLY. Have you tried the rhythm method?

BETTE. But I *want* to get pregnant.

FATHER DONNALLY. What does your doctor say?

BETTE. The problem is that all the babies die. I don't see why I have to go through all this suffering. And Boo never helps me.

FATHER DONNALLY. I give a retreat for young married couples every year in the parish. Why don't you and your husband come to that? I'm sure it will help you if you're having trouble on the marriage couch.

BETTE. All right, I'll bring Booey to the retreat. Thank you, Father.

FATHER DONNALLY. You're welcome, Bette. (FATHER DONNALLY *exits.*)

BETTE. (*Crosses away; calls out.*) Boo. Boo. Booey. Booey. Booey. (*Enter* BOO.)

BOO. What?

BETTE. Booey, I'm pregnant again. Do you think I'm going to die?

(*Lights change.*)

Scene 28

The retreat. Present are BETTE, BOO; *also* MARGARET, EMILY, JOAN, *the dead* PAUL (*with sheet still over him*); KARL, SOOT. *Enter* FATHER DONNALLY.

FATHER DONNALLY. In the name of the Father, of the Son, and of the Holy Ghost, Amen. Good evening, young marrieds. (*Looks about for a moment.*) Am I in the right room?

EMILY. I'm not married, Father. I hope you don't mind that I'm here.

FATHER DONNALLY. On the contrary. I'm delighted.

I'm not married either. (*Laughs.*) The theme of marriage
in the Catholic Church and in this retreat is centered
around the story of Christ and the wedding feast at Cana.
Jesus Christ blessed the young wedding couple at Cana,
and when they ran out of expensive wine, He performed
His first miracle—He took vats of water and He changed
the water into wine. (*Holds up a glass.*) I have some wine
right here. (*Sips it.*)

BOO. (*To* BETTE.) He drinks. Why don't you try to get
him to stop drinking?

BETTE. Be quiet, Boo.

FATHER DONNALLY. (*Laughs, nervously.*) Please don't
talk when I'm talking. (*Starts his speech.*) Young marrieds have many problems to get used to. For some of
them this is the first person of the opposite sex the other
has ever known. The husband may not be used to having
a woman in his bathroom. The wife may not be used to
a strong masculine odor in her boudoir. Or then the wife
may not cook well enough. How many marriages have
floundered on the rocks of ill-cooked bacon? (*Pause.*) I
used to amuse friends by imitating bacon in a saucepan.
Would anyone like to see that? (*He looks around.* JOAN,
KARL, *and* SOOT *raise their hands. After a moment,* EM-
ILY, *rather confused, raises her hand also.* FATHER DON-
NALLY *falls to the ground and does a fairly good—or if
not good, at least unabashedly peculiar—imitation of bacon, making sizzling noises and contorting his body to
represent becoming crisp. Toward the end, he makes
sputtering noises into the air. Then he stands up again.
All present applaud with varying degrees of approval or
incredulity.*) I also do coffee percolating. (*He does this.*)
Pt. Pt. Ptptptptptptptptpt. Bacon's better. But things like
coffee and bacon are important in a marriage, because
they represent things that the wife does to make her husband happy. Or fat. (*Laughs.*) The wife cooks the bacon,
and the husband brings home the bacon. This is how St.
Paul saw marriage, although they probably didn't really
eat pork back then, the curing process was not very well
worked out in Christ's time, which is why so many of
them followed the Jewish dietary laws even though they

were Christians. I know I'm glad to be living now when we have cured pork and plumbing and showers rather than back when Christ lived. Many priests say they wish they had lived in Christ's time so they could have met Him; that would, of course, have been very nice, but I'm glad I live now and that I have a shower. (EMILY, *bothered by what he's just said, raises her hand.*) I'm not ready for questions yet, Emily. (EMILY *lowers her hand; he sips his wine.*) Man and wife, as St. Paul saw it. Now the woman should obey her husband, but that's not considered a very modern thought, so I don't even want to talk about it. All right, don't obey your husbands, but if chaos follows, don't blame me. The tower of Babel as an image of chaos has always fascinated me—(EMILY *raises her hand.*)

BETTE. Put your hand down, Emily. (EMILY *does.*)

FATHER DONNALLY. (*To* BETTE.) Thank you. Now I don't mean to get off the point. The point is husband and wife, man and woman, Adam and rib. I don't want to dwell on the inequality of the sexes because these vary from couple to couple—sometimes the man is stupid, sometimes the woman is stupid, sometimes both are stupid. The point is man and wife are joined in holy matrimony to complete each other, to populate the earth and to glorify God. That's what it's for. That's what life is for. If you're not a priest or a nun, you normally get married. (EMILY *raises her hand.*) Yes, I know, you're not married, Emily. Not everyone gets married. But my comments today are geared toward the *married* people here. (EMILY *takes down her hand.*) Man and wife are helpmates. She helps him, he helps her. In sickness and in health. Anna Karenina should not have left her husband, nor should she have jumped in front of a train. Marriage is not a step to be taken lightly. The Church does not recognize divorce; it does permit it, if you insist for legal purposes, but in the eyes of the Church you are still married and you can never be unmarried, and that's why you can never remarry after a divorce because that would be bigamy and that's a sin and illegal as well. (*Breathes.*) So, for God's sake, if you're going to get married, pay attention to what you're doing, have conversations with the person, figure out if you *really* want to live with that person for years and years and years, because you can't change it. Priests have it easier. If I don't like my pastor, I can apply for a transfer. If I don't like a housekeeper, I can get her fired. (*Looks disgruntled.*) But a husband and wife are *stuck* together. So know what you're doing when you get married. I get so *sick* of these people coming to me after they're married, and they've just gotten to know one another *after* the ceremony, and they've discovered they have nothing in common and they hate one another. And they want me to come up with a solution. (*Throws up his hands.*) What can I do? There is no solution to a problem like that. I can't help them! It puts me in a terrible position. I can't say get a divorce, that's against God's law. I can't say go get some on the side, that's against God's law. I can't say just pretend you're happy and maybe after a while you won't know the difference because, though that's not against God's law, not that many people know how to do that, and if I suggested it to people, they'd write to the Bishop complaining about me and then he'd transfer me to some godforsaken place in Latin America without a shower, and all because these people don't know what they're doing when they get married. (*Shakes his head.*) So I mumble platitudes to these people who come to me with these insoluble problems, and I think to myself, "Why didn't they *think* before they got married? Why does no one ever *think*? Why did God make people stupid?" (*Pause.*) Are there any questions?

(BETTE *raises her hand, as does* EMILY. FATHER DONNALLY *acknowledges* BETTE.)

BETTE. Father, if I have a little girl rather than a boy, do you think it might live? Should I pray for this?

FATHER DONNALLY. You mean . . . a little girl to clean house?

BETTE. (*Irritated.*) No. I don't mean a little girl to clean house. I mean that the doctors say that sometimes a little girl baby fights infection better than a little boy baby, and that maybe if I have a little girl baby, the fighting between the Rh positive blood in her body and the Rh negative blood in my body would not destroy her, and she might live. (*Pause.*) Should I pray for this?

FATHER DONNALLY. By all means, pray for it. Just don't get your hopes up too high, though, maybe God doesn't want you to have any more babies. It certainly doesn't sound like it to me.

BETTE. But I *can* pray?

FATHER DONNALLY. Yes. You can. No one can stop you.

BETTE. That's what I thought.

(EMILY *raises her hand.*)

FATHER DONNALLY. (*Dreading whatever she's going to say.*) Yes, Emily?

EMILY. Do you think maybe it's my fault that all of Bette's babies die? Because I left the convent?

FATHER DONNALLY. Yes, I do.

EMILY. (*Stricken.*) Oh my God.

FATHER DONNALLY. I'm sorry, Emily, I was just kidding. Are there any questions about newly married couples? (*Pause; no one stirs.*) Well, I don't have time for any more questions anyway. We'll take a short break for refreshments, and then Father McNulty will talk to you about sexual problems, which I'm not very good at, and then you can all go home. Thank you for your attention. In the name of the Father, and of the Son, and of the Holy Ghost. Amen. (*Starts to exit.*)

EMILY. Father . . .

FATHER DONNALLY. I was just kidding, Emily, I am sorry. Excuse me, I have to go to the bathroom. (*Exits in a hurry.*)

JOAN. You know, he makes a better piece of bacon than he does a priest.

EMILY. I don't think he should joke about something like that.

MARGARET. He's a priest, Emily.

EMILY. I know you're right, Mom, but everyone should want to meet Our Savior, that's more important than having a shower . . .

MARGARET. Don't talk anymore, Emily.

BETTE. Did that make you feel better, Boo? Are you going to be easier to live with?

BOO. (*Sarcastic.*) Yes, it's all better now.

BETTE. Why won't you let anyone help us?

BOO. What help? He just said that we shouldn't get married, and that if we did, not to bother him with our problems.

BETTE. That's not what he said at all.

MARGARET. Bette, don't talk anymore. Hello, Mrs. Hudlocke. Did you enjoy the talk?

SOOT. I'm sorry, what?

MARGARET. Did you enjoy Father's talk?

SOOT. You know, I can't hear you. I think I'm going deaf. God, I hope so.

MARGARET. What do you mean?

SOOT. I'm sorry, I really can't hear you. (*Laughs.*) I haven't been able to hear Karl for about three days. (*Laughs.*) *It's wonderful.*

BETTE. You should see an ear specialist.

SOOT. What?

BETTE. Oh, never mind.

EMILY. Mom, don't you think . . .

MARGARET. Emily, I said not to talk.

BETTE. Well, if you don't want us to talk, what do you want us to do?

MARGARET. Don't be cranky, Betsy. We'll just all wait for Father McNulty. Maybe he'll have something useful to say.

(*They all wait.* SOOT *smiles.*)

SOOT. (*To audience.*) Little blessings. (*Laughs.*)

(*Lights change.*)

Scene 29

MATT *addresses the audience.* BETTE, BOO, *and the dead* PAUL *stay onstage.*

MATT. Twenty years later, or perhaps only fifteen, Bette files for a divorce from Boo. They have been separated for several years, since shortly after the death of

the final child; and at the suggestion of a therapist Bette
has been seeing, Bette decides to make the separation
legal in order to formalize the breakup psychologically,
and also to get better, and more regular, support pay-
ments. Boo, for some reason, decides to contest the divorce; and so there has to be testimony. Margaret and
Joanie decide that Catholics can't testify in divorce cases,
even though Bette had eventually testified in Joanie's divorce; and so they refuse to testify, frightening Emily
into agreeing with them also. Blah blah blah, et cetera.
So in lieu of other witnesses, I find myself sort of having
to testify against Boo during my sophomore year at college. I am trying to work on a paper on Thomas Hardy,
but find it difficult to concentrate. I fly home for the divorce proceedings. My mother's lawyer reminds me of
my grandfather Paul.

(BETTE *and* BOO *on opposite sides.* MATT *center, tes-
tifies, questioned by* PAUL *who comes to life with no to-
do. He still speaks in* PAUL'*s incomprehensible speech,
but otherwise is quite lawyerly.*)

PAUL. Ehl ee att, oo## oou ing orr agh## er uz acgh
acgha@ @ lehc? [Tell me, Matt, do you think your father
was an alcoholic?]

MATT. What?

PAUL. (*Irritated he can't be understood, as Paul used
to be.*) Oo## oou ing, orr agh# # er uz acgh acgha @ @
lehc? [Do you think your father was an alcoholic?]

MATT. Yes, I do feel he drank a fair amount.

PAUL. Uht us ee acgh acgha @ @ lehc? [But was he
an alcoholic?]

MATT. I'm really not in the position to say if anyone
is actually an alcoholic or not.

BETTE. I have a calendar here from the twelve years
of our marriage. Every time it says "HD," that stands
for "half-drunk." And everytime it says "DD," that
stands for "dead drunk." I offer this as Exhibit A.

PAUL. (*Telling her it's not her turn.*) Eeez own awk
enn oo aht ahn uh ann. [Please don't talk when you're
not on the stand.]

BETTE. What?

Boo. I was never dead drunk. She has this thing about drunks.

MATT. (*To* BETTE.) He said you shouldn't talk when you're not on the stand.

BETTE. I didn't.

PAUL. (*To* BETTE.) Sssh. (*Long question to* MATT:) Ehl ee att, ihd oo# # eheh ee or ah # er ah ehey ohazsn, itt or uher? [Tell me, Matt, did you ever see your father, on any occasion, hit your mother?]

MATT. Yes. Hardy wrote *Tess of the d'Urbervilles* in 1891.

PAUL. (*Irritated.*) As ott ut uh ass. [That's not what I asked.]

MATT. Oh, I'm sorry. I misheard the question.

PAUL. Ihd ee itt er? [Did he hit her?] (*Makes hitting motion.*)

MATT. Yes, I did see him hit her.

PAUL. Ah!

MATT. Of course, she hit him too. They both hit each other. Especially when they were driving. It was fairly harrowing from the back seat.

BETTE. He started it.

Boo. She'd talk and talk like it was a sickness. There was no way of shutting her up.

MATT. Well, I would have appreciated your not arguing when you were driving a car.

PAUL. (*To* BETTE *and* BOO.) Ee i # # #et! [Be quiet!]

MATT. Or at least left me home.

PAUL. Shhh! (*Back to questioning* MATT.) Ehl ee att, oo oo# ih or ohn ihahf eher agh uh ink? [Tell me, Matt, do you in your own life ever have a drink?]

MATT. No, I don't know any happily married couples. Certainly not relatives.

PAUL. (*Irritated.*) As ott ut uh ass. [That's not what I asked.]

MATT. Oh, I'm sorry. I thought that's what you asked.

PAUL. Oo oo# ih or ohn lhahf eher agh uh ink? [Do you in your own life ever have a drink?]

MATT. No, my paper is on whether Eustacia Vye in *The Return of the Native* is neurotic or psychotic, and how she compares to Emily. That isn't what you asked either, is it? I'm sorry. What?

PAUL. *Oo oo# ink?* [Do you drink?]

MATT. Ink?

PAUL. (*Gesturing as if drinking.*) Ink! Ink!

MATT. No, I don't drink, actually.

PAUL. Ehl ee att, urr oo uhaagee ehn or errens epyrateted? [Tell me, Matt, were you unhappy when your parents separated?]

(MATT *is at a loss.* PAUL *must repeat the word "separated" several times, with hand gestures, before* MATT *understands.*)

MATT. No, I was glad when they separated. The arguing got on my nerves a lot. (*Pause.*) I'd hear it in my ear even when they weren't talking. When I was a child, anyway.

PAUL. Ehl ee att, oo oo# ink or aher uz uh goooh aher? [Tell me, Matt, do you think your father was a good father?]

MATT. Yes, I am against the war in Vietnam. I'm sorry, is that what you asked?

PAUL. Doo oo# ink ee uz a goooh ahzer? [Do you think he was a good father?]

MATT. Oh. Yes. I guess he's been a good father. (*Looks embarrassed.*)

PAUL. (*Pointing at* BOO, *pushing for some point.*) Buh dyoo oo# ink ee ad ohme or uh inkng bahblim? [But do you think he had some sort of drinking problem?] (*Makes drinking gesture.*)

MATT. Yes, I guess he probably does have some sort of drinking problem. (*Becoming worked up.*) I mean it became such an issue it seems suspicious to me that he didn't just stop, he kept saying there was no . . . (*Pulls back.*) Well, it was odd he didn't stop. It's really not my place to be saying this. I would prefer I wasn't here.

(*Pause.* MATT *is uncomfortable, has been uncomfortable relating to* BOO *for the whole scene.*)

PAUL. Orr ehcoooz, att. [You're excused, Matt.]

MATT. What?

BETTE. He said you were excused.

MATT. Oh good.

(PAUL *exits, or goes back under sheet.*)

BETTE. Thank you, Skippy. (*Kisses him.*)

Boo. Well, son. Have a good time back at school.

MATT. Thank you. I'm behind in this paper I'm doing. (*Pause.*) I have to get the plane.

Boo. Well, have a good trip. (*Looks embarrassed, exits.*)

MATT. Thank you. (BETTE *exits.* MATT *addresses the audience:*) Eustacia Vye is definitely neurotic. Whether she is psychotic as well is . . . In *Return of the Native*, Hardy is dealing with some of the emotional, as well as physical, dangers in the . . . One has to be very careful in order to protect oneself from the physical and emotional dangers in the world. One must always be careful crossing streets in traffic. One should try not to live anywhere near a nuclear power plant. One should never walk past a building that may have a sniper on top of it. In the summer one should be on the alert against bees and wasps.

As to emotional dangers, one should always try to avoid crazy people, especially in marriage or live-in situations, but in everyday life as well. Although crazy people often mean well, meaning well is not enough. On some level Attila the Hun may have meant well.

Sometimes it is hard to decide if a person is crazy, like Eustacia Vye in *The Return of the Native*, which is the topic of this paper. Some people may seem sane at first, and then at some later point turn out to be totally crazy. If you are at dinner with someone who suddenly seems insane, make up some excuse why you must leave the dinner immediately. If they don't know you well, you can say you're a doctor and pretend that you just heard your beeper. If the crazy person should call you later, either to express anger at your abrupt leave-taking or to ask for medical advice, claim the connection is bad and hang up. If they call back, I'm afraid you'll have to have your phone number changed again. When you call the phone company to arrange this, if the person on the line seems stupid, hostile, or crazy, simply hang up and call the phone company back again. This may be done as many times as necessary *until you get someone sane*. As the phone company has many employees. (*Breathes.*) It is difficult to totally protect oneself, of course, and there are many precautions that one thinks of only when it's too late. But, as Virginia Woolf pointed out in *To the Lighthouse,* admittedly in a different context, the attempt is all.

Sometime after the divorce, five years or fifteen or something, Skippy has dinner with Karl and Soot and Margaret and Paul. Karl is near eighty, Margaret is senile, and Paul and Soot are dead.

Scene 30

MATT *sits at a table with all four.* PAUL *and* SOOT *have their heads on the table, dead.* KARL *seems fairly normal and himself;* MARGARET *is distracted and vague.*

MATT. Hello. Nice to see you all.

MARGARET. Emily! Huh-huh-huh. Tom! Nurse! Huh-huh-huh.

(NOTE: *the "huh-huh-huh" sound is not like laughter, but is a nervous tic, said softly and rather continuously throughout the scene. Technically speaking, it's like a mild vocal exercise using the diaphragm, like an ongoing cough reflex with no real cough behind it. A tic.*)

KARL. You're Skip, aren't you?

MATT. Yes. You remember me?

KARL. Yes, I remember you.

MARGARET. Doctor. Mama. Huh-huh-huh. Huh-huh-huh.

KARL. (*To* MARGARET.) Shut up.

MATT. (*To* KARL *with seriousness.*) What do you think I should do with my life?

KARL. Well, don't marry Soot.

MATT. Yes, but you know—

MARGARET. Emily! Huh-huh-huh.

MATT. Everyone I know is divorced except for you and Soot, and Margaret and Paul. Of course, Soot and Paul are dead, but you all stayed married right up until death.

And I wondered what mistakes you thought I could avoid based on all your experience.

KARL. Don't expect much, that's for starters. Look at Bette and Bore. She kept trying to change Bore. That's idiotic. Don't try to change anybody. If you don't like them, be mean to them if you want; try to get them committed if that amuses you, but don't ever expect to *change* them.

(MATT *considers this.*)

MATT. Do you agree with that, Grandma?

MARGARET. (*Seeing* MATT *for the first time, leaning over to him.*) Go to the baperdy sun ride zone a bat.

MATT. Baperdy?

MARGARET. Lamin fortris trexin home. Emily!

KARL. It's too bad Paul's not still alive. It would be interesting to hear them talk together now.

(MATT *laughs at this.*)

MATT. Grandma, try to be lucid. I think Karl's advice makes sense, sort of, if you're in a bad marriage. But what if you're not in a bad marriage?

MARGARET. When the bob?

MATT. I said, do you agree with Karl? Or do you see something more optimistic?

MARGARET. I want Emily to clean the mirrors with milk of magnesia. I see people in the mirrors and they don't go away.

KARL. At least that was a complete sentence.

MATT. Emily's not here right now.

MARGARET. Everyone's so late. Dabble morning hunting back, Emily. Huh-huh-huh.

MATT. (*Gives up on* MARGARET; *back to* KARL.) You know, I didn't know you and Soot back when you were young, or Margaret and Paul either, for that matter. Maybe your marriages *were* happy. I have no way of knowing.

KARL. I never expected much from life. I wanted to get my way in everything, and that's about all. What did you ask?

MARGARET. Huh-huh-huh. Joan. Emily.

MATT. Why did you marry Soot?

KARL. No reason. She was much prettier when she was younger.

MATT. But surely you didn't marry her because she was pretty.

KARL. Don't tell me what I did.

MATT. And why did everyone call her Soot? How did she get the name "Soot"?

KARL. I don't remember. Was her name Soot? I thought it was something else.

MATT. I think her name was Soot. Do you think I misheard it all these years?

KARL. I couldn't say.

MATT. Why were you so mean to Soot?

KARL. Why do you want to know?

MATT. Because I see all of you do the same things over and over, for years and years, and you never change. And my fear is that I can see all of you but not see myself, and maybe I'm doing something similar, but I just can't see it. What I mean to say is: did you all *intend* to live your lives the way you did?

KARL. Go away. I don't like talking to you. You're an irritating young man.

(MATT *leaves the scene.* KARL, MARGARET, SOOT, *and* PAUL *exit or fade into darkness.*)

Scene 31

MATT. (*Trying to find his place, to audience.*) Back into chronology again. Bette had the first baby, that is, the first dead baby, in 1951 or something. And then the second one in 1953 or 4 or something, and then . . . (*Enter* EMILY.)

EMILY. Hello, Skippy, dear. How does this sound to you? (*Reads from a note.*) "Please forgive my annoying qualities. I know that I talk too much about a thing and that I make people nervous that I do so. I am praying that I improve that fault and beg that you be patient with me."

MATT. Who is that to, Emily?

EMILY. I don't know. Who do you think it should be to?

MATT. I don't know. It would be up to you.

EMILY. Do you think it's all right?

MATT. I don't think you should be so hard on yourself, but otherwise I think it's fine.

EMILY. Oh, thank you. (*Exits.*)

MATT. Okay. Just as dreams must be analyzed, so must the endless details of waking life be considered.

Having intelligence allows one to analyze problems and to make sense of one's life. This is difficult to achieve, but with perseverance and persistence it is possible not even to get up in the morning. To sleep. "To sleep, perchance to dream," to take the phone off the hook and simply be unreachable. This is less *dramatic* than suicide, but more *reversible*.

I can't make sense out of these things anymore. Um, Bette goes to the hospital for the third time, and there's the second dead baby, and then the fourth time, and the third dead baby, and then sometime after Father Donnally's marriage retreat, Bette goes to the hospital for the fifth time. The *last* child of Bette and Boo.

Scene 32

Enter BOO. *He and* MATT *are in their "waiting" positions back in the hospital.*

BOO. You don't have to wait here, Skip, if you don't want.

MATT. It's all right.

BOO. Who knows, maybe it will live. The doctors say if it's a girl, girls sometimes fight harder for life. Or something. (*Pause.*) You doing well in school?

MATT. Uh huh.

(*The* DOCTOR *throws the baby, in a pink blanket, in from offstage.*)

DOCTOR. (*Offstage.*) It was a girl.

BOO. You have any problems you want to talk over, son? Your old man could help you out.

MATT. I'll be outside a minute. *(Exits. Enter* BETTE.*)*

BOO. Bette, let's not have any more. *(Mournfully.)* I've had enough babies. They get you up in the middle of the night, dead. They dirty their cribs, dead. They need constant attention, dead. No more babies.

BETTE. I don't love you anymore, Boo.

BOO. What?

BETTE. Why do you say what? Can't you hear?

BOO. Why do they never have a bar in this hospital? Maybe there's one on another floor.

BETTE. I'm tired of feeling alone talking to you.

BOO. Maybe I'll take the elevator to another floor and check.

BETTE. They don't have bars in hospitals, Boo.

BOO. I think I'll walk down. See you later. *(Exits.)*

BETTE. I feel alone, Boo. Skippy, are you there? Skippy?

(Enter MATT.*)*

MATT. Yes.

BETTE. Would you move this for me? *(She indicates the dead baby on floor. He gingerly places it offstage.)* Your father's gone away. All the babies are dead. You're the only thing of value left in my life, Skippy.

MATT. Why do you call me "Skippy"? Why don't you call me "Matt"?

BETTE. It's my favorite movie.

MATT. *(With growing anger.)* My favorite movie is *Citizen Kane*. I don't call you "Citizen Kane."

BETTE. Why are you being fresh?

MATT. I don't know.

BETTE. I don't want to put any pressure on you, Skippy, dear, but you're the only reason I have left for living now.

MATT. Ah.

BETTE. You're so unresponsive.

MATT. I'm sorry. I don't know what to say.

BETTE. You're a typical Capricorn, cold and ungiving. I'm an Aries, we like fun, we do three things at once. We make life decisions by writing our options on little pieces of paper and then throwing them up in the air and going "Wheeee!" Wee wee wee, all the way home. I should have had more babies, I'm very good with babies. Babies *give* to you, then they grow up and they don't give. If I'd had more, I wouldn't mind as much. I don't mean to be critical, it's just that I'm so very . . . *(Looks sad, shakes her head.)* I need to go to bed. Come and read to me from A. A. Milne until I fall asleep, would you?

MATT. All right.

(BETTE starts to leave.)

BETTE. *(Suddenly tearful.)* I don't want to call you "Matt."

MATT. That's all right. It's fine. I'll be in to read to you in a minute, okay?

BETTE. Okay. *(BETTE exits.)*

MATT. So I read her to sleep from *The House at Pooh Corner*. And then I entered high school, and then I went to college, and then they got divorced, and then I went to graduate school. I stopped studying Thomas Hardy for a while and tried Joseph Conrad. Oh, the horror, the horror. I'm afraid what happened next will sound rather exaggerated, but after she divorced Boo, Bette felt very lonely and unhappy for several years, and then she married another alcoholic, and then after two years that broke up, and then she got cancer. By this time I'm thirty, and I visit her once more in the hospital.

Scene 33

EMILY *pushes* BETTE *on in a wheelchair.* BETTE *doesn't look well.*

EMILY. Doesn't Bette look well today?

MATT. Very well.

EMILY. Let's join hands. *(Holds* MATT's *and* BETTE's *hands.)* In the name of the Father, and of the Son, and of the Holy Ghost, Amen. Heavenly Father, please lift this sickness from our beloved Bette. We place ourselves in Your hands. Amen. *(To* BETTE.*)* Do you feel any better?

BETTE. The pain is a little duller.

EMILY. Well, maybe I better go to the hospital chapel and pray some more.

BETTE. That would be nice, Emily. Thank you. (EMILY *exits*.) I've spent a lot of time in hospitals.

MATT. Yes.

BETTE. I sometimes wonder if God is punishing me for making a second marriage outside the Church. But Father Ehrhart says that God forgives me, and besides the second marriage is over now anyway.

MATT. I don't think God punishes people for specific things.

BETTE. That's good.

MATT. I think He punishes people in general, for no reason.

BETTE. *(Laughs.)* You always had a good sense of humor, Skippy. The chemotherapy hasn't been making my hair fall out after all. So I haven't needed those two wigs I bought. The woman at Lord and Taylor's looked at me so funny when I said I needed them because my hair was going to fall out. Now *she* didn't have a good sense of humor. Emily brought me this book on healing, all about these cases of people who are very ill and then someone prays over them and places their hand on the place where the tumor is, and there's this feeling of heat where the tumor is, and then the patient gets completely cured. Would you pray over me, and place your hand on my hip?

MATT. I'm afraid I don't believe in any of that.

BETTE. It won't kill you to try to please me.

MATT. All right. *(Puts his hand on her hip.)*

BETTE. Now say a prayer.

MATT. *(Said quickly as befits a parochial school childhood.)* Hail Mary, full of grace, the Lord is with thee. Blessed art thou amongst women, and blessed is the fruit of thy womb, Jesus. Holy Mary, mother of God, pray for us sinners, now and at the hour of our death, amen.

BETTE. I think I feel a warmth there.

MATT. *(Noncommittal.)* That's good.

BETTE. You're so cold, you won't give anything.

MATT. If I don't believe in prayer, you shouldn't make me pray. It feels funny.

BETTE. You're just like your father—unresponsive.

MATT. Let's not argue about this.

BETTE. All right. *(On a pleasanter subject.)* Do you remember when you used to smell your father's breath to see if he'd been drinking? You were such a cute child. I saw your father last week. He came to the hospital to visit.

MATT. Oh, how is he?

BETTE. Well, he's still mad at me about my second marriage, but in some ways he's always been a sweet man. I think the years of drinking have done something to his brain, though. He'll be talking and then there'll be this long pause like he's gone to sleep or something, and then finally he'll go on again like nothing's happened.

(Enter Boo, holding flowers.)

Boo. Bette?

BETTE. Oh, Boo, I was just talking about you. Look, Skippy's here.

Boo. Oh, Skip. How are you?

MATT. I'm fine. Hi. How are you?

Boo. You look good.

MATT. Oh yes? Do you want a chair?

Boo. What?

MATT. I'll get you a chair. *(He does.)*

Boo. Skip looks good.

BETTE. Yes.

MATT. Do you want to sit? *(Boo looks uncomprehending.)* I've brought you a chair.

Boo. Oh, thank you. *(Sits.)*

BETTE. The flowers are lovely.

Boo. I brought you flowers.

BETTE. Thank you. *(Boo hands them to her.)*

Boo. *(to MATT.)* Your mother still looks very pretty.

MATT. Mother said you came to visit last week.

Boo. I came last week.

BETTE. He repeats himself all the time.

Boo. What?

BETTE. I said, you repeat yourself. *(Boo looks annoyed.)* But it's charming. *(To MATT.)* Your father flirted with the second-shift nurse.

Boo. Your old man still has an eye for the ladies. I

was here last week and there was this . . . *(Long pause; he stares, blank.)*

BETTE. *(To* MATT.*)* See, he's doing it now. Boo, are you there? Boo? *(Sings to herself.)* God bless Bette and Boo and Skippy, Emily and Boo . . .

Boo. *(Comes back, continues.)* . . . nurse, and she liked your old man, I think.

BETTE. She thought he was her grandfather.

Boo. What?

BETTE. You're too old for her.

Boo. What?

MATT. Maybe he's gone deaf.

Boo. No, I can hear. I think it's my brain.

BETTE. Do you remember when you tried to vacuum the gravy?

Boo. No.

BETTE. Well, you did. It was very funny. Not at the time, of course. And how you used to keep bottles hidden in the cellar. And all the dead babies.

Boo. *(Smiles, happy.)* Yes. We had some good times.

BETTE. Yes, we did. And do you remember that time after we got divorced when I came by your office because Mrs. Wright died?

MATT. Mrs. Wright?

BETTE. You were at college, and I didn't have her very long. She was a parakeet. *(*MATT *suddenly comprehends with an "ah" or "oh" sound.)* And I called her Mrs. Wright because she lived in a Frank Lloyd Wright birdcage, I think. Actually it was a male parakeet but I liked the name better. Anyway, I kept Mrs. Wright free on the screen porch, out of the cage, because she liked it that way, but she'd always try to follow me to the kitchen, so I'd have to get to the porch door before Mrs. Wright, and I always did. Except this one time, we had a tie, and I squashed Mrs. Wright in the door. Mary Roberts Rinehart wrote a novel called *The Door,* but I like her *Tish* stories better. Well, I was very upset, and it almost made me wish I was still married to Boo so he could pick it up. So I went to Boo's office and I said, "Mrs. Wright is lying on the rug, squashed, come help," and he did.

(To Boo, *with great affection.)* You were very good. *(To* Matt.*)* But I think he went out and got drunk.

Boo. I remember that parakeet.

Matt. *(To* Boo.*)* Why did you drink? *(To* Bette.*)* Why did you keep trying to have babies? Why didn't Soot leave Karl? Why was her name "Soot"?

Bette. I don't know why her name was "Soot." I never had a parakeet that talked. I even bought one of those records that say "Pretty blue boy, pretty blue boy," but it never picked it up. Boo picked Mrs. Wright up. As a joke, I called people up and I played the record over the phone, pretty blue boy, pretty blue boy; and people kept saying, "Who is this?" Except Emily, she tried to have a conversation with the record.

Boo. I remember that parakeet. You shut the door on it.

Bette. We moved past that part of the story, Boo. Anyway, then I called Bonnie Wilson and I played the record for her, and she knew it was me right away, she didn't even have to ask. It's nice seeing your parents together again, isn't it, Skippy?

Matt. *(Taken aback, but then it is nice.)* Yes, very nice.

Boo. *(To* Matt.*)* I was just remembering when you were a little boy, Skip, and how very thrilled your mother and I were to have you. You had all this hair on your head, a lot of hair for a baby; we thought, "We have a little monkey here," but we were very happy to have you, and I said to your mother . . . *(Pause; he has another blackout; stares . . .)*

Bette. Ooops, there he goes again. Boo? Boo? *(Feels pain.)* I better ring for the nurse. I need a shot for pain.

Matt. Should I go?

Bette. No. Wait till the nurse comes.

Boo. *(Coming back.)* . . . to your mother, "Where do you think this little imp of a baby came from?"

Bette. We finished that story, Boo.

Boo. Oh.

Matt. I do need to catch my train.

Bette. Stay a minute. I feel pain. It'll go in a minute.

(MATT *smiles, looks away, maybe for the nurse.* BETTE *closes her eyes, and is motionless.*)

BOO. Bette? Bette?

MATT. Is she sleeping?

(MATT, *with some hesitation, feels for a pulse in her neck. Enter* EMILY.)

EMILY. Oh, hello, Boo. It's nice to see you. Are you all right, Skippy?

MATT. She died, Emily.

EMILY. Then she's with God. Let's say a prayer over her.

(EMILY *and* BOO *pray by* BETTE's *body. Music to "Bette and Boo" theme is heard softly.* MATT *speaks to the audience.*)

MATT. Bette passed into death, and is with God. She is in heaven, where she has been reunited with the four dead babies, and where she waits for Boo, and for Bonnie Wilson, and Emily, and Pooh Bear and Eeyore, and Kanga and Roo; and for me.

(*Lights dim. End of play.*)

Wallace Shawn

AUNT DAN
AND LEMON

W ALLACE Shawn simplifies in order to reveal com-
plexity. He renounces judgment in order to express his convictions. He allows his characters to speak
for themselves in order to expose their flaws. In *Aunt Dan
and Lemon*—his exploration of the psychic sources of
brutality, of the intellectual and emotional genesis of
man's inhumanity to man—Shawn shows how ever-so-
slightly careless assumptions, each seemingly logical,
lead inexorably to the next assumption, to the next, to
the next, until the chain of choices, beginning in all innocence, ends in ultimate evil. So in the final paradox,
this most morally concerned of all our playwrights is also
our least moralistic, allowing his play to articulate hor-
rific attitudes without challenging them. Any dispute with
the points of view voiced by the characters, any argument, any refutation, must come from the members of
the audience, who are thus forced to seek in themselves
not only resistance to evil but its very source.

We can all too easily cheer on the playwright's exposure and denunciation of irrational, destructive ideolo-
gies and impulses, Shawn implies—but this reassuring
form of theater allows us to blame others and to evade
our own culpability. "It would be flattering to believe
that we are superior in some way to the audiences who
cheered for Hitler," Shawn has written, "but I think it
would be more prudent to make the assumption that perhaps we're not. . . . If we look into the mirror, we just
might observe a rapacious face." So if the price of liberty is eternal vigilance, that responsibility belongs to
the theatergoer as well as to the playwright. "If everyone
were just like you," Lemon says to the audience in her

opening monologue, "perhaps the world would be nice again"—but her flattery is deceptive, merely lulling us until we're ready to accept Shawn's deeper flattery, that perhaps we're capable of dealing with the ways in which we're *not* so nice.

Shawn's difficult task was to embody these philosophical abstractions in a theatrical narrative, for his goal wasn't so much to analyze issues and win our intellectual assent as to dramatize dilemmas and energize our emotional commitment. Persuading our minds, after all, is less effective than touching our hearts. No one ever gave a standing ovation to an essay.

Shawn's first decision, to structure the play as the story of Lemon's education by Aunt Dan, allowed him to personalize his points. Lemon's mind is a kind of tabula rasa upon which Aunt Dan's precepts are imprinted, and persuasive precepts they initially seem, sensible, kindly, even inarguable—we should treat everyone with respect, certain jobs in our society may not be pleasant but someone has to perform them, and so on. But Lemon hardly notices the subtle permutations by which Aunt Dan soon arrives at her problematic politics—don't her reasonable premises lead to these rational conclusions?

Shawn's second decision, to show alternating scenes of Aunt Dan with her London friends, briefly baffles us (all the more so because they're so funny). What do these decadent people have to do with Lemon's education? Doesn't their despicable behavior clash with Aunt Dan's moral precepts? But of course their private conduct "logically" derives from the same simple assumptions as Aunt Dan's political convictions.

And Shawn's third decision, to frame the play with Lemon's reflections on Naziism, reveals the consequences of lapses in moral vigilance. Her initial monologue acknowledges brutality, her final monologue virtually justifies it, and it is Shawn's greatest achievement to show how the one, by almost imperceptible gradations, leads inevitably to the other, to demonstrate the moral implications of even the most innocuous choices, to reveal that evil doesn't always reside in other people but potentially in all of us.

* * *

WALLACE SHAWN's *Our Night Out, Marie and Bruce,*
and *The Fever*—winner of the 1991 Obie as best new
American play—have established his reputation as one of
our most intellectually provocative and morally challenging playwrights. Also well-known as a character actor,
Shawn has appeared in dozens of movies, most promi-
nently *Manhattan* and *Radio Days*.

Aunt Dan and Lemon was produced by The New York Shakespeare Festival at the Public Theater. It opened on October 21, 1985, with the following cast (in order of appearance):

LEMON	*Kathryn Pogson*
MOTHER	*Linda Bassett*
FATHER	*Wallace Shawn*
AUNT DAN	*Linda Hunt*
MINDY	*Lynsey Baxter*
ANDY	*Larry Pine*
FREDDIE	*Wallace Shawn*
MARTY	*Larry Pine*
RAIMONDO	*Mario Arrambide*
FLORA	*Linda Bassett*
JUNE	*Linda Bassett*
JASPER	*Wallace Shawn*

This production was directed by Max Stafford-Clark; set designed by Peter Hartwell; costumes by Jennifer Cook; lighting by Andy Phillips and Christopher Toulmin; sound by John Del Nero and Andy Pink; stage managers, Peter Gilbert, Jill MacFarlane, and Bethe Ward. The assistant director was Simon Curtis.

NOTE: The action of this play is continuous. There should be no pauses at all, except where indicated, despite the fact that the setting changes.

London. A dark room. A woman named Lemon, born in 1960. She sits in an armchair, weak and sick.

LEMON. Hello, dear audience, dear good people who have taken yourselves out for a special treat, a night at the theater. Hello, little children. How sweet you are, how innocent. If everyone were just like you, perhaps the world would be nice again, perhaps we all would be happy again. (*Pause.*) Dear people, come inside into my little flat, and I'll tell you everything about my life. (*Pause.*) Maybe you're wondering about all these glasses, all these drinks? They're all sweet fruit and vegetable juices, my friends. I spend all my money on these wonderful drinks—lime and celery and lemon and grape—because I'm a very sick girl, and these juices are almost all I can take to sustain this poor little body of mine. Bread and juices, and rolls, of course. (*Pause.*) I've always had a problem with regular meals—I mean, regular food at regular hours. Maybe it's only a psychological problem, but it's destroyed my body all the same. (*Pause.*) My parents both died in their early fifties, and it wouldn't surprise me if I were to die even younger than that. It wouldn't surprise me, and it wouldn't bother me. My father was an American who lived most of his life over here, in England. He worked very hard at his job, and he made some money, which I inherited, but it's very, very little with today's prices. It allows me to live, but not much more. (*Pause.*) Maybe because I have nothing to do all day, I sleep very little, and I make a lot of effort just trying to sleep. I used to read mysteries—detective novels—to put myself to sleep, but I don't anymore. Lately I've been reading about the Nazi killing of the Jews instead. There are a lot of books about the Nazi death camps. I was reading one last night about the camp called Treblinka. In Treblinka, according to the book, they had these special sheds where the children and women undressed and had their hair taken off, and then

they had a sort of narrow outdoor passageway, lined by
fences, that led from these sheds all the way out to the
gas chambers, and they called that passageway the Road
to Heaven. And when the children and women were un-
dressing in the sheds, the guards addressed them quite
politely, and what the guards said was that they were
going to be taken outside for a shower and disinfection—
which happens to be a phrase you read so often in these
books, again and again, "a shower and disinfection."
"A shower and disinfection." The guards told them that
they didn't need to be worried about their clothes at all,
because very soon they would be coming back to this
very same room, and no one would touch their clothes
in the meanwhile. But then once the women and children
stepped out of the sheds onto the Road to Heaven, there
were other guards waiting for them, and those guards
used whips, and the women and children were made to
run rapidly down the road and all the way into the chambers, which were tiled with orange and white tiles and
looked like showers, but which were really killing chambers. And then the doors would be slammed shut, and
the poison would be pumped in until everyone was dead,
twenty minutes later, or half an hour later. So apparently
the Nazis had learned that it was possible to keep everyone calm and orderly when they were inside the sheds,
but that as soon as they found themselves outside, naked,
in that narrow passageway, they instinctively knew what
was happening to them, and so guards were stationed
there with whips to reduce the confusion to a sort of
minimum. The strategy was to deal with them politely
for as long as possible, and then to use whips when po-
liteness no longer sufficed. Today, of course, the Nazis
are considered dunces, because they lost the war, but it
has to be said that they managed to accomplish a great
deal of what they wanted to do. They were certainly successful against the Jews. (*Pause.*) The simple truth about
my life is that I spend an awful lot of time in this room
just doing nothing, or looking at the wall. I can't stand
the noise of television or even the radio. I don't have
visitors, I don't do crossword puzzles, I don't follow
sports, and I don't follow the news. I hate reading the

daily papers, and actually people who *do* read them in a way seem like idiots to me, because they get wildly excited about every new person or thing that comes along, and they think that the world is about to enormously improve, and then a year later they're shocked to learn that that new thing or that new person that was going to make everything wonderful all of a sudden was in fact just nothing or he was just a crook like everyone else, which is exactly what I would probably have guessed already. So the fact is that I spend a lot of time just staring into space. And you know, when you do that, all of your memories come right back to you, and each day you remember a bit more about them. Of course I haven't lived much of a life, and I would never say I had. Most of my "sex," if you can call it that, has been with myself. And so many of my experiences have had to do with being sick, like visiting different doctors, falling down on my face in public buildings, throwing up in hallways in strange places, and things like that. So in a way I'm sitting here living in the past, and I don't really have much of a past to live in. And also, of course, I should say that I'm not a brilliant person, and I've never claimed to be one. And actually most of the people I've known as an adult haven't been that brilliant either, which happens to suit me fine, because I don't have the energy to deal with anybody brilliant today. But it means that I'm really thrown back on my childhood, because my most intense memories really go back to my childhood, but not so much to things that I did: instead I remember things I was told. And one of the times that was most intense for me—and that I've been thinking about especially in the last few days—is a certain summer I want to tell you about. And to describe that summer I have to tell you a little about my background and go a bit farther back into things. And you know, people talk about life as if the only things that matter are your own experiences, the things *you* saw or the things *you* did or the things that happened to *you*. But you see, to me that's not true. It's not true at all. To me what matters really is the people you knew, the things you learned from them, the things that influenced you deeply and made you what you are.

So I may not have done very much in my life. And yet I really feel I've had a *great* life, because of what I've learned from the people I knew. (LEMON *drinks. A long silence. Very faintly in the darkness three seated figures begin to be visible.*) How far do your memories go back? Mine start when I was three: A lawn. The sun. Mother. Father. And Aunt Dan. (*The seated figures stand and form another picture.* MOTHER *and* FATHER *have their arms around each other.* AUNT DAN *is slightly apart.*) Then a little later, sort of at twilight, everyone walking, then suddenly stopping to look at the sky. Mother. Father. And Aunt Dan. (MOTHER *points at something in the sky.* FATHER *and* AUNT DAN *look.*) And then there are the things that happened to other people, but they're mine now. They're my memories. (RAIMONDO, *a Hispanic man in his forties, and* MINDY, *an English woman in her twenties, are seated at a table. Music in the background.*)

RAIMONDO. (*To* MINDY.) What absolutely wonderful music—really delightful—

MINDY. Yes—isn't it?

RAIMONDO. It reminds me of—er—Brasilia Chantelle—do you know that group?

MINDY. No—

RAIMONDO. They have a vibraphone, a banjo, a sax, and a harp. Not your ordinary combo—eh? (*They laugh.*)

MINDY. You seem to know a lot about music, Mr. Lopez.

RAIMONDO. Well, music is one of my passions, you see—you know, I'm afraid I didn't catch your last name.

MINDY. Er—Gatti.

RAIMONDO. Italian?

MINDY. On my father's side Italian. My mother was English.

RAIMONDO. She's no longer living?

MINDY. Yes—she died last winter. A terrible illness.

RAIMONDO. I'm very sorry.

MINDY. Oh, thank you, really. Do you like this wine?

RAIMONDO. It's delicious. It's special.

MINDY. Yes, it's Italian.—The sparkling wines of that region are always—

RAIMONDO. You picked it?

MINDY. Yes.

RAIMONDO. You like wine, don't you?

MINDY. Not *too* much, no—

RAIMONDO. I didn't say *too* much—

MINDY. You were thinking it, though—You were thinking I look like the kind of person—

RAIMONDO. *Every* person is that kind of person. I'm a student of the subject. Ha ha! Believe me. But I like it, too. When a wine is good—and the company's amusing—

MINDY. When the company's amusing, *any* wine is good. (*They laugh. These figures fade.* JUNE, *an English woman in her twenties,* JASPER, *an American man in his forties, and* ANDY, *an American in his early thirties, are now visible, seated in the midst of a conversation.*)

ANDY. (*To* JUNE.) Tell us your opinion.

JUNE. Jasper seems to me an attractive man. He's extremely polite, he's extremely friendly. I'd be very surprised if he had any diseases—diseases, Jasper?

JASPER. Absolutely not. Do you think this kind of thing is my normal life? I *never* do this. I'm on vacation. (*These figures fade, as Lemon speaks.*)

LEMON. (*To the audience.*) But to tell you about myself, I have to tell you something about my father. I can't avoid it. And the first thing he'd want me to tell you about him is that he loved England. That's what he always said. He came here first to study at Oxford, and then he met my mother, an English girl. And then, when they were married, they decided to live in England for good, and Father got a job in a huge company that made parts for cars. Jack and Susie. My father and mother. (*Pause.*) But poor Father always felt that his old friends, the people he'd known, when he was a student at Oxford, had no understanding of the work he did. He would always tell us they didn't have a clue. He used to say that over and over and over again. (FATHER *smiles at the audience, finally speaks.*)

FATHER. I love England. It's a beautiful place. The gardens are lovely. Those English roses. The way they have strawberry jam and that clotted cream with their high teas. And crumpets particularly are very wonderful, I think. There's no American equivalent to crumpets at all—the way they seem to absorb butter like some living creature—the way they get richer and richer as you add all that butter. Well, you can't get anything like that in America at all. But you know, it's interesting that there are some fantastic misconceptions about English life, and one of them is the amazing idea that economic life in England is somehow relaxed—not very intense! Well! Ha! When I hear that, I have a big reaction, I have to tell you. And when I tell people about economic life in England today, the first thing I say is, it's *very* intense. It's *very* intense. You see, the first fact to know about economic life in England today is that it's very, very hard to get a really good job over here. And the second thing that people just don't seem to know is that if you *have* a good job, it is very, very hard to keep *hold* of it. Because people don't realize that if you *have* a good job, then to *keep* that job, you have to *perform*. You really have to *perform*! If you're on the executive level, you have to perform. You do your job right, you get the results, or out you go, I don't care what school you went to, my friend—that stuff about the schools doesn't count anymore—you can just forget it! The thing is now, they look at the figures: Are the orders up? Great. You're okay. Are they down? Believe me, you're out, my friend. I always say, if you don't think I'm right, try sitting in my office for just one week. You'll know what I'm talking about then, you see. That's just what I say to all my old friends when they ask me about it, in that somewhat awkward way that they have. They're all academics, they're scholars, they're writers—they think *they're* using their brains every day, and *I'm* somehow using—?—well, what?—my feet? And that's why I say, I wish you would sit in my office for just one week and do my job and then see whether you need your brains to do it or not. Well, maybe you're so smart you won't *need* your brains—I really don't know. Maybe I'm stupid! But just try it out. Try it for a week and give me a report. Those lazy bastards would drop to their knees with exhaustion after a single day of the work I do. Because the amazing thing about the work *I* do is that you don't just do your work and then say to yourself, "Well done, my boy. That was

very well done!'' You see, that's what scholars do. That's
what writers do. And if you're a scholar or a writer—
great—fine—no one in the world can say, ''No, No, but
your work was bad.'' Or they can say it, maybe, but then
you can say, ''Oh no, you're wrong, it really was good.''
But in *my* work there's an actual test, a very simple test
which tells you without any doubt or question or debate
at all whether your work was in fact ''good,'' or whether
it was, in fact, very very ''bad''—And the test is, how
did your product do in the market? Did people buy it?
Well, your work was good. What? They didn't? Well, I'm
very, very sorry, your work was *bad*. It was *very bad*.
You did a *bad job*. You see, it's no good saying, ''But
the public doesn't understand me, in twenty years they'll
know I was right.'' Because in twenty years the product
won't be on the shelves, you see, so it will be perfectly
irrelevant in twenty years. In twenty years that product
will be out of date—it will be worthless garbage. So the
judgment that's passed on the work I do is extremely
harsh, and the punishment for doing badly is very simple: you have to leave. So at the executive level, you can't
relax. You work hard. You work hard, you pay attention,
and the next day you go in and you work hard again and
pay attention again. And if you miss a day—if you go in
one day and you just don't feel like working hard, and
you just don't feel like paying attention—well, that could
very well be the day when you make the mistake that
costs you your job, the whole thing. I've seen it happen
to a lot of people. I've seen it happen about a thousand
times.

LEMON. Some people have warm memories of their
family table. I can't say I do! There was a problem about
that family table for me. (*At the dinner table,* MOTHER,
FATHER, *and* LEMON *are silent. Mother and Father eat.
Lemon just plays with her food.*)

MOTHER. What's wrong, my love?

LEMON. Mummy, it's raw.

MOTHER. That lamb?—Raw?—But it's *overcooked,*
darling—I was trying—please—I wanted—

LEMON. I'm sorry, Mummy.

MOTHER. But you have to eat—if you don't eat—please—I can't stand this—

LEMON. May I be excused? (*She leaves the table, but stands nearby, where her parents can't see her. To the audience.*) Father was sure that my problem was caused by the very anxiety which my mother expressed when I didn't eat. (*She eavesdrops on her parents' conversation.*)

FATHER. Susie. Susie. I know how you feel! I know how you feel! But you've got to get yourself under control! Yes, it's a *terrible, terrible situation*—but *you're causing* it!

MOTHER. Oh no—please—

FATHER. Yes! Yes! I am right about this! I am right about this! You've got to get yourself under control! Because if you don't, we're going to have a really sick girl around here! And I mean *really sick*! Do you hear what I'm saying? I mean it, I mean it! If you don't get yourself under control, we're going to have a really sick girl, and doctors will have to come here and *take her away*. And I mean *far away*. For a *long time*. So control your feelings! When she *leaves* this room, you can cry, you can scream—and I'll cry too, I'll cry right along with you—but when she's *in* the room, you *keep quiet*! We're dealing here with a sick child, a helpless child, *she* can't help feeling *sick*! Don't you *know* that? She would like to be well! She would like to be well!

MOTHER. Love—please—you mustn't—don't—darling—you're becoming—

FATHER. No. You leave me alone. You leave me alone right now. Don't you start telling me what I'm becoming. Don't you dare. I'm not nothing. Don't you say that I'm nothing. Don't you ever *dare* say to me that I'm nothing.

LEMON. (*To the audience.*) I listened in the way that children listen. I didn't actually hear the points they were making, point for point. It was more of a sound I heard. There was a certain sort of sound she made, and a certain sort of sound from him. My mother was a saint—she loved him very dearly. But my father was a kind of caged animal, he'd been deprived of everything that would keep him healthy. His life was unsanitary in every way. His

entire environment—his cage . . . was unclean. He was
never given a thorough washing. So no wonder . . . his
fur was falling out, he was growing thinner and thinner
every day. His teeth were rotten, his shit was rotten, and
of course he stank. He stank to hell. When we sat at the
table, as if everything was normal, everything was fine,
there was an overpowering stench that was coming from
my father. My mother ignored it, but you have to say,
she did get sick and die at the age of fifty. (LEMON, *as a
young child, is in bed.* MOTHER *is talking to her.*)

MOTHER. I loved the dawn at Oxford. I loved the way
my room looked when I would draw the curtain, and that
little bit of gray light would come in and spill over my
books. I loved the way the books looked in that dim
light—dusty, cold, delicious. I remember there was a
whole winter when every morning I got up at dawn,
brushed my teeth, made myself a big pot of coffee, and
then sat down at my desk, which was right by the window, and I wouldn't get up until it was almost noon. And
I remember that sometimes when I would stand up after
so many hours of reading poetry—it was the English poetry of the seventeenth century—I would be giddy and
unsteady on my feet until I had rushed to my cupboard
and eaten a hard-boiled egg and a bun and a big square
of chocolate, all in about a minute and a half. And then
I would go out, and that same winter I'd discovered this
huge meadow near the edge of town where I used to take
walks. And one afternoon as I walked along I saw another girl who was walking also, and as I was looking at
her, she looked over at me. And then a few days later, I
saw her again, and we found ourselves staring at each
other. Finally it happened again a few days later, and the
other girl decided to introduce herself. She marched up
with a sort of mischievous grin, extended her hand, and
announced in a forthright American accent, ''My name's
Danielle.'' And you know, Dan in those days used to
wear these delicate white Victorian blouses and these
rough nineteenth-century men's caps, and I'd never met
anyone quite like her in my life. So we walked together
for a little while, and then I said to her, ''Well why don't
you come back to my room for tea?'' And so we went

back, and we talked for a very long time, and we drank a lot of tea and got very excited, and we drank some sherry that I'd put away somewhere, and I told her things I hadn't told people whom I'd known for years. I was shocked at first when she said she was a tutor, but I quickly got used to it, and a week or so later she came back again, and then she came once again. And a few weeks later she brought one of her friends—another American—and it was your father, of course.

LEMON. My parents had named me Leonora, but when I was very little Aunt Dan started calling me Lemon, and then I called myself that, and it became my name. And when I was still very little, five or six or seven or eight, I remember how close Aunt Dan and my parents were. (MOTHER, FATHER, AUNT DAN, *and* LEMON *are at the table.*)

AUNT DAN. Dear God, thank you for this meal we are about to eat. Thank you for this table, thank you for these knives and forks and spoons and these plates and glasses, thank you for giving us all each other. Dear God, thank you for giving us not only life, but the ability to know that we *are* alive. May we never spend any moment of these hours together ungrateful for the—(*She hesitates.*)—for the splendors which you have given us—here—in this garden of life. (*Pause for a moment; she looks around.*) Now, let's have lunch.

LEMON. (*To the audience.*) My father had romantic feelings about the English countryside. But the spot he chose for our house, not too far from London, was, I always felt, strangely un-English. Particularly in the summer, it seemed to me like a bit of swamp near the Mississippi which had somehow been transported into the English landscape. The air was sticky and hot, the grass and the weeds were as sharp as knives, and as far as the eye could see, a thick scum of tiny insects formed a sort of solid haze between us and the sun. You could hear their noise even inside the house, and when you went outside they were like a storm of tiny pebbles striking your face. All the same, we had a small garden, and when I was five or six or seven or eight, I remember that Aunt Dan and my parents would spend long, long evenings talking in the garden, and I would sit in the grass and listen. (*The garden. Night.*) They used to agree about everything then. (MOTHER, FATHER, *and* AUNT DAN *are laughing.* LEMON *is apart.*)

FATHER. Did you read that review?

MOTHER. Well, isn't it just the sort of book that Williams would love? He doesn't know a thing about those people himself, but he assumes Antonescu has got it all right.

AUNT DAN. And when Antonescu reads the review, he'll say to himself, "Well then I *did* get it right!" (*They all laugh.*)

LEMON. And they used to play these hilarious games. (*The garden. Night.* MOTHER, FATHER, *and* AUNT DAN *are playing a game.* AUNT DAN *is slowly circling around, imitating some animal, and meanwhile tearing some strips of paper.* MOTHER *and* FATHER *also hold sheets of paper.* LEMON *is apart, watching.*)

MOTHER. A cat!

FATHER. No, it's sort of a *sea* monster—isn't that it?

MOTHER. A sea *lion*!

FATHER. No—a lion! A lion! (*He rips up pieces of paper.*)

AUNT DAN. Right! A lion!

FATHER. Lion! Lion! (MOTHER *crumples her sheets of paper and throws them at* FATHER *and* AUNT DAN. *They are all laughing.*)

LEMON. And then there was a time when they stopped playing. And I don't think anyone said, "We shouldn't do this again. We don't enjoy it anymore." I think that even a year later or two years later if you'd asked one of them about it they would have said without any hesitation, "Oh yes, we *love* those games. We play them all the time." (*Pause.*) And then there were wonderful evenings when Aunt Dan and my father and I would listen to my mother reading out loud. (*The garden. Night.* MOTHER *is reading out loud inaudibly. Listening are* FATHER, LEMON *and* AUNT DAN. LEMON *speaks to the audience over the reading.*) The sound of her voice was so beautiful. It was so soothing. It made everyone feel calm and at peace. (*As* LEMON *pauses, the reading becomes audible.*)

MOTHER. Across the dark field the shepherd strode,
His pipe gripped tightly in his gnarled hand,
Heedless of the savage winter rain
Which smote the desolate, barren land.
The sheep had gone; he knew that much,
And out across the tangled wood he struck . . .

LEMON. (*As* MOTHER *continues reading inaudibly.*) And then there was a time when she stopped reading. I suppose it was like the games, in a way. There was one evening, some evening, which was the very last time she read to us all, but no one remembered that evening or even noticed it. (*Pause.*) Well, across the garden from the main house was a little house which was also ours. My father had built it to use as a study, but it turned out that he never went near it. And so, somehow, over the years, little by little, I found that I was moving all of my things from my own room in the main house across the garden to this little house, till finally I asked to have my bed moved as well, and so the little house became mine. And it was in that little house, whenever Aunt Dan would come to visit our family, that she and I would have our evening talks, and when I look back on my childhood, it was those talks which I remember more than anything else that ever happened to me. And particularly the talks we had the summer I was eleven years old, which was the last time my parents and Aunt Dan were friends, and Aunt Dan stayed with us for the whole summer, and she came to visit me every night. And in a way it was an amazing thing that a person like Aunt Dan would spend all that time talking to an eleven-year-old child who wasn't even that bright, talking about every complicated subject in the world, but listening to Aunt Dan was the best, the happiest, the most important experience I'd ever had. (*Pause.*) Of course, Aunt Dan wasn't really my aunt. She was one of the youngest Americans to ever teach at Oxford—she was just a couple of years older than my parents—and she was my father's best friend, and my mother's too, and she was always at our house, so to me she was an aunt. Aunt Dan. But my mother and father had other friends, and they had their own lives, and they had each other, and they had me. But I had only Aunt Dan. (*Silence.*) The days that summer were awful and hot. I would sit in the garden with Aunt Dan and Mother, squinting up at the sun to see if it had made any progress in its journey toward the earth. Then, eventually, I would wolf down some tea and bread and by six o'clock I'd be in my little house, waiting for Aunt Dan to come and visit. Because Aunt Dan didn't spend her evenings talking in the garden with my parents anymore. And as I waited, my mind would already be filling with all the things she'd told me, the people she'd described. (*Pause.*) Usually there'd still be some light in the sky when I would hear her steps coming up to the little house. And then she would very ceremoniously knock on the door. ''Come in!'' I'd shout. I'd already be in my pajamas and tucked in under the covers. There'd be a moment's pause. And then she'd come in and sit on my bed. (*Night. The little house.* LEMON *and* AUNT DAN *are laughing.*)

AUNT DAN. (*To* LEMON.) You see, the thing was, Geoffrey was the most fantastic liar—I mean, he was so astonishingly handsome, with those gorgeous eyes and those thick, black eyebrows—he just had to look at a woman, with those eyes of his, and she immediately believed every word that he said. And he didn't mind lying to his wife at all, because she'd trapped him into the marriage in the first place, in the most disgusting way, and she just lived off his money, you know—she just lay in bed all day long in a pink housecoat, talking on the telephone and reading magazines and ordering the servants around like slaves. But he knew she'd go mad if he left for the week, so he went to her looking totally tragic, and he said, ''Sadie, I've *got* to go to Paris for a conference for at least three days, and I'm so upset, I just hate to leave you, but some professors over there are attacking my theories, and if I don't defend myself my entire reputation will be just destroyed.'' So she cried and wailed—she was just like a baby—and he promised to bring her lots of presents—and the next thing was, I heard a little knock on my tiny door, and in came Geoffrey into my basement room. I mean, you can't imagine—this tiny room with

nothing in it except all my laundry hanging out to dry—
and here comes this gigantic prince, the most famous
professor in the whole university, a great philosopher,
coming to see me, a starving second-year student who
was living on a diet of brown bread and fruit and occasionally cheese. Well, for the first two days we didn't
move from bed—I mean, we occasionally reached across
to the table and grabbed a pear or an apple or something—and then on the third day we called a taxi, and we
went all the way into London to this extraordinary shop—
I'd never seen anything like it in my life—and while the
taxi waited we simply filled basket after basket with all
this incredible food—I mean, outrageous things like hams
from Virginia and asparagus from Brussels and paté from
France and olives and caviar and boxes of marrons
glacés, and then we just piled it all into the taxi, along
with bottles and bottles of wine and champagne, and
back we went to my tiny basement and spent the rest of
the week just living like pigs.

LEMON. The light from the window—the purplish light
of the dusk—would fall across her face.

AUNT DAN. Now Lemon, I have to tell you something
very important about myself. And there aren't many
things I'm sure of about myself, but this is something I
can honestly say with absolute confidence, and it's something that I think is very important. It is that I *never*—
no matter how annoyed or angry I may be—I *never, ever
shout at a waiter*. And as a matter of fact, I never shout
at a porter or a clerk in the bank or anybody else who is
in a weaker position in society than me. Now this is very,
very important. I will never even use a *tone of voice* with
a person like that which I wouldn't use with you or your
father or anyone else. You see, there are a lot of people
today who will simply *shout* if they're angry at a waiter,
but if they happen to be angry at some powerful person
like their boss or a government official, well then they'll
very respectfully disagree. Now to me that's a terrible
thing, a horrible thing. First of all, because I think it's
cowardly. But mainly because it shows that these people
don't recognize the value and importance of all those
different jobs in society! They think a waiter is less *im-*

portant than a president. They look down on waiters!
They don't admire what they do! They don't even notice
whether someone is a good waiter or a bad waiter! They
act as if we could sort of all afford to have no respect for
waiters now, or secretaries, or maids, or building super-
intendents, because somehow we've reached a point
where we can really just *do without* these people. Well,
maybe there's some kind of a fantasy in these people's
minds that we're already living in some society of the
future in which these incredible robots are going to be
doing all the work, and every actual citizen will be some
kind of concert pianist or a sculptor or a president or
something. But I mean, where are all these robots, actually? Have you ever seen one? Have they even been
invented? Maybe they *will* be. But they're not here *now*.
The way things are *now*, everybody just can't *be* a president. I mean—I mean, if there's no one around to cook
the president's lunch, he's going to have to cook it himself. Do you know what I'm saying? But if no one has
put any food in his kitchen, he's going to have to go out
and buy it himself. And if no one is waiting in the shop
to sell it, he's going to have to go out into the countryside
and *grow* it himself, and, you know, that's going to be a
full-time job. I mean, he's going to have to resign as
president in order to grow that food. It's as simple as
that. If every shop clerk or maid or farmer were to quit
their job today and try to be a painter or a nuclear phys-
icist, then within about two weeks *everyone* in society,
even people who used to *be* painters or nuclear physi-
cists, would be out in the woods foraging for berries and
roots. Society would completely break down. Because
regular work is not one tiny fraction less necessary today
than it ever was. And yet we're in this crazy situation
that people have gotten it into their heads that regular
work is somehow unimportant—it's somehow worth
nothing. So now almost everyone who isn't at *least* a
Minister Of Foreign Affairs feels that there's something
wrong with what they do—they feel ashamed of it. Not
only do they feel that what they do has no value—they
feel actually *humiliated* to be doing it, as if each one of
them had been singled out for some kind of unfair, de-

grading punishment. Each one feels, I shouldn't be a laborer, I shouldn't be a clerk, I shouldn't be a minor official! I'm better than that! And the next thing is, they're saying, "Well, I'll show them all—I won't work, I'll do nothing, or I'll do *almost* nothing, and I'll do it badly." So what's going to happen? We're going to start seeing these embittered typists typing up their documents incorrectly—and then passing them on to these embittered contractors, who will misinterpret them to these huge armies of embittered carpenters and embittered mechanics, and a year later or two years later, we're going to start seeing these ten-story buildings in every city collapsing to the ground, because each one of them is missing some crucial screw in some crucial girder. Buildings will collapse. Planes will come crashing out of the sky. Babies will be poisoned by bad baby food. How can it happen any other way?

LEMON. I would watch the wind gently playing with her hair.

AUNT DAN. Well, that same theater showed vampire films all night long on Saturday nights, and of course all the students would bring these huge bottles of wine into the theater with them, and by the time we got out at dawn on Sunday, your parents and I would be absolutely *mad*. We'd sort of crawl out—dripping with blood—and we'd walk through that freezing town, with everyone asleep, to your father's rooms, and then we'd just close the door and put on some record like Arnold Schoenberg's *Transfigured Night,* as loud as we could. I mean, Lemon, you know, that *Transfigured Night* could just make you squeal, it's just as if Arnold Schoenberg was inside your dress and running his hands over your entire body. And then when we'd drunk about twenty cups of coffee we'd all bicycle out to see some other friends of ours called Phyllis and Ned who lived in a kind of abandoned monastery way out of town, and we would sit outside, and Ned would read us these weird items from the week's papers—you know, he collected horrible stories like "Mother Eats Infant's Head While Father Laughs" and things like that—and Phyllis would serve these gigantic salads out on the grass.

LEMON. And then, as we were talking, night would fall.

AUNT DAN. Well, the telephone thing we worked out was great. Alexander could call me right from his office at the laboratory, no matter who was there, or even from a cozy Sunday afternoon by the fire with his wife, and he'd just say something like, "I need to speak with Dr. Cunningham, please," and that would mean we would meet at Conrad's, a place we used to go to, and then he'd say, "Oh hi, Nat," and that would mean we would meet at nine. Or of course, if I called *him* and his wife answered, I'd just say something like, "I'm awfully sorry, Mrs. Waldheim, it's Dr. Vetzler's office again," and then he'd get on, and I'd say whatever I had to say, and then he'd say something jaunty like, "Oh hi, Bob! No, that's all right, I don't mind a bit!"

LEMON. But her friends were the best. The people she'd known when she was young and wild and living in London. Amazing people. I felt I knew those people myself. (ANDY *appears next to* LEMON.)

ANDY. (*To* LEMON.) Do you remember Mindy? Do you remember June? Do you remember the night that Mindy introduced us to *Jasper*?

LEMON. There was nothing Aunt Dan didn't tell me about them.

ANDY. (*To* LEMON.) Well, June was nice. How could anyone not like June? She was always good-tempered. A wonderful girl. Now, Mindy—Mindy was another story. Mindy could really be sort of annoying, but there were some awfully good reasons for liking her too. For one thing, frankly, she was very, very funny when we were having sex, and that's not nothing. I mean, you know, she thought the whole thing was basically a joke. She just thought bodies were funny, and their little parts were funny, and what they did together was ridiculous and funny. There was just no pressure to make it all work with Mindy, because she really didn't care whether it worked or not. Well, that might be because she used to spend half her day in bed just playing with herself, and she was going out with about six other men as well as me at the time, but from my point of view, I didn't care *why* she was so relaxed about it all, it was just a pleasure, because that was the time when everyone was madly serious about sex, and it was like some kind of terrible hell we all had to go through at the end of each day before we were allowed to go to sleep. And Mindy was different. Mindy thought it was all funny. And you know something else? I really enjoyed giving money to Mindy, because she didn't have it, and she really wanted it, and she loved to get it.

LEMON. Usually Aunt Dan didn't care about politics. In fact, I remember her saying, "When it comes to politics, I'm an ignoramus." But there were certain people Aunt Dan really loved, and one of them was the diplomat Henry Kissinger, who was working for the American government at the time I was eleven. And it reached a kind of point that she was obsessed with Kissinger. When people would criticize him, she would really become extremely upset. Well, this was the time the Americans were fighting in Vietnam, and people even used to attack Kissinger because while all sorts of awful things were happening over there in the war, he was leading the life of a sort of cheerful bachelor in Washington and Hollywood and going out with lots of different girls. People used to say he was an arrogant person. But Aunt Dan defended him.

AUNT DAN. You see, I don't *care* if he's vain or boastful—maybe he is! I don't *care* if he goes out with beautiful girls or likes to ride around on a yacht with millionaires and sheikhs. All right—he enjoys life! Is that a bad thing? If he enjoys life, maybe he'll be even more inspired to do his job of *preserving* life, to help us all lead the life we want! I mean, you can hardly call him a frivolous man. Look at his face! Look at that face! He can stay up night after night after night having a wonderful time with beautiful girls, but he will always have that look on his face, my Lemon, that look of *melancholy*—that look that can't be erased, because he has seen the power of evil in the world.

LEMON. But despite the pain it often caused her, it seemed to me that Aunt Dan just couldn't resist combing every newspaper and every magazine, English and

American, to see what they were saying about Kissinger every day.

AUNT DAN. I mean, all right now, Lemon, you know, let's face it—we all know there are countries in this world that are not ideal. They're poor. They're imperfect. Their governments are corrupt. Their water is polluted. But the people in some of these countries are very happy—they have their own farms, they have their own shops, their own political parties, their own newspapers, their own lives that they're leading quietly day by day. And in a lot of these countries the leaders have always been friendly to us, and we've been friendly to them and helped them and supported them. But then what often happens is that there are always some young intellectuals in all of these countries, and they've studied economics at the Sorbonne or Berkeley, and they come home, and they decide to become rebels, and they take up arms, and they eventually throw out the leaders who were friendly to us, and they take over the whole country. Well, pretty soon they start closing the newspapers, and they confiscate the farms, and they set up big camps way out in the country. And people start disappearing. People start getting shot. Well now, this is exactly the kind of situation that Kissinger faces every day. What should he do? Should he give some support to our old friends who are trying to fight these young rebels? Or should he just accept the situation and let the young rebels do what they like? Well Lemon, do you know—it's as if these journalists don't care *what* he does, so long as they can think of a way to put it in some horrible light! I mean, does he decide to let the rebels do what they like? Well then, everyone will say, "This is very unpleasant! All our old friends are being rounded up and slaughtered! Why didn't Kissinger do something to protect these people? They were counting on us, and we betrayed them!" But does he decide instead to help our old friends and fight the young rebels? Well then, he's a bully! He's a thug! He's a warped, raging, vengeful pig who's trying to show off his masculinity by staging a battle with these pitiful, weak, tiny rebels! You know, it's the hypocrisy of it all that makes me want to just crawl to the toilet and vomit, Lemon. I can't believe people can sink so low!

LEMON. And she loved to explain Kissinger's strategies to me.

AUNT DAN. He's trying to get the North Vietnamese in a corner, so they'll have to negotiate on *his terms*. I mean, these North Vietnamese don't care how long this war goes on! *They* don't care how many men they lose! But *we care*. So let's make it worth their while to stop it now! That's why he's being so friendly to the *Chinese* all of a sudden—it's not because he likes Chinese food! Those Chinese are scared of the Russians, so let's help them out—let's give them the feeling they can *relax* a little. Yes, we'll save you from the Russians! Sure! We're glad to! But for God's sake, stop annoying us by being so helpful to those crazy, maniacal North Vietnamese. Please cut it out! And, of course, the Chinese are thrilled to cooperate. It's a small price to pay for an important friendship with us. And so now *we're* in a position to turn around and say to the Russians, "Listen Russians, these damned Chinese are being awfully friendly to us, and we really don't like them, but while this goddamned war in Vietnam is going on, you know, what can we do? We'd much rather be friends with you, but, let's face facts, the way you're supplying these North Vietnamese with guns and tanks, you're actually helping to kill our soldiers every single day, so how can you be shocked if we have some talks with the Chinese—at least they're helping us to end this war!" And the result of all these talks with the Russians and the Chinese is simply going to be that the North Vietnamese are going to be cut off, they're going to be isolated, they're going to *starve*. No supplies from the Chinese! No supplies from the Russians! Pretty soon they're going to understand that. And if they don't understand it, and they keep on acting as if they can do what they like, well, all the better. We'll bomb their harbors, we'll bomb their cities, and then we'll sit and watch while the Russians and Chinese make a few little critical noises and proceed to do absolutely *nothing* to help them. And when the North Vietnamese feel *that* knife in the heart from their supposed allies, then they'll finally, finally understand that they have *no options*.

LEMON. And there was a story she told me more than once.

AUNT DAN. It was utterly amazing. I could hardly believe it, my little Lemon. It was last winter, and I had a date to have lunch one day at this club in Washington. Well, as I entered the rather formal room where one waited for one's luncheon partner in this rather disgusting, rather unbearable club—and I was waiting to meet a rather disgusting, rather unbearable friend, a member of the club—I saw, sitting in an armchair, reading a large manuscript, Henry Kissinger. At first I couldn't believe it was really Kissinger—why in the world would he be there in this terrible place? But, of course, it *was* him, and he undoubtedly had come for the very same reason that I had—a sense of loyalty, a sense of obligation, to some old but now perhaps rather stupid friend. And it was possible that Kissinger was early, but it was also possible that that friend of Kissinger's was indeed *so* stupid that he actually was late to his own lunch with Henry Kissinger. Of course I tried not to stare. I took a seat far across the room. But every now and then I would just peep over and look. And the most striking thing was that, seated in an uncomfortable position in this uncomfortable chair, Kissinger was utterly immobile. Each time I looked over, his position was exactly the same as it had been before. His pose was more or less determined by what he was doing—he was reading the manuscript held in his lap—but to me the downward-looking angle of his entire head, so characteristic of Kissinger, expressed something more—my feeling was that it expressed the habitual humility of a man whose attitude to life was, actually, prayerful, a man, I felt, who was living in fear of an all-knowing God. The boastful exuberance of the public Kissinger was nowhere to be seen in this private moment. Kissinger's thoughts were not on himself, they were on what was written in that large manuscript—and from that same downward look you could tell that the manuscript was not some theoretical essay, not some analysis of something that had happened a hundred years ago, but a document describing some crucial problem which had to be dealt with by Kissinger soon; and in Kissinger's heart I felt I could see one and only one question nervously beating—would he make the right decision about that problem? Would he have the wisdom to do the thing that would help to resolve it, or would he be misled, would he make an error in judgment and act, somehow, so as to make things worse? Let me tell you, there was no arrogance in the man who sat in that uncomfortable, ridiculous armchair, waiting for his stupid friend to come to lunch; that was a man saddened, almost *terrified,* by the awful thought that he might just possibly do something wrong, that he might just possibly make some dreadful mistake. Then, suddenly, Kissinger's friend arrived—stupid, just as I'd predicted, but so much *more* stupid than I would ever have imagined—a huge, vulgar, crew-cutted, red-faced, overgrown baby who greeted Kissinger with a twanging voice and pumped his hand about twenty times. But, my God, the warmth with which Kissinger leapt up and greeted this man! It was almost impossible to believe. I was utterly stunned by the sheer *joy* which turned Kissinger's face as red as his friend's and seemed to banish from his mind all thought of the heavy manuscript which he still clutched mechanically in his left hand. But then, yes, I realized—this is a man who loves his country, and he loves the people of his country. To Kissinger, I felt, the very crudeness and grossness of this man were his most American, and therefore almost his most wonderful, features, and that was why Kissinger now was smiling like Punch himself in a puppet show as he chatted and laughed with this ignorant, brutal, piglike American friend. And then off they went to the dining room, and I stayed behind and waited for my own stupid friend, and he got from me a greeting that was much less generous, much less kind. But am I proud of myself, Lemon, for my chilly, indifferent greeting toward my stupid friend? No, I'm not. And do I admire Kissinger for his ardent love of a country and a people that have offered him, and perhaps could still offer the entire world, the hope of a safe and decent future? Yes. Yes. I admire him for that.

LEMON. Naturally, at that time, I often used to dream about running away from my parents and going to live with Aunt Dan in London, and I must admit I often pictured that Kissinger would be dropping in on us fairly regularly there. At least, I imagined, he would never think of missing Sunday breakfast, Aunt Dan's favorite meal. For Kissinger, I imagined, she'd always prepare something very special, like some little tarts, or eggs done up with brandy and cream. And Kissinger, I felt, would be at his very most relaxed around Aunt Dan. He would stretch himself out on the big couch with a sleepy sort of smile on his face, and he and Aunt Dan would gossip like teenagers, both of them saying outrageous things and trying their best to shock each other. As for myself, the truth was that I was quite prepared to serve Kissinger as his personal slave—I imagined he liked young girls as slaves. Well, he could have his pleasure with me, I'd decided long ago, if the occasion ever arose. Few formalities would need to be observed—he didn't have the time, and I knew that very well. An exchange of looks, then right to bed—that would be fine with me. It wasn't how I planned to live as a general rule, but for Kissinger, I thought, I would make an exception. He served humanity. I would serve him. (*Pause.*) But a lot of people didn't feel about Kissinger the way we did, and after a while we realized something that we both found rather surprising. As it turned out, one of the people who didn't like Kissinger was actually Mother! In fact, Mother didn't like him even at all—just not one bit—and throughout that summer, when Mother and Aunt Dan would chat in the garden in the afternoons, whenever the conversation turned to the subject of Kissinger, as it often did— and more and *more* often, it seemed to me—things would suddenly become extremely tense. And, naturally, at the time I wasn't in a position to see these conversations as steps toward a final split between Mother and Aunt Dan, but that, of course, was exactly what they were. (*The garden. A silence before* AUNT DAN *speaks.*)

AUNT DAN. Susie, do you think he *likes* to bomb a village full of poor peasants?

MOTHER. (*After a long pause.*) Dan, if you're asking

whether I think he personally enjoys it—I have no idea.
I don't know. I don't know him.

AUNT DAN. Susie! My God! What a horrible thing to
say!

MOTHER. Well Dan, after all, there *are* people who for
one reason or another . . . just can't control their lust for
blood, or they just give in totally to that side of their
nature. They convince themselves that it's necessary—

AUNT DAN. You think that *Kissinger*—

MOTHER. No, Dan, I don't know him, really. I have
no idea. (*Pause.*) I'm sure he believes that what he's doing is right—that he can't avoid it—

AUNT DAN. Mmm-hmm—

MOTHER. But you know, he could believe that he had
to do it—he could feel that he was only striking out
against a danger, an immediate, terrible danger, a threat,
to America—or the world—but you know still it could be
. . . a delusion, actually. I mean, what if the threat is a
fantasy, Dan, or what if it isn't really—so utterly crucial?

AUNT DAN. But Susie, he assesses that. That's exactly
what he does all day.

MOTHER. No, I'm sure he does, but sometimes people
don't assess things carefully enough, because they've really already made up their minds about them a long time
ago. They think they're studying all the information, but
actually their preconceptions are so strong that they're
not really paying very close attention—do you know what
I mean? (AUNT DAN *is silent.*)

LEMON. And so the hot afternoons in the garden got
worse and worse, and the cool, blessed evenings in the little
house, where Aunt Dan would tell me about her friends,
by contrast, seemed nicer and nicer. And the amazing
thing is that still, in my memory, the afternoons and evenings of that long summer keep following each other, on
and on, in an endless alternation. (MINDY *appears next to*
LEMON.) And as the early days of August grew into the
late days, Aunt Dan told me more and more about her
friend Mindy.

MINDY. (*To* LEMON.) I was living a sort of dog's life
at that time, quite frankly. I always seemed to be making
furious love on top of ugly bedspreads and then taking

these awful showers with strange men. But Andy was always so sweet to me.

AUNT DAN. (*To* MOTHER.) Susie, look, he has to make a choice. He has to fight or not fight. One or the other. Do you want him not to fight? Fine—then any country in the world will be free from now on to do anything they like, and we'll be free to do nothing. If they want to invade other countries, or conquer other people's territory, or kill all our friends, well then that's all okay, that's all fine. But some day somebody is going to lose their patience. Do you see what I'm saying? And then you just might find yourself falling into a war that is suddenly so big that you can't stop it.

MOTHER. I understand, you *think* that if America doesn't fight in Vietnam today, then more and more countries in the world will come to be America's enemies. In ten years. In twenty years. But that's just a prediction. It's just a guess.

AUNT DAN. Yes. It's a prediction.

MINDY. (*To* LEMON.) And it would be late at night, and I'd be sitting in some quiet flat with the clock ticking gently, and I'd be looking at some man whom I'd caressed and hugged, and whose beautifully wrapped presents I'd opened in a gay flurry of shrieks and cries— jewelry, perfume, or lingerie—and he'd be dressed in some endearing underwear, and he'd be telling me quietly about the secrets of his life, and suddenly something would come over me, and a cold sweat would break out on my face, and the most incredible lies, or strange insults, would come out of my mouth, and I would rush to the door and go out into the street. And it was a wonderful thing, on a night like that, to find a telephone and call Andy. And he would always tell me to come right over. And it was really nice on those particular nights to just stick my hand in the air and hail a taxi and go over and play with Andy and his friends.

AUNT DAN. (*To* MOTHER.) Susie, he is not a private individual like you and me—he works for the *government*! I mean, you're talking here as if you were trying to tell me that you and I are so nice every day and why can't our governments be just like us! I can't believe

you're saying that! Don't you understand that you and I
are only able to be nice because our governments—our
governments are *not* nice? Why do you think we've set
these things up? I mean, a state, policemen, politicians—
what's it all for? The point is so we don't all have to
spend our lives in some ditch by the side of the road
fighting like animals about every little thing. The whole
purpose of government is to use force. So we don't have
to. So if I move into your house and refuse to leave, you
don't have to kick me or punch me, you don't have to go
find some acid to throw in my face—you just nicely have
to pick up the phone and call the police! And if some
other country attacks our friends in Southeast Asia, you
and I don't have to go over there and fight them with
rifles—we just get Kissinger to fight them for us.

MOTHER. But Dan—

AUNT DAN. These *other* people use force, so we can
sit here in this garden and be incredibly nice. Otherwise
we'd be going around covered with scars and bruises and
our hair all torn out, like stray cats.

MOTHER. But are you saying that governments can do
anything, or Kissinger can do anything, and somehow it's
never proper for us to say, Well we don't like this, we
think this is wrong? Do you mean to say that we don't
have the right to criticize this person's decisions? That
no one has the right to criticize them?

AUNT DAN. No, I don't say that. Go right ahead. Criticize his decisions all you like. I don't know. Go ahead
and criticize everything he does.

MOTHER. I don't—

AUNT DAN. Particularly if you have no idea what you
would do in his place.

MOTHER. Dan, I'm not . . . (*Silence.*)

AUNT DAN. Susie, I'm simply saying that it's terribly
easy for us to criticize. It's terribly easy for us to sit here
and give our opinions on the day's events. And while we
sit here in the sunshine and have our discussions about
what we've read in the morning papers, there are these
certain *other* people, like Kissinger, who happen to have
the very bad luck to be society's leaders. And while we
sit here chatting, they have to do what has to be done.

And so *we* chat, but *they* do what they *have* to do. *They* do what they *have* to do. And if they have to do something, they're prepared to do it. Because I'm very sorry, if you're in a position of responsibility, that means you're responsible for doing whatever it is that has to be done. If you're on the outside, you can wail and complain about what society's leaders are doing. Go ahead. That's fine. That's your right. That's your privileged position. But if you are the one who's in power, if you're responsible, if you're a leader, you don't have that privilege. It's your job to do it. Just to do it. Do it. Do it. Don't complain, don't agonize, don't moan, don't wail. Just do it. Everyone will hate you. Fine. That's their right. But you have to do it. Of course, you're defending *those very people*. *They're* the ones you're defending. But do you expect to be *understood*? You must be nuts! You must be crazy!—insane! All day long you're defending *them*—defending, defending, defending—and your reward is, they'll spit in your face! All right—so be it. That's the way it is. The joy of leadership. But you can bet that what Kissinger says when he goes to bed at night is, Dear God, I wish I were nothing. Dear God, I wish I were a little child. I wish I were a bird or a fish or a deer living quietly in the woods. I wish I were anything but what I am. I am a slave, but they see me as a master. I am sacrificing my life for them, but they think I'm scrambling for power for myself. For myself! Myself! *None* of it is for myself. I *have* no self. I am a leader—that means I am a slave, I am less than dirt. *They* think of themselves. *I* don't. They think, what would *I* like? What would be nice for *me*? I think, what has to be done? What is the thing I *must* do? I don't think, what would be nice for *me* to do? No. No. Never. Never. Never that. Only, what is the thing I *must* do? What is the thing I *must* do. (*Silence*.) And then these filthy, slimy worms, the little journalists, come along, and it is so far beyond their comprehension—and in a way it's so unacceptable to them—that anyone could possibly be motivated by dreams that are loftier than their own pitiful hopes for a bigger byline, or a bigger car, or a girlfriend with a bigger bust, or a house with a bigger game-room in the basement, that, far from feeling gratitude to this man who has taken the responsibility for making the most horrible, shattering decisions, they feel they can't rest till they make it impossible for him to continue! They're out to stop him! Defying the father figure, the big daddy! Worms! Worms! How *dare* they attack him for killing peasants? What decisions did *they* make today? What did *they* have to decide, the little journalists? What did *they* have to decide? Did they decide whether to write one very long column or two tiny little columns? Did they decide whether to have dinner at their favorite French restaurant or to save a little money by going to their second-favorite French restaurant instead? Cowards! Cowards! If anyone brought them a decision that involved human life, where people would die whatever they decided, they would run just as fast as their little legs would carry them. But they're not afraid of trying to stop *him*, of making people have contempt for *him*, of stirring up a storm of loathing for *him*, of keeping him so busy fending off their attacks that he can't breathe, he can't escape, he just has to collapse or resign! I would love to see these cowards face up to some of the consequences of their murder of our leaders! I would love to see them face some of the little experiences our leaderless soldiers face when they suddenly meet the North Vietnamese in the middle of the jungle. That might make the little journalists understand what they were doing, the little cowards. Have they ever felt a bayonet go right through their chest? Have they ever felt a knife rip right through their guts? Would they be sneering then, would they be thinking up clever ways to mock our leaders? No, they'd be squealing like pigs, they'd be begging, begging, "Please save me! Please help me!" I would love to be hiding behind a tree watching the little cowards screaming and bleeding and shitting in their pants! I would love to be watching! Those slimy cowards. So let's see them try to make some decisions. Let's see them decide that people have to die. They wouldn't have the faintest idea what to do. But they just sit in their offices and write their little columns. They just sit in their offices and toss them off. Well, do you think Kissinger is just sitting in *his* office casually making his *decisions*? Do you think he makes those decisions lightly? What do you think? Do you think he just sits in his office and tosses them off? Do you think he just makes them in two minutes between bites of a sandwich? (*A long silence.*)

MOTHER. Dan, I'm sure he makes his decisions thoughtfully. And I'm sure he believes himself to be justified. But I was asking, is he *actually* justified, as far as *I* am concerned? I'm sure he's weighed those lives in the balance against . . . some large objective. But I was asking, has he weighed them, actually, at—at what I would consider their correct measure? (*A silence.*) Does he have a heart which is capable of weighing them correctly?

AUNT DAN. What? What? I don't believe this! I don't believe what I'm hearing from you! Look, I'm sorry, Susie, but all I can say to you is that if he sat at his desk weeping and sobbing all day, I don't think he'd be able to do his job. That's all I can say. He has just as much of a heart as anyone else, you can be sure of that, but the point is that the heart by itself cannot tell you what to do in a situation like that. The heart just responds to the present moment—it just sees these people in a village who've been hit by a bomb, and they're wounded and dying, and it's terribly sad. But the mind—the mind sees the story through to the end. It sees that yes, there are people who are wounded and dying in that village. But if we *hadn't* bombed it, some of those same people would have been marching tomorrow toward the *next* village with the grenades and machine guns they'd stored in that pretty little church we blew up, and when they *got* to that village, they would have burned it to the ground and raped the women and tortured the men and killed whole families—mothers and children. Of course, those things aren't actually happening now, so the heart doesn't care about them. But the things that will happen tomorrow are real too. When it *is* tomorrow, they'll be just as real as the things that are happening now. So I'm asking you, Susie, here is Kissinger. Here is the man who must make the decisions. What do you want this man to do? I am only asking what you want him to do. What is it that you want him to do?

MOTHER. (*After a long pause.*) Well, I suppose I want

him to assess the threat he is facing . . . with scrupulous
honesty . . . and then I want him to think about those
people. Yes, I suppose I do want him to weep and sob at
his desk. Yes. Then let him make his decisions.

LEMON. There were times when Aunt Dan just stared
at Mother. She just sat and stared. (ANDY *appears next
to* LEMON.)

ANDY. Well, Mindy would do almost anything, you
know, to get hold of money, but with all the good will
in the world she still ended up at times without a penny
in her purse. And it was at times like that that the phone
would ring in the middle of the night, and there would
be Mindy asking what I was up to. Well, I was usually
flat on my back being fucked by some girl, if you'll pardon my French, or maybe two, but that didn't bother
Mindy a bit. She'd come by for some money, and half
the time she'd stay to have sex with the rest of us as well.
The one thing the girls I liked seemed to have in common
was they all liked Mindy—but I mean, who wouldn't?
She was so thin she never took up any room, and she
never asked anyone for anything but money. In my book,
she was okay. Well, you see, they say the English are
stuffy, but that's not my experience. (ANDY*'s flat. Late
night.* MINDY *and* JASPER *are coming in the door, amidst
hilarity.* ANDY, JUNE, *and* AUNT DAN—*in her early
thirties—are hastily putting on dressing gowns or long
sweaters.*)

ANDY. Well, well, well—hello, Mindy. What's this?

MINDY. Hello, Andy. I've brought you Jasper. (*Pre-
senting him with a grand gesture. Whoops from everyone.* ANDY *makes introductions.*)

ANDY. Delighted, Jasper. June and Dan. (*Everyone
mock formally shakes hands, murmuring loudly.*)

MINDY. (*To* ANDY.) You see, Jasper's new in town,
passing through, a countryman of yours.

ANDY. What, mine?

MINDY. Say hello, Jasper. Show Andy you're one of
his.

ANDY. Now don't be rude, Mindy—he may be shy!
Don't make him talk like a puppet. I think he *is* shy. Let
him take his time. Shall we have some drinks? June, help

me, dear, ask Jasper what he'd like—what about you, Mindy?

MINDY. Vodka, please.

ANDY. A beer for me—

AUNT DAN. Bourbon for me.

JASPER. Oh, can I help? (JUNE *and* JASPER *exit.*)

ANDY. So who's this Jasper?

MINDY. Well I just met him. He's got a hundred thousand pounds in his trouser pocket.

ANDY. What? Really?

MINDY. He won it. Gambling.

AUNT DAN. My my.

ANDY. Yes, good for you. I hope you get twenty off him at least.

MINDY. Jesus Christ, I'd really like it all.

ANDY. Well, not *all*. That's not fair, Mindy. Leave him a little.

MINDY. If the poor guy would just have a heart attack and die on your floor, we could keep every penny and no one would know. I mean, he's here as a tourist, all by himself. We met in the park. He's been wandering around since he won the money. He's lived a good life! And he's a worthless person, I promise you no one would miss him. He's already told me, his wife hates his guts.

ANDY. Why don't you tell him you need the money?

MINDY. I tried that—it didn't work. (JASPER *and* JUNE *return.*)

JUNE. Jasper's telling me the most amazing story. I think he's frightfully clever.

JASPER. Look, Andy, I won a hundred thousand pounds tonight, from about six guys in a gambling casino. I don't know how it happened, unless they rigged the deck, and somehow it worked out wrong—I mean, they made some mistake and instead of them getting the cards it turned out to be me. I mean, I just kept winning—I'd win one hand, and then I'd win again, and then I'd win again, and each time the stakes kept getting bigger—I think they must have thought that each time it would go against me, but it never did. God damn—my mother would have loved to hear this story—she never saw money in her whole life.

JUNE. God damn—neither did *my* mother, come to think of it.

MINDY. Mine neither.

ANDY. Well, since you ask, *my* mother is quite all right. And how about yours, Dan—is she doing all right?

AUNT DAN. Oh, not too bad.

JASPER. I mean, I'll tell you, Andy, these British men really like to spend money. They're wild as hell.

ANDY. I've found that myself, I must admit.

JUNE. Where have I been all my life?

ANDY. Oh come on, June, now what about that fellow you were telling me about just last week? A Member of Parliament, Jasper, who took June to Africa to study some natives on an important commission about something or other. He used to buy elephants' tusks as if they were pencils—he gave you so many presents you had to hire a little boat to carry them all through the swamps, you told me.

JUNE. Not the swamps, dear, that was the *vaal*.

ANDY. Well pardon me, the *vaal* then.

JUNE. I can't stand how these Yankees can't speak the language.

ANDY. Oh we do all right, we know the major phrases.

JASPER. Yeah, like, "Place your bets," "Let's try another hand"—

ANDY. Yes, right, exactly, things like that—

JUNE. But what part of America do you come from, Jasper?

JASPER. Oh, I'm from Chicago—

AUNT DAN. Aha—

JUNE. Great. I've heard they make the most marvelous steaks. It's just like being a cave man again, a friend of mine said.

JASPER. What do you mean?

ANDY. I think you're thinking of Poughkeepsie, dear.

JUNE. No, that's where they make that white cheese that you put on top of fish.

AUNT DAN. Philadelphia.

JUNE. No, that sounds Greek. Wait—it's a Greek island! Yes, I went there once with a big fisherman. I didn't understand a word he said, but he certainly knew how to catch fish.

AUNT DAN. That's *not* Philadelphia.

ANDY. Well it *might* be, somehow. Is that where you learned how to mend nets? Didn't you once tell me you could mend nets?

JUNE. Who, me?

MINDY. Look, Jasper, you're neglecting that scotch.

JASPER. God you're pretty—you know, I really like you.

MINDY. I told you, Jasper—I have a serious boyfriend, you're not allowed to think of me like that—don't look at me like that, I'm telling you, Jasper, or I'm just going to send you home in a cab.

ANDY. She's serious, Jasper—it's hopeless, my friend, I've tried for years.

JASPER. Years? What? You don't really have a boyfriend, do you, you weasel? I mean, what is this ''years''? If it's been all these years, then where's the boyfriend? He's just an excuse. He doesn't exist. Does he, Andy?

ANDY. Well, I must admit, *I've* never met him. But she's sure been faithful to the guy, I'll say that much.

JASPER. But is there really a guy, or are you just a tease?

MINDY. What is this, Jasper, are you calling me a liar?

JASPER. Yes, I am. You know you'll have me if I give you money.

MINDY. Hey, wow—now don't insult me.

JASPER. Well, I'd love to have you without the money, but you told me no. So now I'm asking you *with* the money.

MINDY. Is that what you're saying? And you think I would?

JASPER. For a thousand pounds, no. That would be too cheap—just prostitution. But *ten* thousand pounds, that's more like marriage. That would be like an intensely serious, permanent relationship, except it wouldn't last beyond tomorrow morning.

MINDY. No, Jasper.

JASPER. What is this no? Are you totally nuts?

MINDY. Give me all of it!

JASPER. Get lost!

JUNE. I think this discussion is going in circles.

ANDY. Friends, please! Let's try to approach our problems sensibly, all right? Now, Jasper, you're asking very little of Mindy, in my opinion. You merely want to strip her clothes off for a few hours and probably fuck her twice at the most, and for this you are offering her ten thousand pounds. Mindy, *my* opinion is, the exchange would be worth it. June, don't you think so? Tell us your opinion.

JUNE. Jasper seems to me an attractive man. He's extremely polite, he's extremely friendly. I'd be very surprised if he had any diseases—diseases, Jasper?

JASPER. Absolutely not. Do you think this kind of thing is my normal life? I *never* do this. I'm on vacation. Now here's the situation: I'm going back home tomorrow morning, and I'm going to put this money in the bank, and right now I'd like to spend some—ten thousand pounds.

JUNE. I think it's a good idea.

MINDY. For ten thousand pounds you can see my tits.

ANDY. Please, Mindy, let's not turn my flat into an oriental market. Either go to bed with the nice man or send him home, but please don't sit on my sofa and sell different parts of yourself. Besides, if you start dividing yourself into pieces, how do you know we won't each take a section and end up tearing you to bits?

MINDY. I don't want your money—I want his.

JUNE. I notice she doesn't mention mine. I'll bet she's guessed I don't *have* any. (*A pause.*)

AUNT DAN. I'll throw in five pounds just to watch.

ANDY. Well, I'll pay a hundred pounds *not* to watch, and here it is. (*He puts it on the table and gets up.*) Come on, June.

AUNT DAN. (*To* LEMON.) Well, Mindy was a terribly clever girl, and she managed to get an awful lot of money from poor Jasper. She really did get ten thousand for taking off her shirt, and by the time he'd screwed her she'd got sixty thousand. Meanwhile, he was trying to pay *me* just to leave the room, but I wouldn't budge. Finally he was so drunk and exhausted he fell asleep, and Mindy sat there on that sofa stark naked and told me stories about her life. Outside the window the city was sleeping, but Mindy's eyes sparkled as she talked on and on. There wasn't much that she hadn't done, and there were things she didn't tell anyone about, but she told me. (MINDY *is seen with* FREDDIE, *an American man.*)

MINDY. (*To* FREDDIE.) All right, I'll do it. Sure. Why not. But you're giving me the money now, right?

FREDDIE. Sure. Of course. I'll see you at Morley's to-morrow evening at nine o'clock. We'll work it so when we come in you'll have a date already—it's more fun that way. And we'll call you Rosa.

MINDY. Okay, Freddie. Whatever you like. (*Morley's, a night club.* RAIMONDO, FREDDIE, *and* FLORA *enter.* MINDY *and* MARTY *are already at a table.* MARTY *is an American man.* FLORA *is a young American woman.*)

MARTY. Hey! Freddie!

FREDDIE. Marty! Rosa! How unexpected!

MARTY. Oh—you know Rosa?

FREDDIE. I've known her for years. A marvelous girl—what's she doing with a guy like you, Marty? (*They all laugh.*) Marty, Rosa, this is Flora Mansfield, and this is my very good friend Raimondo Lopez.

MARTY. Flora. Raimondo.

RAIMONDO. Delighted. Señorita—

MINDY. Enchantée, I'm sure.

MARTY. Say, but where the hell is your wife, Freddie?

FREDDIE. My what? No, no, just kidding, Marty, Corrine's in the country with all the boys—

MARTY. Great. Great. But—er—listen, Freddie, why don't you and your friends join Rosa and me—

FREDDIE. Oh we'd hate to trouble you—

MARTY. No, really—

FREDDIE. Really? Do you think—? Well—er—Raimondo—would you like—?

RAIMONDO. Well yes—yes—certainly—yes. (*Music. They sit down.*)

FLORA. (*To* MARTY.) Say—do you have a brother who sells room dividers over on Bamberger Street?

MARTY. Well—no.

FLORA. Gosh—there's a guy over there who looks exactly like you.

FREDDIE. Er—just imagine. (*They all listen to the music for a while.*)

RAIMONDO. (*To Mindy.*) What absolutely wonderful music—really delightful—

MINDY. Yes—isn't it?

RAIMONDO. It reminds me of—er—Brasilia Chantelle—do you know that group?

MINDY. No—

RAIMONDO. They have a vibraphone, a banjo, a sax, and a harp. Not your ordinary combo—eh? (*They laugh.*)

MINDY. You seem to know a lot about music, Mr. Lopez.

RAIMONDO. Well, music is one of my passions, you see—you know, I'm afraid I didn't catch your last name.

MINDY. Er—Gatti.

RAIMONDO. Italian?

MINDY. On my father's side Italian. My mother was English.

RAIMONDO. She's no longer living?

MINDY. Yes—she died last winter. A terrible illness.

RAIMONDO. I'm very sorry.

MINDY. Oh, thank you, really. Do you like this wine?

RAIMONDO. It's delicious. It's special.

MINDY. Yes, it's Italian.—The sparkling wines of that region are always—

RAIMONDO. You picked it?

MINDY. Yes.

RAIMONDO. You like wine, don't you?

MINDY. Not *too* much, no—

RAIMONDO. I didn't say *too* much—

MINDY. You were thinking it, though—You were thinking I look like the kind of person—

RAIMONDO. *Every* person is that kind of person. I'm a student of the subject. Ha ha! Believe me. But I like it, too. When a wine is good—and the company's amusing—

MINDY. When the company's amusing, *any* wine is good. (*They laugh.*)

RAIMONDO. You're single, then, Miss Gatti? That's almost Italian for cat, isn't it? It's the same word in Spanish—

MINDY. Yes. Yes. I'm single. Miss Cat, if you like.

RAIMONDO. Yes—yes—I'll call you Miss Cat. (*They laugh.*) And when you put that fur around your neck, I'll bet that you look like one too, Miss Cat.

MINDY. Oh come on.

RAIMONDO. No, I mean it. Your smile is a little bit catlike too.

MINDY. You've just got the idea in your head, Mr. Lopez.

RAIMONDO. What idea? Now what idea do I have in my head? (*They are both laughing.*) Are you telling me what ideas I have in my head now? (*They both laugh loudly.*) You're a very unusual woman, Gatti. I think you can *put* ideas inside people's heads if you really want to.

MINDY. Say—now what in the world are you talking about? Eh?

RAIMONDO. If you only *knew* the ideas you've put in my head.

MINDY. I think you're crazy! That's what I think, Mr. Lopez—I think you're absolutely mad!

RAIMONDO. I think you're a witch! I think you're a devil!

MINDY. (*A roar of laughter from the other side of the table.*) Say—it looks like Marty is flirting with your date!

RAIMONDO. My date? Are you crazy? That's not my date! That's a friend of Freddie's wife, a very close friend of his family, Gatti!

MINDY. Oh she is, eh?

RAIMONDO. Yes!—she is! A friend of his family!

MINDY. Really!

RAIMONDO. Yes!

MINDY. Well, all right, Mr. Lopez, then I think Marty is flirting with a very close friend of Freddie's family. (*Outside of Morley's. The same group.*)

MARTY. Well, Rosa, let me take you home. Ha ha— we've hardly had a chance to talk all evening! Now—you live on the South Side, don't you, Rosa?

FREDDIE. Well, why don't we all share a cab? Flora lives on the South Side too—

FLORA. Yes—good—

MARTY. That's fine—great—

MINDY. Well, Freddie, actually, I live on the North Side, actually—

MARTY. Oh—well—

RAIMONDO. So Marty—why don't you drop Freddie and Flora, and *I'll* take Rosa along with me—

MARTY. Oh well, really—oh no—(*to* MINDY) are you sure you wouldn't mind?

MINDY. No no—not at all—

MARTY. Well then—er—all right—well then, come along, Flora—you come along with us—

FLORA. Oh I see—all right—

RAIMONDO. (*To* MINDY.) And you come with me. (MINDY'*s apartment.* RAIMONDO *and* MINDY *are standing at different sides of the room. They have come in a few minutes before. A silence.*) Do you know the first glimpse I had of you tonight?

MINDY. No—what was it?

RAIMONDO. I was standing in the entrance to the restaurant, and Flora was checking her coat, and I looked into the room, and I mostly saw these men in their boring jackets and ties and these dull-looking women—and just through a crack between all those people I suddenly saw a pair of lavender stockings, and I wondered, who is the person who belongs to those stockings? (*They both laugh.*) Because I'm a connoisseur of women's clothing, Gatti. From a woman's clothing, you can see everything. Because some clothing is inert and dead, just dead cloth, like dead skins. And some clothing is alive. Some clothing is there just to cover the body. And some is there to—to describe the body, to tell you about it—like a beautiful wrapping on something sweet. (*There is a silence. He walks toward her. Then he crouches on the floor in front of her and slides his hands along her stockings. He puts his head up her skirt.*) Oh—so warm. (*She stays absolutely still, neither encouraging nor resisting. After a moment, he removes his head and looks at her. Then he helps her take off her shoes, and he removes her stockings. He puts them over the back of a chair.*)

MINDY. Would you like a drink?

RAIMONDO. Well—would you?

MINDY. Thank you. Yes. There's some brandy—

there—(*She points to the brandy. He gets up, gets them both a drink. He sips his.*)

MINDY. Won't you take off that jacket?

RAIMONDO. Oh—thank you—yes. (*He takes off his jacket and tie.*)

MINDY. Sit down, why don't you. (*He sits. There is a silence.*)

RAIMONDO. You're so gorgeous—so sweet. You know, when I get hungry, I'm just like a bear. I start to sweat till I get to the honey.

MINDY. Finish your brandy. There's plenty of time. (*She wipes his forehead with a napkin as he sips his drink. As he finishes, she lowers herself to the floor in front of him, unzips his trousers and starts to kiss his crotch.*)

RAIMONDO. Oh God—yes—yes—oh, please—(*After another moment, she looks up.*)

MINDY. It's chilly in here. And you're still sweating. Come lie down. (RAIMONDO *starts to stand.*)

RAIMONDO. I feel dizzy.

MINDY. Just relax. (*They head toward the bedroom. She turns back for her stockings.*)

RAIMONDO. I feel dizzy. (*In the darkness, his cries of ecstasy.*) Oh, beautiful. Oh, good. (*The bedroom. The light from the window falls on the stockings.* MINDY *is standing by the bed, dressed in a robe, looking down at* RAIMONDO, *who is out cold. She shakes him roughly, and he groans slightly but doesn't wake up. Then she opens a drawer, pulls on a pair of jeans, takes out some pieces of rope, and loops them around the knobs at the head of the bed and the knobs at the foot. She slips the nooses around Raimondo's wrists and ankles. She picks up a pair of stockings, and he suddenly speaks. His voice is indistinct.*) Rosa? Rosa? (*She freezes. After a moment, he feels the ropes, then speaks again, a bit louder.*) What are you doing? Rosa? (*She steps onto the bed behind him.*) Rosa! Please! No! No! (*She puts her feet on his shoulders, leans back against the headboard, puts the stockings around his neck and starts to strangle him. She looks straight ahead of her, not at his face, as he struggles and gags.*)

AUNT DAN. (*To* LEMON.) She had to put the guy in this plastic sack, kick him down her back stairs, haul him outside, and stick him into the trunk of a car that was parked in an alley. Apparently he'd been working with the police for some time against her friend, Freddie. (*A silence.*) Well. My teeth were chattering as I listened to the words of this naked goddess, whose lipstick was the dreamiest, loveliest shade of rose. Then she fell silent for a long time, and we just looked at each other. And then she sort of winked at me, I think you would call it, and I wanted to touch that lipstick with my fingers, so I did. And she sort of grabbed my hand and gave it a big kiss, and my hand was all red. And then we just sat there for another long time. And then, to the music of Jasper snoring on the couch, I started to kiss her beautiful neck. I was incredibly in love. She kissed me back. I felt as if stars were flying through my head. She was gorgeous, perfect. We spent the rest of the night on the couch, and then we went out and had a great breakfast, and we spent a wonderful week together. (*Pause.*)

LEMON. (*To* AUNT DAN.) Why only a week?

AUNT DAN. Huh?

LEMON. Why only a week? (*Pause.*)

AUNT DAN. Lemon, you know, it's because . . . (*Pause.*) Because love always cries out to be somehow expressed. (*Pause.*) But the expression of love leads somehow—nowhere. (*A silence.*) You express love, and suddenly you've . . . you've dropped off the map you were on, in a way, and onto another one—unrelated—like a bug being brushed from the edge of a table and falling off onto the rug below. The beauty of a face makes you touch a hand, and suddenly you're in a world of actions, of experiences, unrelated to the beauty of that face, unrelated to that face at all, unrelated to beauty. You're doing things and saying things you never wanted to say or do. You're suddenly spending every moment of your life in conversations, in encounters, that have no connection with anything you ever wanted for yourself. What you felt was love. What you felt was that the face was beautiful. And it was not enough for you just to feel love, just to sit in the presence of beauty and enjoy it.

Something about your feeling itself made that impossible. And so you just didn't ask, Well, what will happen when I touch that hand? What will happen between that person and me? What will even happen to the thing I'm feeling at this very moment? Instead, you just walked right off that table, and there was that person, with all their qualities, and there was you, with all *your* qualities, and there you were together. And it's always, of course, extremely fascinating for as long as you can stand it, but it has nothing to do with the love you originally felt. Every time, in a way, you think it will have *something* to do with the love you felt. But it never does. It never has anything to do with love. (*Silence.*)

LEMON. (*To the audience.*) My father didn't know about my mother's conversations with Aunt Dan in the garden. He had other things on his mind. The friendship ended, it faded away, and it didn't bother him. Aunt Dan never came back to visit us after the summer I was eleven, but a couple of times a year I would take the train into London and visit her, and she would take me out to dinner at some beautiful restaurant, and we'd sit together and have a lovely meal and talk for hours. When I was just eighteen, Aunt Dan got sick, and then when I was nineteen she finally died. (*Pause.*) In the year or two before Aunt Dan got sick there would sometimes be some odd moments, some crazy moments, in those beautiful restaurants. Some moments when both of us would just fall silent. Well, it was really quite straightforward, I suppose. I think there were crazy moments, sitting at those restaurant tables, when both of us were thinking, Well, why not? We adore each other. We always have. There you are sitting right next to me, and isn't this silly? Why don't I just lean over and give you a kiss? But of course Dan would never have touched me first. I would have to have touched her. Well, neither of us really took those moments seriously at all. But sure, there were moments, there were silences, when I could feel her thinking, Well, here I am sitting on this nice lawn, under this lovely tree, and there's a beautiful apple up there that I've got my eye on, and maybe if I just wait, if I just sit waiting here very quietly, maybe the apple will drop right into my lap. I could feel her thinking it, and I could feel how simple and natural it would be just to do it, just to hold her face and kiss her on the lips, but I never did it. It never happened. So there was me and Aunt Dan in the little house, and then there was me and Aunt Dan not touching each other in all those restaurants, and finally there was one last visit to Aunt Dan just before she died, in her own flat, when she was too sick to touch anybody. (*Music.* AUNT DAN's *flat.*) There's a nice melody playing on her record-player when I go in. She's smiling. My dress surprises her. Well, I thought it would be right to wear a dress. Who is she now? Is she someone I've ever known? I can't tell. Filthy from the train, I go into her bedroom and wash my hands. And in the bathroom there are a thousand things I don't want to see—what pills she takes, what drops, what medicines—with labels I don't want to read—how many, how often to be taken each day. Have there ever been so many things to hide my eyes from in one small room? Soap that has touched her hands, her face; the basin over which she has bent; the well-worn towel, bearer of the imprint of her nose, her mouth—I feel no need now ever to see her again. (*The music has ended.* LEMON *sits down by* AUNT DAN.) It was the nurse's day off. (*A silence; then to* AUNT DAN.) Er—um—does she clean the flat as well, Aunt Dan? (*A silence.*)

AUNT DAN. She's a wonderful woman. She's been coming here for over a year. I can't tell you. Her kindness . . . She serves me as if she were a nun.

LEMON. A nun?

AUNT DAN. Going to the toilet. My meals. I know her. No secrets. No talking. She hears my thoughts. What would be the point of talking? Lemon, do you know the number of things going on in this room right now? There are hundreds! But while I'm talking, you hear only one—me. It's insanity to live like that. Insane. But she's listening to everything. We listen together. The insects, the wind, the water in the pipes. Sharing these things. Literally *everything*. The whole world. (*The dark room, as at the beginning of the play.*)

LEMON. (*To the audience.*) There's something that

people never say about the Nazis now. (*She drinks.*) By the way, how can anybody like anything better than lime and celery juice? It is the best! The thing is that the Nazis were trying to create a certain way of life for themselves. That's obvious if you read these books I'm reading. They believed that the primitive society of the Germanic tribes had created a life of wholeness and meaning for each person. They blamed the sickness and degeneracy of society as *they* knew it—before they came to power, of course—on the mixture of races that had taken place since that tribal period. In their opinion, all the destructive values of greed, materialism, competitiveness, dishonesty, and so on, had been brought into their society by non-Germanic races. They may have been wrong about it, but that was their belief. So they were trying to create a certain way of life. They were trying to create, or recreate, some sort of society of brothers, bound together by a certain code of loyalty and honor. So to make that attempt, they had to remove the non-Germans, they had to eliminate interbreeding. They were trying to create a certain way of life. Now today, of course, everybody says, "How awful! How awful!" And they were certainly ruthless and thorough in what they did. But the mere fact of killing human beings in order to create a certain way of life is not something that exactly distinguishes the Nazis from everybody else. That's just absurd. When any people feels that its hopes for a desirable future are threatened by some other group, they always do the very same thing. The only question is the degree of the threat. Now for us, for example, criminals are a threat, but they're only a small threat. Right now, we would say about criminals that they're a serious annoyance. We would call them a problem. And right now, the way we deal with that problem is that we take the criminals and we put them in jail. But if these criminals became so vicious, if there got to be so many of them, that our most basic hopes as a society were truly threatened by them—if our whole system of prisons and policemen had fallen so far behind the problem that the streets of our cities were controlled and dominated by violent criminals—then we would find ourselves forgetting the prisons and just killing the criminals instead. It's just a fact. Or let's take the Communists. There are Communists, now, who meet in little groups in America and England. They don't disrupt our entire way of life. They just have their meetings. If they break a law, if they commit a crime, we punish them according to the penalty prescribed. But in some countries, they threaten to destroy their whole way of life. In those countries the Communists are strong, they're violent, they're actually fanatics. And usually it turns out that people decide that they have to be killed. Or when the Europeans first came to America, well, the Indians were there. The Indians fought them for every scrap of land. There was no chance to build the kind of society the Europeans wanted with the Indians there. If they'd tried to put all the Indians in jail, they would have had to put all their effort into building jails, and then, when the Indians came out, they would undoubtedly have started fighting all over again as hard as before. And so they decided to kill the Indians. So it becomes absurd to talk about the Nazis as if the Nazis were unique. That's a kind of hypocrisy. Because the fact is, no society has ever considered the taking of life an unpardonable crime or even, really, a major tragedy. It's something that's done when it has to be done, and it's as simple as that. It's no different from the fact that if I have harmful or obnoxious insects—let's say, cockroaches—living in my house, I probably have to do something about it. Or at least, the question I have to ask is: How many are there? If the cockroaches are small, and I see a few of them now and then, that may not be very disturbing to me. But if I see big ones, if I start to see them often, then I say to myself, they have to be killed. Now some people simply hate to kill cockroaches, so they'll wait much longer. But if the time comes when there are hundreds of them, when they're crawling out of every drawer, when they're in the oven, when they're in the refrigerator, when they're in the toilet, when they're in the bed, then even the person who hates to kill them will go to the shop and get some poison and start killing, because the way of life that that person had wanted to lead is now really being threatened. Yes, the fact is, it is very unpleasant to kill another creature—let's admit it. Each one of us has his own fear of pain and his own fear of death. It's true for people and for every type of creature that lives. I remember once squashing a huge brown roach—I slammed it with my shoe, but it wasn't dead and I sat and watched it, and it's an awful period just before any creature dies—any insect or animal—when you're watching the stupid, ignorant things that that creature is trying to do to fight off its death—whether it's moving its arms or legs, or it's kicking, or it's trying to crawl to another part of the floor, or it's trying to lift itself off the ground—those things can't prevent death!—but the creature is trying out every gesture it's capable of, hoping, hoping that something will help it. And I remember how I felt as I watched that big brown roach squirming and crawling, and yet it was totally squashed, and I could see its insides slowly come oozing out. And I'm sure that the bigger a thing is, the more you hate to see it. I remember when I was in school we did some experiments on these big rats, and we had to inject them with poison and watch them die—and, of course, no matter what humane method you use in any laboratory to kill the animals, there's a moment that comes when they sense what's happening and they start to try out all those telltale squirming gestures. And with people, of course, it's the same thing. The bigger the creature, the harder it is to kill. We know it takes at least ten minutes to hang a person. Even if you shoot them in the head, it's not instantaneous—they still make those squirming movements at least for a moment. And people in gas chambers rush to the doors that they know very well are firmly locked. They fight each other to get to the doors. So killing is always very unpleasant. Now when people say, ''Oh the Nazis were different from anyone, the Nazis were different from anyone,'' well, perhaps that's true in at least one way, which is that they observed themselves extremely frankly in the act of killing, and they admitted frankly how they really felt about the whole process. Yes, of course, they admitted, it's very unpleasant, and if we didn't have to do it in order to create a way of life that we want for ourselves, we would never be involved in killing at all. But since we have to do it, why not be truthful about it, and why not admit that yes, yes, there's something inside us that likes to kill. Some part of us. There's something inside us that likes to do it. Why shouldn't that be so? Our human nature is derived from the nature of different animals, and of course there's a part of animal nature that likes to kill. If killing were totally repugnant to animals, they couldn't survive. So an enjoyment of killing is somewhere inside us, somewhere in our nature. In polite society, people don't discuss it, but the fact is that it's enjoyable—it's enjoyable—to make plans for killing, and it's enjoyable to learn about killing that is done by other people, and it's enjoyable to think about killing, and it's enjoyable to read about killing, and it's even enjoyable actually to kill, although when we ourselves are actually killing, an element of unpleasantness always comes in. That unpleasant feeling starts to come in. But even there, one has to say, even though there's an unpleasant side at first to watching people die, we have to admit that after watching for a while—maybe after watching for a day or maybe for a week or a year—it's still in a way unpleasant to watch, but on the other hand we have to admit that after we've watched it for all that time—well, we don't really actually care anymore. We have to admit that we don't really care. And I think that that last admission is what really makes people go mad about the Nazis, because in our own society we have this kind of cult built up around what people call the feeling of "compassion." I remember my mother screaming all the time, "Compassion! Compassion! You have to have compassion for other people! You have to have compassion for other human beings!" And I must admit, there's something I find refreshing about the Nazis, which is partly why I enjoy reading about them every night, because they sort of had the nerve to say, "Well, what *is* this compassion? Because I don't really know what it is. So I want to know, really, what is it?" And they must have sort of asked each other at some point, "Well say, Heinz, have *you* ever felt it?" "Well no, Rolf, what about you?" And they all had to admit that they really didn't know what the hell it was. And I find it sort of relaxing to read about those people, because I have to admit that I don't know either. I mean, I think I've felt it reading a novel, and I think I've felt it watching a film—"Oh how sad, that child is sick! That mother is crying!"—but I can't ever remember feeling it in life. I just don't remember feeling it about something that was happening in front of my eyes. And I can't believe that other people are that different from me. In other words, it was unpleasant to watch that pitiful roach scuttling around on my floor dying, but I can't say I really felt *sad* about it. I felt revolted or sickened, I guess I would say, but I can't say that I really felt sorry for the roach. And plenty of people have cried in my presence or seemed to be suffering, and I remember wishing they'd *stop* suffering and *stop* crying and leave me alone, but I don't remember, frankly, that I actually cared. So you have to say finally, well, fine, if there are all these people like my mother who want to go around talking about compassion all day, well, fine, that's their right. But it's sort of refreshing to admit every once in a while that they're talking about something that possibly doesn't exist. And it's sort of an ambition of mine to go around some day and ask each person I meet, Well here is something you've heard about to the point of nausea all of your life, but do you personally, actually remember feeling it, and if you really do, could you please describe the particular circumstances in which you felt it and what it actually felt *like*? Because if there's one thing I learned from Aunt Dan, I suppose you could say it was a kind of honesty. It's easy to say we should all be loving and sweet, but meanwhile we're enjoying a certain way of life—and we're actually *living*—due to the existence of certain other people who are willing to take the job of killing on their own backs, and it's not a bad thing every once in a while to admit that that's the way we're living, and even to give to those certain people a tiny, fractional crumb of thanks. You can be very sure that it's more than they expect, but I think they'd be grateful, all the same. (*The lights fade as she sits and drinks.*)

Maria Irene Fornes

The Danube

IRENE Fornes was walking along West 4th Street in New York, passed a thrift shop, noticed some 78 rpm records in a bin, and on an impulse—without even knowing what they were—bought one for a dollar. When she got home, she put it on her record player and discovered that it was a decades-old Hungarian language lesson, the simplest sentences, first in Hungarian, then in English. Telling each other their names and occupations, discussing the weather, learning how to order in restaurants—the people on the record moved step by step through the ritualistic exchanges of everyday life. And when, a few weeks later, Fornes was commissioned to write an antinuclear play, her mind kept returning to that record. "There was such tenderness in those little scenes," she recalls. "I thought how sorrowful I felt for its bygone era, how sorrowful it would be to lose the simple pleasures of our own era."

The dialogue of *The Danube* consists almost entirely of commonplace communication in basic sentences very much like those of a language lesson—initially, in fact, phrases are repeated in Hungarian and English—and tells the simple story of Paul and Eve, who meet, fall in love, and get married. Gradually, however, ominous signs begin to appear—the weather turns bad, the characters become oddly disoriented, their health starts to fail. Between each scene, smoke comes up from the stage floor, and all too soon the characters—still speaking in formal, stilted sentences, conveying only the most basic information—are wearing goggles to protect their eyes, notice spots on their skin, have to shake ash off their clothes. At the end of the play, just as Paul and Eve realize "there's no place to go," a brilliant white flash of light briefly illuminates the stage, followed by a blackout.

The threat of nuclear annihilation has rarely been evoked with such unutterable anguish, for as the characters deteriorate before our eyes, their seemingly barren and rigid language becomes a kind of poignant poetry. Fornes's achievement is all the more remarkable in that she has not only conveyed a political point without a hint of polemics, but she has expressed emotional devastation solely through formal inventiveness. The disjunction between language and feeling—between the flat, ritualistic, elemental, depersonalized, deemotionalized, depsychologized dialogue and the increasingly horrifying events it describes—is infinitely more eloquent than any rhetorical appeal or explicit "message." The play proceeds, in effect, from "How are you?" "I am fine," to "I am dying," "I am sorry."

Yet far from a simplistic warning, *The Danube* contains a multitude of subtleties, ironies, and ambiguities. For much of its length the Danube serves as the border between Western and Eastern Europe and near its center it runs through the bipartite city of Budapest. The puppets in the final scenes re-double the duplication of tape and speech, Hungarian and English, that is Fornes's striking formal innovation. And the elementary structures of language are seen as both the building blocks of civilized discourse and as an inadequate mechanism for dealing with civilization's discontents.

Unproduced by most of the country's major cultural centers, and rarely anthologized, Fornes has nevertheless established herself, to a loyal and ardent following of Off-Off-Broadway theatergoers, as one of the half-dozen most gifted playwrights in the American theater. As Lanford Wilson puts it, "She's one of our very very best—it's a shame she's always worked in such obscurity. Her work has no precedents. It isn't derived from anything. She's the most original of us all."

In a sense, the very experiments in form and content that have made Fornes's career so exemplary, the very shifts in style that have kept her work so compelling—

from giddy insouciance to lethal brutality, from exuberant fantasy to spare documentation, from antic verbal gaiety to the denuded verbal severity of *The Danube*—are precisely the reasons she's received so little recognition. There's no Fornes "signature" to capture the attention of casual theatergoers, nothing but her uncompromising creativity.

As Susan Sontag says, "One of the few agreeable spectacles which our culture affords is to watch the steady ripening of this beautiful talent."

IRENE FORNES has won so many Obies that playwright Harvey Fierstein, hosting the ceremonies one year, welcomed the audience to "the Irene Fornes Show." Originally a painter, Fornes turned to theater in the early sixties. Her musical *Promenade,* one of the first productions of the legendary Judson Poets Theater, was instrumental in defining the Off-Off-Broadway sensibility in its formative years. Active as a writer, director, translator, and teacher for three decades, she won the Obie for Lifetime Achievement in 1982—and has kept on working.

The Danube was performed at The American Place Theatre under the direction of the playwright, Maria Irene Fornes, with the following cast (in order of appearance):

MR. SANDOR .... *Sam Gray*
PAUL GREEN .... *Richard Sale*
EVE SANDOR-GREEN .... *Kate Collins*
KOVACS, WAITER, DOCTOR, BARBER . *Thomas Kopache*
ENGLISH TAPE .... *W. Scott Allison*
HUNGARIAN TAPE .... *Stephan Balant*
Music by Berg, Berlioz and Guy Lombardo.

AUTHOR'S NOTE

A tape which follows the language record convention is played where indicated in this script. Each sentence is heard in English, then in Hungarian, then there is enough blank tape for the actors to speak the same line.

The lesson number and title which head the scenes indicated should be heard on the recording in English only and should not be repeated by the actors.

In order to maintain a flow of life on stage through the recorded speeches it is recommended that the actors do not appear to be aware of the recorded voices. This can be achieved as follows:

1) The style of speaking of the recorded voices should be in the style of speaking of recorded language lessons. But the style of speaking of the actors should be naturalistic.

2) The actors should hear and assimilate a line when it is delivered to them, but they should not respond or react to it till it is time for them to reply. If they should react to it immediately but not speak, it would be apparent that the recording is impeding their speaking and that their behavior is not autonomous. It would not be difficult to maintain a liveliness during the recorded interval if the actor imagines the other person elaborating further on what he or she has just said.

3) The actors should deliver their lines with a different sense, a different emphasis, or a different reading from that on the tape.

4) The actors' lines should slightly overlap the recorded Hungarian lines.

This sign in the script "//" indicates where the recorded voices are heard.

The set is a playing platform with four vertical posts. Two are on the upstage side of the platform two feet from each side. The other two are on each side of the platform four feet from the downstage side. Painted backdrops, in a style resembling postcards, depict the different locations. A drop with a theater curtain is hung on the downstage posts. At each change of scenery smoke will go up from three places on the stage floor. The play starts in 1938. However, it soon departs from chronological realism.

THE SCENES

1. *A neighborhood café*
2. *On the banks of the Danube*
3. *A restaurant*
4. *A garden*
5. *Paul's room (Bed)*
6. *By a castle*
7. *Paul's room (Doctor)*
8. *Paul's room (Dinner)*
9. *A sanatorium*
10. *Mr. Sandor's living room (Coffee)*
11. *A barbershop*

CHARACTERS

PAUL GREEN, *a well-meaning American, age 30*
MR. SANDOR, *a Hungarian bureaucrat, age 50*
EVE SANDOR, *Mr. Sandor's daughter, age 24*
MR. KOVACS, *a friend of Mr. Sandor, age 48*
THE WAITER
THE DOCTOR
THE BARBER
All the above are members of a well-mannered working class. It is suggested that Mr. Kovacs, the Waiter, the Doctor and the Barber be played by the same actor.

Scene 1

A neighborhood café in Budapest. MR. SANDOR *sits at a table. He wears a brown suit, a white shirt and a black tie and shoes. On the table is a shot glass containing spirits and a newspaper which he has folded to a manageable size.* PAUL *approaches him. He wears a tweed jacket and hat, a wool plaid shirt and wool tie and trousers.*

ON TAPE. *"Unit One. Basic sentences. Paul Green meets Mr. Sandor and his daughter Eve." Also include dialogue in English and Hungarian up to "Are you Hungarian?"*

PAUL. //Good afternoon Mr. Sandor.// I believe we met at the Smiths' last night.

MR. SANDOR. //Yes, I remember. Your name is Paul Green.

PAUL. //Yes.

MR. SANDOR. (*Standing and shaking Paul's hand.*) // Please, take a seat. (*They sit.*)

PAUL. Thank you.

MR. SANDOR. //Are you Hungarian?

PAUL. Oh no. I'm from the U.S.

MR. SANDOR. What is new in the U.S.?

PAUL. The weather is bad.

MR. SANDOR. Is that so?

PAUL. Yes, we have not had good weather.

MR. SANDOR. I see.

PAUL. And how is the weather in Budapest?

MR. SANDOR. It has been bad. We have not had good weather. Are you visiting Budapest?

PAUL. No. I have come here to study and work. My company has sent me here.

MR. SANDOR. What is your line of work, Mr. Green?

PAUL. Metal production.

MR. SANDOR. I am glad to hear that. I have a son and two daughters and they all study. The eldest, my son, works and studies; my eldest daughter studies and she is not working presently. And my youngest daughter is studying and she has not yet started to work.

PAUL. What do they study?

MR. SANDOR. My eldest daughter studies German, English and Hungarian. The youngest studies accounting.

PAUL. And what does your son study?

MR. SANDOR. My son is an aviator and he studies German. Some say German is the language of the future. Others say English is the language of the future. That is why Eve studies both.

PAUL. Hungarian is the language of the future. (*They laugh.*)

MR. SANDOR. Hungarian may be the language of poetry but not of the future. I don't see very much poetry in the future. Do you?

PAUL. No, I don't.

MR. SANDOR. You must be a practical man.

PAUL. Yes. I think so.

MR. SANDOR. So is my son. He flies a commercial plane. Yesterday he went up with his youngest daughter. Have you ever been up in a plane, Mr. Green?

PAUL. No, I haven't.

MR. SANDOR. I haven't either. One day I may go up with my son. I am looking forward to being so high up in the air that a house would look like a speck in the distance. Would you care for a cigarette? (*He offers Paul a cigarette.*)

PAUL. (*Taking it.*) Thanks. Hungarian cigarette?

MR. SANDOR. No, this is a German cigarette. It is from a German factory like airplanes and shoes.

PAUL. Thank you very much. (*He puts the cigarette in his pocket.*) Thanks.

MR. SANDOR. What have you seen in Budapest?

PAUL. I have not seen very much yet. Since I arrived I have worked and I have attended school. I also spent time looking for a place to live.

MR. SANDOR. Have you found a place?

PAUL. Yes, I have found a room in a hotel on Maria Street.

(EVE *enters. She wears a lightweight two-piece suit. She stands at the door looking out.*)

MR. SANDOR. Here is my daughter Eve. Eve, please come here. (EVE *approaches.*) I should like to introduce Mr. Paul Green from the U.S. (PAUL *stands.*)

EVE. (*Shaking hands.*) Glad to meet you.

PAUL. Thank you.

EVE. But, please, take a seat. (*They sit.*)

PAUL. Thanks. Very gladly.

EVE. Do you understand Hungarian? I speak English.

PAUL. I understand Hungarian.

MR. SANDOR. She understands German, English and Hungarian.

EVE. Do you understand German?

PAUL. I don't understand German.

EVE. But you speak Hungarian very well.

PAUL. I studied Hungarian in the U.S. My firm had me take special courses in Hungarian. They have a Hungarian affiliated firm.

(*She offers him a cigarette.*)

EVE. Would you care for a cigarette?

PAUL. (*Taking it.*) Thanks. (*Putting it in his pocket.*) Thank you very much. I believe I have seen you on Baross Street, Miss Sandor.

EVE. Oh, yes. We live on Baross Street.

PAUL. I live on Maria Street.

EVE. We live near each other. Maria Street crosses Baross Street.

PAUL. How far is my house from yours?

EVE. Your house is five minutes from ours.

PAUL. I saw you in the bakery.

EVE. I go there each day. I buy bread in the bakery on Baross Street.

PAUL. How fortunate.

EVE. Yes. Have you lived here long?

PAUL. Not very long. I have lived here two weeks.

EVE. This is not the most elegant part of Budapest.

But it is very convenient. We are near the shops and it is economical. We have nice parks and the streets are clean.

PAUL. Maybe you'll be so good as to show me the parks, Miss Sandor.

EVE. I'll be glad to.

PAUL. Thank you.

EVE. I am free in the early evening, before dinner.

PAUL. Would you be free tomorrow at this time?

EVE. Yes.

PAUL. How very fortunate. (*To* MR. SANDOR.) Mr. Sandor, at what time is dinner in Budapest?

MR. SANDOR. Dinner is around eight p.m. Breakfast around eight o'clock. Lunch between twelve and one.

EVE. Sometimes we eat a morning snack too.

PAUL. What do you eat for breakfast as a rule?

EVE. For breakfast, we drink tea or coffee. Sometimes we eat an egg too, with bread or a roll and butter.

MR. SANDOR. In the afternoon, women especially drink coffee. They customarily do. In the morning before work men usually drink palinka in a cafe.

PAUL. Will you be free tomorrow till eight, Miss Sandor?

EVE. I will be free tomorrow till eight. I usually go home at seven. But tomorrow my father will cook. On Thursdays he likes to cook goulash. My father is a very good cook.

PAUL. Are you a good cook, Miss Sandor?

EVE. I am also a good cook. Do you like to cook, Mr. Green?

PAUL. I am not a very good cook. I only know how to make eggs, toast, boiled potatoes and a steak. What forms of entertainment are there in Budapest, Miss Sandor?

EVE. In Budapest there is dancing. There is swimming in the baths. There is music in the parks and concert halls. There are picnics in the countryside and there are theaters and movies.

PAUL. Do you enjoy the movies, Mr. Sandor?

MR. SANDOR. I do.

PAUL. Do you, Miss Sandor?

EVE. Oh yes.

PAUL. (*To Eve.*) May I invite you to the movies?

EVE. Yes, thank you.

PAUL. Mr. Sandor, would you come to the movies also?

MR. SANDOR. I would be glad to. I often go to the movies.

PAUL. Would you like to go tonight?

MR. SANDOR. Not tonight. I am expecting my friend Mr. Kovacs tonight. He is coming for dinner. But Eve may join you. She likes the movies very much.

PAUL. (*To* EVE.) Do you know at what time the movie starts?

EVE. I believe it begins at eight.

PAUL. Do you know what is playing?

EVE. We can look in the evening paper.

MR. SANDOR. This is the morning paper.

EVE. It is not evening yet.

PAUL. I will bring the paper when I come.

MR. SANDOR. We must leave now. (*Giving* PAUL *a card.*) 9 Baross Street. First floor. Second door to the left.

PAUL. Thank you.

(MR. SANDOR *and* EVE *stand.* PAUL *stands.*)

MR. SANDOR. We have a dining room, two bedrooms, a kitchen and a bathroom. The bathroom is very good because it has hot and cold water.

(PAUL *gives* MR. SANDOR *his own card.*)

PAUL. This is my card.

MR. SANDOR. (*Giving the card to* EVE.) Thank you.

PAUL. Thank you.

MR. SANDOR, PAUL, EVE: Good-bye.

(EVE *and* MR. SANDOR *exit left.* PAUL *exits right.* "*The Blue Danube*" *is heard. As the scenery is changed, smoke goes up from the stage floor.*)

Scene 2

On the banks of the Danube. There is a view of Budapest. There is a bench. MR. SANDOR, EVE, MR. KOVACS *and* PAUL *enter.*

ON TAPE. *"Unit Two. Basic sentences. Mr. Sandor, Kovacs, Eve and Paul discuss their relatives by the Danube."* *The scene is performed without a tape.*

KOVACS. Of my sons, one is a doctor, one is a soldier, and the other is a clerk.

EVE. When I have a son, I would like for him to be a teacher.

KOVACS. I always wanted one of my sons to be a soldier, like my father. And one did become a soldier.

MR. SANDOR. Was that Stephen?

KOVACS. No, Stephen is not a soldier.

MR. SANDOR. He is a clerk.

KOVACS. He works in a factory. George is the soldier. What does your brother do, Mr. Green?

PAUL. My brother is a farmer and so is my father. And my sister is a nurse.

KOVACS. I am a tailor.

PAUL. And is your brother a tailor too?

KOVACS. No, my brother isn't a tailor. He's a shoemaker. He makes shoes. I have one cousin who is a tailor, and another who is a mason.

MR. SANDOR. My father's father was a mason. But he also did plumbing like his cousin.

EVE. My father's cousin was a seamstress and her daughter was a teacher. They live in Paks. Is your niece married, Mr. Kovacs?

KOVACS. Yes. She's married. Her husband is a carpenter. He has his own shop. And she is a stenographer. Today women work as well as men.

MR. SANDOR. Yes, my brother works in an armament factory and his wife works in the same plant.

KOVACS. My nephew also works in the same factory. And his brother is a waiter. He works the early shift.

MR. SANDOR. I am a clerk in the custom house. I have worked there since I was young.

KOVACS. I have a nephew who is a barber. He owns his own shop. Another cousin is a doctor. He is a good doctor. Well, good-bye now. I want to buy cigarettes before the stores close. (*To* EVE.) Good-bye. (*To* PAUL.) I enjoyed the movies, Mr. Green. I like American movies.

PAUL. Thank you.

KOVACS. Good-bye.

MR. SANDOR. I'll go with you. Good-bye.

ALL: Good-bye.

(KOVACS *and* MR. SANDOR *exit. There is a pause.*)

PAUL. The city is very beautiful.

EVE. Yes, it is. Budapest lies on two sides of the Danube. Buda is on the right side. Pest is on the left. Between the two towns there are six bridges. From the mountains of Buda you can see Pest. On the Pest side is Parliament. The cathedral is not far. Budapest is full of baths. For example the one on Margaret Island. That bath is very beautiful. There's hot and cold water. The island lies in the middle of the Danube.

PAUL. Eve, come with me to a café. There's one not far from my hotel.

EVE. Let's go. (*They start to go.*) You can bathe in the Danube but the water is too cold. The weather is bad. It has changed.

(*They exit. "The Blue Danube" is heard. As the scenery is changed, smoke goes up from the stage floor.*)

Scene 3

The restaurant. It is a working class restaurant. There is a table and two chairs. The table is set with glasses, silver dishes and napkins. PAUL *and* EVE *enter. They are cheerful.*

ON TAPE. *"Unit Three. Basic sentences. Paul and Eve go to the restaurant." Also include dialogue in English and Hungarian up to "Yes, here's one."*

PAUL. //Here comes the waiter.

WAITER. //What do you wish?

PAUL. //Have you a table for two?

WAITER. //Yes, here's one.

(*They sit. The* WAITER *gets a water pitcher and a menu. He walks to the table, gives them the menu and pours water.*)

WAITER. Will you have lunch?

PAUL. Yes, both of us.

EVE. What soup do you have?

WAITER. Beef broth.

PAUL. Bring two beef broth.

EVE. What sort of meat is there?

WAITER. There is chicken with paprika. There is cold and hot ham.

PAUL. I'd like fish.

WAITER. I'm very sorry but there is no fish.

EVE. Then bring the chicken.

WAITER. Would you like some wine?

EVE. I only want a glass of water.

PAUL. I would like a glass of white wine. (*The* WAITER *exits.*)

PAUL. Where shall we go this afternoon?

EVE. We could go to a museum.

PAUL. Which museum?

EVE. The economic museum is very interesting.

PAUL. Where is the economic museum?

EVE. Not very far. (*The* WAITER *enters with soup and puts it on the table.*)

PAUL. Thank you.

WAITER. With pleasure.

PAUL. Shall we go by car?

EVE. The streetcar is much cheaper. And you can see the town from the window. One comes every minute.

PAUL. I would also like to do some shopping.

EVE. What would you like to buy?

PAUL. A present for my sister. Another for my mother. I also have to buy something for my brother and presents for my niece and nephew.

EVE. . . . Paul . . . (PAUL *looks at* EVE.) Are you leaving Budapest?

PAUL. Yes. I have been asked to return to the U.S.

(*There is a sudden sound of plaintive music which continues playing through the following dialogue.* PAUL *and* EVE *are distressed.*)

EVE. Oh, no.

PAUL. Yes.

EVE. How soon?

PAUL. In two weeks.

EVE. Please, don't go.

PAUL. I don't want to go.

EVE. Please, don't go.

PAUL. I want to stay.

EVE. It will never be the same without you. I feel cold. Is it winter yet? (*The* WAITER *enters with the menu.*)

WAITER. We have no more chicken. Would you like the hot ham?

EVE. No, thank you.

WAITER. Would you like some hot ham?

PAUL. No, thank you.

WAITER. You should eat when you can. The crops have not been good. Would you like some dessert?

PAUL. What desserts do you have?

WAITER. We have apple pie, ice cream, and fresh fruit. May I suggest the fresh fruit?

(*The* WAITER *and* EVE *freeze. The music stops.*)

PAUL. (*Speaking rapidly.*) I came from a country where we hear out suggestions. We invented the suggestion box. The best suggestion may come from the least expected place. We value ideas. We don't hesitate to put ideas to practice. We consider ideas that are given to us. We don't hold back our suggesting of ideas for fear of appearing foolish. We are not afraid to appear foolish, as good ideas disguise themselves in foolishness. We are not afraid to appear foolish. We are the foolish race.

EVE. (*As if in a trance.*) I'll have fresh fruit.

WAITER. Sir?

PAUL. I'll have fresh fruit.

WAITER. You are foolish but oh how fast you move forward.

EVE. Please, let's go to a café.

(*As she stands, her chair falls to the floor.* PAUL *picks up the chair and turns to where the* WAITER *exited.*)

PAUL. Waiter, please, give me the bill.

(*The* WAITER *enters.* EVE *faints.*)

WAITER. You don't want fresh fruit?

PAUL. No, thank you.

(*The* WAITER *starts writing the bill.* PAUL *starts to pay. He is distressed and disoriented. He drops bills and coins, picks them up, puts a bill on the* WAITER'*s*

tray, takes money from another pocket, drops more coins
and bills, and puts two bills on the WAITER*'s tray.*)

WAITER. Thank you. (*The* WAITER *moves to the up left*
corner and stands in a very straight stylized position.
PAUL *picks up* EVE*'s napkin, puts it on the table, and*
freezes with knees bent in an almost squatting position.
EVE *also freezes. The* WAITER *speaks rapidly in a de-*
clamatory manner. Through the course of the speech he
gradually raises the tray which he holds with both hands
in front of him.) We are concerned with quality. That
which is lasting. Craftsmanship. A thing of quality always ends up being heavy. We have preferred quality to
anything else. We wish for things to last but we tire of
them. We are buried under the stones of buildings, iron
grates, heavy shoes, woolen garments, heavy sheets,
foods that smell potent like the caves in the black forest.
Hands that cut, knead and saw and measure and chisel
and sweat into everything we see. Pots that are too heavy
to use. Shoes that delay our walk. Sheets that make our
sleep a slumber.—Americans sleep light and wake up
briskly. You create life each day. Here, the little trousers
a boy wears to school are waiting for him at the store
before he is born. We are dark. Americans are bright.—
You crave mobility. The car. You move from city to city
so as not to grow stale. You don't stay too long in a
place. A person who lives too long in the same house
is suspect. It's someone who is held back. Friction keeps
a stone polished. Mobility. You are alert. You get in
and out of cars limberly. That is your grace. Our grace
is weighty. Not yours. You worship the long leg and
loose hip joint. How else to jump in and out of cars.
You dress light. You travel light. You are light on your
feet. You are light-hearted and a light heart is a pump
that brings you to motion. You aim to alight, throw the
load overboard. Alight the flight. You are responsible.
That is not a burden. You are responsible to things that
move forward. You are responsible to the young. Not
so much to the old. The old do not move forward. You
will find a way for the old to move forward, have them
join in your thrust. Solving a problem is not a burden
to you. A problem solved is a lifting of a burden. Egyp-

tians lifted heavy stones to build monuments. You lift them to get rid of heavy stones. Get rid of them! Obstacles! You are efficient. You simplify life. Paperwork. Your forms are shorter, so is your period of obligation. Work. Your hours are shorter and you have more time to sit on the lawn in your cotton trousers. (*He lowers the tray.* EVE *comes to.* PAUL *helps her up.*)

EVE. Let's take a streetcar.

PAUL. Let's go.

(*They exit. Music plays. The* WAITER *exits. As the scenery is changed smoke goes up from the stage floor.*)

Scene 4

In the garden. There are dried leaves. There is a cement pillar, the top of which is cut at a slant with a cloth sculpted over it. The word "True" is engraved on the base. The sound tape contains only the Hungarian phrases.

EVE.//This may be the last time I come here.// Here is where I first kissed you.// I kissed you that day, you know.// I kissed you because I could not help myself.// Now again I try to exert control over myself// and I can't.// I try to appear content and I can't.// I know I look distressed.// I feel how my face quivers. And my blood feels thin.// And I can hardly breathe. And my skin feels dry.// I have no power to show something other than what I feel.// I am destroyed. And even if I try,// my lips will not smile.// Instead I cling to you and make it harder for you.// Leave now.// Leave me here looking at the leaves.// Good-bye.// If I don't look at you it may be that I can let you go.

(PAUL *kisses her. Music plays. Lights fade. As the scenery is changed smoke goes up from the stage floor.*)

Scene 5

PAUL's *bedroom. It is almost dawn.* EVE *and* PAUL *lie on a cot by the window.* EVE's *head lies on* PAUL's *chest. They are covered with a sheet. The sound tape includes the complete dialogue in both English and Hungarian.*

EVE. Silence . . . // Silence . . . // Adieu . . . // Adieu . . . // Hold me this last time.// And kiss me.// Kiss me one more time. (*They kiss. She puts her head down on his chest again and caresses his eyes with her fingers.*) //Adieu . . . Farewell to your eyes.// I will never see them.// Farewell, sweet eyes.

PAUL. This cannot be.// I will stay.// I must stay.// Marry me, sweet Eve.// I will marry you.

EVE. //Oh, Paul, you love me.// You do. You love me.// You do.// You will be happy since I love you so.

PAUL. //I'll never say adieu again.

(*The sky outside the window is lit.*)

PAUL. //Look, here is the dawn.

(*Lights fade. Music plays. As the scenery is changed, smoke goes up from the stage floor.*)

Scene 6

By a castle. EVE *looks out to the left. There is the sound of a fox-trot. She dances a little in place.* PAUL *enters with two glasses. He puts the glasses down and takes her by the waist. They dance for a while. The music ends. They continue dancing. The scene is performed without a language tape.*

EVE. The music ended.

PAUL. If I tried, I could not stop.

(*Lights fade. There is the sound of* EVE's *panting. The lights come up.* EVE *is standing against the wall. She holds a drink in her hand. Her mouth and eyes are wide open.* PAUL *is lying on the floor. His body is contorted. His face is in a grimace. There is an eerie sound.*)

EVE. . . . Paul!—

(Lights fade. There is music. As the scenery is changed, smoke goes up from the stage floor.)

Scene 7

It is PAUL*'s room. There is a table and two chairs.* PAUL *has a blood pressure device attached to his arm. He is sitting on the upstage side of the table. The* DOCTOR *sits to the right. There is a doctor's case on the floor to the right of the* DOCTOR. *They both suffer slight physical contortions, an ankle, a shoulder, a few fingers. All other characters suffer the same contortions. As the play advances these contortions will become more extreme.*

ON TAPE. *"Unit Seven. Basic sentences. Paul Green is examined by the Doctor." The sound tape includes the complete dialogue in both English and Hungarian.*

DOCTOR. //Your blood is thin.// Have you been eating well?

PAUL. //Yes. (*The* DOCTOR *looks into* PAUL*'s eyes.*)

DOCTOR. //Come here, closer to the light. (*They go upstage to the window, he looks again at his eye. He takes his pulse.*) //Let me see your tongue. (PAUL *sticks his tongue out. The* DOCTOR *puts a tongue depressor on it.*) //Say ahh.

PAUL. Ahh. (*The* DOCTOR *walks back to the table.*)

DOCTOR. (*Thoughtfully.*) //It's nothing serious.// Sit down.// (PAUL *sits.*) What you have is common.// Thin blood.// A white throat.// The eyes secrete mucus.// You feel very ill.// And yet the symptoms are not serious.// Do you excrete normally?

PAUL. //No.

DOCTOR. //This is common.

PAUL. //What is causing it? (*The* DOCTOR *writes.*)

DOCTOR. //Does your wife suffer from this too?

PAUL. //I think so.

DOCTOR. //Not as severely?

PAUL. //No.

DOCTOR. (*Still writing.*) //Take a train to Fured.// There, repose yourself.// Drink this tonic four times a day.// Sleep. And don't worry. (*He takes his bag and stands up to leave. He takes a last look at* PAUL's *eyes, ears, teeth. He feels his forehead. He looks at his fingernails. He then takes a handkerchief from his pocket and puts it over* PAUL's *nose.*) //Blow your nose on this. (PAUL *does. The* DOCTOR *looks at the secretion in the handkerchief, puts it in his pocket and exits. Lights fade. There is music. As the scenery is changed, smoke goes up from the stage floor.*)

Scene 8

PAUL's *room. There is a table set with soup dishes.* MR. SANDOR *sits on the up right side.* MR. KOVACS *sits on the down left side.* PAUL *stands stage right.* EVE *stands stage left.*

ON TAPE. *"Unit Eight. Basic sentences. Paul and Eve Green invite Mr. Sandor and Mr. Kovacs for dinner." The scene is performed without a language tape.*

EVE *starts to exit left.* PAUL *follows her.*

EVE. Please, you don't need to come. I can serve.

(EVE *exits.* PAUL *follows her.*)

KOVACS. (*To* MR. SANDOR.) Do you know how to cook?

MR. SANDOR. Of course. When my wife died I learned to cook. Eve was only seven. The boy and I did the housework.

KOVACS. I also know how to cook and so does my younger brother. We Hungarians like good food. (EVE *and* PAUL *enter carrying soup in metal cups. They pour the soup and sit,* EVE *on the down side,* PAUL *on the up left side.*) Do you know how to cook, Mr. Green?

PAUL. I only know how to make eggs, toast, boil potatoes and cook a steak; fried or grilled in the oven or barbequed.

KOVACS. That is plenty.

PAUL. It would not be interesting to eat this every day.

KOVACS. What?

PAUL. Eggs, toast, boiled potatoes and steak.

KOVACS. That would be too much.

PAUL. Do you know how to cook, Mr. Kovacs?

KOVACS. I know how to make chicken paprika and beef goulash.

MR. SANDOR. I make cabbage soup with beef.

EVE. Is the soup good?

KOVACS. It is good.

MR. SANDOR. It is as good as I ever had.

KOVACS. I have a feeling Honved is not winning today.

MR. SANDOR. I think Honved is winning.

KOVACS. How could Honved win? It is not a good team.

MR. SANDOR. Honved is a very good team. It is better than MTK.

KOVACS. Oh no. MTK is better than Honved.

MR. SANDOR. Not at all. Honved is the leading team. It wins all the time.

KOVACS. It is not better. It is worse. They just have better luck.

MR. SANDOR. You don't win soccer with luck, Kovacs.

KOVACS. Honved does.

MR. SANDOR. Paul, what is it Americans call a bad loser? Is Kovacs a bad loser . . . is he? (PAUL *smiles.* MR. SANDOR *speaks to* KOVACS.) You're a bad loser.

KOVACS. Do you play soccer, Paul?

PAUL. In the U.S., we don't play soccer. We play football, baseball and basketball.

KOVACS. (*To* MR. SANDOR.) I never knew that. Did you know that, Henry?

MR. SANDOR. I did. Football, baseball and basketball are American games. Soccer is not.

(PAUL *faints.* EVE *stands and looks at him alarmed.*)

EVE. He has not been well. (*Pause.*) And neither have I.

(MR. SANDOR *and* KOVACS *look at each other and lower their heads. Lights fade. There is music. As the scenery is changed, smoke goes up from the stage floor.*)

Scene 9

A sanatorium. There is a small desk and chair. To the left there is a cot. On the back wall there is a moonlit mountain peak. PAUL is wearing pajamas, a robe, and slippers. He is at the desk writing.

PAUL. Dearest Eve. How are you? Have you missed me? What is new? How is work? I am still under constant observation. I must see the doctor at two each day. I am always hopeful. The doctors say that my teeth have caused it. It is not true. There is something in the air. It is natural I feel sad. Nothing I do makes me feel right. All my hours go into longing for you and the hour of my return. I have little hope. What do you think? All my love. Paul.

(Lights fade. There is music. Smoke goes up from the stage floor. The stage is lit. PAUL lies on the cot. He is covered with a sheet. A sound tape contains only the Hungarian phrases.)

PAUL. //Eve, I feel much worse.// I have a high fever.// My vision is blurred. (EVE *appears by* PAUL's *side. He holds her.*) //Who knows why, but suddenly I am here next to you.// I just left Fured and suddenly here I am next to you.// Write to the captain in regard to this.// Tell him that I cannot bear it any longer.// That I am dying.// That I am going mad.// Tell him that he must release me.// That I cannot be of any use to Hungary.// That I am a peaceful man. (*Short pause.*) //Oh, no. I know that is not possible.// Every man must do his share. (*He cries.*) //There is no point.// We are all useless to Hungary.// We cannot save her.// Oh, Hungary, we cannot save you.

(Lights fade. There is music. Smoke goes up from the stage floor. The stage is lit. EVE is sitting at the table writing and PAUL lies in bed unconscious. The following is performed without a language tape.)

EVE. Paul Green, private, front line. A long time has passed and things are not any clearer. I know there is no front line and I know there is no war. I wish there were one. A war would end and you would return to me. I don't know where you are. You are where I am but never at the same time. My dearest, life escapes from us like blood out of a wound. Will we ever be whole again and in each other's arms? All my love, Eve.

(*Lights fade. There is music. As the scenery is changed, smoke goes up from the stage floor.*)

Scene 10

MR. SANDOR's *living room. There is a table and two chairs.* MR. SANDOR *enters right. He carries a tray with a coffee pot and two cups. He stands with his back to the left, places the tray on the table and pours. All characters will wear goggles from here on. Their speech will be progressively convoluted. Their skin will show reddish spots as if of burns. Their clothes appear to have been exposed to ash dust and strange drippings.*

ON TAPE. *"Unit Ten. Basic sentences. Paul Green visits Mr. Sandor. They discuss the weather." The scene is performed without a language tape.*

MR. SANDOR. Hello, Paul. (PAUL *enters,* MR. SANDOR *turns.*) Would you like some coffee?

PAUL. Yes, thanks. (PAUL *sits.* MR. SANDOR *gives* PAUL *a cup, and takes the other to his chair. He sits.*) Perhaps tomorrow the weather will be good.

MR. SANDOR. Yes, the weather is bad. Perhaps tomorrow the weather will be good.

PAUL. In the morning I was warm. Now in the evening it's cold. Where's Eve?

MR. SANDOR. She went to town.

PAUL. But it's raining. In the winter she works. In the summer she studies. I haven't seen her since spring.

MR. SANDOR. Would you have a cigarette?

PAUL. Yes, please. (MR. SANDOR *gives him a cigarette.*)

MR. SANDOR. Of course. Here's a match. How's the coffee?

PAUL. Very good. (PAUL *turns suddenly.*) I think it's snowing.

MR. SANDOR. I don't think so. In the fall it doesn't snow.

PAUL. I hope so. This year was bad enough. I'd like some more coffee.

MR. SANDOR. Certainly. (MR. SANDOR *starts to pour.*)

PAUL. Thanks. What time is it?

MR. SANDOR. Not six yet. Five.

PAUL. There's time for a movie from six to eight.

MR. SANDOR. It's raining very hard.

PAUL. That's true.

MR. SANDOR. (*Offering him another pack of cigarettes.*) Have another cigarette. (*Handing him matches.*) Here is a match. (MR. SANDOR *sits.*) There's still more coffee.

PAUL. This cigarette is wet.

MR. SANDOR. Oh, I beg your pardon. (*Handing him a cigarette.*) Here's another one. You look much better.

PAUL. I am better.

MR. SANDOR. Is Fured a good hospital?

PAUL. Yes, very good. (PAUL *looks in the cup.*) What's this? (MR. SANDOR *looks in the cup.*)

MR. SANDOR. Oh, I beg your pardon. (MR. SANDOR *takes an amorphous black object from the cup and looks at it carefully. He puts it in his pocket and sits.*)

PAUL. This coffee is cold. It may be my last cup and it's cold. Which is the way to the toilet? (MR. SANDOR *points to the up left corner.*)

MR. SANDOR. The toilet is to the left.

(PAUL *exits.* EVE *enters from the up right corner and walks to the down left center.*)

EVE. Where is Paul?

MR. SANDOR. I haven't seen him since yesterday.

EVE. Paul . . .

(*Lights fade. There is music. As the scenery is changed, smoke goes up from the stage floor.*)

Scene 11

The barbershop. The BARBER *sits on a chair on the left. Paul enters stage right, takes a few steps and stops. He wears a brown-green shirt and tie and a band around his arm.*

ON TAPE. *"Unit Eleven. Basic sentences. Paul Green goes to the barbershop." The sound tape contains only the Hungarian phrases.*

PAUL. //Please, cut my hair.

BARBER. //Please, take a seat. (PAUL *sits. The* BARBER *puts a white cloth around his neck.*) //Are you Hungarian?

PAUL. //No. I am from the United States.

BARBER. //Are you a soldier?

PAUL. //Why yes. (PAUL *lifts the cloth.*) //Look at my clothes.

BARBER. //Shall I cut it short in the back?

PAUL. //Please.

(*The* BARBER *cuts* PAUL'*s hair. Neither speaks for a while.* PAUL *looks front.*)

PAUL. // . . . What's this . . . ? //Eve is coming. . . . //She's coming. . . . (*Turning to look at* EVE.) // . . . Eve. . . . (*The* BARBER *turns* PAUL'*s head down. He cuts his hair.* EVE *appears on the up right corner.*)

BARBER. (*Speaking close to* PAUL'*s ear. He loses control progressively. He goes on his knees and grabs* PAUL *by the leg.*) //Tell me.// Is it permitted?// For me to ask you.// Please, tell me.// What does one say?// I want?// I want milk?// Please, give me beer?// Meat?// I'm very hungry?// It is the heart of the nation.// It is cold.// The earth is cold.//

PAUL. (*Standing abruptly.*) //I'm very sorry.// I have to go now.// How much does a haircut cost?

BARBER. //This was a plain haircut.// The price is fifty filler.

PAUL. //That's cheap enough.// Have you cigarettes or matches?

BARBER. //I'm sorry but we have no cigarettes or

matches.// We only cut hair and shave.// Would you like a shave, sir?

PAUL. (*Handing money to the* BARBER.) //No, thank you. That's cheap enough. (*He turns his head towards* EVE.)

EVE. //Let's go.

(EVE *exits.* PAUL *turns towards the exit slowly. He lifts his arm as if reaching for* EVE. *He has lost her. He exits. Lights fade. There is music. As the scenery is changed, smoke goes up from the stage floor.*)

Scene 12

EVE *lies on a blanket on the floor down right. There is a table and chair next to her.* MR. SANDOR *sits on a chair up left. He sleeps.* PAUL *enters. He is in his underwear. He carries a drawer with clothes, places it on the floor and walks to* EVE. *The scene is performed without a language tape.*

PAUL. Eve, I'm leaving. I can't take this any longer. You take care of the place or burn it if you want. I don't care what you do.

EVE. Why don't you take me with you? (*He sits.*)

PAUL. If you go, we'll never get anywhere. It is you who has polluted me. I am clean of body and mind.

EVE. That's not so. I have not polluted you.

PAUL. It is you who have caused all the trouble.

EVE. You are losing your brain, Paul. You are talking like a machine. You are saying what machines say.

PAUL. It must be true if machines say it. (*She screams and hits him repeatedly.*) I am sorry, Eve. I don't know what made me say that. (*He hits the table with his fist. It breaks apart. He cries.*) I didn't mean any of it. I don't have a mind. And I don't have a soul.

MR. SANDOR. (*Startled as if awakened from a nightmare. He remains so through the following scene.*) What happened!

EVE. Paul got angry, father, and he smashed the table. (EVE *has a coughing attack.*)

MR. SANDOR. Is she ill!

PAUL. Why do you ask that?

MR. SANDOR. She's coughing!

PAUL. She always coughs.

MR. SANDOR. What's wrong with that!

PAUL. Nothing. She coughs, I throw up, and you have diarrhea.

MR. SANDOR. Let's call a doctor!

(PAUL *emits a loud and plaintive sound. Lights fade. There is music. As the scenery is changed, smoke goes up from the stage floor.*)

Scene 13

There is a theater curtain placed on the downstage posts. A puppet stand is placed on stage. On the floor of the puppet stage down right is a blanket. To the left of the blanket and facing it is a chair. To the right of the chair is a breakaway table. On the up left corner is a chair. PAUL, EVE, *and* MR. SANDOR *operate puppets whose appearance is identical to theirs. The following scene, which is the same as scene 12, is performed by the puppets.*

PAUL. Eve, I'm leaving. I can't take this any longer. You take care of the place or burn it if you want. I don't care what you do.

EVE. Why don't you take me with you? (*He sits.*)

PAUL. If you go, we'll never get anywhere. It is you who has polluted me. I am clean of body and mind.

EVE. That's not so. I have not polluted you.

PAUL. It is you who have caused all the trouble.

EVE. You are losing your brain, Paul. You are talking like a machine. You are saying what machines say.

PAUL. It must be true if machines say it. (*She screams and hits him repeatedly.*) I am sorry, Eve. I don't know what made me say that. (*He hits the table with his fist. It breaks apart. He cries.*) I didn't mean any of it. I don't have a mind. And I don't have a soul.

MR. SANDOR. (*Startled as if awakened from a night-*

mare. He remains so through the following scene.) What happened!

EVE. Paul got angry, father, and he smashed the table. (EVE *has a coughing attack.*)

MR. SANDOR. Is she ill!

PAUL. Why do you ask that?

MR. SANDOR. She's coughing!

PAUL. She always coughs.

MR. SANDOR. What's wrong with that!

PAUL. Nothing. She coughs, I throw up, and you have diarrhea.

MR. SANDOR. Let's call a doctor!

(PAUL *emits a loud and plaintive sound. Lights fade. There is music. As the scenery is changed, smoke goes up from the stage floor.*)

Scene 14

The actors set up for another puppet scene. There is a table center and a chair to the left and facing it. There are two drawers on the floor against the back wall, one to the right and one to the left. The puppet representing EVE *sits at the table. The puppet representing* PAUL *enters.*

ON TAPE. *"Unit Thirteen. Basic sentences. Paul and Eve pack their suitcase." The scene is performed without a language tape.*

PAUL. Eve.

EVE. Yes.

PAUL. Let's go.

EVE. Yes.

(PAUL *gets a suitcase and puts it on the table. They each get the items of clothing indicated in the script from the drawers and put them in the suitcase.*)

EVE. Stockings. Five pairs of underpants.

PAUL. Eight pairs of socks.

EVE. Five shirts. Three blouses.

PAUL. Trousers.

EVE. Shorts. Six pairs of shorts. A skirt. A dress.

PAUL. Handkerchiefs. Seven handkerchiefs.

EVE. Everything is here.

PAUL. Let's go.

(MR. SANDOR *enters*.)

MR. SANDOR. What's this?

EVE. Please, Father, come with us.

MR. SANDOR. Don't go. (EVE *embraces* MR. SANDOR.)

EVE. Good-bye, father. (*Walking to* PAUL.) Good-bye.

(*Lights fade. There is music. As the scenery is changed, smoke goes up from the stage floor. The puppet stage is removed.*)

Scene 15

MR. SANDOR'*s living room. There is a table center and a chair to the left.* EVE *sits on the chair.* PAUL *enters. They are both in a state of physical and emotional restraint which hampers their speech and movement.*

ON TAPE. *"Unit Fourteen. Basic sentences. Paul and Eve Green pack their suitcase." The scene is performed without a language tape.*

PAUL. Eve.

EVE. Yes.

PAUL. Let's go.

EVE. Yes. (PAUL *gets a suitcase and puts it on the table. They each get the items of clothing indicated in the script from the drawers and put them in the suitcase.*) Stockings. Five pairs of underpants.

PAUL. Eight pairs of socks.

EVE. Five shirts. Three blouses.

PAUL. Trousers.

EVE. Shorts. Six pairs of shorts. A skirt. A dress.

PAUL. Handkerchiefs. Seven handkerchiefs.

EVE. Everything is here.

PAUL. Let's go.

EVE. (*Taking a revolver from the suitcase.*) What's this?

PAUL. (*Reaching for the gun.*) A gun. (*First she resists. Then she releases it. He puts it in his pocket.* MR. SANDOR *enters.*)

MR. SANDOR. What's this?

PAUL. (*Taking the suitcase.*) Good-bye.

EVE. (*Embracing Mr. Sandor.*) Good-bye, Father.

MR. SANDOR. Don't go.

EVE. Please come with us.

MR. SANDOR. I live here and work here. My family lives here.

EVE. Please, Father, come with us.

MR. SANDOR. It doesn't matter, Eve. There's no place to go.

EVE. Good-bye. (*Eve walks downstage and speaks front.*) My Danube, you are my wisdom. My river that comes to me, to my city, my Budapest . . . I say good-bye. As I die, my last thought is of you, my sick friend. Here is your end. Here is my hand. I don't know myself apart from you. I don't know you apart from myself. This is the hour. We die at last, my Danube. Good-bye. (*She joins Paul. They start to exit right.*)

MR. SANDOR. Eve!

(*There is a brilliant white flash of light. Black out.*)

END

Suzan-Lori Parks

Imperceptible Mutabilities in the Third Kingdom

AT first glance, Suzan-Lori Parks's *Imperceptible Mutabilities in the Third Kingdom* seems as idiosyncratic—and as difficult—as its title. Yet Parks writes out of two intertwined if apparently disparate traditions: the "black English" spoken by millions of Americans for centuries and the black poetry best expressed in our theater by Adrienne Kennedy and Ntozake Shange. And she has that rarest of playwright's gifts, the ability to make a seemingly opaque text emerge with stunning clarity on stage. First produced at Brooklyn's BACA Downtown in 1989, Parks's surrealist tetraptych almost immediately established its author, still in her mid-twenties, as one of the most provocative new voices in the experimental theater scene and as a consciousness—and a conscience—that might help us disentangle racial images from racial realities.

All five sections of *Imperceptible Mutabilities* address issues of black history and black identity, in particular the distance between individual experience and social representation. Since this means that the disjunction between the spoken text and the projected slides is a crucial component of Parks's theatrical strategy, readers should try to visualize a performance as they turn the pages. "You have these fixed pictures projected up there," Parks has said, "and down below there's a little person mutating like hell on the stage. I'm obsessed with the gap between these two things"—between, in other words, preconceptions and people.

"Snails," the first section, set in the present, depicts an apparently random conversation between three African American women, but the title hints at the defining metaphor of animal life. An infestation of insects, the viewing of the TV program *The Wild Kingdom,* most notably the sudden appearance of a white male naturalist observing the women in their natural habitat—in such an environment, the single word *exterminator* becomes unutterably chilling.

"Third Kingdom," the second section—reprised and continued as the fourth section in one of the play's many fugues—shows a group of blacks in a slave ship "lost between the two shores" of Africa and America. "Where I comed from," one of the characters says, "didnhut look nowhere like I been."

In "Open House," the single image of smiling white teeth—white America's view of the "darkie"—expands into a former slave's vision of her life as a sequence of agonizing tooth extractions, as if she herself were being extracted from history. For one way blacks approach the historical, Parks points out, is to regard it as the "histironical."

"Greeks," the final section, has aspects of autobiography—Parks was raised in a military family—and even in its title repeats her "histironical" approach, intimating at once the alienation of blacks in America and their links to the roots of Western civilization. What "distinction" is Sergeant Smith awaiting, and who is empowered to bestow it?

Far more is going on in Parks's world than these clues suggest—Sergeant Smith, she writes, in a phrase used more than once, "deals in a language of codes"—yet the mystery is not meant to be "solved," it's woven into the very fabric of her style. Incantatory like a balladeer, evoking the Bible like a preacher, lyrical as a singer and visual as a painter, she possesses, above all, the poet's wonder at words, and recognizes that the quest for identity, for the reality behind the image, requires first of all a reclaiming of language. "He didnhut have no answer cause he didnhut have no speech."

"Who are we?" Parks is asking—who are we beneath our imperceptibility, beyond our mutabilities?

Suzan-Lori Parks, who was born in Fort Knox, Kentucky, in 1963 and educated at Mt. Holyoke, credits a class with James Baldwin with inspiring her to become a writer. *Imperceptible Mutabilities in the Third Kingdom,* her second play, was produced while she was still in her mid-twenties, and her fourth play, *The Death of the Last Black Man in the Whole Entire World,* has received numerous productions across the country.

Imperceptible Mutabilities in the Third Kingdom was produced at BACA DOWNTOWN, September 1989, directed by Liz Diamond, with the following cast:

VERONICA/US-SEER/ARETHA/MRS. SMITH
....*Pamala Tyson*
CHARLENE/SHARK-SEER/ANGLOR/BUFFY
.... *Shona Tucker*
MOLLY/KIN-SEER/BLANCA/MUFFY .... *Kenya Scott*
ROBBER/SOUL-SEER/MISS FAITH/MR. SMITH
.... *Jasper McGruder*
NATURALIST/OVER-SEER/CHARLES/DUFFY
.... *Peter Schmitz*

"Or as the snail, whose tender horns being hit,
Shrinks backward in his shelly cave with pain,
And there, all smoth'red up, in shade doth sit,
Long after fearing to creep forth again. . . ."

—*Venus and Adonis*

Part 1:

Snails

THE PLAYERS

Molly/Mona
Charlene/Chona
Veronica/Verona
The Naturalist/Dr. Lutzky
The Robber

A.
Slide show: Images of MOLLY *and* CHARLENE. MOLLY
and CHARLENE *speak as the stage remains dark and the
slides continue to flash overhead.*

CHARLENE. How dja get through it?

MOLLY. Mm not through it.

CHARLENE. Yer leg. Thuh guard. Lose weight?

MOLLY. Hhh. What should I do Cho-na should I jump
should I jump or what?

CHARLENE. You want some eggs?

MOLLY. Would I splat?

CHARLENE. Uh uh uhnnnn.

MOLLY. Twelve floors up. Whaduhya think?

CHARLENE. Uh uh uhn. Like scrambled?

MOLLY. Shit.

CHARLENE. With cheese? Say "with" cause ssgoin in.

MOLLY. I diduhnt quit that school. HHH. Thought:
nope! Mm gonna go on—go on ssif nothin ssapin yuh
know? "S-K" is /sk/ as in "ask." The-little-lamb-
follows-closely-behind-at-Mary's-heels-as-Mary-boards-
the-train. Shit. Failed every test he shoves in my face.
He makes me recite my mind goes blank. HHH. The-
little-lamb-follows-closely-behind-at-Mary's-heels-as-
Mary-boards-the-train. Aint never seen no woman on no
train with no lamb. I tell him so. He throws me out. Stuff
like this happens every day y know? This isnt uh special
case mines iduhnt uh uhnnn.

CHARLENE. Salami? Yarnt veg anymore.

MOLLY. "S-K" is /sk/ as in "ask." I lie down you lie down he she it lies down. The-little-lamb-follows-closely-behind-at-Mary's-heels. . . .

CHARLENE. Were you lacto-ovo or thuh whole nine yards?

MOLLY. Whole idea uh talkin right aint right no way. Aint natural. Just goes tuh go. HHH. Show. Just goes tuh show.

CHARLENE. Coffee right?

MOLLY. They—expelled—me.

CHARLENE. Straight up?

MOLLY. Straight up. "Talk right or youre outa here!" I couldnt. I walked. Nope. "Speak-correctly-or-you'll-be-dismissed!" Yeah. Yeah. Nope. Nope. Job sends me there. Basic Skills. Now Job don't want me no more. Closely-behind-at-Mary's-heels. HHH. Everythin in its place.

CHARLENE. Toast?

MOLLY. Hate lookin for uh job. Feel real whory walkin thuh streets. Only thing worse n workin sslookin for work.

CHARLENE. I'll put it on thuh table.

MOLLY. You lie down you lie down but he and she and it and us well we lays down. Didnt quit. They booted me. He booted me. Coundnt see thuh sense uh words workin like he said couldnt see thuh sense uh workin where words workin like that was workin would drop my phone voice would let things slip they tell me get Basic Skills call me breaking protocol hhhhh! Think I'll splat?

CHARLENE. Once there was uh robber who would come over and rob us regular. He wouldnt come through thuh window he would use thuh door. I would let him in. He would walk in n walk uhround. Then he would point tuh stuff. I'd say "help yourself." We developed us uh relationship. I asked him his name. He didnt answer. I asked him where he comed from. No answer tuh that neither. He didn't have no answers cause he didnt have no speech. Verona said he had that deep jungle air uhbout im that just off thuh boat look tuh his face. Verona she named him she named him "Mokus." But Mokus whuduhnt his name.

MOLLY. Once there was uh me named Mona who wanted tuh jump ship but didn't. HHH. Chona? Ya got thuh Help Wanteds?

CHARLENE. Flies are casin yer food Mona. Come eat.

MOLLY. HELP WANTEDS. *YOU GOT EM?*

CHARLENE. Wrapped thuh coffee grinds in em.

MOLLY. Splat.

B.

Lights up on stage with canned applause. At the podium stands the NATURALIST.

NATURALIST. As I have told my students for some blubblubblub years, a most careful preparation of one's fly is the only way by in which the Naturalist can insure the capturence of his subjects in a state of nature. Now for those of you who are perhaps not familiar with the more advanced techniques of nature study let me explain the principle of one of our most useful instruments: "the fly." When in Nature Studies the fly is an apparatus which by blending in with the environment under scrutiny enables the Naturalist to conceal himself and observe the object of study—unobserved. In our observations of the subjects which for our purposes we have named "Molly" subjects and "Charlene" subjects we have chosen for study in order that we may monitor their natural behavior and after monitoring perhaps—modify the form of my fly was an easy choice: this cockroach modeled after the common house insect *hausus cockruckus* fashioned entirely of corrugated cardboard offers us a place in which we may put our camera and observe our subjects—unobserved. Much like the "fly on the wall."

C.

Slide show: Images of MOLLY *and* CHARLENE. *Actors speak as stage remains dark and slides flash overhead.*

MOLLY. Once there was uh me named Mona who wondered what she'd be like if no one was watchin. You got thuh Help Wanteds?

CHARLENE. Wrapped thuh coffee grinds in um. —Mona?

MOLLY. Splat. Splat. Splatsplatsplat.

CHARLENE. Mm callin thuh ssterminator for tomorrow. Leave it be for now.

MOLLY. Diduhnt even blink. I threatened it. Diduhnt even blink.

CHARLENE. They're gettin brave. Big too.

MOLLY. Splat!

CHARLENE. Mona! Once there was uh little lamb who followed Mary good n put uh hex on Mary. When Mary dropped dead, thuh lamb was in thuh lead. You can study at home. I'll help.

MOLLY. Uhnn! I'm all decided. Aint gonna work. Cant. Aint honest. Anyone with any sense dont wanna work no how. Mm gonna be honest. Mm gonna be down n out. Make downin n outin my livelihood.

CHARLENE. He didnt have no answers cause he didnt have no speech.

MOLLY. Wonder what I'd look like if no one was lookin. I need fashions. "S-K" is /sk/ as in "ask." The-little-lamb-follows-Mary-Mary-who . . . ?

CHARLENE. Once there was uh one Verona named "Mokus." But "Mokus" whuduhnt his name. He had his picture on file at thuh police station. Ninety-nine different versions. None of um looked like he looked.

MOLLY. Splat! Splat! Diduhnt move uh muscle even. Don't even have no muscles. Only eyes. Splat! Shit. I woulda been uhcross thuh room out thuh door n on tuh thuh next life. Diduhnt twitch none. Splat! I cant even talk. I got bug bites bug bites all over! I need new styles.

CHARLENE. Once there was uh one named Lutzky. Uh exterminator professional with uh Ph.D. He wore white cause white was what thuh job required. Comes tuh take thuh roaches uhway. Knew us by names that whuduhnt ours. Could point us out from pictures that whuduhnt us. He became confused. He hosed us down. You signed thuh invoice with uh X. Exterminator professional with uh Ph.D. He can do thuh job for $99.

MOLLY. Mm gonna lay down, K?

CHARLENE. Youre lucky Mona.

MOLLY. He thuh same bug wasin thuh kitchen?

CHARLENE. Uh uhnn. We got uh infestation problem. Youre lucky.

MOLLY. He's watchin us. He followed us in here n swatchin us.

CHARLENE. I'll call Lutzky. Wipe-um-out-Lutzky with uh PhD. He's got uh squirt gun. He'll come right over. He's got thuh potions. All mixed up. Squirt in uh crack. Hose down uh crevice. We'll be through. Through with it. Free of um. Wipe-um-out Lutzky with thuh PhD. He's got uh squirt gun. He'll come right over.

MOLLY.   Uh—the-cockroach-is-watching-us,-look-Chona-look! Once there was uh me named Mona who wondered what she'd talk like if no one was listenin.

CHARLENE. Close yer eyes, Mona. Close yer eyes n think on someuhn pleasant.

D.

The NATURALIST *at the podium.*

NATURALIST. Thus behave our subjects naturally. Thus behave our subjects when they believe we cannot see them when they believe us far far away when they believe our backs have turned. Now. An obvious question should arise in the mind of an inquisitive observer? Yes? HHH. How should we best accommodate the presence of such subjects in our modern world. That is to say: How. Should. We. Best. Accommodate. Our subjects. If they are all to live with us—all in harmony—in our modern world. Yes. Having accumulated a wealth of naturally occurring observations knowing now how our subjects occur in their own world *(mundus primitivus),* the question now arises as to how we of our world *(mundus modernus)* best accommodate them. I ask us to remember that it was almost twenty-five whole score ago that our founding father went forth tirelessly crossing a vast expanse of ocean in which there lived dangerous creatures of the most horrible sort tirelessly crossing that sea jungle to find this country and name it. The wilderness was vast and we who came to teach, enlighten and tame were few in number. They were the vast, we were the few. And now. The great cake of society is crumbling. I ask us to realize that those who do not march with us do not march not because they will not but because they cannot. . . . I ask that they somehow be—taken care of for there are too many of them—and by "them" I mean of course "them roaches." They need our help. They need our help. Information for the modern cannot be gleaned from the primitive, information for the modern can only be gleaned through ex-per-i-men-tation. This is the most tedious part of science yet in science there is no other way. Now. I will, if you will, journey to the jungle. *Behavioris distortionallus-via-modernus*. Watch closely:

E.
On stage. During this part E the ROBBER *enters, steals the roach, and exits.*

CHONA. Verona? Hey honeyumm home?

VERONA. Chona Chona ChonaChonaChona. Mona here?

CHONA. Laying down.

VERONA. Heart broken?

CHONA. Like uh broken heart. Thuh poor thing. I'll learn her her speech. Let's take her out n buy her new styles.

VERONA. Sounds good.

CHONA. She wants fashions.—We got roaches.

VERONA. Shit! Chona. Thats uh big one. I got some motels but. I got some stickys too—them little trays with glue? Some spray but. Woo ya! Woo ya woo ya?! They gettin brave.

CHONA. Big too. Think he came through that crack in thuh bathroom.

VERONA. Wooya! Wooya! Shit. You call Lutzky? Thuh Ph.D.?

CHONA. On his way. We'll pay. Be through. He's got uh squirt gun.

VERONA. We'll all split thuh bill. He gonna do it for 99?

CHONA. Plus costs. Mona dunht know bout thuh Plus Costs part. Okay?

VERONA.—K. Maybe I can catch uh few for our Lutzky shows.

CHONA. Once there was uh woman who wanted tuh get unway for uwhile but didnt know which way tuh go tuh get gone. Once there was uh woman who just layed down.

VERONA. Traps. Place um. Around thuh sink corner of thuh stove move move yer feet threshole of thuh outside door. Yeauh. Mm convinced theyre comin in from uhcross thuh hall—slippin under thuh door at night but I aint no professional—see?! Lookit im go—movin slow-ly. He's thuh scout. For every one ya see there are thousands. Thousands thousands creepin in through thuh cracks. Waiting for their chance. Watchim go. Goinsslow. We gotta be vigilant: sit-with-thuh-lights-out-crouch-in-thuh-kitchen-holdin-hard-soled-shoes. GOTCHA! Monas got bug bites on her eyelids? Mmputtin some round her bed. Augment thuh traps with thuh spray.

CHONA. Once there was uh woman was careful. Once there was uh woman on thuh lookout. Still trapped.

VERONA. Vermin free by 1990! That means YOU!

CHONA. *Wild Kingdom*s on.

VERONA. YER OUTTA HERE!

CHONA. Yer shows on.

VERONA. Great. Thanks.

CHONA. Keep it low for Mona. K?

VERONA. Perkins never shoulda uhlowed them tuh scratch his show. Wildlife never goes outta style. He shoulda told em that. Fuck thuh ratings. Oh, look! On thuh trail of thuh long muzzled wildebeast: mating season. Ha! This is uh good one. They got bulls n cows muzzles matin close-ups—make ya feel like you really right there with em. Part of thuh action. Uh live birth towards thuh end. . . .

CHONA. You want some eggs?

VERONA. They got meat?

CHONA. —Yeauh—

VERONA. I'm veg. Since today. Kinder. Cheaper too. Didja know that uh veg—

CHONA. Eat. Here. Ssgood. Ssgood tuh eat. Eat. Please eat. Once there was uh one name Verona who bit thuh hand that feeds her. Doorbell thats Lutzky. I'll get it.

VERONA. Mona! Our shinin knights here!

MONA. THE-LITTLE-LAMB-FOLLOWS-MARY-CLOSELY-AT-HER-HEELS—

VERONA. Wipe-um-out Dr. Lutzky with uh P uh H and uh D. Baby. B. Cool.

MONA. B cool.

CHONA. Right this way Dr. Lutzky. Right this way Dr. Lutzky Extraordinaire Sir.

LUTZKY. I came as quickly as I could—I have a squirt gun, you know. Gold plated gift from the firm. They're so proud. Of me. there was a woman in Queens—poor thing—so distraught—couldn't sign the invoice—couldn't say "bug"—for a moment I thought I had been the un-witting victim of a prank phone call—*prankus callus*—her little boy filled out the forms—showed me where to squirt—lucky for her the little one was there—lucky for her she had the little one. Awfully noble scene, I thought. You must be Charlene.

CHONA. Char-who? Uh uhn. Uh—It-is-I,-Dr.-Lutzky,-*Chona.*

Lutzky. Ha! You look like a Charlene you look like a Charlene you do look like a Charlene bet no one has ever told that to you, eh? Aaaaaaah, well. I hear there is one with "bug bites all over." Are you the one?

CHONA. I-am-Chona. Mona-is-the-one. The-one-in-the-livingroom. The-one-in-the-livingroom-on-the-couch.

LUTZKY. What's the world coming to? "What is the world coming to?" I sometimes ask myself. And—

CHONA. Eggs, Dr. Lutzky?

LUTZKY. Oh, yes please. And—and am I wrong in making a livelihood—meager as it may be—from the ver-min that feed on the crumbs which fall from the table of the broken cake of civilization—oh dear—oh dear!

CHONA. Watch out for those. We do have an infestation problem. Watch out for those.

LUTZKY. Too late now—oh dear it's sticky. It's stuck—oh dear—now the other foot. They're stuck.

MONA. THE-LITTLE-LAMB—

VERONA. SShhh.

CHONA. Make yourself at home, Dr. Lutzky. I'll bring your eggs.

LUTZKY. Can't walk.

CHONA. Shuffle.

LUTZKY. Oh dear. Shuffleshuffleshuffle. Oh dear.

VERONA. Sssshhh!

LUTZKY. You watch *Wild Kingdom*. I watch *Wild Kingdom* too. This is a good one. Oh dear!

MONA. Oh dear.

CHONA. Here is the Extraordinaire, Mona. Mona, the Extraordinaire is here. Fresh juice, Dr. Lutzky Extraordiniare?

LUTZKY. Call me "Wipe-em-out."

MONA. Oh dear.

VERONA. SSSSShhhhh.

LUTZKY. Well. Now. Let's start off with something simple. Who's got bug bites?

MONA. Once there was uh me named Mona who hated going tuh thuh doctor.—I-have-bug-bites-Dr.-Lutzky-Extra-ordiniare-Sir.

LUTZKY. This won't take long. Step lively, Molly. The line forms here.

CHONA. I'll get the juice. We have a juice machine!

LUTZKY. I have a squirt gun!

VERONA. He's got uh gun—Marlin Perkinssgot uh gun—

MONA. Oh, dear. . . .

LUTZKY. You're the one, aren't you, Molly? Wouldn't want to squirt the wrong one. Stand up straight. The line forms here.

CHONA. I am Chona! Monas on the line!—Verona? That one is Verona.

LUTZKY. ChonaMonaVerona. Well well well. Wouldn't want to squirt the wrong one.

VERONA. He's got uh gun. Ssnot supposed tuh have uh gun—

MONA. "S-K" IS /SK/ AS IN "AXE." Oh dear. I'm Lucky, Dr. Lutzky.

LUTZKY. Call me "Wipe-em-out. Both of you. All of you.

CHONA. Wipe-em-out. Dr. Wipe-em-out.

LUTZKY. And you're "Lucky"?

VERONA. He got uh gun!

MONA. Me Mona.

LUTZKY. Mona?

MONA. Mona Mokus robbery.

CHONA. You are confusing the doctor, Mona. Mona, the doctor is confused.

VERONA. Perkins ssgot uh gun. Right there on thuh Tee V. He iduhnt spposed tuh have no gun!

MONA. Robbery Mokus Mona. Robbery Mokus Mona. Everything in its place.

CHONA. The robbery comes later, Dr. Wipe-em-out Extraordinaire, Sir.

LUTZKY. There goes my squirt gun. Did you feel it?

VERONA. I seen this show before. Four times. Perkins duhnt even own no gun.

CHONA. Once there was uh doctor who became confused and then hosed us down.

LUTZKY. I must be confused. Must be the sun. Or the savages.

MONA. Savage Mokus. Robbery, Chona.

CHONA. Go on Mokus. Help yourself.

LUTZKY. I need to phone for backups. May I?

VERONA. He duhnt have no gun permit even. Wait. B. Cool. I seen this. Turns out alright. I think. . . .

CHONA. Juice? I made it myself!

MONA. I am going to lie down. I am going to lay down. Lie down? Lay down. Lay down?

LUTZKY. Why don't you lie down.

MONA. I am going to lie down.

CHONA. She's distraught. Bug bites all over. We're infested. Help yourself.

LUTZKY. You seem infested, Miss Molly. Get in line, I'll hose you down.

MONA. MonaMokusRobbery.

LUTZKY. Hello Sir. Parents of the Muslim faith? My fathers used to frequent the Panthers. For sport. That was before my time. Not too talkative are you. Come on. Give us a grunt. I'll give you a squirt.

VERONA. Ssnot no dart gun neither—. Holy. Chuh! Mmcallin thuh— That is not uh dart gun, Marlin!!!

MONA. Make your bed and lie in it. I'm going to lay down.

CHONA. Lie down.

MONA. Lay down.

CHONA. LIE, Mona.

MONA. Lie Mona lie Mona down.

CHONA. Down, Mona down.

MONA. Down, Mona, bites! Oh my eyelids! On-her-heels! Down Mona down.

VERONA. Call thuh cops.

LUTZKY. That will be about $99. Hello. This is Dr. Lutzky. Send ten over. Just like me. We've got a real one here. Won't even grunt. Huh! Hmmm. Phone's not working. . . .

VERONA. Gimmie that! Thank-you. Hello? Marlin-Perkins-has-a-gun. I-am-telling-you,-Marlin-Perkins-has-a-gun! Yeah it's loaded course it's loaded! You listen tuh me! I pay yuh tuh listen tuh me! We pay our taxes, Chona?

CHONA. I am going to make a peach cobbler. My mothers ma used to make cobblers. She used to gather the peaches out of her own back yard all by herself.

LUTZKY. Hold still, Charlene. I'll hose you down.

CHONA. Go on Mokus. Help yourself.

VERONA. *HE'S SHOOTIN THUH WILD BEASTS!*

MONA. Oh dear.

VERONA. He-is-shooting-them-for-real! We diduhnt pay our taxes, Chona.

LUTZKY. Here's my invoice. Sign here.

CHONA. X, Mona. Help yourself.

MONA. Splat.

CHONA. Cobbler, Dr. Lutzky? Fresh out of the oven????!!!

MONA. Splat.

LUTZKY. Wrap it to go, Charlene.

MONA. Splat.

LUTZKY. What did you claim your name was dear?

MONA. Splat.

CHONA. I'll cut you off a big slice. Enough for your company. Youre a company man.

LUTZKY. With back-ups, Miss Charlene. I'm a very lucky man. Molly's lucky too.

MONA. Splat. Splat. Splatsplatsplat.

VERONA. Cops dont care. This is uh outrage.

LUTZKY. Here's my card. There's my squirt gun! Did
you feel it? I need backups. May I?

VERONA. Don't touch this phone. It's bugged.

LUTZKY. Oh dear!

CHONA. Cobbler, Verona?

LUTZKY. Well, good night.

VERONA. We pay our taxes, Chona?

LUTZKY. Well, good night!

VERONA. We pay our taxes, Chona??!!!!?

MONA. Tuck me in. I need somebody tuh tuck me in.

F.

Slide show. VERONA *speaks at the podium.*

VERONA. I saw my first pictures of Africa on TV: Mu-
tual of Omaha's *Wild Kingdom.* The thirty-minute filler
between Walt Disney's wonderful world and the CBS
Evening News. It was a wonderful world: Marlin Perkins
and Jim and their African guides. I was a junior guide
and had a lifesize poster of Dr. Perkins sitting on a white
Land Rover surrounded by wild things. Had me an 8 ×
10 glossy of him too, signed, on my nightstand. Got my
nightstand from Sears cause I had to have Marlin by my
bed at night. Together we learned to differentiate African
from Indian elephants the importance of hyenas in the
wild funny looking trees on the slant—how do they stand
up? Black folks with no clothes. Marlin loved and re-
spected all the wild things. His guides took his English
and turned it into the local lingo so that he could con-
verse with the natives. Marlin even petted a rhino once.
He tagged the animals and put them into zoos for their
own protection. He encouraged us to be kind to animals
through his shining example. Once there was uh me name
Verona: I got mommy n dad tuh get me uh black dog n
named it I named it ''Namib'' after thuh African sands
n swore tuh be nice tuh it only Namib refused tuh be
trained n crapped in corners of our basement n got up on
thuh sofa when we went out n Namib wouldnt listen tuh
me like Marlins helpers listened tuh him Namib wouldnt
look at me when I talked tuh him n when I said someuhn
like ''sit'' he wouldnt n ''come'' made im go n when I
tied him up in thuh front yard so that he could bite the

postman when thuh postman came like uh good dog
would he wouldnt even bark just smile n wag his tail so
I would kick Namib when no one could see me cause I
was sure I was very very sure that Namib told lies uhbout
me behind my back and Namib chewed through his rope
one day n bit me n run off. I have this job. I work at a
veterinarian hospital. I'm a euthenasia specialist! Someone brought a stray dog in one day and I entered "black
dog" in the black book and let her scream and whine
and wag her tail and talk about me behind my back then
I offered her the humane alternative. Wiped her out! I
stayed late that night so that I could cut her open because
I had to see I just had to see the heart of such a disagreeable domesticated thing. But no. Nothing different. Everything in its place. Do you know what that means?
Everything in its place. That's all.

  (Lights out.)

Part 2:

Third Kingdom

THE PLAYERS

KIN-SEER
US-SEER
SHARK-SEER
SOUL-SEER
OVER-SEER

KIN-SEER. Kin-Seer.
US-SEER. Us-Seer.
SHARK-SEER. Shark-Seer.
SOUL-SEER. Soul-Seer.
OVER-SEER. Over-Seer.

KIN-SEER. Kin-Seer.
US-SEER. Us-Seer.
SHARK-SEER. Shark-Seer.
SOUL-SEER. Soul-Seer.
OVER-SEER. Over-Seer.

KIN-SEER. Last night I dreamed of where I comed from. But where I comed from diduhnt look like nowhere like I been.
SOUL-SEER. There were 2 cliffs?
KIN-SEER. There were.
US-SEER. Uh huhn.
SHARK-SEER. 2 cliffs?
KIN-SEER. 2 cliffs: one on each other side thuh world.
SHARK-SEER. 2 cliffs?
KIN-SEER. 2 cliffs where thuh world had cleaved intuh 2.
OVER-SEER. The 2nd part comes apart in 2 parts.
SHARK-SEER. But we are not in uh boat!

Us-Seer. But we iz.

Soul-Seer. Iz. Uh huhn. Go on—

Kin-Seer. I was standin with my toes stuckted in thuh dirt. Nothin in front of me but water. And I was wavin. Wavin. Wavin at my uther me who I could barely see. Over thuh water on thuh uther cliff I could see my uther me but my uther me couldnt see me. And I was wavin wavin wavin sayin gaw *gaw gaw gaw eeeeeee-uh.

Over-Seer. The 2nd part comes apart in 2 parts.

Shark-Seer. But we are not in uh boat!

Us-Seer. But we iz.

Soul-Seer. Gaw gaw gaw gaw eeeee—

Kin-Seer. Ee-uh. Gaw gaw gaw gaw eeeee—

Soul-Seer. Ee-uh.

Us-Seer. Come home come home dont stay out too late. Bleached Bones Man may get you n take you far uhcross thuh waves, then baby, what will I do for love?

Over-Seer. The 2nd part comes apart in-to 2.

Shark-Seer. Edible fish are followin us. Our flesh is edible tuh them fish. Smile at them and they smile back. Jump overboard and they gobble you up. They smell blood. I see sharks. Ssssblak! Ssssblak! Gaw gaw gaw eee-uh. I wonder: are you happy?

All. We are smiling!

Over-Seer. Quiet, you, or youll be jettisoned.

Soul-Seer. Duhduhnt he duhduhnt he know my name? Ssblak ssblak ssblakallblak!

Over-Seer. Thats your *self* youre looking at! Wonder #1 of my glass-bottomed boat.

Kin-Seer. My uther me then waved back at me and then I was happy. But my uther me whuduhnt wavin at me. My uther me was wavin at my Self. My uther me was wavin at uh black black speck in thuh middle of thuh sea where years uhgoh from uh boat I had been—UUH!†

Over-Seer. Jettisoned.

Shark-Seer. Jettisoned?

Kin-Seer. Jettisoned.

Us-Seer. Uh huhn.

---

*"Gaw" is expressed by a glottal stop.

†"UUH!" is a sharp intake of air.

SOUL-SEER. To-the-middle-of-the-bottom-of-the-big-black-sea.

KIN-SEER. And then my Self came up between us. Rose up out of thuh water and standin on them waves my Self was standin. And I was wavin wavin wavin and my Me was wavin and wavin and my Self that rose between us went back down in-to-the-sea.

KIN-SEER. FFFFFFFFF.

US-SEER. Thup.

SHARK-SEER. Howwe gonna find my Me?

KIN-SEER. Me wavin at Me. Me wavin at I. Me wavin at my Self.

US-SEER. FFFFFFFFF.

SOUL-SEER. Thup.

SHARK-SEER. I dream up uh fish thats swallowin me and I dream up uh me that is then becamin that fish and uh dream of that fish becamin uh shark and I dream of that shark becamin uhshore. UUH! And on thuh shore thuh shark is given shoes. And I whuduhnt me no more and I whuduhnt no fish. My new Self was uh third Self made by thuh space in between. And my new Self wonders: am I happy? Is my new Self happy in my new-Self shoes?

KIN-SEER. MAY WAH-VIN ET MAY. MAY WAH-VIN ET EYE. MAY WAH-VIN ET ME SOULF.

OVER-SEER. Half the world had fallen away making 2 worlds and a sea between. Those 2 worlds inscribe the Third Kingdom.

KIN-SEER. Me hollering uhcross thuh cliffs at my Self:

US-SEER. Come home come home dont stay out too late.

SHARK-SEER. Black folks with no clothes. Then all thuh black folks clothed in smilin. In between thuh folks is uh distance thats uh wet space. Two worlds: Third Kingdom.

SOUL-SEER. Gaw gaw gaw gaw gaw gaw gaw gaw.

KIN-SEER. May wah-vin et may may wah-vin et eye may wah-vin et me sould.

SHARK-SEER. How many kin kin I hold. Whole hull full.

SOUL-SEER. Thuh hullholesfull of bleachin bones.

US-SEER. Bleached Bones Man may come and take you far uhcross thuh sea from me.

OVER-SEER. Who're you again?

KIN-SEER. I'm. Lucky.

OVER-SEER. Who're you again?

SOUL-SEER. Duhduhnt-he-know-my-name?

KIN-SEER. Should I jump? Shouldijumporwhut?

SHARK-SEER. But we are not in uh boat!

US-SEER. But we iz. Iz iz iz uh huhn. Iz uh huhn. Uh huhn iz.

SHARK-SEER. I wonder: are we happy? Thuh looks we look look so.

US-SEER. They like smiles and we will like what they will like.

SOUL-SEER. UUH!

KIN-SEER. Me wavin at me me wavin at my i me wavin at my soul.

SHARK-SEER. Chomp chomp chomp chomp.

KIN-SEER. Fffffffffff—

US-SEER. Thup.

SHARK-SEER. Baby, what will I do for love?

SOUL-SEER. Wave me uh wave and I'll wave one back blow me uh kiss n I'll blow you one back.

OVER-SEER. Quiet, you, or youll be jettisoned!

SHARK-SEER. Chomp. Chomp. Chomp. Chomp.

KIN-SEER. Wa-vin wa-vin.

SHARK-SEER. Chomp chomp chomp chomp.

KIN-SEER. Howwe gonna find my Me?

SOUL-SEER. Rock. Thuh boat. Rock. Thuh boat. Rock. Thuh boat. Rock. Thuh boat.

US-SEER. We be walkin wiggly cause we left our bones in bed.

SOUL/US/SHARK/KIN/OVER. Gaw gaw gaw gaw gaw gaw gaw gaw gaw gaw gaw gaw gaw gaw gaw gaw gaw/

OVER-SEER. I'm going to yell ''Land Ho!'' in a month or so and all of this will have to stop. I'm going to yell ''Land Ho!'' in a month or so and that will be the end of this. Line up!

SHARK-SEER. Where to?

OVER-SEER. Ten-Shun!

SOUL-SEER. How come?

OVER-SEER. Move on move on move—. LAND HO!

KIN-SEER. You said I could wave as long as I see um. I still see um.

OVER-SEER. Wave then.

Part 3:

Open House

THE PLAYERS

Mrs. Aretha Saxon
Anglor Saxon
Blanca Saxon
Charles
Miss Faith
(Notes for Part 3 appear on pages 282–283.)

A.
A double-frame slide show: Slides of ARETHA *hugging* ANGLOR *and* BLANCA. *Dialogue begins and continues with the slides progressing as follows: (1) they are expressionless; next (2) they smile; next (3) they smile more; next (4) even wider smiles. The enlargement of smiles continues. Actors speak as the stage remains dark and the slides flash overhead.*

ARETHA. Smile, honey, smile.

ANGLOR. I want my doll. Where is my doll I want my doll where is it I want it. I want it now.

ARETHA. Miss Blanca? Give us uh pretty smile, darlin.

BLANCA. I want my doll too. Go fetch.

ARETHA. You got such nice white teeth, Miss Blanca. Them teeths makes uh smile tuh remember you by.

ANGLOR. She wont fetch the dolls. She wont fetch them because she hasnt fed them.

ARETHA. Show us uh smile, Mr. Anglor. Uh quick toothy show stopper.

BLANCA. She wont fetch them because she hasnt changed them. Theyre sitting in their own filth because they havent been changed they havent been fed they havent been aired theyve gone without sunshine.

ANGLOR. Today is her last day. Shes gone slack.

BLANCA. Is today your last day, Aretha?

ANGLOR. Yes.

ARETHA. Smile for your daddy, honey. Mr. Charles, I cant get em tuh smile.

BLANCA. Is it? Is it your last day?!

ANGLOR. You see her belongings in the boxcar, dont you?

BLANCA. Where are you going, Aretha? Youre going to get my doll!

ARETHA. Wish I had me some teeths like yours, Miss Blanca. So straight and cleaned. So pretty and white. —Yes, Mr. Charles, I'm trying. Mr. Anglor. Smile. Smile for show.

BLANCA. Youre going away, arent you? ARENT YOU?

ANGLOR. You have to answer her.

BLANCA. You have to answer me.

ARETHA. Yes, Missy. Mm goin. Mm goin uhway.

BLANCA. Where?

ARETHA. Uhway. Wayuhway.

ANGLOR. To do what?

ARETHA. Dunno. Goin uhway tuh—tuh swallow courses uh meals n fill up my dance card! Goin uhway tuh live, I guess.

BLANCA. Live? Get me my doll. My doll wants to wave good-bye. Who's going to sew up girl doll when she pops?!

ANGLOR. Who's going to chastise boy doll!? Boy doll has no manners.

BLANCA. Who's going to plait girl doll's hair?! Her hair should be plaited just like mine should be plaited.

ANGLOR. Who's going to clean their commodes?! Who's going to clean our commodes?! We wont visit you because we wont be changed! We'll be sitting in our own filth because we wont have been changed we wont have been fed we wont have been aired we wont have manners we wont have plaits we'll have gone without sunshine.

ARETHA. Spect your motherll have to do all that.

BLANCA & ANGLOR. Who!??!

ARETHA. Dunno. Smile, Blanca, Anglor, huh? Lets see them pretty white teeths.

(Camera-clicking noises.)

B.

On stage. MRS. ARETHA SAXON.

ARETHA. Six seven eight nine. Thupp.* Ten eleven twelve thirteen fourteen fifteen sixteen. Thupp. Seventeen. Eighteen nineteen twenty twenty-one. And uh little bit. Thuuup. Thuup. Gotta know thuh size. Thup. Gotta know thuh size exact. Thup. Got people comin. Hole house full. They gonna be kin? Could be strangers. How many kin kin I hold. Whole hold full. How many strangers. Depends on thuh size. Thup. Size of thuh space. Thuup. Depends on thuh size of thuh kin. Pendin on thuh size of thuh strangers. Get more mens than womens ssgonna be one number more womens than mens ssgonna be uhnother get animals thuup get animals we kin pack em thuup. Tight. Thuuup. Thuuuup. Mmmm. Thuuup. Count back uhgain: little bit twenty-one twenty nineteen eighteen seventhuup sixteen fifteen fourteen twelve thuup eleven ten uh huh thuuup three two thuuup one n one. Huh. Twenty-one and one and one. And thuh little bit. Thuuup. Thup. Thirty-two and uh half.

MISS FAITH. Footnote #1: The human cargo capacity of the English slaver, the *Brookes,* was about 3,250 square feet. From James A. Rawley, *The Transatlantic Slave Trade,* G. J. McLeod Limited, 1981, page 283.

ARETHA. 32 ½[1] Thuuup! Howmy gonna greet em. Howmy gonna say hello. Thuup! Huh. Greet em with uh smile! Thupp. Still got uh grin. Uh little bit. Thup. Thuuup. Twenty-three and uh little bit. 32 ½. Better buzz Miss Faith. Miss Faith?

MISS FAITH. Yeahus—.

MRS. SAXON. Thuup. Sss Mrs. Saxon. 2D.

MISS FAITH. Yes, Mrs. Saxon. Recovering? No more bleeding, I hope.

MRS. SAXON. You wanted tuh know thuh across.

MISS FAITH. Holes healing I hope.

MRS. SAXON. Twenty-three and uh half.

MISS FAITH. Is that a fact?

MRS. SAXON. Thup. Thatsuh fact. Twenty-three feets and uh half on the a cross! Thats uh fact!

---

*"Thupp" is a sucking-in sound.

MISS FAITH. Thank you, Ma'am!

MRS. SAXON. You say I'm tuh have visitors, Miss Faith? You say me havin uh visitation is written in thuh book. I say in here we could fit—three folks.

MISS FAITH. Three. I'll note that. On with your calculations, Mrs. Saxon!

MRS. SAXON. On with my calculations. Thuup.

MISS FAITH. Mrs. Saxon? I calculate— we'll fit six hundred people.[2] Six hundred in a pinch. Footnote #2: 600 slaves were transported on the *Brookes,* although it only had space for 451. *Ibid;* page 14.

MRS. SAXON. Miss Faith, six hundred in here won't go.

MISS FAITH. You give me the facts. I draw from them, Ma'am. I draw from them in accordance with the book. Six hundred will fit. We will have to pack them tight.

MRS. SAXON. Miss Faith—thuup—Miss Faith—

MISS FAITH. Mrs. Saxon, book says you are due for an extraction Mrs. Saxon an extraction are you not. Gums should be ready. Gums should be healed. You are not cheating me out of valuable square inches, Mrs. Saxon, of course you are not. You gave me the facts of course you did. We know well that "She who cheateth me out of some valuable square inches shall but cheat herself out of her assigned seat asside the most high." We are familiar with Amendment 2.1 are we not, Mrs. Saxon. Find solace in the book and—bid your teeth good-bye. Buzz me not.

MRS. SAXON. Thup. Thup. 2.1[3]

MISS FAITH. Footnote #3: The average ratio of slaves per ship, male to female was 2.1.

ARETHA. "Then she looketh up at the Lord and the Lord looketh down on where she knelt. She spake thusly: 'Lord, what proof canst thou give me that my place inside your kingdom hath not been by another usurpt? For there are many, many in need who seek a home in your great house, and many are those who are deserving.' " Thuuuuup! Thuup. "And the Lord looketh upon her with" Thuuuup! "And the Lord looketh upon her with kind azure eyes and on his face there lit a toothsome—a toothsome smile and said, 'Fear not, Charles, for your place in my kingdom is secure.' '' Thup. Thuuup! Charles? Miss Faith?

MISS FAITH. Buzz! BUZZZ!

(Buzzer.)

C.

CHARLES *appears.* BLANCA *and* ANGLOR *hum the note of the buzz.*

ARETHA. And she looketh up at the Lord—

CHARLES. And the Lord looketh downeth oneth whereth sheth knelth—

ARETHA. What proof can yuh give me, Lord? I wants uh place.

CHARLES. A place you will receive. Have you got your papers?

ARETHA. Thuh R-S-stroke-26?[4]

CHARLES. Let us see. It says "Charles." "Charles Saxon."

ARETHA. Had me uh husband names Charles.

CHARLES. Funny name for you, Mrs. Saxon. "Charles"?

ARETHA. My husband's name. We's split up now.

CHARLES. Divorce?

ARETHA. Divorce?

CHARLES. The breakup of those married as sanctioned by the book. Illegal, then. Non legal? I see. Were you legally wed, Charles? Wed by the book? Didn't—"jump the broom" or some such nonsense, eh? Perhaps it was an estrangement. Estrangement? Was it an estrangement? Estrangement then? You will follow him, Mister Sir, I suppose.

ARETHA. He's— He's dead, Mister Sir.

CHARLES. I'll mark "yes," then. Sign here. An "X" will do, Charles.

ARETHA. I dunno.

CHARLES. There is a line—

ARETHA. Mehbe—

CHARLES. —that has formed itself behind you—

ARETHA. Mehbe—do I gotta go—mehbe—maybe I could stay awhiles. Here.

CHARLES. The book says you expire. No option to renew.

ARETHA. And my place?
CHARLES. Has been secured.
ARETHA. Where?
CHARLES. Move on.
ARETHA. Where to?
CHARLES. Move on, move on, move on!
(Humming grows louder.)

D.

Humming is replaced by buzzer buzz.

MRS. SAXON. How many—extractions this go, Sister Faith?

MISS FAITH. Open up. ALL. Don't look upon it as punishment, Mrs. Saxon, look on it as an integral part of the great shucking off. The old must willingly shuck off for the sake of the new. Much like the snakes new skin suit, Mrs. Saxon. When your new set comes in—and you will be getting a new set, that the book has promised—they will have a place. We will have made them room. Where would we go if we did not extract? There are others at this very moment engaged in extracting so that for us there may be a place. Where would we go if we did not extract? Where would they go? What would happen? Who would survive to tell? The old is yankethed out and the new riseth up in its place! Besides, if we didn't pluck them we couldnt photograph them. To be entered into the book they must be photographed. Think of it as getting yourself chronicled, Mrs. Saxon. You are becoming a full part of the great chronicle! Say that, Mrs. Saxon. You don't want to be forgotten, do you?

MRS. SAXON. Thuup! I was gonna greet em with uh grin.

MISS FAITH. An opened jawed awe will do. Open? Yeauhs. Looks of wonder suit us best just before we're laid to rest. AAAh! Open. Hmmm. Canine next, I think. Find solace in the book. Find order in the book. Find find find the book. Where is the book. Go find it. Find it. Go on, get up.

MRS. SAXON. Thuuuuup.

MISS FAITH. Read from it.

MRS. SAXON. Thuuuuuup?

MISS FAITH. Now.

MRS. SAXON. Thup. Thuuuuppp! "The woman lay on
the sickness bed her gums were moist and bleeding. The
Lord appeared to her, as was his custom, by dripping
himself down through the cold water faucet and walking
across the puddle theremade. The Lord stood over the
sickness bed toweling himself off and spake thusly:
'Charles, tell me why is it that you. . . .' '' Thuuuuuup!
"Charles" uhgain. Thup. Wonder why he calls her
"Charles," Miss Faith? Now, I had me uh husband
named Charles wonder if it says anything uhbout Retha
Saxons husband Charles in thuh book. Still. Havin uh
husband named Charles aint no reason for her tuh be
called—

MISS FAITH. Open! She is named what her name is.
She was given that name by him. The book says your
Charles is dead. Sorry. Never to return. Sorry. That is
a fact. A fact to accept. The power of the book lies in
its contents. Its contents are facts. Through examination of the facts therein we may see what is to come.
Through the examination of what comes we may turn to
our book and see from whence it came. Example: the
book has let us know for quite some time that you expire
19–6–65,[6] do you not, Mrs. Saxon. You expire. Footnote #5: "Juneteenth," June 19th in 1865, was when,
a good many months after the Emancipation Proclamation, the slaves in Texan heard they were free. You
expire. Along with your lease. Expiration 19–6–65 with
no option to renew.

MRS. SAXON. Thuuup?

MISS FAITH. You expire. Yes, Ma'am!

MRS. SAXON. Yahs Maam.

MISS FAITH. Yes, Ma'am. 19–6–65. That's a fact. And
now we know you're to have visitors. And now we know
that those visitors are waiting on your doorstep.

MRS. SAXON. Naaaa?

MISS FAITH. Now. 32.5. 19–6–65? Now. Open! Now.
Close!

MRS. SAXON. Now. Howmy gonna greet em? Was

gonna greet em with uh smile . . . Awe jawll do. I guess.

MISS FAITH. Youre expiring. It's only natural. That's a fact. Amendment 1807,[6] Mrs. Saxon. A fact. You sit comfortably. I'll buzz them in.

(Buzzer.)

E.

CHARLES appears.

CHARLES. You know what they say about the hand that rocks the cradle, dont you, Aretha?

ARETHA. Nope.

CHARLES. Whats that?

ARETHA. No suh. No Mr. Charles suh. I dont.

CHARLES. Well well well. ''No suh. I dont.'' Well well well well that's just as well. How about this one, eh? ''Two hands in the bush is better than one hand in—''

ARETHA. Sssthey feedin time, Mistuh Charles.

CHARLES. —Go on. Feed them. Ooooh! These will make some lovely shots—give the children some wonderful memories. Memory is a very important thing, dont you know. It keeps us in line. It reminds us of who we are, memory. Without it we could be anybody. We would be running about here with no identities. You would not know that youre my—help, youd just be a regular street and alley heathen. I would not remember myself to be master. There would be chaos, chaos it would be without a knowledge from whence we came. Little Anglor and little Blanca would—well, they would not even exist! And then what would Daddy do? Chaos without correct records. Chaos. Aaaah. You know what chaos is, dont you.

ARETHA. No suh. I dont.

CHARLES. He he he! Aaaaah! Ignorance is bliss! They say ignorance is bliss—only for the ignorant—for those of us who must endure them we find their ignorance anything but blissful. Isnt that right.

ARETHA. Yes suh.

CHARLES. ''Yes suh. Yes suh.'' Heh heh heh heh. Hold

them up where I can see them. Thaaaats it. You will look back on these and know what was what. Hold em up. There. Thaaaaaats just fine. Smile. Smile! Smile? Smiiiiiile—

(Clicking of camera.)

F.

On stage. Clicking of camera is replaced by buzzing of door.

ANGLOR. Very nice!

BLANCA. Very nice!

MISS FAITH. As the book promised: very well lit, views of the land and of the sea, a rotating northern exposure—

ANGLOR. Very very nice!

BLANCA. OH yes very nice! Blanca Saxon—

ANGLOR. Anglor Saxon.

MRS. SAXON. I'm Mrs. Saxon.

MISS FAITH. —Expires 19-6-65.

ANGLOR. Very nice.

BLANCA. We're newlyweds.

MRS. SAXON. I'm Mrs. Saxon.

BLANCA. Newly weds. Newly wedded. New.

ANGLOR. Very new.

MISS FAITH. Very nice.

BLANCA. Blanca and Anglor Saxon.

MRS. SAXON. Thuup! I'm—

MISS FAITH. Very nice. 32.5 19-6-65. By the book. As promised.

BLANCA. We read the book. The red letter edition. The red herring.[7] Cover to cover. We read the red book.

ANGLOR. We're well read.

MRS. SAXON. You ever heard of Charles? He's in thuh book—

MISS FAITH. Five walk-in closets. Of course, theyre not in yet.

BLANCA. Does she come with the place?

MISS FAITH. She's on her way out.

BLANCA. She has no teeth.

ANGLOR. Havent I seen her somewhere before?

BLANCA. Anglor Saxon! —He's always doing that. When we met he wondered if he hadnt seen me somewhere before. And he had! We had to make an Amendment.

MISS FAITH. The closets will go here here there and thar. We will yank her out to make room for them.

ANGLOR. Thus says the book. Amendment 2.1. Always liked that amendment. It's very open—open to interpretation.

MISS FAITH. We will put in some windows, of course.

BLANCA. Of course.

ANGLOR. Yanking out the commode?

MISS FAITH. Commodes just for show.

MRS. SAXON. Just for show.

BLANCA. We might like to have a bathroom. We're planning to have a big family.

MRS. SAXON. A family. Had me uh family once. They let me go.

ANGLOR. Meet our children: Anglor and Blanca. Theyre so nice and quiet they dont speak unless theyre spoken to they dont move unless we make them.

MISS FAITH. This is where we plan the bathroom.

ANGLOR. You'll never guess where we met.

BLANCA. Love at first sight.

MISS FAITH. Plenty of room for a big family.

ANGLOR. Guess where we met!

MISS FAITH. We'll rip out this kitchen if you like leave it bare youll have more space.

MRS. SAXON. Charles got you tuhgether.

ANGLOR. Close. I told you we know her, Blanca.

MISS FAITH. We'll put in the commode and rip it out then put it back again. If you so desire.

BLANCA. Guess!

ANGLOR. We're going to need someone to mind that commode. We're going to need help.

MRS. SAXON. I raised uh family once. I raised uh boy. I raised uh girl. I trained em I bathed em. I bathed uh baby once. Bathed two babies.

BLANCA. We're childhood sweethearts. From childhood. We met way back. In the womb.

ANGLOR. We need help.

BLANCA. We're twins!

MRS. SAXON. That iduhnt in thuh book.

ANGLOR. We're related. By marriage. It's all legal. By the book.

MISS FAITH. We will put the commode closer to the bath. Put the commode in the bath. Youll have more space.

MRS. SAXON. We got different books.

ANGLOR. We have the same last name! Saxon! Blanca Saxon—

BLANCA. Anglor Saxon. Blanca and Anglor Saxon—

MRS. SAXON. I'm Mrs. Saxon. Howdeedoo.

ANGLOR. Mrs. Saxon, we need help.

BLANCA. We're going to have children. We're going to breed. We've bred two we'll breed more.

MISS FAITH. It's all a part of the great shucking off—

MRS. SAXON. You wouldnt know nothin uhbout uh Charles, wouldja? Charles was my husband. Charles Saxon?

MISS FAITH. The old must willingly shuck off to make way for the new. Much like the snakes new skin suit. The new come in and we gladly make them room. Where would they go if we did not extract?

ANGLOR. I dont suppose youve nowhere to go? We need help. You seem like a sturdy help type. I suppose you can shuffle and serve simultaneously? Wet nurse the brood we've bred? A help like you would be in accordance with the book. Make things make sense. Right along with the record. More in line with what youre used to. I would be master. Blanca: mistress. Thats little master and little missy. Yes, that's it! Give us a grin!

MISS FAITH. Shes on her way out.

ANGLOR. Give us a grin!

BLANCA. Anglor, shes toothless.

MRS. SAXON. Charles sscome back! I see im down there wavin—no—directin traffic. Left right left right left—he remembers me right right he's forgiven me right left right right he wants tuh see me.

MISS FAITH. Charles is dead.

ANGLOR. Thus says the book?

MRS. SAXON. Make uh amendment. Charles ssdown thuh street. Oh thuh street down thuh street.

MISS FAITH. Not in my book.

BLANCA. We've got different books.

MRS. SAXON. We got differin books. Make uh amendment. I'm packin my bags. I left him. Had to go. Two babies to care for.

ANGLOR. We know her from somewhere.

MRS. SAXON. Had tuh go. He gived me his name. Make uh amendment.

BLANCA. We've got the same name.

ANGLOR. WE KNOW HER FROM SOMEWHERE! Too bad she cant grin.

MRS. SAXON. Had to go. Have tuh go. Make thuh amendment, Sister Faith, Charles is back.

MISS FAITH. You need help. She comes with the place. She can live under the sink. Out of mind out of sight.

BLANCA. Shes toothless.

ANGLOR. Not a good example for the breed. Make the amendment.

MRS. SAXON. Miss Faith? Make uh uhmendment. Charles's waitin—

MISS FAITH. Charles is dead! Never to return. Thus says the—

MRS. SAXON. Buchenwald! Buchenwald! I—I showed em my blue eyes n they hauled me off anyway—

BLANCA. Stick to the facts, help! Shes bad for the brood. Make that amendment.

MISS FAITH. An amendment.

MRS. SAXON. Nine million just disappeared![8] That's uh fact!!

BLANCA. Six million. Six! Miss Faith? The amendment! I would like another child. I would like to get started!

MRS. SAXON. They hauled us from thuh homeland! Stoled our clothes!

MISS FAITH. Amendment! Amendment XIII.[9] You have been extracted from the record, Mrs. Saxon. You are free. You are clear. You may go.

ANGLOR. Free and clear to go. Go.

MISS FAITH. Go.

BLANCA. Go.

MRS. SAXON. Oh. How should I greet him? Should greet im with uh—

BLANCA. GIT! Wave good-bye, children! That's it.
That's it! They're so well mannered.

ANGLOR. Wife? Brood? Isn't this a lovely view? And
the buzzer! It works!

(*Buzzer.*)

G.

CHARLES appears.

CHARLES. You let them take out the teeth youre giving
up the last of the verifying evidence. All'll be obliter-
ated. Alls left will be conjecture. We wont be able to tell
you apart from the others. We wont even know your
name. Things will get messy. Chaos. Perverted. People
will twist around the facts to suit the truth.

ARETHA. You know that they say bout thuh hand that
rocks thuh cradle?

CHARLES. I didnt rock their cradles.

ARETHA. You know how thuh sayin goes?

CHARLES. "Rocks the cradle—rules the world," but I
didnt rock—

ARETHA. Dont care what you say you done, Charles.
We're makin us uh histironical amendment here, K? Give
us uh smile. Uh big smile for thuh book.

CHARLES. Historical." An "Historical Amendment,"
Ma'am.

ARETHA. Smile, Charles.

CHARLES. Where are you going, Miss Aretha?

ARETHA. Mmm goin tuh take my place aside thuh most
high.

CHARLES. Up north, huh?

ARETHA. Up north.

CHARLES. Sscold up there, you know.

ARETHA. Smile, Charles! That's it! You think Marys
Jesus done what she wanted?

CHARLES. Mary's Jesus? The Jesus? The book says—

ARETHA. You think that Jesus had hisself uh twin sister
and Madame Mary culled it? Think she culled it tuh make
room?

CHARLES. Room for whom?

ARETHA. Just some things tuh consider, Charles.

CHARLES. Chaos! You know what chaos is?! Things cease to adhere to—

ARETHA. SMILE. Smile, Charles. Smile! Show us them pretty teeths. Good.

CHARLES. I cant get the children to smile, Ma'am.

ARETHA. You smile.

CHARLES. Theyre crying, Miss Mary!

ARETHA. Smile! Smile! SMILE!! There. Thats nice.

CHARLES. Theyre crying.

ARETHA. Dont matter none. Dont matter none at all. You say it's uh cry I say it's uh smile. These photographics is for my scrapbook. Scraps uh graphy for my book. Smile or no smile mm gonna remember you. Mm gonna remember you grinnin.

(Whir of camera grows louder.)
(Lights fade to black.)

NOTES TO PART 3

1. The "human cargo" capacity of the English slaver, the *Brookes,* was about 3250 square feet. (From James A. Rawley, *The Transatlantic Slave Trade,* G. J. McLeod Ltd., 1981, p. 283.)

2. 600 slaves were transported on the *Brookes* although it only had the space for 451. *(Ibid.)*

3. The average ratio of slaves per ship, Male: Female, was 2:1. *(Ibid.,* p. 14.)

4. A common form from the Division of Housing and Community Renewal (DHCR).

5. "Juneteenth." June 19, I think, was when, in 1865, a good many months after the Emancipation Proclamation, the slaves in Texas heard that they were free.

6. In March of 1807, England's slave trade was abolished.

7. Red herring. In co-op sales, a preliminary booklet explaining the specifics of sale.

8. An estimated 9 million Africans were taken from Africa into slavery. (Rawley, *The Transatlantic Slave*

Trade.) An estimated 6 million Jewish people were killed in the concentration camps of WWII.

9. Amendment XIII abolished slavery in the United States.

Third Kingdom

(reprise)

THE PLAYERS

KIN-SEER
SHARK-SEER
US-SEER
SOUL-SEER
OVER-SEER

OVER-SEER. What are you doing?

US-SEER. Throw-ing. Up.

KIN-SEER. Kin-Seer sez.

SHARK-SEER. Shark-Seer sez.

US-SEER. Us-Seer sez.

SOUL-SEER. Soul-Seer sez.

OVER-SEER. Over-Seer sez.

KIN-SEER. Sez Kin-Seer sez.

SHARK-SEER. Sezin Shark-Seer sez.

US-SEER. Sez Us-Seer sezin.

SOUL-SEER. Sezin Soul-Seer sezin sez.

OVER-SEER. Sez Over-Seer sez.

KIN-SEER. Tonight I dream of where I be-camin from. And where I be-camin from duhduhnt look like nowhere like I been.

SOUL-SEER. The tale of how we were when we were—

OVER-SEER. You woke up screaming.

SHARK-SEER. How we will be when we will be—

OVER-SEER. You woke up screaming.

US-SEER. And how we be, now that we iz.

ALL. You woke up screaming out—you woke me up.

OVER-SEER. Put on this. Around your head and over your eyes. It will help you sleep. See? Like me. Around your head and over your eyes. It will help you see.

KIN/US/SHARK. Gaw gaw gaw gaw—eeeee-uh. Gaw gaw gaw gaw eeeeeee-uh.

SOUL-SEER. Howzit gonna fit? Howzitgonnafit me?!

US-SEER. Bleached Bones Man has comed and tooked you. You fall down in-to-the-sea.

KIN-SEER. Should I jump? Should I jump?? Should I jump shouldijumporwhut?

SHARK-SEER. I dream up uh fish thats swallowin me—

SHARK/KIN. And I dream up uh me that isthen be-camin that fish and I dream up uh dream of that fish be-camin uh shark and I dream up that shark be-camin uhshore.

ALL. UUH!

SOUL-SEER. And where I be-camin from duhduhnt look like nowhere like I been.

KIN/SHARK. And I whuduhnt me no more and I whu-duhnt no fish. My new Self was uh 3rd Self made by thuh space in between.

ALL. UUH!

KIN-SEER. Rose up out uh thuh water and standin on them waves my Self was standin. And my Self that rose between us went back down in-to-the-sea.

US-SEER. EEEEEEEEE!

SHARK-SEER. Me wavin at me me wavin at I me wavin at my Self.

US-SEER. Bleached Bones Man has comed and tooked you. You fall down in-to-the-sea. . . .

KIN-SEER. Baby, what will I do for love?

OVER-SEER. Around your head and over your eyes. This piece of cloth will help you see.

SHARK-SEER. BLACK FOLKS WITH NO CLOTHES. . . .

US-SEER. This boat tooked us to-the-coast.

SOUL-SEER. THUH SKY WAS JUST AS BLUE!

KIN-SEER. Thuuuup!

SHARK-SEER. Eat eat eat please eat.

SOUL-SEER. THUH SKY WAS JUST AS BLUE!

KIN-SEER. Thuuuup!

SHARK-SEER. Eat eat eat please eat. Eat eat eat please eat.

OVER-SEER. Around your head and over your eyes.

US-SEER. This boat tooked us to-the-coast.

SOUL-SEER. But we are not in uh boat!

US-SEER. But we iz. Iz uh-huhn-uh-huhn-iz.

OVER-SEER. There are 2 cliffs. 2 cliffs where the Word has cleaved. Half the Word has fallen away making 2

Words and a space between. Those 2 Words inscribe the Third Kingdom.

KIN-SEER. Should I jump shouldijumporwhut.

US-SEER. Come home come home don't stay out too late.

KIN-SEER. Me hollerin uhcross thuh cliffs at my Self:

SOUL-SEER. Ssblak! Ssblak! Ssblakallblak!

OVER-SEER. That's your *soul* you're looking at. Wonder #9 of my glass-bottomed boat. Swallow it, you, or you'll be jettisoned.

SOUL-SEER. UUH! UUH!

KIN-SEER. This boat tooked me from-my-coast.

US-SEER. Come home come home come home come home.

SOUL-SEER. The tale of who we were when we were, who we will be when we will be and who we be now that we iz:

US-SEER. Iz-uhhuhn-uhhuhn-iz.

KIN-SEER. You said I could wave as long as I see um. I still see um.

OVER-SEER. Wave then.

OVER/KIN/SOUL/SHARK/US. Gaw gaw gaw gaw ee-uh. Gaw gaw gaw gaw ee-uh.

SHARK-SEER. This is uh speech in uh language of codes. Secret signs and secret symbols.

KIN-SEER. Wave wave wave wave. Wave wave wave wave.

SHARK-SEER. Should I jump shouldijumporwhut? Should I jump shouldijumporwhut?

KIN-SEER.	SHARK-SEER.
Wave wave wave wave.	Should I jump shouldijumporwhut
Wavin wavin	Should I jump should I jump
wavin wavin	shouldijumporwhut?

[:]US-SEER. Baby, what will I do for love?

SOUL-SEER. Rock. Thuh boat. Rock. Thuh boat.

KIN-SEER.	SOUL-SEER.	SHARK-SEER.	US-SEER.
Wavin wavin.	Rock. Thuh boat.	Shouldijump	Thuh sky

wavin	Rock.	shouldijump	was just
wavin	Thuh boat.	orwhut?	blue!
			THUP!

Wavin wavin	Rock. Thuh boat.	Shouldijump	Thuh sky
wavin	Rock.	shouldijump	was just
wavin	Thuh boat.	orwhut?	blue!

OVER-SEER. HO!
(*Repeat from* [:])

KIN/SOUL/SHARK/US/OVER. Gaw gaw gaw gaw gaw gaw gaw gaw.

OVER-SEER. I'm going to yell "Land Ho!" in a day or so and all of this will have to stop. I am going to yell "Land Ho!" in a day or so and that will be the end of this.

KIN/SOUL/SHARK/US. Gaw gaw gaw gaw-ee-uh. Gaw gaw gaw gaw-eeeee-uh.

OVER-SEER. What are you doing? What'reya doin. What'reyadoeeeeee! *WHAT ARE YOU DO-EEE-NUH???!*

KIN-SEER. (*Throwing kisses.*)

Part 4:

Greeks (or The Slugs)

THE PLAYERS

Mr. Sergeant Smith
Mrs. Sergeant Smith
Buffy Smith
Muffy Smith
Duffy Smith

A.

MR. SERGEANT SMITH. I'll have four. Four shots. Four at thuh desk. Go ahead—put in thuh colored film. Mmsplurgin. Splurging. Uh huh. Wants em tuh see my shoes as black. Shirt as khaki. Stripes is green. No mop n broom bucket today! I'll sit first. No. Stand. I kin feel it. In here. Mmm gettin my Distinction today. Thuh events of my destiny ssgonna fall intuh place. What events? That I dont know. But they gonna fall intuh place all right. They been all along marchin in that direction. Soon they gonna fall. Ssonly natural. Ssonly fair. They gonna fall intuh place. I kin feel it. In here. This time tomorrow mm gonna have me my Distinction. Gonna be shakin hands with thuh Commander. Gonna be salutin friendly back n forth. Gonna be rewarded uh desk cause when uh mans distinguished he's got hisself uh desk. Standin at thuh desk. My desk. Sssgonna be mines, any-how. Fnot this un then one just liekit. Hands in pockets. No—out. Ready for work. Here is Sergeant Smith at his desk. Ready. Ready for work. Next, second shot: right hand on the desk. Like on the Bible. God and Country. Here is a man who loves his work. The name of this man is the name of Smith. You get the stripes in? They gonna be bars by evenin! Ha! Bars by evenin! Having a desk is distinguished. All of us have them. Because when there is danger from above, we stop. We look. We listen. Then we—dive underneath our desk (being careful that we do not catch our heads on the desk lip). Dive! Dive under our desks where it is safe. Like turtles. In our shells we wait for the danger to pass.—I dont wanna do uh shot uh that—dont want em tuh worry. Next, third shot: Here—oh. I will sit. Hands folded. Here I am—no. Arms folded. Next, shot number four. Ready? Hands on books and books open. A full desk and a smiling man. Sergeant Smith has got stacks of papers, but, not to worry, he is a good worker and will do well. Wait. Uh smile. Okay. Go head. Take it. Smiling at work. They like smiles.

(Airplane sounds.)

B.

MRS. SERGEANT SMITH *and* BUFFY. *A lovely home.*

BUFFY. Mommie, what should the Biloxie Twins wear today?

MRS. SMITH. Sumthin nice.

BUFFY. The green one with pink stripes orange and yellow fuzzy sweater sets. Blue coat dresses. Double breasted. Which ones nicest?

MRS. SMITH. They all perm press? Put em in permanent press. You dont want em arrivin wrinkled. I vote for them two sharp little brown n white polka-dotted numbers. Put em both in thuh brown n white dotted swisses.

BUFFY. There iduhnt any brown and white swiss.

MRS. SMITH. Perm press is best. Put em in thuh swiss.

BUFFY. I'll press em with my hands. My hands get as hot as uh iron sometimes, Mommie. Here they go—ssss—tuh! Hot enough! Press press press.

MRS. SMITH. Dont press on thuh desk. Gotta keep your daddys desk nice for im. Use starch? Starch!

BUFFY. Starch—starchstarch! Ooooh—starch made uh tab come off.

MRS. SMITH. Sssokay. Itll hold with three tabs.

BUFFY. What if thuh wind blows her dress? What if three tabs wont hold? She'll be naked. Thuh windll steal her clothes and then she'll be naked.

MRS. SMITH. Ssit pressed? Bring it here. Lemmie feel. Good, Buffiena—

BUFFY. But what if her dress whips off? What if she is

naked? Cant be outside and naked people will see her she'll be shamed—

MRS. SMITH. Good tuh be pressed. Dont like crinkles—

BUFFY. What if thuh wind pulls like this and this and then she is naked and then—

MRS. SMITH. She kin hide behind her twin. They look just alike, dont they. They look just alike then Miss-Naked-Biloxie-with-thuh-three-tabs kin hide behind Miss-Fully-Clothed-Biloxie-with-thuh-four. Nobodyll notice nothin.

BUFFY. Where the Biloxie Twins off to, Mommie?

MRS. SMITH. Off out.

BUFFY. Off out where?

MRS. SMITH. Off out to thuh outside.

BUFFY. Off outside when they go who're they gonna meet?

MRS. SMITH. Their Maker. Theyre gonna meet their Maker. Huh! Sssimportant. Last furlough your daddy had, I tooked you tuh see him. Remember? Two thousand, oh hundred fifty-three stops. Three days on one bus. Was uh local. Missed thuh express. Changed in Castletin. Most folks waited in thuh depot. We waited outside. In thuh snow. Wanted tuh be thuh first tuh see thuh bus round thuh bend. That bus tooked us to thuh coast. Last tuh get on. Sat in thuh—rear. More even ride in thuh rear. Tooked us to thuh coast. Saw your daddy. Remember?

BUFFY. Uh huhn. The Biloxie twins are gonna—

MRS. SMITH. Huh! Good memory you got. —That was before you was born. I tooked you to see your Maker. Put on my green n white striped for thuh busride—it got so crinkled. Had tuh change intuh my brown with thuh white dots. Changed right there on thuh bus. In thuh restroom, of course. Theres some womens thatll change anywheres. With anybody. Not this one. Not this Mrs. Smith. I gotta change my dress I goes to thuh restroom no matter how long thuh line. Goin to thuh mobile restrooms uh privilege, you know. They let me privy to thuh privilege cause I wanted tuh look nice for your daddy. Wanted tuh look like I hadnt traveled uh mile or sweated uh drop.

BUFFY. Biloxie Twinsss gonna wear their brown and whites—

MRS. SMITH. Got off that bus at thuh coast. Sky was shinin. Real blue. Didnt see it. All I seen was him. Mr. Smith. Your daddy. He tooked up my whole eye. "Mrs. Smith!" he yelled, loud enough for everyone tuh hear, "you aint traveled a mile nor sweated a drop!"

BUFFY. You were just as proud.

MRS. SMITH. I was just as proud.

BUFFY. You were just as proud.

MRS. SMITH. I was just as proud. "Aint traveled a mile nor sweated a drop!"

BUFFY. I'm gonna be just as proud.

MRS. SMITH. As what?

BUFFY. —As proud—.

MRS. SMITH. Uh huhnn. We're gonna have us uh big family. Your fathers got uh furlough comin up. Howd you like uh—uh sister, Buffeena?

BUFFY. The Biloxie Twins dont need uh sister cause then they wouldnt be twins.

MRS. SMITH. We can put her in uh bed next tuh yours.

BUFFY. Where would the Biloxie Twins sleep?

MRS. SMITH. Men from thuh Effort come by?

BUFFY. 0800.

MRS. SMITH. Whatja give em.

BUFFY. Thuh floor lamp.

MRS. SMITH. With thuh curlicues? Huh. Dont need it nohow. Whatcha need is uh—uhnother girl. You and her—youll have uh—uh sister. Get your twins off thuh desk, Buffy. Gotta keep it nice for your daddy. Two girlsll make things even. And thuh next time your daddy comes home we'll all do it up in brown and white.

(Airplane sounds rise up.)

C.

MR. SERGEANT SMITH.

SMITH. Here I am on a rock. As you can see, the rock is near water! We of the 20–53rd are closer to water than you can guess. We are in the water! But, we are not on a boat! But, we are not on a submarine! We of the 20–53rd are on an ISLAND!! A big rock in the middle of the ocean. Next time your mother takes you to visit the ocean, Buffeena, look very far out over the water and give me a wave. I will waaaave back! You may have to put on your glasses to see me, and I expect that to you I'll look like just a little speck. But if you look very far, youll see me and if you wave very hard, I will waaaaaaave back! Next time your mother takes you to visit the ocean, Buffeena, throw me a kiss and I will throooooow one back! Now, Buffy, to reach me at the 20–53rd you are going to have to throw me a BIG kiss. Ask your Mother to help you. She will help you just as we here at the 20–53rd help each other, working together, to get the good job done. Here at the 20–53rd different men have different jobs. Some read maps. Some fly airplanes. Some watch guard over our island home. It is my job to keep watch over this rock. The rock I'm standing on right now. Our Commander, the man in charge, likes a clean rock. See my broom? See my mop? It is my job to keep this rock clean! My rock is very clean. My rock is the cleanest of all the rocks on our island home. I make the Commander very happy because I do a good job. I help him and in turn he will help me. My Commander, when the time is right, will reward me for a good job well done. My Commander will award me soon and put me in charge of bigger and more important—more important aspects of our island home. And your daddy will then have his Distinction. And your daddy will then come home. He will come home with bars instead of stripes and you and your Mommie will be just as proud! Well, it is time for work! Your daddy loves you, Buffy, and sends a big kiss and a big smile.

(Airplane sounds rise up.)

D.
    MRS. SMITH, BUFFY, *and* MUFFY. *A lovely home.*
    MUFFY. How come he didnt write tuh me?
    BUFFY. Say "why is it that," Muffy, not "how come."
    MUFFY. Why is that he didnt write tuh me? He didnt include me.

MRS. SMITH. You got thuh ledger, Buffeena? ''Subject'': uh letter. Check thuh ''non bill'' column. ''From'': ? Write—

MUFFY. How come he didnt say Muffy too?

BUFFY. Get out from under the desk, Muff. Mrs. Smith, write ''Sergeant Smith''?

MRS. SMITH. Right.

MUFFY. Duhdunt he know my name? I'm Muffy. Duhdunt he know my name?

BUFFY. ''Contents''?

MUFFY. Duddunt he know me?! I'm Muffy.

MRS. SMITH. Write—uh—''general news.''

BUFFY. General news.

MRS. SMITH. Slash—''Report of duties.''

BUFFY. Good.

MUFFY. He duhdnt like me. Sergeant Smith dudhnt like me, Buffy. He only likes Mrs. Smith he only likes Buffy Smith he only likes his desk. He duduhnt like Muffy. I'm Muffy. He duduhnt like me.

BUFFY. He likes you.

MRS. SMITH. ''Signs of Distinction'': —uh—uh—put ''——.'' Whatd we put last time?

MUFFY. He duhuhunt love me. HE DUDUHNT LOVE HIS DESK!

BUFFY. Helovesyouheloveshisdesk.

MRS. SMITH. I hear you kickin Sergeant Smith's desk, Mufficent! I'm comin over there tuh feel for scuff marks and theyre better not be uh one! ''Signs of Distinction''? Whatd we put last time.

MUFFY. Why dudnt he love me? If he really loved Muffy he'd say Muffy. If he really loved me he would I'm Muffy why dudnt—

BUFFY. Last letters signs of distinction were ''on the horizon.''

MRS. SMITH. Before that?

BUFFY. . . . ''Soon.'' Before that he reported his distinction to be arriving quote any day now unquote.

MUFFY. Mm wearin my brown and white. You said he likes his girls in their brown and whites.

MRS. SMITH. On thuh horizon any day now soon. Huh. You girls know what he told me last furlough? Last fur-

lough I got off that bus and thuh sky was just as blue—
wooo it was uh blue sky. I'd taken thuh bus to thuh coast.
Rode in thuh front seat cause thuh ride was smoother up
in thuh front. Kept my pocketbook on my lap. Was nervous. Asked thuh driver tuh name out names of towns
we didnt stop at. Was uh express. Uh express bus.
"Mawhaven!" That was one place—where we passed
by. Not by but through. "Mawhaven!" Had me uh front
seat. Got to thuh coast. Wearin my brown and white.
"You aint traveled a mile nor sweated a drop!" Thats
exactly how he said it too. Voice tooked up thuh whole
outside couldnt hear nothin else. We got tuh talkin. He
told me that over there, where he's stationed, on his island home, over there they are uh whole day ahead of us.
Their time aint our time. Thuh sun does—tricks—does
tricks n puts us all off schedules. When his times his own
he tries tuh think of what time it is here. For us. And
what we're doin. He's in his quarters stowin away his
checkers game and it's dark but youre whinin out thuh
lumps in your Cream of Wheat, Buffy and Muffy, youre
tearin at your plaits and it's Tuesday mornin and it's yesterday. And thuh breakfast goes cold today. I redo Miss
Muffs head and fasten it with pins but it aint today for
him. Ssstomorrow. Always tomorrow. Iduhnt that somethin?

BUFFY. I'll put "expected." How's that.

MUFFY. I like his desk. I love his desk. I kiss it see?
I hug it. Uuh! Hear me, Mommie, I'm kissing Sergeant
Smiths desk. I am hugging it. Uuuhh! He likes his girls
in their swisses, right? Dont you, Sergeant Smith? I'm
their swisses! I'm their swisses!!

MRS. SMITH. "Mention of work": check "yes."

BUFFY. Check.

MUFFY. "Mention of family": check NO.

MRS. SMITH. Check "yes," Buffeena.

BUFFY. Check.

MUFFY. Did not mention Muffy.

BUFFY. Censors, Muff.

MRS. SMITH. Scissors?

BUFFY. Censors. The Censors—theyre uh family. Like
us. Theyre uh family with Mr. Censor at thuh lead. Mr.

Censor is a man who wont let Sergeant Smith say certain things because certain things said may put the Effort in danger. Certain things said and certain ways of saying certain things may clue-in the enemy. Certain things said may allow them to catch Sergeant Smith unawares. Sergeant Smith, Muff, deals in a language of codes—secret signs and signals. Certain ways with words that are plain to us could, for Sergeant Smith, spell the ways of betrayal, right, Mrs. Smith? Notice he only says "Commander." He isn't allowed to mention his Commander by name. We say "Muffy" every day but for Sergeant Smith saying your name would be gravely dangerous.

MUFFY. Muffys not gravely dangerous.

MRS. SMITH. Muffy—Muffy—Muffy sounds like minefield. Whats uh mine, Mufficent?

MUFFY. A mine is a thing that dismembers. Too many mines lose the war.

MRS. SMITH. Good girl.

MUFFY. Remember the Effort.

MRS. SMITH. Good girl!

BUFFY. We all gotta make sacrifices, Muffy.

MRS. SMITH. Wouldnt uh named you "Muffy," but they hadnt invented mines when you came along.

MUFFY. They name mines after me?

MRS. SMITH. Go put on your brown n white. We're goin tuh thuh beach.

BUFFY. Shes got it on, Mrs. Smith.

MUFFY. Sergeant Smiths comin?!?

MRS. SMITH. Youre not wrinkled are you Mufficent? Comeer. Lemmie feel. Hmmmm. Ssall right. Wouldnt want tuh be crinkly for Sergeant Smith. Huh. I remember when he first saw you. We traveled for miles and—when we walked off that bus! Brown-and-White polka dots uh swiss! Lookin like we hadnt traveled uh mile nor sweated uh drop!

MUFFY. Was he just as proud?

BUFFY. He was.

MRS. SMITH. Your Sergeant ssgonna be furloughin soon. Howd my two girls like uh—uh brother, huh? Seems like three is what this family needs. He always wanted uh—boy. Boy. Men from thuh Effort come by already, huh?

BUFFY. 0800.

MRS. SMITH. Whatyuh give em?

BUFFY. Floor lamp.

MRS. SMITH. Thuh one with thuh green brass base?

BUFFY. And thuh phonograph.

MRS. SMITH. Records too? HHH. Dont need em no how. What we need is uh—

BUFFY. Uh brother.

MRS. SMITH. Uh brother! Your Sergeant Smith ssgonna be furloughin soon. Whatduhyuh say, Buffy? Muffy? Buffy? Muffy?

(Airplane sounds rise up.)

E.

MR. SERGEANT SMITH.

SMITH. I expect it's today for you by now. Last night it comed to me: theres four hours every day that I kin say "today" and youll know what today I mean. We got us whatcha calls "uh overlap." We got us uh overlap of four hours. Times when my days yours—and yours is mines. Them four hours happens real quick and they look just like thuh other twenty-odd so you gotta watch for em real close. That little bit uh knowledge comed tuh me last night. Along with—my Distinction. Mrs. Smith, your Sergeant Smith's now—distinguished. Theyre etchin "Sergeant Smith" on thuh medals right this very moment as I speak I expect. Sssmy desk. Sssmy desk, this. Hhh. I saved uh life, ya know. Not every man kin say that, Mrs. Smith. I know youre gonna be proud. Make no mistake. Just as proud. Just as proud as—. Not every man saves uh life!

(Airplane sounds rise up.)

F.

MRS. SMITH, BUFFY, MUFFY, *and* DUFFY. *A lovely home.*

MRS. SMITH. You ironed thuh Sergeants desk today, Buffeena?

BUFFY. Yes, Mrs. Smith.

MRS. SMITH. Dont want it wrinkled.

BUFFY. No, Mrs. Smith. We'll get him another one tomorrow, K Muff? Duff too.

MRS. SMITH. Another what?

DUFFY. Are turtles mammals, Mommie?

MRS. SMITH. Mammals? Waas uh mammal?

MUFFY. Live births. Nurse their young.

MRS. SMITH. Waas today, Buffeena?

BUFFY. No, Duffy, theyre not mammals. Todays Friday, Mrs. Smith.

MUFFY. Mind if I yo yo, Buff?

BUFFY. Be careful, K?

MRS. SMITH. Be careful of thuh desk. Sergeant Smiths comin home n all we needs for it tuh be scored with your yo yo welts, you!

DUFFY. Sergeant Smith uh mammal?

MRS. SMITH. Waas uh mammal?

MUFFY. Live births—round the world—whooosh!

BUFFY. No, Duffy.

MUFFY. Nurse their young. Whoosh! Whoosh!

MRS. SMITH. Today Friday?

BUFFY. Yes, Mrs. Smith.

DUFFY. He said he was uh turtle.

MRS. SMITH. Turtle?! Todays Friday. Waas uh turtle?

MUFFY. Masquerade as fish, Mrs. Smith. Round the world! Round the world!

MRS. SMITH. They catch on my line when I cast it out. Todays Friday. Fish on Friday. We'll have fish.

BUFFY. When Sergeant Smith said he was uh turtle that was uh figure of speech, Duffy. Sergeant Smith was figuring his speech.

MRS. SMITH. We'll go out. Out. Out. Have fish. Youll wear your swiss, Duffy. Same as us.

DUFFY. How do they breathe?

MRS. SMITH. Same as us.

DUFFY. Underwater?

MRS. SMITH. Same as us. Smiths. Same as us. Sergeant comin. Soon. Today. Sergeant Smiths comin soon today soon.

MUFFY. Soon today today soon on the horizon today

soon on the horizon today soon round the world round the world.

DUFFY. All winter through gills?

BUFFY. In summer they suck up lots of air. They store it. In the winter they use the stored air. Like camels use water.

DUFFY. Camels breathe water? Camels have gills?

MRS. SMITH. Course they got gills. You heard of thuh overlap, aintcha? Overlaps uh gap. Uh gap overlappin. Thuh missin link. Find thuh link. Put out thuh cat. Close thuh kitty cat flap mm feelin uh breeze. Seal up thuh flap mm feelin uh breeze.

BUFFY. Flap is sealed.

MRS. SMITH. Sscold. Mm feelin uh breeze. Mm feelin uh breeze.

MUFFY. She's feeling a breeze we're all gonna freeze round the world round the world.

BUFFY. Flap is sealed.

MUFFY. Round the world.

MRS. SMITH. Look for thuh overlap!

MUFFY. Round the world.

DUFFY. Overlaps uh gap!

BUFFY. Isnt!

DUFFY. Is!

MUFFY. Round the world round the world.

DUFFY. Overlaps uh gap!

BUFFY. Isnt!

DUFFY. Is!

MUFFY. Round the world round the—

MRS. SMITH. FREEZE!

MUFFY. —world.

MRS. SMITH. Sound off.

BUFFY. Buff-y!

MUFFY. Muff-y!

DUFFY. Duff-y!

MRS. SMITH. Mm feelin uh breeze. Stop that yoin, Mufficent, or youll have thuh Sarge tuh answer to. Still. Still thuh breeze. Anyone by at 0800? Whatja give em? Dont need it no how. What we need is uh—. There was uh light in thuh sky last night. Dont suppose no one seen it. You alld gone out. Through thuh gap. I was waitin

up. There was uh light in thuh sky. I stopped. I looked.
I heard. Uh man was fallin fallin aflame. Fallin at mid-
night. There wasnt uh sun. He was comin from another
world. I stopped. I looked. I heard but couldnt do nothin.
It all happened so far away. It all happened before you
was born. Go put on your brown and white, son. The
Sergeant likes his family in their brown and whites.

MUFFY. Walk thuh dog.

MUFFY. Walking the dog walking the dog.

MRS. SMITH. Thuh Sergeantll want to see things in
order. Nothin more orderly than uh walked dog.

MUFFY. Walk the dog. Walk the dog. Round the world.
Walk the dog.

MRS. SMITH. Stand me in my walker. Go on—my
walker, private! Sarge is comin, gotta snap to attention.

DUFFY. Turtles lay eggs in thuh sand at night. Then
they go away. How do they know which ones are theirs?
Which eggs? Thuh eggs hatch and thuh baby turtles go
crawlin out into thuh sea. How do thuh parents know em?
How do thuh parents know em, Buff?

BUFFY. I dont think they much care.

MRS. SMITH. TEN-SHUN!

SMITH. Hello, honey. I'm home.

BUFFY. Daddy is home!

MUFFY. Daddy is home!

DUFFY. Daddy is home!

BUFFY/MUFFY/DUFFY. Hello, Daddy!

MRS. SMITH. Hello, Mr. Smith. How was your day?

SMITH. Just fine, Mrs. Smith. Give me uh kiss. Why,
Mrs. Smith, youve lost your eyes. Youve lost your eyes,
Mrs. Smith. When did you lose your eyes?

BUFFY. What did you bring me, Daddy?

MRS. SMITH. For years. I had em lost for years.

SMITH. When?

MRS. SMITH. YEARS. Years uhgo.

MUFFY. What did you bring me, Daddy?

SMITH. Shoulda wroten.

DUFFY. What did you bring me, Daddy?

SMITH. Shoulda called.

BUFFY. Daddy promised me uh china doll!

SMITH. Shoulda given me some kinda notice, Mrs.

Smith. Iduhnt no everyday uh wife loses her eyes. Where did you lose them and when did they go? Why havent we ordered replacements? I woulda liked tuh hear uhbout that.

Mrs. Smith. Thought theyd come back afore you did. Shoulda informed me you was stoppin by.

Smith. I wrote. I called.

Buffy. I'll get thuh ledger.

Mrs. Smith. What do you think of our brown and whites, Mr. Smith?

Smith. Who're you uhgain?

Duffy. Duffy. You promised me an airplane.

Muffy. I'm Muffy.

Mrs. Smith. You are Mr. Smith. You are our Mr. Smith? What do you think of our brown and whites, our Mr. Smith?

Duffy. I'm your spittin image. Did you bring my airplane?

Smith. I was uh fine lookin man—like you—once. I got pictures. Uh whole wallet full. There. Thats me.

Duffy. Nope. Thats me. We look uhlike.

Buffy. They took thuh ledger. Thuh ledger was in thuh desk.

Mrs. Smith. Ssstoo bad. We needs documentation. Proof.

Smith. I wrote! I called!

Mrs. Smith. Theres lots uh Smiths. Many Smiths. Smithsss common name.

Duffy. You promised me uh air-o-plane!

Smith. I visited. We had us uh family. Thats proof.

Mrs. Smith. Lots uh visits. Lots uh families.

Smith. I got my Distinction. See? Here are my medals here in my name. They let me be uh Mister. Mr. Smiths got his bars!

Mrs. Smith. Distinction? Waas uh distinction?

Buffy. You promised me uh Chinese doll.

Smith. Uh distinctions when ones set upart. Uh distinctions when they give ya bars. Got my bars! See?

Mrs. Smith. Lemmie feel.

Smith. I saved uh life! Caught uh man as he was fallin out thuh sky!

MRS. SMITH. You catched uh man? Out thuh sky? I seen uh light last night. In thuh sky. From uhnother world. I dont suppose you catched it. Dont suppose youre our distinctioned Mr. Smith?

SMITH. Was standin on my rock. I stopped. I heard. I seen him fallin—

MUFFY. You stepped on a mine. I read it in the paper. A mine is a thing that remembers. Too many mines lose the war. Remember the Effort. The mine blew his legs off.

SMITH. You one uh mines?

BUFFY. He lost his legs.

SMITH. You one uh mines?

DUFFY. He lost thuh war.

SMITH. You one uh mines?

MRS. SMITH. Why, Mr. Smith, youve lost your legs, why, Mr. Smith, youve lost thuh war. When did you lose your legs, Mr. Smith, Mr. Smith, when did you lose thuh war? Men come by at 0800. What do we give em? What we dont need nohow. BuffyMuffyDuffy? Your father's got hisself uh furlough comin up soon. Thats just what we need. Uhnother boy. Always thought things should come in fours. Fours. Fours. All fours. I'll put it to him when he comes home. Whatduhyasay?

DUFFY. Are we turtles? Are we turtles, Mr. Smith?

BUFFY. Duffy—

SMITH. No. No—uh—boy we iduhnt turtles. We'se slugs. We'se slugs.

(Airplane noises rise up.)

G.

MR. SMITH.

SMITH. Always wanted to do me somethin noble. Not somethin better than what I deserved—just somethin noble. Uh little bit uh noble somethin. Like what they did in thuh olden days. Like in thuh olden days in olden wars. Time for noble seems past. Time for somethin noble was yesterday. There usta be uh overlap of four hours. Hours in four when I'd say "today" and today itd be. Them four hours usta happen together, now, they scatters theirselves all throughout thuh day. Usta be uh flap tuh slip through. Flaps gone shut. I saw that boy fallin out thuh sky. On fire. Thought he was uh star. Uh star that died years uhgo but was givin us light through thuh flap. Made uh wish. Opened up my arms—was wishin for my whole family. He fell on me. They say he was flyin too close to thuh sun. They say I caught him but he fell. On me. They gived me uh distinction. They set me apart. They say I caught him but he fell. He fell on me. I broked his fall. I saved his life. I aint seen him since. No, boy— Duffy—uh—Muffy, Buffy, no, we aint even turtles. Huh. We'se slugs. Slugs. Slugs.

(Airplane sounds rise up.)

Samuel Beckett

Ohio Impromptu

SAMUEL Beckett and a friend once went for a walk—
or so the story goes—and Beckett exclaimed, "What
a lovely day!" "It's the kind of day," his friend replied,
"that makes you glad to be alive!" "Ah," Beckett mur-
mured, "I wouldn't go so far as to say *that*."

Among the many clichés surrounding Beckett, the most
persistent, and the most inaccurate, is that his work is
pervaded by gloom. He was preoccupied with the inevi-
tability of death, certainly, obsessed with the inexorable
passage of time, haunted by memories of loss. But this
poet of loneliness and grief was also suffused with a kind
of patient serenity, blessed with an eschatological wit,
and enamored of the gorgeous expressiveness of language.

Another cliché frequently applied to Beckett is that his
plays are "difficult." But the more familiar his work becomes, the more obvious it is that his major innovation
was a radical *simplification* of theatrical conventions, eliminating everything he considered superfluous—traditional
forms of narrative and characterization in particular—and
focusing only on the irreducible elements of drama, image, actor, and mystery. At first, audiences were bewil-
dered, not by the complexities of what he'd added but by
the absence of what he'd subtracted. With none of the familiar theatrical conventions remaining between theatergoer and stage, they looked so intensely for what wasn't
there that they couldn't see what was. Within a decade,
however, plays that had seemed impenetrable to the most
sophisticated intellectuals became accessible to the most
callow freshmen. (Among the first theatergoers to appreciate *Waiting for Godot*, in fact, were uneducated prison

inmates. Not taught what to expect of theater, they weren't confused by what he'd omitted but simply experienced what was taking place in front of their eyes.)

In the sculpted tableau of *Ohio Impromptu*, only a few things are "clear." The two characters are so similar in appearance they're virtually two aspects of a single person—there's only one hat on the table, and the two arms of "the receding stream" "conflowed and flowed united on." The Reader, near the end of his days, is reading from a volume very much like the book of life, or perhaps from the collected works of a writer much like Beckett himself—"Little is left to tell" is the first sentence of the play, "Nothing is left to tell" the last. The Listener interrupts the Reader several times with knocks on the table—at first the Reader goes back a phrase or two to repeat what he's already read before resuming the text, but the last time the knock is greeted by silence. Finally, the play concerns the search for solace against the "terror of night"—"a last attempt to obtain relief," "his slow steps retrace," the repeated appearance of a man "to comfort you"—until finally comes the dawn that "shed no light."

Yet these few certainties serve only as the ground for overriding *uncertainties*, for the intimations, for the evocations, for the vibrations that constitute the emotional texture of the play—and of life itself. So many questions can be asked of this so short play. What is the relationship between the two characters? Who is the visitor and to whom does "the dear name" refer? What solace can we find for our lost loves and dwindling lives? But of course there are no answers, or rather, whatever answers we supply are at best only the most tentative of guesses, the dimmest of glimpses. On one level, among the multiplicity of possibilities, the play concerns a bereaved lover, on another the playwright's creation of a listening self (as in *Krapp's Last Tape*), on yet another the existence of the soul, the reappearance of Christ, and the consolations of religion—yet these guesses, these glimpses, remain enigmas that can never be explained.

Intimations, evocations, vibrations—eloquently but unsparingly, Beckett tells us that we can know nothing of the repeated cycles of life, the same old "sad tales" told over and over and over again, except that they eventually cease. Beckett's supreme artistry lay in his articulation of the unfathomable silence at the heart of existence. "No, not thoughts," he writes, "profounds of mind."

SAMUEL BECKETT, novelist and playwright, was awarded the Nobel Prize for Literature in 1969. Several of his plays have won Obies, including *Endgame, Krapp's Last Tape,* and *Happy Days.*

Ohio Impromptu was produced by Lucille Lortel at The Harold Clurman Theatre, in New York, on June 15, 1983. It was directed by Alan Schneider and had the following cast:

READER..................................... *David Warrilow*
LISTENER.................................... *Rand Mitchell*

L = *Listener*
R = *Reader*
As alike in appearance as possible.
Light on table midstage. Rest of stage in darkness. Plain white deal table, say 8' × 4'. Two plain armless white deal chairs.
L *seated at table facing towards end of long side audience right. Bowed head propped on right hand. Face hidden. Left hand on table. Long black coat. Long white hair.*
R *seated at table in profile center of short side audience right. Bowed head propped on right hand. Left hand on table. Book on table before him open at last pages. Long black coat. Long white hair.*
Black wide-brimmed hat at center of table.
Fade up.
Ten seconds.
R *turns page.*
Pause.
R. *(Reading.)* Little is left to tell. In a last—
*(**L** knocks with left hand on table.)*
Little is left to tell.
(Pause. Knock.)
In a last attempt to obtain relief he moved from where they had been so long together to a single room on the far bank. From its single window he could see the downstream extremity of the Isle of Swans.
(Pause.)
Relief he had hoped would flow from unfamiliarity. Unfamiliar room. Unfamiliar scene. Out to where nothing ever shared. Back to where nothing ever shared. From this he had once half hoped some measure of relief might flow.
(Pause.)
Day after day he could be seen slowly pacing the islet. Hour after hour. In his long black coat no matter what the weather and old world Latin Quarter hat. At the tip he would always pause to dwell on the receding stream. How in joyous eddies its two arms conflowed and flowed united on. Then turn and his slow steps retrace.
(Pause.)

In his dreams—

(Knock.)

Then turn and his slow steps retrace.

(Pause. Knock.)

In his dreams he had been warned against this change. Seen the dear face and heard the unspoken words. Stay where we were so long alone together, my shade will comfort you.

(Pause).

Could he not—

(Knock.)

Seen the dear face and heard the unspoken words. Stay where we were so long alone together, my shade will comfort you.

(Pause. Knock.)

Could he not now turn back? Acknowledge his error and return to where they were once so long alone together. Alone together so much shared. No. What he had done alone could not be undone. Nothing he had ever done alone could ever be undone. By him alone.

(Pause.)

In this extremity his old terror of night laid hold on him again. After so long a lapse that as if never been. *(Pause. Looks closer.)* Yes, after so long a lapse that as if never been. Now with redoubled force the fearful symptoms described at length page forty paragraph four. *(Starts to turn back the pages. Checked by L's left hand. Resumes relinquished page.)* White nights now again his portion. As when his heart was young. No sleep no braving sleep till—*(turns page)*—dawn of day.

(Pause.)

Little is left to tell. One night—

(Knock.)

Little is left to tell.

(Pause. Knock.)

One night as he sat trembling head in hands from head to foot a man appeared to him and said, I have been sent by—and here he named the dear name—to comfort you. Then drawing a worn volume from the pocket of his long black coat he sat and read till dawn. Then disappeared without a word.

(Pause.)

Some time later he appeared again at the same hour with the same volume and this time without preamble sat and read it through again the long night through. Then disappeared without a word.

(Pause.)

So from time to time unheralded he would appear to read the sad tale through again and the long night away. Then disappear without a word.

(Pause.)

With never a word exchanged they grew to be as one.

(Pause.)

Till the night came at last when having closed the book and dawn at hand he did not disappear but sat on without a word.

(Pause.)

Finally he said, I have had word from—and here he named the dear name—that I shall not come again. I saw the dear face and heard the unspoken words. No need to go to him again, even were it in your power.

(Pause.)

So the sad—

(Knock.)

Saw the dear face and heard the unspoken words. No need to go to him again, even were it in your power.

(Pause. Knock.)

So the sad tale a last time told they sat on as though turned to stone. Through the single window dawn shed no light. From the street no sound of reawakening. Or was it that buried in who knows what thoughts they paid no heed? To light of day. To sound of reawakening. What thoughts who knows. Thoughts, no, not thoughts. Profounds of mind. Buried in who knows what profounds of mind. Of mindlessness. Whither no light can reach. No sound. So sat on as though turned to stone. The sad tale a last time told.

(Pause.)

Nothing is left to tell.

*(Pause. **R** makes to close book.*
Knock. Book half-closed.)

Nothing is left to tell.

(Pause. **R** *closes book.*
Knock.
Silence. Five seconds.
Simultaneously they lower their right hands to table,
raise their heads and look at each other. Unblinking.
Expressionless.
Ten seconds.
Fade out.)

Eric Bogosian

Sex, Drugs, Rock & Roll

"PERFORMANCE art" was perhaps the most overhyped and ill-defined theatrical trend of the eighties. If, by the end of the decade, it appeared to be little more than a voguish name for solo performers, many of whom were essentially stand-up comics in a dramatic context—and if, in retrospect, its motivation seems as much economic as aesthetic, allowing underfunded theaters to cut expenses to the marrow—still, at its best, as in the monologues of Eric Bogosian, performance art was a significant expression of personal vision in a theater scene too often dominated by commercial comedies, mercenary melodramas, and computer-activated musicals.

Many monologists perform stereotypical characters from the outside, distancing themselves from their maligned creations, satirizing their shabby values without any sense of complicity. Bogosian's genius is not merely to invent a wide range of personae—in *Sex, Drugs, Rock & Roll,* a pathologically self-effacing panhandler, an ego-bloated rock star, a debris-obsessed derelict, a loonily self-destructive urban redneck, a maniacally phone-wielding executive, an artist slowly sinking into a kind of mellow paranoia, and several more—but to inhabit them from the *inside,* to embody them with the same self-satisfaction they bestow upon their own lives, to express their values with wholehearted conviction. Paradoxically, this "honoring" of his characters makes them more horrifying, for in seeing them as wholly rounded people rather than as stick-figure targets, Bogosian reveals the full scope of their anger, their fear, their *danger.*

In another paradox, Bogosian focuses on characters at the top and bottom of the social scale in order to explore the emotional impulses and psychological conflicts of the vast majority in the middle—including not only his audience but himself. "I've spent most of my life stuck between idealism and hedonism," Bogosian has written, "between selfishness and selflessness, between love and sex, between chaos and clarity. . . . I write about those things I can't figure out. The monologues in *Sex, Drugs, Rock & Roll* are my open meditation on the conflicts in my life. They are an attempt to take the nasty sides of myself and put them out there for everyone to see. . . . I take a good look at myself by grabbing the disturbing traits and personifying them in a character. . . . Then I slam one character up against the next and hope that some kind of meditation will evolve. Provocation in the guise of a good time."

In yet another paradox, Bogosian stresses the monstrous self-infatuation of his characters in order to expose their hypocrisies, insecurities, and self-doubts. Over and over they insist on their honesty—"Drugs are no good for anybody," says the rock star who lived for years loaded to the gills, and "Would I lie to you?" asks the executive immediately before lying. And over and over they reveal the scary ambiguities beneath their gloating self-assurance—"Don't make no difference," says the man reduced to collecting bottles for a living, and "Feeling good makes me feel good" smirks a man after committing murder with a screwdriver.

In a sense, the secret of Bogosian's success is that as a writer he dislikes his characters but that as a performer he loves them—that as a writer he exposes their greed, cruelty, and immorality but that as a performer he relishes their idioms, their vitality, their excess. The tension between these two attitudes releases the hilarious and terrifying ironies of his work, creating a compelling composite of our culture at once morally scathing and theatrically exhilarating, revealing its bottom-line materialism, savage sexuality, testosterone violence, and me-first morality.

Scariest of all, in the words of one of Bogosian's alter

egos, "the only difference between you and me is that you're on the ups and I'm on the downs." Anything else, as another puts it, is just "icing on the gravy."

Sex, Drugs, Rock & Roll is only one of several performance art pieces written and performed by ERIC BOGOSIAN in the last decade—others include *Funhouse, Men Inside,* and *Drinking in America.* Bogosian has also written a play, *Talk Radio,* which was turned into a film by Oliver Stone. Bogosian himself played the leading role in both versions.

Sex, Drugs, Rock & Roll had a workshop at P.S. 122 in New York and was produced at the Orpheum Theatre on February 8, 1990, directed by Jo Bonney.

(Lights go down.
An amplified voice is heard. A raucous deejay.)
Hey, you're listening to WRXX, the home of hard rock and roll! I don't know about you, but I want to *party*, I want to rock the house, I want to take care of business—if you know what I mean, and I hope you do! So buckle your belts, grab your hats, zip your pants, and hoist your bats—we got some rockin' to do too-night!
(Amplified hard rock blasts at the audience.
A man appears in silhouette, holding a stick.
He begins a frenzied ''air guitar'' mime to the music.
The lights change. The man is hobbling toward the audience on the stick. . . .
Segue . . .)

Grace of God

(A man is revealed hobbling on a cane, holding an empty paper cup; he addresses the audience.)

Good afternoon, ladies and gentlemen. I only want a few minutes of your time. It doesn't cost you anything to listen. Please be patient with me.

I just got released from Riker's Island, where I was unjustly incarcerated for thirty days for acts I committed during a nervous breakdown due to a situation beyond my control. I am not a drug addict.

This is the situation: I need your money. I could be out robbing and stealing right now; I don't want to be doing that. I could be holding a knife up to your throat right now; I don't want to be doing that. . . . And I'm sure you don't want that, either.

I didn't choose this life. I want to work. But I can't. My medication costs over two thousand dollars a week, of which Medicaid only pays one-third. I am forced to go down to the Lower East Side and buy illegal drugs to stop the pain. I am not a drug addict.

If you give me money, if you help me out, I might be able to find someplace to live. I might be able to get my life back together. It's really all up to you.

Bad things happen to good people. Bad situations beyond my control forced me onto the streets into a life of crime. I won't bore you with the details right now. But if you don't believe me, you can call my parole officer, Mr. Vincent Gardello. His home number is 555-1768.

The only difference between you and me is that you're on the ups and I'm on the downs. Underneath it all, we're exactly the same. We're both human beings. I'm a human being.

I'm a victim of a sick society. I come from a dysfunctional family. My father was an alcoholic. My mother tried to control me. My sister thinks she's an actress. You wouldn't want the childhood that I had.

The world is really screwed up. Things get worse every day. Now is your chance to *do* something about it . . . help out somebody standing right in front of you instead of worrying about South fuckin' Africa ten thousand miles away. Believe me when I tell you God is watching you when you help someone less fortunate than yourself, a human being, like me.

I'm sorry my clothes aren't clean. I'm sorry I'm homeless. I'm sorry I don't have a job. I'm sorry I have to interrupt your afternoon. But I have no choice, I have to ask for help. I can't change my life—you can. Please, please look into your hearts and do the right thing! . . . Thank you.

(He addresses people in the front row, begging to one or two while holding out his cup, saying "Thank you very much, God bless you" repeatedly. If money is given, he says, "Stay guilty." If money is withheld, he says, "I really feel sorry for you, man." Finally, he leaves, repeating over and over again, "Thank you, God bless you" . . . segueing into the "Thank you"'s that begin the next piece.)

Benefit

(The "thank you"'s from the last segment introduce this segment as a man addresses an imaginary "host" on-stage, then seats himself in a chair stage left. His accent is "British.")

Thank you, Bill, thank you. . . .
(Sits, attaches lavaliere microphone to shirt.)
Yes, yes, yes, yes, yes, yes . . . we're very excited about the success of the new album. It's nice having a number-one album again, you know, considering the band really hasn't done anything for about ten years . . . it's a real breath of fresh air. . . .
(Picks up a glass of water from a small table on his left, sips the water.)
No . . . I don't, Bill . . . and I'm glad you asked me that question. . . .

(Returns the glass of water and picks up a pack of cigarettes and a lighter; taps out a cigarette as he speaks.)

I used to do quite a few drugs. . . . But you know, Bill, drugs are no good for anybody. I've seen a lot of people get really messed up on drugs, I've seen people die on drugs. . . .

(Lights cigarette, inhales deeply.)

I was saying to Trevor just the other day—I said, "Trevor, how is it that we managed to survive?" After Jimi died and Janis died and John died, I said to myself, "Why didn't *we* die?'' We shoulda died. All the stuff we used to do.

Yes, Bill, I was. I was a bona fide drug addict. I used drugs every single day for five years.

What was it like? Well, I tell you, Bill. I used to get up every morning, before I even brushed my teeth, I would smoke a joint. While I was smoking the joint, I'd pop a beer. While I was sipping the beer, I'd cook up a spoon of cocaine, heroin—whatever was lying around. Shoot it right into my arm, get completely wasted. . . . Flip on the telly, get high some more . . . maybe order up some lunch . . . have some girls over, get high with them . . . fool around with the girls, get high some more.

I did that every single day for five years.

It was horrible . . . it was horrible. . . . I mean, it was wonderful too, in its own way. I won't lie to you, Bill— my life is based on honesty today.

Yes, we did . . . we saw many tragic consequences. People very close to us. We had a sound engineer who had major problems with drugs . . . Hoover, we called him. His problem was that he wasn't just our sound engineer, he was also in charge of getting the drugs for the band, because we always used to get very high whenever we cut an album. And I'll never forget, we were cutting the *Wild Horses* album, and Hoover shows up—

Oh, thank you, Bill . . . yes, it is a great album. A real rock classic.

—So we're cutting *Wild Horses*, and Hoover shows up with a coffee can full of the most amazing white flake Peruvian cocaine . . . absolutely pure, very wonderful. . . . I don't know if you've ever done white flake Peruvian, Bill, but it's an experience.

Wouldn't mind having a little bit of it right now! (*Laughs out loud, then remembers the audience.*) Just joking, just joking!

So we took that can of cocaine, dumped it onto a table in the middle of the studio, cut out some lines two, three feet long. . . . Hoover would do three or four in each nostril . . . what a beast. Don't know where he had room in his skull for the stuff.

And we started to play. . . .

Of course, in those days we didn't just do coke. We did everything—it was heaven! Trevor was smoking Afghani hash round the clock. Nigel was in his crystal meth period, so we had that. Ronnie showed up with a large bottle of NyQuil. We were blind, we were so high . . . completely wasted.

And we started to play, and you know, Bill, we never played better. It was like we all had ESP; it was historic. . . . Myself, I looked down at my fingers and I'm thinking, "It's not me playing this guitar, it's not me playing this guitar. It's God playing." . . . It was awe-inspiring.

(*Long pause, loses his train of thought.*) What was I talking about? . . . Oh right—Hoover!

So we're playing this brilliant music for about an hour, and I happened to look up and there's Hoover in the sound booth, and well . . . he was smashing his head up against the glass. Blood is running down off his forehead all over his nose. His nose is all red with blood. Cocaine is shooting out of his nostrils onto his beard. His beard was all white. He looked like a deranged Sandy Claus.

Well, see, the thing is, the thing is, he forgot to push the "record" button. And he went completely stark raving mad. They had to take him away in a straitjacket. Took him to a sanitarium.

And the sad thing is, Bill, he was one of my closest friends in the whole world.

(*Puts out cigarette.*)

What's that? . . . No . . . no . . . I don't know where he is today. I know he's somewhere. Probably still in an institution somewhere. . . . Maybe he's watching right now.

Hoover, if you're watching . . . (*Makes a thumbs-up gesture to an imaginary TV camera, then laughs.*)

You see, Bill, that's the insidious thing about drugs—you don't realize . . . uh . . . I mean, you're having such a good time, you don't realize what a bad time you're having.

I got straight while I was on tour. Woke up one morning . . . typical tour situation: luxury hotel room, I don't even know where I am . . . beautiful naked girl lying next to me in the bed, I don't know who she is, I don't know how she got there . . . champagne bottles all over the floor, cocaine on every horizontal surface. I hardly have the strength to pick up my head. So I pick up the remote control and I flip on the telly.

And I was saved, Bill, I was saved.

You have a man on in this country, on TV all the time. Saved my life. White hair. A genius . . . Donahue, Donahue was on. . . . What he said really hit me. He said: "If you haven't met your full potential in this life, you're not really alive." The profoundness struck me like a thunderbolt. I thought, "That man is talking about me. He's talking about me."

Because here I was, young, talented, intelligent, wealthy, good-looking, very intelligent . . . and what am I doing with my life? I'm on drugs, day and night. I mean, I can understand if you're talking about some Negro guy or Puerto Rican guy in the ghetto on drugs—I can understand that. But in my case it was such a tragedy when you think about it. Such a waste of human potential. Such a waste.

Because, Bill, you can have your caviar breakfast, lunch, and dinner, you can have your stretch limousines, your Concorde flights back and forth to London. Wads of cash, everyone treating you like God. Women willing to do whatever you want them to do . . . wherever you want them to do it. House in London, house in L.A., apartment in New York . . . home in the Bahamas . . .

Bill, if it doesn't mean anything, what's the point?

You know what I'm saying?

Maybe not.

I straightened up and I went cold turkey. Had all my blood changed. And I feel like I've been reborn. I can say today, "I like myself today. I'm not such a bad guy, in fact, I'm an amazingly wonderful human being." I'm honest enough to say that today. I've really come to terms with my own brilliance—it's not a burden anymore.

The rest of the band got straight too, and today, we're

just one big happy family. We just want to help other people.

Yes, yes . . . Well, that's why we're doing the benefit to aid the Amazonian Indians. I think they're Indians . . . the people down there in the Amazon . . . that we're helping . . . in the jungle . . . whatever. . . .

Yes! Well, Trevor has a home down in Rio, we go there every winter when it's summer down there. He has this lovely houseboy takes care of the house for him—Nacho, we call him. He's actually not a boy; he's about fifty or so . . . lovely little guy, very brown, always smiling, very helpful.

Nacho knew we were into the environment, so he hired a boat to take up the Amazon, take a look at the birds and the trees and the flowers and all that shit. . . . So we're going along in this boat and we come to a turn in the river and there was this clearing, turned out it was an Indian village . . . whatever, and we all got out and took a walk around.

Bill, I've never seen such depressing poverty . . . the children running around barefoot with the dogs in the dirt, they have no shoes . . . the women, half naked, breast-feeding their infants straight from their breasts. . . . No running water. Couldn't even get a glass of water. I was parched. No Coke, no Pepsi.

The chief of the whole village came out to greet us. Man owned no clothing whatsoever. Completely naked— everything's showing, his willy hanging out and everything. All he had on was this carved piece of wood on his head with a feather sticking out.

Couldn't even speak English. It was heartbreaking.

I turned to Trevor and I said, "Trevor, we have to do something about this. We have to help these people. It's up to us, after all—'We are the world,' so to speak."

And so we decided to do the benefit. Now, I hate to say this, but so many of these benefits, they're just ego trips. They raise the money and just throw it at these people. Well, these poor buggers are primitive people— they've never seen money before. They don't know what to do with money. We found when we were down there that there were many things we had they really liked:

digital wristwatches, Sony Walkmans, cigarette lighters, cigarettes . . . they love cigarettes.

So we're going to be buying these things for them up here with the money. Shipping them down. Try to improve their lives in a substantial way. Do some good for a change.

Thank you, Bill, thank you. It's nothing. . . .

So I hope everyone watching can tune in when we're on MTV. Brought to you by Kronenbrau Beer, Remington Cigarettes. . . . Have to say it, Bill, have to say it—sorry! The cigarette people have been fantastic, donated a truckload of cigarettes to hand out to the Indians. . . . Or buy the album when it comes out. And remember that for every dollar you donate, fully twenty percent goes directly to the Amazonian Indians.

Bill, I'd like to say one more thing about drugs if I may.

A lot of the kids watching right now buy our albums, learn the lyrics, memorize them, live their lives by them. So I know that everything I have to say is very, very important. And I'd like to say this about drugs:

(He looks directly and "meaningfully" at the audience.)

I've done a lot of drugs. I had a lot of adventures on drugs. Some of my music has been inspired by drugs. In fact, I think it's safe to say I had some of the best times of my life on drugs.

That doesn't mean *you* have to do them.

We were recently invited to the White House to do a special concert for Vice-President Quayle and his lovely wife, Marilyn.

Oh, yes, she's hot . . . she's very hot. *(Aside.)* I'll tell you a little story when we get off the air. . . .

He's a wonderful man who, whatever you think of him publicly, in person is a very caring, very sensitive, very intelligent man.

He shared something with us that I would like to share with all of you tonight: The next time someone offers drugs, remember you can always just . . . turn them

Thank you, Bill. Good night.

(Stands and gives the peace sign.)

Cheers.

(Walks off.)

Dirt

(A man shuffles and rants, scratching and coughing, grumbling in a gruff derelict's voice.)

Fuckin' ya shit fuck piss, ya shit fuck piss, ya shit fuck piss . . . *(Coughs and spits, points at the ground.)* What's that? What's that? It's shit, that's what it is. . . . Shit on the ground, shit in the air, it's a bunch of shit if you ask me! You know what I'm talking about, you know what I'm talking about—we're living in a human garbage can, that's what I'm talking about . . . we're living in a human sewer. . . .

(Back to the audience, he picks at the crack in the seat of his pants, talking continuously.)

You can't walk down the street without stepping in some garbage, some dog mess, lumps and smears everywhere ya go . . . some cat piss . . . everything's drenched in piss. Pools of piss. Streams of piss. Rivers of piss. Rivers . . . rivers, the rivers!

The rivers are polluted. They are! You know what I'm talking about. . . . And where do the rivers come from, huh? They come out of the mountains, and the mountains are full of hikers and hunters and cross-country skiers. What are they doing? Pissing on every tree, shitting behind every bush. What do they care? Trees are gonna die from the acid rain anyway!

But you know what happens? You know what happens?

(He indicates his storytelling with a kind of energetic mime.)

The acid rain, the acid rain runs down the tree and mixes with the piss and it makes a little brook and the little brooks flow into little streams. And the streams—where's the stream go, huh? Streams go down by the condos, where the pipes come out filled with more piss and shit and soap suds and tampons and puke from the drunken parties they have on Saturday night 'cause the houses are so ugly they have to be drunk just to live in 'em.

And the streams pour into the rivers and the rivers go by the factories, where they got bigger pipes spewing out chemicals and compounds and compost and arsenic and . . . and NutraSweet . . . and all that goes into the river.

And then the river gets bigger and it goes by the *city,* where they got even bigger pipes choked with all the slop from millions of toilets and garbage disposals and hospital bed pans and laundromats and car washes and fried-chicken places and pizza parlors and whorehouses and Ukrainian restaurants. . . . And all this goes into the river, and the river goes down to the ocean.

And the ocean! What's the ocean? The ocean is just one big oil slick with all this shit being poured into it. But if that isn't enough—no, no, no . . .

(Scratches and coughs.)

. . . they gotta drag out these giant garbage scows filled with tons of burning plastic bags of garbage—they drag those around for a couple of months until they stink and are full of maggots and mildew and dump those in too.

And then rich guys ride around in their pleasure boats with their fishing poles and they're drinking their beers and getting drunk and throwin' the empties over the side and pissing over the side and then they get seasick and puke up their steak tartare and caviar and crème brulée and their pâté! *(He pretends to vomit over the edge of the stage.) Braaaaaaahhhhhhh!!!!!* And all this stuff is going into the water!

And what else is in the water? Huh?

Fishies, that's what.

Millions and millions of little fishies are swimming

around trying to get past the chicken bones and the orange peels and the syringes, and the little balled-up pieces of toilet paper floating by get stuck in their eye! They can't even see, there's so much stuff down there!

And they want to wipe their eyes but they can't 'cause they don't got hands, they got fins. . . . So they go up to the top of the water to look around and they get all covered with oil and it goes in their gills and their hair and they get all greasy and they drown. . . .

And this seagull is flying by and he sees this greasy little fish floating there, so he comes down to get a free meal . . . oooops! Now he's stuck in the oil too! And then a seal, he sees the seagull, now he's stuck in the oil too, he drowns! Then the polar bear, he sees the seal, comes to eat him, he's stuck in the oil too! Then . . . then the lion comes to eat the polar bear, he gets stuck in the oil too. . . .

And there you have it! That's the ocean: just a giant vat of oil, garbage, and dead animals . . . just sloshing around there.

And then a hurricane comes. Then a tidal wave comes. And the whole mess splashes all over the beaches.

And there you've got it. That's it. Millions and millions of dead fishes all over the beaches. . . .

(Pause.)

And then you know what happens?

The rats come, the rats come and they eat the fishies . . . and then, then the cats come and they eat the rats! And then the dogs come and they eat the cats! And then the dogs—you know what the dogs do?

You know what they do! They shit all over the place, that's what they do!

Dog shit, horse shit, pigeon shit, rat shit. You can't go down the street without steppin' in something! *(Mumbling.)* Fuckin' shit fuck piss. Shit fuck piss . . .

(He notices something on his foot, scrapes his foot on the edge of the stage.)

We're living in a human cesspool, we're living in a human septic tank. Living in a human toilet.

You know what I say? Flush the toilet, that's what I say! Flush the toilet! Flush the toilet!

That's what I say!

(He hobbles upstage, back to the audience.)

That's what I say . . .

(In the darkness, he vomits.)

BRAAAHHHHHHHHHGGGGGH!

The Stud

(A man speaks directly to the audience in a slow, easy-going drawl. He's drinking from a long-necked beer bottle.)

Sometimes, when I'm in a bar, having a drink with some fellas, one will make an idle comment like "How does that guy do it? He always gets the girls!"

I remain quiet when I hear such remarks. I like to keep a low profile with regard to my "extracurricular activities." I don't need to advertise. I know what I've got. And the ladies . . . hell, they know better than I do.

I'm not so good-lookin'. I was athletic when I was younger, but I'm no Mr. Universe. I'm medium height, medium weight. Never really excelled at anything, certainly not school. As far as my job goes, they can all screw themselves.

But you know what? I don't give a shit. 'Cause I've got what every guy—and every woman—wants. And all the looks, brains, money in the world can't buy it.

I'm "endowed."

(Takes a swig from his bottle.)

I've got a long, thick, well-shaped prick. The kind girls die for.

You're laughing. So what? Fuck you. Facts are facts. I'll hang out in some bar down on Wall Street around six o'clock, and in they all come, the guys with their health-club bodies and expensive Italian suits. Trying to compensate. The women—smart, fresh, pretty. I especially like the ones with the big bow ties and the Adidas sneakers.

I pick out the prettiest one in the room. We start talking about this or that. I act like I'm going to buy her a drink, then save myself the money and say: "Why don't we get the hell out of here?"

Two hours later, I'm in some strange bedroom, blowin' smoke rings at the ceiling.

(He takes a swig from the bottle, puts it down on the floor.)

They love to tell me about their boyfriends and husbands. What wonderful men they are. So nice, so gentle, so dependable . . . so boring.

And they love to tell me what a wonderful cock I've got. So big, so hard, so unlike anything they've got at home. And they love to beg for more . . . and I love to give it to 'em.

Ever see a girl cry 'cause she's so happy? Ever have a girl beg to tear your clothes off? Ever see a woman faint because she's had such an intense orgasm?

(Scans the audience as if looking for an answer.)

I have.

It's like in school—that Greek guy—what was his name?—Plato, said everything in the world has a perfect example after which it is modeled. That's my sex life. Platonic perfection.

I know what you're thinking. This guy is pretty screwed up. He's lonely. He's obsessed. He's got no love in his life.

Don't tell me about love. I got love. I always keep the choicest for a daily visit . . . that's love. Right? Same as you, same as everybody.

But the point is, I got love, and I got all the others too. I see a girl walkin' down the street, I like the way she smiles—bingo, she's mine.

Some of 'em get scared after a while, go back to their boyfriends. That's fine with me. I understand—it's a lot to handle. Some get addicted, I get rid of them too.

But most of the time, they are very cool about it. Whenever I call 'em up, they drop whatever they're doin', whatever they're doin', and come to me. A couple of times, girls stopped screwing their boyfriends when I gave 'em a ring. They understand that this kind of quality and quantity is in limited supply. . . .

Let's be honest—sex is what everyone is basically interested in. Great sex with great-looking, great fucks. There are only so many to go around. . . .

I am one.

Sometimes I feel sorry for other people. *(Adjusts his crotch.)* Sometimes I feel guilty. It's like I'm living in a color movie, everybody else is living in black and white. But then I think, someone has to live out the dream. Somebody's got to have it all. Might as well be me.

Stag

(A man wearing a T-shirt with sleeves rolled stands poised in the middle of the stage, a beer in one hand, an imaginary football in the other. He's about to throw the ball.)

Terry! Terry! Go out for a long one! Go back! Go back! Go way back! *(Throws the ball.)* Hey, watch out for the truck, man, watch out for the—oh . . . shhhhh . . . I told you to watch out for the truck! . . . Hey, I can't help it if you're uncoordinated. . . .

Yo, Terry, Terry, Terry, Terry, if you're goin' to the store to get bandages, get me a pack of cigarettes, please? Winston, hard pack . . . *(He contorts his posture.)* Come on, man, *pleeeeeeasssse*! . . . Thank you.

(He sips from his beer and walks away from the audience toward upstage right, then notices someone behind him downstage left. He spins and gives the high five.)

Hey, Joey, my man, that pot was great last night, man—you got to get us some more! Yeah, we smoked it all up . . . half-pound only goes so far. . . .

Aaah, the party was great, it was great! You shoulda been there! Me and Frankie, we goes down the corner, we grabs Louie, we kidnaps him. We brings him up to the apartment. We got five cases of beer, three cases of champagne, four bottles of Jack Daniel's, an ounce of blow, and the half-pound of pot. For the three of us, right?

Louie looks around, he goes, "What's all this?" I

says, " 'What's all this?'! You're gettin' married tomorrow, man—this is your surprise stag party!"

Louie's lookin' around . . . he goes, "I gotta be at the church by ten o'clock—I can't get too wasted." And Frankie—Frankie's so funny, man, he's cutting lines on the counter, he's cutting lines and he goes, "Don't worry, man, we won't get you *too* wasted."

(Laughs a long, horsey laugh.)

Then Frankie—Frankie's so cool, man, he just goes like this . . . *(Snaps his fingers.)* The bedroom door opens up and these three beautiful babes come waltzing out of the bedroom wearing bikinis. . . . *(Laughs.)* You shoulda seen Louie's face. He looked like he was gonna cry! . . . Yeah, yeah, they're friends of Frankie's—he told 'em if they hung out for the night he'd introduce 'em to Bruce Springsteen. I didn't even know he *knew* Bruce Springsteen. *(Pause.)* Oh, he doesn't? Oh . . . So anyways . . .

So we start partying, man . . . champagne, cocaine. . . . Frankie gets out these porno tapes, to warm up the ladies? The nice ones, man—the kind with, like, stories in 'em? One of 'em was so funny, man. How'd it go? Oh, yeah . . . There's this girl, right? And, uh, this chick, she's in her house, ironing her clothes, and there's a knock on the door and the guy goes, "It's the milkman—I have something for you!" Right? And he comes in . . . I don't think it was a real milkman . . . and they start screwing right on the ironing board. Very sensuous, very nicely done. . . .

So then he leaves and there's another knock on the door. And she goes, "Who is it?" and the guy outside goes, "It's—" wait a minute . . . oh, yeah—"It's UPS, I have something for you!" And this guy comes in and he's holding this package like this *(indicates carrying a heavy box)* and she opens it up and *his dick's inside*! Joe, what a riot! I never woulda guessed it in a million years. Huh? There was a hole in the box! And they do it. . . . Then he leaves . . . takes his dick with him. . . . And there's another knock on the door . . . and she says, "Who is it?" And . . . there's no answer. So she goes over to look out the door—there's nobody there! She opens the door—there's nobody there! She looks down, Joey—there's a *dog* out there! The dog comes trotting in . . . starts licking her feet, licking her legs . . . I can't watch it. . . .

I mean, what am I gonna tell the priest in confession? "Oh, yeah, I was watchin' dog porno tapes." "That's fifteen million Hail Marys, twenty million Our Fathers. . . ."

Hey, man, I don't got the time!

But listen, Joe . . . the girl I'm sittin' with? She's watchin' the whole thing! Oh, yeah, man . . . she's watchin' it. I turns to her, I says, "This stuff turn you on?" She says, "Sure—why not?" Like it's the most normal thing in the world. The rest of the night, man, I'm like checking myself out for fleas!

Great party, man—we had food. I got the food together. You know how you always run out of potato chips? I bought fifty bags of potato chips. The ripple kind, the good kind? Clam dip . . . from the 7-Eleven. . . . We spared no expense.

I'm sittin' there on the couch, man, and I'm thinkin' to myself, "This is the best party I ever been to, man. I'm doing everything I love to do in the whole world!" I got a beautiful girl sitting next to me . . . I'm watchin' TV . . . I'm eating clam dip . . . with a rippled potato chip! I'm smoking joints, I'm snortin' coke, I'm tossin' shots of Jack Daniel's and I'm chasin' 'em with glasses of champagne! I'm thinking to myself, "This is civilized!"

It doesn't get any better than that, man. What more could you want?

And all of a sudden I got depressed, man. You know why? Because I looked over and I saw Louie on the couch and I thought to myself, "He's never gonna have it like this again for the rest of his life." Really, man—think about it. Guys get married and they never have any fun anymore. Might as well shoot 'em in the head and bury 'em. . . . No, come on, Joey—I'm gonna call up Louie six months from now and you know what he's gonna say? I'm gonna call him up and say, "Louie, come on, let's go out, let's play some pool or something." And he's

gonna say, "No, I can't . . . I gotta go up to the mall
with my wife, look for towels and sheets." Guy's had
one towel, one sheet for twenty-five years, now he needs
new towels and sheets. . . . Who puts those ideas in a
guy's head? You know who! *(Sips beer.)* You know fucking who!

(Pause.)

So me and Frankie, we're getting wasted. Playing all
the old party games—you know: who can snort the most
coke, who can make his nose bleed first, who can toss
the most shots, who can see double first. . . . Getting
totally hammered.

You know when you're like *(indicates)* this close to
puking, but you don't puke? We were *there*, man—we
were there all fucking night. Just sitting there feeling the
brain cells die . . . "Oh, there goes the right side of my
brain! *I'm a moron!*" *(Laughs.)*

It was nice, man. Blacked out three times! Woke up,
Louie's over with this babe we hooked him up with, this
Angela, he's kissing her, he's got his tongue in her ear,
his hand up her shirt. . . . Next thing we know, he's going in the bedroom with her. . . . Hey, okay with me—
he's not married yet, he's normal, he's got hormones. Go
in the bedroom.

So I'm hungry, so I goes into the kitchen. I always get
really hungry whenever I'm doing Quaaludes, so I'm frying up these steaks. *(Mimes frying the steaks.)* Joey, the
whole trick to frying up steaks when you're on 'Ludes is
keeping your face outa the frying pan. *(Mimes nodding
into the frying pan.)* "Whoooooa! Keep burnin' my
nose!"

Five minutes goes by . . . Angela comes tearing out
of the bedroom, she says, "You guys gotta do something
about your friend in there." "What? What?!"

Me and Frankie go running into the bedroom. . . .
Louie's sitting in the middle of the bedroom floor, shit-
faced, crying his eyes out. No, Joey—really crying. He's
sitting there going: "I changed my mind . . . I changed
my mind . . . I don't want to get married anymore." I
says, "Louie, Louie, you gotta get married, they already hired the hall. . . . You gotta get married, Louie—

ya grandmother made lasagne for four hundred people!''

"I don't care! I don't care! I'm in love with *her*!" *(Points.)*

He's in love with this Angela! Great! I'm trying to figure this thing out, I'm getting one of those brain tumor headaches . . . all of a sudden, I smell my steaks burning! We runs into the kitchen, and the kitchen, Joe, the kitchen was all like . . . fire . . . all different kinds of fire, burning everything up. So we're taking, like, champagne, we're pouring that on it, we're throwin' beer on it. Frankie goes and gets the TV set, throws that on it. . . .

We finally get the fire out, right? The place stinks, it smells. . . . Steaks stuck to the wall with clam dip . . . place is wrecked. . . . Frankie goes, he goes *(laughing)*, ''Fuck the fuckin' party, man, the fuckin' party's fucked.''

How does he think up those lines, man? He's funny—he should be on TV. . . .

I says, ''Wait a minute—apartment's finished, but the party's not finished! Let's go somewhere, have a nice sit-down dinner, have our party there.'' . . . So anyways, make a long story short, we decide to go down to the new McDonald's.

So we walks into the McDonald's, first thing I see, four Hell's Angels sitting over there having something to eat. Fine, great. We sit over here. . . . The girls are fooling around—you know the way girls get when they're drunk—they get silly. Louie, he's not eatin', he's in love with Angela, he's never gonna eat again for the rest of his life. Frankie, he's not eatin' 'cause every time he gets near Hell's Angels, that scar next to his eye starts to throb.

Me, I'm eatin'. I'm in a McDonald's, I'm gonna eat, I'm not gonna miss the opportunity.

So one of the girls, she takes my ketchup thing—you know, those things of ketchup, whatever you call 'em, ketchup bag—and she squeezes it, and the ketchup goes way up in the air, comes down, goes all over Frankie's shirt. She starts laughin' like this is the funniest thing she ever saw in her whole life. Right? Now all the girls, they start going hysterical.

The Hell's Angels, they see what happened, they start laughin', the manager of the McDonald's, he starts laughin', everybody who works there, they're all laughing. People out in the parking lot, they're laughin'. Everybody in the whole world is laughing at Frankie. Great, let's make an atom bomb while we're at it.

I goes over to Frankie, I says, "Frankie, let's go out and get some fresh air?" He says, "In a minute." I says, "Frankie, there's four of them, there's three of us, let's get out of here now." He says, "In a minute."

Frankie stands up, he walks over to the biggest Hell's Angel, guy isn't even a human being, he's just this side of a mountain, sitting there.

Guy's got a shaved head, a tattoo of like Satan or Jesus or some fuck on his forehead, big bushy beard, ring through his nose. Guy's just sitting there *(imitates the Angel)*, "Rah-blah-blah."

Frankie goes up to him like this: "Yo, Chief . . . you lose this?" And he's got one of those like ketchup things in his hand? He just goes *splllllt, frlllllllt* . . . right in the guy's face!

(He acts all of this out, laughing as he tells the story.)

Before the guy can even shake his head, Frankie's like *BANG! BANG! BANG!* right in the guy's face, kickin' his ass. Fortunately I thought ahead—I picked up one of those Ronald fucking McDonald trash cans, I toss it into the teeth of the guy sitting next to him. So I'm standing there crunching this guy's head, Louie comes over, he's good for nothing, falls on a guy.

The girls, they're throwing french fries, hamburgers. The manager of the McDonald's, he comes running out with a fire extinguisher, sticks it in my ear, turns it on! Like I started it or something! What a rush! Frankie, he jumps over the counter, runs in the back, gets a big potful of that hot french-fry grease, throws it all over these guys. . . .

Me, Frankie, and Louie, we go running out to my car . . . Frankie jumps in, tries to start my car, trying to start the car, car won't start, as usual—gotta get a new starter. I'm sitting there, I'm praying. . . . Louie's in the backseat, he's got the door wide open, hanging out the door, he's goin', "*Angela!* ANGELA!" I says, "Louie, get inside the car, lock the door, come on!"

And that guy, that inhuman mountain guy? Like nothing even happened to him, Joey. He just stands up, starts walkin' right at us in the car *(mimes a Frankenstein-style walk)*—right through the plate-glass window of the McDonald's, man! Boom!

We're just about to take off, the guy reaches out, grabs Louie's leg, Louie grabs me around the neck, Frankie hits the gas, we're pulling this whale all over the parkin' lot. Frankie's trying to scrape the guy off on trash cans, the curb, over those little McDonald bushes they got everywhere. Nothing's workin'. I'm going, "Louie, Louie, hit the guy, kick him, do something!" And Louie—I don't know if he did it on purpose or what—he just turns around, pukes all over the guy's face. . . . *(Laughs.)* He let go of him *then*, man!

Louie passes out into the backseat of the car—we slam the door shut, take off like a bat outa hell!

(Laughing, really enjoying himself.)

It was fuckin' great, man!

(Catches his breath.)

But you know what was really great, man? What was like the icing on the gravy?

We're driving, we're like five miles away, the action's behind us. We're not even going that fast—maybe seventy, seventy-five. And I turns to Frankie and I says, "Frankie, why'd you start all that shit, man? I mean, we coulda gotten killed back there!" And you know what he says, Joey? He doesn't even look at me—he just keeps drivin' and he goes, "Sometimes you gotta spit in the devil's eye . . . just to make sure you're alive."

(Slow smile.)

Think about that. Hit my brain like a rock. I'm sitting there and I looks at Louie passed out in the back-

seat, dreamin' about towels and sheets . . . I looks at
Frankie drivin' the car, smokin' a joint, a beer between
his legs, the music's blastin', and I thinks to myself,
"Yeah, man, yeah—this guy knows what he's talking
about. He's never gonna sell out. He's gonna live until
the day he dies." *(Raises his fist.)* Rock on, man, no
surrender!

We drove all the way out to the beach, man . . . we
made a little fire on the beach and we just stayed up all
night smokin' joints. Smoked up that whole half-pound
of pot, man. Didn't even talk. I thought about what he
said all night, man. It was heavy.

Watched the sun come up. And I thought about all the
water in the ocean. There's a lot of water out there. And
that water's just little drops. And I'm like a little drop of
water in the world. So I might as well party, man. Might
as well party. *(Laughs.)* Sun comes up and Louie wakes
up, stumbles down to the beach. He goes: "I gotta be at
the church at ten o'clock."

He's got puke all over him, he wants to go to church!

So we throw Louie in the backseat of the car, we start
driving to the church, run outa gas a mile down the
road. . . . Huh? Naw, we got there, we got there. A little
late . . . around twelve-thirty. . . .

Yeah, they gotta postpone it to next Saturday. Big deal.
It's okay. Louie's okay. . . . Louie's grandmother got one
of those little heart attacks.

But listen, Joey—next week, Friday night, we're gonna
have another surprise stag party for Louie. Don't tell nobody. . . .

Listen, Joey—one thing. *(He turns and pees against
the back wall, then turns to face the audience, zips
up.)* . . . If you're gonna come . . . no girls. . . . They
cause too much trouble. . . .

Bottleman

(A man talks quickly, nervously, rarely looking at the audience. He constantly hitches his pants and pats his hair. His overcheerful manner covers his fear. He's making conversation with an imaginary listener.

He begins by talking to the wall.)

I don't like to complain. I'm not a complaining kind of guy, I'm a happy kind of guy—runs in my family, happiness. Never been sick in my life. Not one day. Unless you count broken bones, which I don't. But I like to stay positive. Stay on the sunny side of the street. You give me a pack of cigarettes, egg salad sandwich, cup of coffee, a newspaper, someplace to sit down, and I'm happy—I'm happy.

(Turns, paces, then stops.)

I don't even need the cigarettes. I should quit anyway. It's a dirty habit. Unhealthy. Expensive. Of course you can always find cigarettes. People always have cigarettes—they'll give 'em to you. Food's another subject altogether. People aren't exactly walking around with an egg salad sandwich in their pocket—unless they're crazy! And you figure, egg salad sandwich's gonna run you maybe seventy-eighty bottles. I'm findin' maybe fifty bottles a day—you're talking a short fall of about twenty bottles . . . or cans . . . bottles or cans, it doesn't make much difference.

(Now another direction, paces, stops.)

Back in the old days, I used to weigh a lot more than I do now. Used to be on a diet all the time. Always trying to lose weight. I don't have that problem anymore. I'm on the egg salad sandwich diet now. One egg salad sandwich every two days . . . you lose weight like crazy. The fat just flies off . . . and it stays off. I'm gonna patent it. Get a copyright and put an ad in the newspaper. Make a little money.

See, newspapers—newspapers, you can get. You can always find a newspaper, people just leave 'em around. And I read 'em. I wanna know about the world.

(His pacing has him facing completely upstage, his back to the audience.)

It's important to stay informed. I read about a train in Japan goes three hundred miles an hour, gets you there in no time. They got hotels for cockroaches now, hotels for mice. I stay away from hotels. Too much money— who's got that kinda money? Ten bucks a night, forget it. You figure that's two hundred bottles—bottles or cans—and that's not in my budget.

(Now he's facing the audience, talking to the audience in a detached way.)

But it's not a problem. You can always find some-place—there's always someplace to stay. You wedge yourself in someplace. The real problem is the concrete. The stone. They make everything out of rocks and ce-ment! Too hard. What ever happened to wood? Used to be all the buildings were made out of wood. Used to make benches outa wood. But no more. Because they make wood outa trees, and trees, they don't got them no more.

I saw this tree . . . there was this tree, beautiful tree . . . they dug a hole and put it in the sidewalk. Every day I come to say hello. And this guy was backing up his truck. The truck was making that beep sound— *beep-beep-beep-beep*—right over the tree, 'cause, see, the tree can't hear that. See? That was it for the tree. That was it. What are you gonna do? It's just in the nature of a tree that if you run 'em over they die. They're not like people—they can't take the abuse.

Take a tree, replace it with a metal pole, then there's

no problem. Truck hits the pole, that's it. But you lose the leaves. You lose the leaves and the twigs. You lose the wood. Wood is good.

(Paces, suddenly:)

Dogs like wood. I know—I used to have a dog. Walked him every day. I used to say *(miming walking the dog):* "Come on! Come on! . . . Who takes care of you? Who takes care of you? *I* take care of you. . . . Who's gonna take care of *me* in my old age? Who's gonna take care of me?" That's what I used to ask him. . . .

He ran away. But that's okay—they gotta eat too, the little ones. Everybody's gotta eat, sooner or later. It's human nature. It's human nature. I like to eat. I like to eat. Kind of a habit of mine, food.

(He holds an imaginary sandwich before his face.)

Nice egg salad sandwich. Cup a coffee . . . Cream. Sugar.

I'm cutting down on the coffee. I don't drink much coffee these days. Sixty cents a cup. Where did they come up with that figure, that's the question I want to ask. Should be ten cents! But they got ya, see, they got ya. 'Cause they got the beans. They got the beans. You got no choice. They got a cartel. This OPEC.

But I don't need coffee. I don't need the coffee. People drink coffee to stay awake—I don't need to stay awake. I'm awake, I'm awake. When I'm asleep I'm awake. You gotta keep your eyes open when you're sleeping, 'cause you find a place to lie down and you don't keep your eyes open and a guy comes back with a baseball bat and that's it—*bang bang,* you're dead!

No more coffee, no more cigarettes—that's it!

See, these guys on the street, they like to fight. I don't got that luxury. I'm on my second set of teeth, I'm missing a kneecap, I can't hear in one ear. I'm like the bionic man without the hardware. I'm no Cassius Clay. I'm no Cassius Clay.

(Pause.)

But I stay on the sunny side of the street. I stay on the

sunny side of the street. A guy once told me, "Life is
like a half a glass of water . . . half a glass of water . . ."

*(He loses his train of thought; his hand is shaking,
holding the imaginary glass.)*

You got a half a glass a water. . . . "And . . . uh . . .
you should drink the water," that's what he said. . . .

*(Sheepish—he didn't get the saying right—he turns
away, then laughs at himself.)*

No, that isn't what he said. . . . He said . . . he said
. . . "Half a glass of water is better than no water at
all!" That's it. "Half a glass of water is better than no
water. . . ."
(Full of energy again.)
I look at it this way—I could be living in Ethiopia.
Those poor people got it terrible. They got nothing to
eat. Starving all the time. They just sit in the sand all
day long. . . . It's too sunny, too many flies . . . it's not
for me. It's not my bag. I prefer it here . . . it's better
here.
(Lost in thought, convincing himself.)
It's good here, it's good. It's good. Thank God!

*(Pause. He's just standing, staring at the ground.
He snaps out of it—sunny, cheerful again, he
addresses the audience.)*

Well, I gotta get going, got to get to work. You know
what they say: "The early bird catches the can!"
Or bottles . . . bottles or cans, it don't make no dif-
ference. . . .
(He walks off upstage, still talking.)
It don't make no difference at all. . . .

Candy

(The sound of a push-button phone being dialed; then a recorded sexy voice is heard.)

Hi, I'm Candy. I'm glad you called. I was just about to take a really, really erotic bath, and I thought, "Wouldn't it be nice if a really, really horny guy called up so I could tell him all about it?" . . . I can't think of anything sexier than having a really, really horny guy listening to my deepest and most . . . intimate . . . erotic fantasies. . . . It gets me *sooooo* excited, I feel all tingly and pink, it makes me just want to pull off all my clothes and dance around the room listening to some really, really *hard* rock. Ooooooh, I get goose bumps just thinking about it! Sometimes when I'm really, really horny I have to call just two or three of my best girlfriends up and they come over and we just take all our clothes off and rub olive oil all over our bodies and then do really really vigorous aerobics. Ohhhh, my bathtub's all filled up, and I'm ready to jump in and scrub myself all over. If you want to "come" along, call me back and press two on your touch-tone phone for more erotic adventures. I can't wait.

Rock Law

(Lights up on a man sitting in an office chair, rolling across the stage. He jumps out of the chair, shouting into a hand-held phone. He paces, he contorts his body, as he yells into the phone.)

Frank, Frank, Frank . . . what did he say? He's gonna sue me? He's gonna sue me? Did you tell him who he's messing with here, Frank? Did you tell him who he's *fucking* with here, Frank? He's fucking with *God,* Frank—did you tell him that? Did you tell him what God *does* when he gets fucked with, Frank? Ever hear of Sodom and Gomorrah, Frank? That's what I'm gonna do to his *face!*

No, no, no, no, no, Frank—I don't want to hear it. Sue me? Sue me? I'm gonna blow him away, Frank, I'm gonna peel his skin off, I'm gonna chew his bones, I'm gonna drink his blood, I'm gonna *eat his children,* Frank!

And I'm gonna enjoy myself—you wanna know why? Because he's a schmuck, a schlemiel, and shithead for fucking with me, that's why! He should know better! . . .

No, no, no, Frank—I'm not listening to another word! *(Sings loudly: La-la-la-la, la-la-la-la!)* Sue me? *Sue me?* Call him back right now and tell him . . . tell him . . . *Wait*—don't call him back, don't call him. . . . Call his children, call his children and tell them to *get ready to be eaten*! Good-bye, Frank!

(He strides over to a small table stage left and yells into an intercom.)

DIANE! DIANE! Who's on line one? . . . My wife? Put her on hold . . . What's for lunch? I'm starving to

death. . . . I don't care, anything. . . . I don't care, Diane, anything—*I am starving to death! (Pause.)* No, I
don't want that! *(Pause.)* No, I don't want that, either
. . . no monkfish . . . no monkfish, no arugula, no sun-
dried tomatoes, no whole-wheat tortellini. . . . I want
food, Diane—you know what I mean when I say "food"?
Diane, unlike you I am a human being, I need food, I
need coffee—please get me some. . . . Call Jeff Cava-
naugh, put him on line two—call Dave Simpson, put him
on line three . . . *thank you*!

*(Taps a button on his hand-held phone, becomes
cordial and familiar.)*

Hi, honey. . . . I know! I tell her time and time again,
"Don't put my wife on hold," she puts you on hold. I'm
sorry. What did you do today? . . . That's nice—how
much did that cost? . . . No, no, no! Spend the money—
that's what it's there for. . . . That's what it's there
for. . . . *(Rubs his forehead.)*

How's Jeremy? . . . Why did he do that? No, no—why
did he bite the kid, Sonia? . . . I told him to? I did not
tell him to bite anybody. . . . Sonia, I did not tell him—
. . . Don't tell me what I tell him. . . . I told him— . . .
Can I talk, please? I told him, "The next time a little
boy does something to you, do twice as much back to
him," that's what I told him. I don't care what his therapist says! I don't care what his therapist says—his therapist is a co-dependent dysfunctional fraud! . . . No, no,
wait—you know what I'm going to tell Jeremy? I'm gonna
say, "Jeremy, bite your therapist!" Let him work on that
for a while.

What else? . . . How did she do that? How did she get
it in the microwave, Sonia? . . . No, wait, that's what?—
three microwave ovens in two years? . . . We have to buy
another microwave now? . . . No, no, I just want to say
something: If you hired people who came from a country
where they had electricity, we wouldn't have this problem. . . . Well, you gotta tell her. . . . What do you
mean, "She'll quit"? . . . She won't quit—she's got it

great. She spends all day in a luxury New York apartment! I spend all day in this office killing myself so she
can spend all day in my luxury New York apartment! She
spends more time there than I do!

I AM NOT SHOUTING! *(Lowers his voice.)* I am not
. . . this is not shouting. . . . Am I shouting? Now wait
a minute, am I shouting? Is this shouting? This is not
shouting—this is discussing. We are discussing . . . we
are having a discussion.

(Patronizing.) Well, obviously you're too agitated to
have a normal conversation right now, so why don't we
wait until I get home. . . . I'm gonna be a little late tonight. . . . Around nine. . . .

I have a lot of work to do! Sonia, do you think I like
slaving and sweating here all hours of the night and day
so that you and Jeremy can be safe and free? Do you?

It hasn't been two weeks . . . It hasn't been two weeks,
we just did it the other—

Okay, okay . . . we'll have sex tomorrow night, all
right? . . . I won't forget—I'll put it in my book!

Listen, honey, I've been working very hard. Next
month, we'll go down to Saint Bart's, we'll get a place
by the beach, we'll make love every day on the beach.

You won't get sand in your crotch! Look, I gotta get
off, I got twenty people on hold. . . .

Huh? . . . No, don't color your hair—no, don't cut
your hair, either! Nothing with your hair. . . . Don't start
with the hair blackmail now. . . . No henna, nothing! I
want you to look the same when I get home tonight as
you did when I left this morning, that's what I want. . . .
I gotta get off. . . .

Give Jeremy a kiss good night for me, okay? Say hi to
your mother for me, too. . . . Okay, all right. . . .
What?! . . . Orange juice. Fine. Okay. . . . I love you
too . . . I'll be home around ten-thirty. . . . Bye!

(Goes over to intercom.)

Diane, what are you doing in there, *growing the food*?!
Come on! I feel like a poster child for Ethiopian relief.
My ribs are sticking out, flies are crawling all over
me, I'm gonna be dead in five minutes—come on!

(Punches a button on his phone, starts to speak, then relaxes into chair stage right and carries on a very casual conversation.)

Jeff? Hey, man, how they hanging? . . . Not bad, not bad. . . . Yeah, I finished that deal yesterday. . . . No, I made twenty grand—chump change. Listen to this, man—this morning I cut a deal I made seventy-five grand. You know what they say: "A hundred grand here, a hundred grand there—pretty soon you're talking real money." . . .

I don't know—maybe I'll buy a Porsche for the country house, park it in front of the tennis court, piss off my neighbors. Not even drive it, just leave it there all the time. . . . Huh? No, I can't drive it—I don't drive a stick. . . . That's an idea—Range Rover, they're good. Very ecological, right? Maybe I'll get one of those.

Naw, I can't, not tonight. I'm doin' something. . . . *Who* am I doin'? I'm not telling you. Jeff, I tell you, you're gonna tell Nadine and she'll tell Sonia. . . . Very beautiful. . . . Better. . . . Better than her. . . . Better than her. . . . Yeah, she has breasts—yeah, she has legs, she has arms, she has a head. I got the whole package. Jeff, the closest you ever came to a girl this beautiful is that time you bought the scratch-and-sniff picture of Vanna White . . . ha-ha . . . And get this, she's an artist. She's very, very sensitive. She picked me up in a bar—how could I say no?

Jeff, unlike you, I am still committed to my sixties idealism. I'm still committed to experience and exploration. . . . Unfortunately, you gave up the struggle a long time ago; but for me, it's a matter of principle.

Why don't we get together tomorrow night, play some handball, have a couple of pops over at my club? . . . No, *my* club, my club, Jeff. My club is nicer than your club—it's safer, it's cleaner, it's more exclusive. . . .

(Stands up.)

Okay? I gotta get off the phone, I have a lot of work to do, unlike you. . . . Thank you . . . thank you. I am a genius. I am the best. No one can get close to me. I'll let *you* get close to me, Jeff, you can blow me. . . . Bye!

(Pushes more buttons on his phone and keeps talking, with a more aggressive, impatient tone, pacing once again.)

Dave, Dave, can I say just one thing here? I agree with you one hundred and fifty percent! . . . No, no, Dave, the man is a wonderful human being, he's a mensch, he's a lovely person. . . . I love him, I felt terrible having to let him go. . . .

Yes, I understand that, I know he's fifty-eight years old. . . . I know he's gonna lose his pension. . . . I understand that, but Dave, Dave, Dave, Dave! . . .

There's two sides to this argument—don't forget the human side of the equation! . . .

Now, when I first came to work at this company, this man was like a father to me—he's like my own father, this guy. I love him—we're like blood relatives. . . . It broke my heart to *have to have to fire him, Dave*! . . .

Yes, yes, yes . . . I know he's going in for major surgery next week—that's not my problem, I'm not his doctor, Dave, I'm his boss.

No . . . no . . . no . . . but—but—but—but Dave! Dave! Now you've been talking for five minutes straight, can I get a word in edgewise here? The guy . . . the guy is not performing anymore. He's not hustling anymore. He's easy listening and this place is rock and roll! I need heavy metal here, Dave—I need production—I need performance!

Yes, but Dave, Dave, Dave!

Let me make it a little clearer for you: You like your Mercedes station wagon? You like your country house? You like your swimming pool? You like skiing in Aspen? You like long lunches, your car phone, that horsey school you send your daughter to? What pays for those things, Dave? Now, wait—what do you think pays for those things?

Profits, that's what—say "profits," Dave! Say "profits" . . . I just want to hear you say it . . . Say it! Thank you. . . .

Now, now, now, Dave, when the profit ax comes down, anybody's head can roll. I could lose my job tomorrow, you could lose your job tomorrow. You could lose your job today, you could lose your job in the next five minutes if we keep up this stupid conversation. Because, to tell you the truth, Dave, I want to get rid of the guy even more now, because now he's wasting *your* time as well as mine. You're wasting your time, I'm wasting my time, all these people in this company are wasting their time around here, and I have to say to myself, "What's the point?" What's the point, Dave—what's the point. What is your fucking goddamn point!? WILL YOU TELL ME WHAT YOUR FUCKING GODDAMN POINT IS, PLEASE?

Dave? . . .

You're not sure? Well, let me ask you this: Are you happy working for this company? . . . No, I mean, are you happy working for this company? . . . You are? Good, because I just want you to be happy . . . so get back to work.

(Suddenly laughs.)

Okay. . . . All right. . . . No, no—no hard feelings. We've all been working hard. . . . Okay. . . . All right, I understand. . . . Call anytime. . . . Say hi to Judy for me. . . . Janet? . . . Say hi to Janet. . . . Okay . . . All right. . . . Take care.

(He switches off, then yells into the intercom.)

DIANE, LET ME MAKE IT EASY FOR YOU: TAKE YOUR HAND, PUT IT IN THE MICROWAVE, GRILL IT, BRING IT IN TO ME!

WHO'S ON LINE FOUR? . . .

I GOT IT.

(Pushes more buttons on his phone; then, very relaxed, sultry:)

Hi . . .

Nothing . . . I'm making money—what else do I do? . . . I'm working very hard . . . now that you called it's getting harder and harder. . . . Um-hmmmm. . . .

(Sits in his chair.)

You being a good girl? . . . Oh, yeah? What are you doing? . . . Making a sculpture, that's interesting. What kind of sculpture? . . . You made a sculpture of a horse and you wrote the word "horse" all over it? That's very conceptual, Yvette. . . .

(He checks his watch, stifles a yawn.)

What do you mean, I sound bored? Of course I'm not bored, I love talking about your art! I was just telling someone ten minutes ago what a wonderful art you have. . . . Yvette, Yvette, can I just say something? . . . No, can I say something?

If you were ninety-five years old and you were in a wheelchair, I would still love you, and you want to know why? Because I love your art, that's why. . . . Of course I mean it, of course I mean it—and when you say these means things to me I get all angry and confused . . . and . . . and I feel like coming over there and . . . giving you a good spanking!

(The serious look on his face melts into pleasure as he listens to what she's going to do to him.)

Ooohhh . . . that would hurt! All over my body! And then what are you going to do? . . . The whole thing!? The phone is heating up, Yvette—stop it! . . . No, not that! Anything but that *(laughs)* . . .

What did I do to deserve all this attention? I am a pretty nice guy, aren't I? . . .

Um-hmm . . . I love you too. I love you too. . . . Of course I mean it. Yvette, when I say I love you, I mean I love you. No one else in the whole world knows what love means the way that I know what love means when I say from me to you "I love you." No one was ever loved before the way that I love when I love you. Because my life would have no meaning if I didn't love you.

(Through all of the above, he has become fascinated with a smudge of dirt on his shoe. He's been picking at it as he speaks, and now is totally engrossed in the smudge, but he keeps talking without missing a beat.)

Of course I mean it, of course I mean it. Would I lie to you? . . .

(Checks his watch.)

Listen, Yvette, the boss just walked in—I gotta get off. . . . When am I going to see you? . . . Around six? At the loft? Okay . . . I will. . . . Keep making those sculptures. . . . Ciao to you too.

(He blows her a noisy kiss over the phone, switches off, and lurches at the intercom.)

Diane, cut the food, cut the coffee. Send in the Maalox, the shoeshine boy, and hold my calls. Thank you!
(Blackout to silhouette.)

X-Blow

(A man in silhouette declaims to a rap beat.)

I'm a child of nature, born to lose—
people call me "Poison" but that's no
   news.
When I wake up in the morning, I see
   what I see,
I look into the mirror, what I see is me:
A player, a winner, an unrepentant
   sinner—
if you mess with me, I'll eat you for
   dinner.
There are those that rule and those that
   serve,
I'm the boss, baby, 'cause I got the nerve
to take what I want, take what I need,
cut you first, sucker, and make you bleed.
'Cause life's a bitch, that I know.
Don't misunderstand me or then you'll go
to your grave in a rocket, nothing in your
   pocket,
if you got a gun, you better not cock it,
'cause then you'll die, that I know,
what's left of you away will blow
and you will spend eternity
praying to God you never met me!
Huh-huh-huh-huh-huh!

*(He steps into the light and addresses the audience,
telling the story in a friendly manner.)*

Sucker dissed me, man, he dissed me! I had no choice. He showed me his gun, so I walked up to him, I stuck my screwdriver into his stomach, and I ran it right true his heart. He looked surprised, man. Skinny kid like me, killing him like dat. Hah. Didn't even bleed.

Felt good, man, felt better than gettin' laid on a sunny day. And I like to feel good. Feeling good makes me feel good. Don't need no sucker drugs to feel good.

'Fore they locked me up I used to get up every morning and I had me two problems: how to find money, how to spend it. All the rest was gravy. Like the man says, "Don't worry, be happy."

That was the Reagan years, and the Reagan years is over, man, and I miss 'em! Ronnie Reagan, he was my main man. He had that cowboys-and-Indians shit down. Now he's out in L.A. sitting on a horse and we're sitting in the shit he left behind. But it's okay he's gone. New man's in charge! *Batman!* Batman is my man!

Gonna be beaming around like Kirk and Scotty, like the Jetsons, man! Just beaming around, beaming around. Jump into my Batmobile, get behind some smoked bulletproof windshield, stick in the CD, flip the dial to ten, rock the engine, burn the brakes. . . . Man, that's living . . . you can smoke that shit!

You only live once, you gotta grab that gusto shit.

My best friend in school went to work at McDonald's—worked hard too! First he 'came 'sistant manager, than he 'came manager. Guess he figured if he worked hard enough, one day he's gonna be president of McDonald's. Making four-fifty a week, had it nice, man. Had himself a duplex rental 'partment and a Ford Escort.

One Friday night some homeboys came in with a .38 special, greased him for the receipts, man. . . . Bang, bang in the back of the head—execution style!

Sucker! He missed the whole point! He's standing on that platform and that train be gone!

See, you wanna play the game, you gotta think about the big guy, you gotta think about God! God made man same as hisself. You wanna learn how to live, live like God! Check the big guy out!

God, man, he gets up every morning, he don't smoke

no crack, he don't shoot no dope. God don't flip no burgers. No, man—he gets up and he looks down on the world and he says (*hands on hips*), "World, what am I gonna do with you today? *(Stretches out his arms.)* Lessee, how about this, I will make an earthquake today . . . or how about dis, a tidal wave?

Or, lessee, maybe I'm a little bored, I think I will crack up some trains in India, kill me up some dotheads. . . .

Or maybe I'm feeling a little evil, maybe I jus' burn down an elementree school, fry up some nine-year-olds. . . .

Or maybe I'm feeling real evil, I'll mix up some new disease, sprinkle it all over them homosexual faggots, fuck 'em up, make 'em miserable, make 'em cry and die a slow evil death!

See, God's a player, he likes the action! God likes to rock, he likes to get high. . . . But God don't shoot no dope, he don't shoot no dope—he lets the dopes shoot each other!

Man, I *know* how he feels!

'Fore I was in the joint, used to get me a ten-gauge shotgun, shoot me up some sewer rats. You hit one square, they just vaporize. Like with a ray gun! Makes a nice sound too—BOOM! That must be what it's like to be God, lots of noise and destruction and fun!

See—people, they don't *understand* God. Last summer I was running down the street in my home neighborhood. Typical day for me—guy's chasing me, wants to put a bullet in my head. . . . So I jumps inside of this church, middle of the day . . . and there be this buncha little kids in the church with their teacher. Prayin'. In the middle of the day. Little tiny heads, little tiny butts.

I said, "Yo, teacher, whachoo be doin' in this here church for in the middle of the day?" She says, "Boy, we's in here prayin'—we's prayin' for peace, we's praying against nuclear disarmament."

Hah! I starts laughin'. I says, "Baby, you be prayin' in the wrong place! This here's God's house. You best go pray someplace else. Who you think make all that war shit up in the first place? Who you think make that nuclear bomb up, made up the poison gas and dynamite, rockets and bombs? They's his toys, baby!'' I's laughin' so hard, I fell right down on the floor of the church, my gun fell outa my pocket, went off, shot a hole right true the cross on the altar!

See you gotta figure: you wanna run with the big guy, you gotta think big. That's what I do—I think bigger every day. 'Cause God, that's where all the power is. I want to get closer to the power, I want to get more and more spiritual, get closer to God.

That's why next time I gets out, I'm gonna get me some new wheels and an Uzi, man.

Peoples, you gotta wake up, smell the coffee.

(Turns to go.)

''What goes around comes around.'' If you can't dig that shit, you better get out of Gotham City.

(Walks off.)

Live

(A man walks to the edge of the apron, cigar in hand. He stands erect, chest thrust forward. Gruff, ethnic American accent.)

JIMMY! I'm out in the backyard, here! Come out to the backyard!

(Feels his belly.)

Ugghhh . . . every time I have the fried calamari with the hot sauce, I feel like I'm gonna blow up!

So what do you think?

Olympic size, Olympic size! I said to the guy, "I want the best pool you got—gimme the biggest, the best pool you got! I don't care what it cost!"

I got a motto, Jimmy, very simple: "Take care of the luxuries, the necessities will take care of themselves."

You only live once, Jimmy—you gotta go for the best in this life, you gotta grab all the gusto you can.

I dunno, one hundred grand? It's not important.

It's like when I was buying my BMW . . . I says to myself, I can buy the 750 or I can save a little money, buy a 535. . . . But then I thinks to myself, I buy the 535, I'm in the middle of the highway someplace, 750 passes me, I'm gonna get pissed off! Another eight hundred, nine hundred bucks a month—why waste the aggravation, buy the 750!

You should get yourself a BMW, Jimmy. . . . What do you mean you can't afford it, of course you can afford it, don't give me that crap!

You know what's wrong with people like you, Jimmy?—and I'm just trying to be helpful here—you're full of crap, see? The only thing that's stopping you from having the car of your dreams is fear. You're afraid. You're afraid to have, you're afraid to own, you're afraid to live.

How much are you making now a year? Nineteen grand a year? Twenty-two grand a year? Get yourself a BMW! What are you afraid of?

You gotta live, Jimmy—that's what life is all about. I want to buy something, I buy it! I want to go someplace, I go there!

See this cigar? This is a Havana cigar. Why do I smoke Havana cigars? Because it's the best cigar, that's why. I could smoke something else. I could save myself fifteen bucks a pop, I could smoke something else. Why should I? So somebody else can smoke this cigar? Fuck him, it's my cigar.

It's my cigar—it's my life and I'm living it.

I exercise. Now we got the pool, I come out here every morning, I jump in the pool, I swim a whole lap. Then I go in the house, I have a healthy breakfast. I eat those oat bran muffins. I can't stand 'em, but I eat 'em, they're supposed to be good for you. . . . I have four or five muffins, scrambled eggs, bacon, sausage . . . big pot of black coffee, and I'm alive, Jimmy, I'm alive!

I'm fifty-one years old, I still make love to my wife like it's our wedding night. I know guys ten years younger than me, they don't even know they got a dick! They're in the shower in the morning . . . "La . . . la . . . la, la . . . Oh! What's that?" They think it's a growth sticking out of their body!

(Smokes his cigar, contemplates the horizon.)

See that there—you know what that is? That's a gazebo. Guy who sold me the pool, he says you gotta have a gazebo if you're gonna have a swimming pool. That's the best one they make—cost me five grand. I don't even know what it is.

(Puffs contentedly on his cigar.)

See, perfect example of what I'm saying here . . . Vito Schipletti! Never did nothing in his life. He never smoked, he never drank, he never chased skirts, never gambled, never walked when it said "Don't walk!"

You know where he is today with all his money in the

bank? He stands in front of the old candy store from nine o'clock in the morning till nine o'clock at night. He lived his life so good, he forgot to live.

What's the point of being alive like him? You might as well be dead!

Jimmy, they tell you cigars take three years off your life. What three years? What three years? Eighty-six to eighty-nine? Who needs 'em! Gimme the cigars!

There are people, Jimmy, all over the world, starving to death, in Africa and Asia, Armenia, they sit around all day starving . . . just sitting in the dirt. Those people, all they got is dreams. They dream, ''What would it be like to live in America? What would it be like to have a car, a house, food, a swimming pool. . . .'' Jimmy, I can't let those people down. . . . I'm here, I'm living it, I might as well enjoy it. . . .

I read in a magazine about a new resort in Hawaii where you can swim with the dolphins. . . . *Bango!* I'm there. They open a new casino down Atlantic City, I'm there the first day it opens. . . . They make a new TV set, ten feet wide, two stories high, I buy it.

'Cause it's my life, Jimmy, it's my life. If I don't live it, who's gonna?

I'm gonna live until the day I die, then I can rest.

(Steps toward the edge of the stage.)

You know what you need, Jimmy? You need a nice swim in my new swimming pool. . . . Put on your suit, come on! Snap out of it! *(Bends over the edge of the stage and tests the ''water.'')* The water's not cold—jump in!

Dog Chameleon

(A man sits in a chair, talking into a microphone with suppressed anger. He tries to be pleasant.)

Hey, I want to be normal, just like every other guy! Don't leave me out, come on! There's got to be more to life than worrying about the price of cigarettes, getting a job, what's on TV. I know—I know about normalcy. Don't tell me about normalcy!

I want to drive a station wagon with a bunch of kids singing Christmas carols in the backseat. I want to go to the supermarket and compare prices. I want to lose weight while I sleep. I want to buy life insurance. I want to wear pajamas and a bathrobe, sneak into the kitchen in the middle of the night and steal a drumstick out of the refrigerator. Worry about my dog's nutrition. Or maybe just order something from the L.L. Bean catalogue . . . a nice down parka maybe, a flannel shirt . . . something in corduroy!

I know all about normalcy!

I want to yell at my wife when she goes on a spending spree! I want to help my kids with their grades! I want to fertilize my lawn. I want to order my hamburger *my way*! I want to donate money to impoverished minorities!

But all that stuff costs money. Being normal is expensive, you know.

(Short pause.)

There was this rat scratching inside my wall the other night. After a while it sounded like it was inside my head. *And I said, "Wait a minute! Wait one minute! I'm white, I'm an American! I'm a male! I should be doing better than this!"*

Ozzie and Harriet didn't have rats in the wall. There were no roaches in the Beaver's room! Even Mister Ed had *heat*! WHAT THE FUCK IS THIS?

The rat kept scratching and I realized something:

Times have changed.

It's a race to the death now. Anyone waiting around for the good life to show up is a *fool*! Anyone who thinks that playing fair will get you anywhere is *blind*!

Then I said, "Calm down, calm down, you're getting all excited about nothing. Sure you're poor, you're an artist! You have an artistic sensibility! Artists are supposed to be poor."

And the rat-scratch voice inside my head said, "Fuck that!"

I want to be rich. And I want to be famous. These are normal desires, that should not be thwarted. If you thwart them, if you repress them, you get cancer.

Shit, I want *fame*! Look at *me, man*! Fame is what counts. Fame with money. Any jerk can go to the top of some tower with a scope rifle and start shooting at people. That's shitty fame. I want the good kind. The kind with lots and lots of money. Any slob can win the lottery, it takes *skill* and *brains* to get the fame and the money *at the same time* . . . that's success, man. So everyone looks at you, wherever you go, and they say: "That guy, he did it. He got everybody to look at him, admire him and give him money, their money, at the same time!"

I heard about this guy, he made four hundred million dollars. Four hundred million dollars! I'd be happy with fifty million. Most people would still think I was a success, even if I wasn't as successful as that guy. I don't care what they think! I wouldn't even tell them how much money I have! I'd just ride around in my stretch limousine, and when I got tired of that I'd go home and I'd have this enormous mansion with fifty rooms. . . . And . . . and I'd have this room with a trench around it full of pit bulls, and I'd have a chair that tilts back and a TV set with a remote control and a big bowl of potato chips!

And I'd just watch TV all day and change the channels. Maybe I'd just sit in a large bathtub with lots of bubbles. Smoke a cigar like Al Pacino in *Scarface*. . . . But

I wouldn't take drugs or have sex. Too dangerous. Just gimme the money, and the food, and the dark room . . . and the TV set. And a gun—so I can shoot the TV set when somebody I don't like comes on.

I hate people. They get in the way of a good time. Just when everything's getting good, they want something from you!

But I want you all to love *me*. Even though I hate all of you. Just to confirm my deep-seated feeling that you're all scum compared to my beneficence.

Just joking. Just joking. Don't get all excited. Nothing to get excited about. Just love me. Tell me I'm great. And pay me. And then we'll be even. For all the shit you've given me my whole fucking life! I know, I know what you're all thinking. "What a jerk. All he does is talk about himself." Yeah? And what do you do? LISTEN!

I was wronged when I was little. I never really got what I wanted. Now it's time to even the score. Even if I tell you my plans you can't stop me. I'm gonna become so rich and powerful, no one will touch me.

And all those rich fucks who lorded over me, all those muscular jocks who kicked sand in my face, all those big-boobed blondies who laughed at me when I asked them for a date, all those parsimonious paternal patronizing administrators at school and at the unemployment office and at the IRS and the police station . . . you'll all be sorry. You have no idea what I've got in store for you. Hah!

You know what it means to be really, really rich? You walk into a store and the jerk behind the counter gives you some kind of shit like . . . like, I don't know, smirking at you because he thinks you can't afford the most expensive watch in the case. . . . You know the look they give you, they humor you: "Yes, sir, may I help you?"

He doesn't want to help me, he doesn't want to help anybody—he just wants to laugh at me! Won't show me the watch, won't take it out, won't even tell me the price. . . .

Well, when I make it, I'm going to go back to that store and I'm not going to buy one watch, I'm not going to buy ten watches—I'm going to buy the whole store, and then I'm going to fire that patronizing jerk for laughing at me. . . . And then, I'm going to find out where he lives and I'm going to buy his apartment building and I'm going to have him evicted . . . one more pathetic homeless person walking the streets in a state of permanent depression!

Or those big thugs that push into you when you're walking down the street and don't say they're sorry or nothing. Why? Because they think I can't fight back. They think I'm afraid of them. Well, when I make it, I'm gonna get me some bodyguards. They'll walk with me when I'm going down the street. And some fucker pushes into me and I'll just step aside and there's my boy with the sock filled with marbles. Or the straight razor. Or the .38. He won't know what's hit 'im. He'll just end up on the ground, bleeding, looking up at me with glazed eyes, and I'll just lean over and step over 'im and say, "Excuse me."

(Laughs.)

You think I should be ashamed of myself? I HAVE NO GUILT! Because I am not a man. I am a dog.

(Barks a long howl.)

You know what I find fascinating? Human nature. The nature of human beings . . . what they like, what they don't like, what turns them on, what turns them off. What incredible appetites they have. Night after night they stay glued to their TV sets watching some pinheaded newscaster going on and on about today's grisly murder or vicious rape. They munch on popcorn and suck up TV dinners as they absorb the minutiae pertaining to the day's massive mud slide or exploding chemical plant.

(Mimicking the newscaster.)

"Thousands dead and dying! Hundreds blinded!"

Munch . . . munch . . . "Carol, get some more salt while you're in the kitchen! . . . Oh, wait, wait, come here, you have to see this—they're completely buried! Come on, you'll miss it, there's a commercial coming on!"

Then, these same people watch shows on educational TV about dolphins, *then* they cry. . . . Then they stay up

late to watch some old Christmas movie with Jimmy
Stewart standing on a bridge on Christmas Eve; *then* they
go berserk!

The next morning, they jump into their sporty compact
cars, drink ten cups of coffee, and race each other on the
highway while they sing along with some ardent rock
singer screaming and yelling about emaciated, dark-
skinned, hopeless people turning to dung half a world
away.

So they feel so guilty they race home and write out a
check for five dollars and mail it to some post-office box
in New York City and then they feel so good about themselves they go to bed with each other and they kiss and
they lick and they suck each other and they hold each
other really really tight, because they really, really
care. . . .

(Pause.)

I know I'm negative. I know I'm not a nice guy. I know
you all hate me. But I don't care. Because at least I realize I'm a shit, and for that tiny fragment of truth, I
respect myself. That's why normalcy is so far out of my
reach. Because you have to be blind to be normal. You
have to like yourself, and the thought of that is so repellent to me that I'm ecstatic to be in the depressing place
that I am!

Artist

(A man sits cross-legged in the middle of a pool light, downstage center. He mimes smoking a joint and passing it to an unseen companion.)

It's like if a tree falls in the forest—you know what I'm saying, man? It's like if everybody already knows everything, then nothing means anything. Everything's a cliché.

That's why I stopped making art.

(Takes the joint and tokes.)

You know what's wrong with the world today? Why everything's screwed up and you can't do anything about it? Because we don't live in a human world—we live in a machine world.

(Passes the joint.)

There's this guy, I can see him from my apartment, down in his apartment across the street. All night long, every night, he lies on his couch, doesn't move for hours on end, his eyes wide open. . . . Now if I didn't know that guy was watching TV, I'd think there was something seriously wrong with him, like he was paralyzed or hypnotized or something. . . .

All night long he lies there, and messages from outer space go into his brain: "Buy a new car," "Use deodorant," "Work harder," "Your dog has bad breath," "Buy a microwave oven." . . . All night long, man, into his brain.

(Takes the joint and tokes.)

I mean, what's a microwave oven, man? Everybody's got one, nobody knows what it does, nobody knows how

it works, everybody's got one. Why? Why does everybody have a microwave oven?

Because the TV set told 'em to buy it, that's why.

(Tokes and passes.)

I'm telling you, man, the government is building this
computer, biggest computer they ever built. Spending
billions and billions of dollars. It's a secret project, but
I read about it. . . .

When they finish this computer we're all gonna be
dead, man. . . . 'Cause they're gonna hook this huge
computer up to everybody's TV set. Then they're gonna
reverse the TV set so it can see you in your house doing
your thing? Computer's gonna watch you, man, and if
you do something the computer doesn't like, it's gonna
send a message to the TV set. TV set's gonna send a
message to the microwave oven, door's gonna pop open,
you're gonna be *ashes,* man. . . .

Don't believe me? Go in a store, pick something up,
pick anything up, take a look . . . everything's got those
little computer lines on 'em now. Everything. What do
those little lines mean, man?

Nobody knows. Nobody knows what they say—it's not
English, it's computer. All these computers are talking
to each other, man, nobody knows what they're saying.
It's like we're living in an occupied country, man.

All day and all night long, the computers are talking
to each other on the modems and the fax machines and
the satellite link-ups. All day and all night. What are they
talking about? What are they talking about? I'll tell you
what they're talking about. They're talking about you and
me . . . how to use us more efficiently. . . .

See, they don't have feelings, man, they're just machines. All they care about is efficiency.

The worst human being who ever lived had feelings,
man. Genghis Khan had feelings. Adolf Hitler had feelings. Every once in a while he'd get a little bummed out.
Computers never get bummed out, man, never.

(Tokes on the pot, passes it back.)

You know how they make bacon? No, I mean, you
know how they make bacon? They got these giant meat-
packing plants out in Idaho, run by robots and comput-

ers. And way down at the bottom of the assembly line they have to have a human being to hold the meat? 'Cause every piece of meat is different. And these twenty-four razor-sharp blades come down, slice through the meat, and that's how you get a slab of bacon.

So some dude comes into work, isn't thinking about what he's doing—maybe he had a fight with his old lady the night before, whatever—sits down at his spot, down come the twenty-four razor-sharp blades, and instead of a hand, he's got a half-pound of sliced and smoked Armour Star.

(Tokes.)

Bummer, right?

Happens about once a week. And nobody does anything about it. Nobody cares. Who's to care? Machines run everything now, man.

Every day the machines put more oil in the water, more poison in the air, they chop down more jungles. What do they care? They don't breathe air, they don't drink water.

We do.

(He looks at the joint, considers it for a moment, then swallows it. A strange look comes over his face.)

Stoned, man.

Wish we had some music to listen to. I used to love to listen to rock when I got high. All the great old bands—the Jefferson Airplane, the Stones, the Who.

They're all dead now. . . .

What, those bands touring around? You think that's the Stones, man? You think that's the Who?

Robots, man.

They gotta be robots. Listen to the music. The old bands, what did they sing about? Love, Peace, Anarchy, Freedom, Revolution, Get High. . . . What do the new bands sing about? Fear, Paranoia, Work Harder, Buy a Microwave Oven. . . .

They're just trying to brainwash us, man. They're just part of the system—if they weren't part of the system, you'd never even hear about 'em. All the bands that fought the system—Janis, Jimi, Morrison—they killed 'em all, made it look like accidents. They're all gone now, man, all that's left is the system.

And the system only has one message, man—fear. That's all they tell us all day long, fear. Because we're like little mice in our cages, man, running on our wheels as fast as we can, because we're so afraid.

Every day, get up seven A.M., drink two cups of caffeine, jump in the car, get stuck in traffic, get to work, get yelled at by the boss, make a deadline, drink more caffeine, get back in the car, get stuck in traffic again, get home, pay bills you can't afford, eat your microwave dinner, jump into bed. . . . Oh, wait, wait, I forgot the most important thing—watch a little TV—gotta get those messages in the head!

Get up the next morning, do it over again, get up the next morning, do it over again. Do it over again, do it over again, over again, over again. . . .

They call that being responsible, man. Everybody's scared, man—they're afraid they don't do what they're supposed to do, bang, they're homeless.

That's what the homeless people are, man. They're the warning to all of us, "Stay in your cage, don't rock the boat."

Ever talk to any of those guys on the street, man? Everybody says they're crazy. You live on the street for a while, see what kind of ideas *you* come up with. You don't go crazy, man—you start to see the truth. You start seeing the truth, you start telling the truth, you start talking about the way things really are.

That's why they keep those guys out on the street, man. The system's afraid of them. Afraid of their freedom. Freedom is the opposite of responsibility. Freedom is a threat to the system.

That's why nobody smokes pot anymore—everybody's afraid of the freedom. They're afraid they're going to smoke some pot, get high, think a thought or two, realize what bullshit their life is . . . and freak out.

That's why I stopped making art, man. It's hopeless. What can you say about this situation?

You write a book, best book ever written, makes bestseller list, everybody reads it. Two months later it's forgotten, there's some other important book everybody's supposed to read. You write a song, beautiful song, makes Top 40. Next thing you know, it's a jingle in a beer commercial. You paint a painting, millionaire buys it, hangs it on the wall of his corporate headquarters.

In the old days, man, rich people used to get lions' heads and tigers' heads, hang 'em on the wall—made 'em feel powerful, made 'em feel safe.

The system collects artists' minds, man. It sleeps better at night knowing the best and the brightest are dead from the neck up.

That's why I don't give 'em the satisfaction. I keep my mind inside my head where they can't get at it. Everything becomes part of the system, man. The only way to escape the system is not to do anything.

That's what I do. I want to paint a painting, I want to write something, I do it in my head, where they can't see it.

If they ever knew what I was thinking, man . . . I'd be dead.

Craig Lucas

Prelude
to a Kiss

MY wife and I saw *Prelude to a Kiss* in previews and were so enchanted by the gradual unfolding of its "secret"—a plot twist unfortunately revealed by all the subsequent reviews—that I'd advise readers who want to share a luminous revelation with its characters to turn to the play at once and come back to this introduction only after they've finished.

There.

Prelude to a Kiss is a contemporary fairy tale, and, like most fairy tales, has a dark as well as a delightful side. After Rita and the Old Man exchange souls during their kiss at Rita's wedding, Peter realizes he's been exposed to the risks as well as the rewards of love. Lucas skillfully prepares the theatergoer for the transformation so central to fairy tales. In retrospect, for instance, we can see that Rita's inability to sleep ironically evokes the princess awakened by a kiss, and the lovers' exchange early in the play—"What about when I'm a hundred years old with a mustache and yellow teeth?" asks Rita, to which Peter replies, "I'll still love you"—quietly prefigures their destiny. But he unravels and resolves the mystery of Rita's transformation even more skillfully—the craftsmanship of dramaturgy has seldom faced such a seemingly insurmountable challenge, and it is a measure of his mastery that the theatergoer barely notices.

Many critics have found in Lucas's play a provocative and moving metaphor for AIDS—the uneasy relationship between sex and death, the way in which so many young lovers, feeling embowered in happiness and vitality, are

suddenly cast into the realm of misery and disease, their
beloved partners growing old and dying before their eyes.
But the play has other resonances as well—the way our love
is constantly challenged by change, the way our partners'
personalities evolve in unexpected and not always pleasing
directions, the way aspects of their character we never sus-
pected emerge over the years. "I'm sorry," Rita tells Peter
at the end of the first act, "I can't be whatever you want me
to be. This is me. And maybe what you saw wasn't here at
all."

In all his plays—but never more so than in *Prelude to
a Kiss*—Lucas is an artificer of evanescent yearnings that
can't be articulated, of elusive moods beneath the dialogue. At once audacious and exquisite, his plays seem
to take place in the spaces between words, conveying the
unspoken rhythms and inaudible hum of human relation-
ships. With erotic and rapturous delicacy—particularly
apparent in Peter and Rita's courtship and reconciliation—his work invariably reveals the triumph of tenderness over adversity, the testing of love by the specter of
death. And not the least of his gifts is a deft comic touch,
releasing laughter at the very moment of emotional tran-
scendence.

"For better or for worse"—rarely have the ritualistic
words of the marriage ceremony had more theatrical re-
verberation. Love is both precious and precarious, and
one feels this dual blessing more profoundly if one has
entered the world of the play without knowing its secret
beforehand, if one has suffered, along with Peter, Rita's
increasingly disorienting behavior and experienced, along
with Rita, Peter's gradual surrender to his discovery. For
it is the *second* kiss in the play—and our wondrous shiver
as Peter leans slowly forward to gently kiss the Old Man
on the lips—that radiantly foreshadows Peter's final
words: "Never to be squandered . . . the miracle of another human being."

CRAIG LUCAS began his career as a musical comedy
performer, but with the encouragement of Stephen
Sondheim turned to playwriting in the early eighties. Such

plays as *Blue Window* and *Reckless* quickly established his reputation as a quirkily gifted dramatist, and his film script for *Longtime Companion* was one of the first works about AIDS to reach a nationwide audience.

Prelude to a Kiss was produced by the Circle Repertory Company on March 14, 1990. The cast and creative contributors were as follows:

PETER	*Alec Baldwin*
TAYLOR	*John Dossett*
RITA	*Mary-Louise Parker*
TOM	*L. Peter Callender*
MRS. BOYLE	*Debra Monk*
DR. BOYLE	*Larry Bryggman*
MINISTER	*Craig Bockhorn*
AUNT DOROTHY	*Joyce Reehling*
UNCLE FRED	*Michael Warren Powell*
OLD MAN	*Barnard Hughes*
JAMAICAN WAITER	*L. Peter Callender*
LEAH	*Joyce Reehling*
ENSEMBLE	*Kimberly Dudwitt, Pete Tyler*
DIRECTOR	*Norman René*
SETS	*Loy Arcenas*
COSTUMES	*Walker Hicklin*
LIGHTING	*Debra J. Kletter*
SOUND DESIGN	*Scott Lehrer*
HAIR AND WIG DESIGN	*Bobby H. Grayson*
STAGE MANAGER	*M. A. Howard*

CHARACTERS
(in order of speaking)

PETER
TAYLOR
RITA
TOM
MRS. BOYLE
DR. BOYLE
MINISTER
UNCLE FRED
AUNT DOROTHY
OLD MAN
JAMAICAN WAITER
LEAH
Party guests, barflies, wedding guests, vacationers

PLAYWRIGHT'S NOTE

To provide a fluidity of motion and to stress the imaginary leap required to make sense of the story, *Prelude* was originally staged with a minimum of scenery—a chair and lamp to indicate RITA's apartment, a free-standing bar for the Tin Market, a pair of chaise longues for Jamaica—allowing the lighting to do the bulk of the work in transforming the space. We also used a great deal of underscoring with source music and sound effects (surf, traffic, popular songs, marimba bands in Jamaica), again to indicate place and create a kind of magic. PETER often changed clothes in front of our eyes, and the scenery came to him on tracks, gliding quietly. Upstage, a permanent green wall, as if in a garden, suggested that things were more than they might seem; in that wall was a large window looking out on a changing sky—night stars, distorted sunsets for Jamaica—and a twisted vine climbed up alongside the window frame. If lit from the front, the sky behind the window disappeared and a greenish, painted sky of clouds made the window once again part of the wall itself.

ACT I

(Music. We hear a recorded vocalist as the lights go down: "If you hear a song in blue,/Like a flower crying for the dew,/That was my heart serenading you,/My prelude to a kiss.")

(A crowded party. PETER *stands apart, then approaches* TAYLOR*).*

PETER. I'm splitting. . . . Hey, Tay?

TAYLOR. Hey, Pete, did you meet Rita?

PETER. No. Hi.

RITA. Hi.

TAYLOR. *(Overlapping.)* Rita, Peter, Peter, Rita.

PETER. Actually, I . . .

TAYLOR. *(Overlapping.)* What's everybody drinking? Reet? Can I fill you up there?

RITA. Oh, I'll have another Dewar's, thanks.

TAYLOR. Pete?

PETER. No, nothing, thank—

TAYLOR. Don't worry, I've got it taken care of. You two just relax. One Dewar's, one beer . . .

(He moves off. Pause.)

PETER. How do you know the Sokols?

RITA. I don't. I mean, except from the hall.

PETER. Oh, you're a neighbor.

RITA. I couldn't sleep.

PETER. Oh, really? Why? . . . How long have you lived here?

RITA. I haven't slept since I was fourteen. A year and a half.

(Beat.)

PETER. Did you say you hadn't slept since you were fourteen?

RITA. Pretty much.

PETER. You look great!

RITA. Thank you.

PETER. Considering. Rita what?

RITA. Boyle.

PETER. Peter Hoskins.

RITA. Hoskins?

PETER. As in Hoskins disease?

RITA. Oh, Hodgkins.

PETER. No, no, it was just a . . . nonhumorous . . . flail.

RITA. What? *(He shakes his head.)* I like your shirt! *(TAYLOR returns with drinks.)*

TAYLOR. Dewar's, madame?

RITA. Thank you.

TAYLOR. No beer, sorry.

PETER. Wine's fine. Thanks. . . . Rita has insomnia.

TAYLOR. Oh yeah? Listen, I've got to pee, I'm sorry, excuse me. Forgive me. . . .

(He is gone again.)

PETER. What do you do when you're not *not* sleeping?

RITA. Oh, I usually, you know . . . write in my journal or— . . . Oh, for a living, you mean? I'm a bartender.

PETER. Oh. Where?

RITA. *(Overlapping.)* Yeah. At the Tin Market.

PETER. Oh, I know where that is. One for Pete.

RITA. Yeah.

PETER. I guess it's a good place for an insomniac to work. You work Saturdays? *(She nods.)* Well, you must make good money. Well, so you hate it, I'm sorry, I can't help that. What are your aspirations, in that case?

RITA. I'm like a graphic designer.

PETER. Oh, great.

RITA. I studied at Parsons.

PETER. This is good.

RITA. What do you do?

PETER. I make little tiny, transparent photographs of scientific articles which are rolled on film like microfilm only smaller. You'd like it. It's really interesting.

RITA. What are your aspirations in that case?

PETER. I should have some, shouldn't I? No, I I I I I I, uh, can't think of the answer, I'm sorry.

RITA. That's okay!

PETER. So why can't you sleep? You know what's good? I forget what it's called, it's an herb.

RITA. I tried it.

PETER. It didn't work?

RITA. I can't remember what it's called either. My memory is terrible!

PETER. Maybe that's why you can't sleep. You forget how tired you are. Well . . . If you ever need any help getting to sleep. *(Beat.)* Sorry. *(Beat.)* It was nice talking to you.

RITA. You, too.

PETER. Get some sleep.

RITA. I'll try.

(PETER addresses the audience.)

PETER. I stood outside for a while, just listening to the silence. Then I tried to figure out which window was hers and what her life might be like and why she couldn't sleep. Like that. *(Beat.)* The spell was cast.

(The Tin Market)

PETER. Hi.

RITA. Oh, hi.

PETER. Is this all right?

RITA. No, I'm sorry, you can never come in here. . . . What's new?

PETER. Since yesterday? Well, let's see, so much has happened. You look great.

RITA. What'll you drink?

PETER. Do you have Molson? . . . *(She nods.)* So, did you get some sleep?

RITA. Eventually.

(She sets down his Molson.)

PETER. Thank you.

RITA. You?

PETER. Sleep? Oh, I don't have any trouble. But . . . let's see, I read *The White Hotel* today.

RITA. Oh.

PETER. That was pretty much it.

RITA. Yeah.

PETER. You?

RITA. Oh, I slept, mostly. . . . How was *The White Hotel*?

PETER. Did you read it?

RITA. No, but I've read some of the case histories it's based on.

PETER. You have? Freud's? Case histories? You've read Freud.

RITA. Have you?

PETER. No, but . . . This book?

RITA. Uh-huh?

PETER. Starts with this very high-falutin' sexual dream thing, you know?

RITA. Yeah, I've heard everybody beats off when they read it.

(Beat.)

PETER. Uh-huh.

RITA. I'm sorry.

PETER. You heard that?

RITA. Go on.

PETER. . . . It's very depressing, the book.

RITA. Uh-huh.

PETER. This lovely, very neurotic woman goes into therapy with Freud himself—

RITA. Right.

PETER. And he sort of cures her so that she can go on to live for a few years before being killed by the Nazis in a lime pit. Happy. Happy stuff.

RITA. So why were you in Europe for ten years?

PETER. How did you know I was in Europe?

RITA. Word gets around.

PETER. You asked Taylor about me? You were asking around about me? Let's get married.

RITA. Okay.

PETER. I just went, you know.

RITA. He said there was a story and you would have to tell me.

PETER. He did? . . . Okay, this is the story and I'm not making this up.

RITA. Okay.

PETER. And it's not as sad as it sounds.

RITA. Shoot.

PETER. My parents?

RITA. Uh-huh?

PETER. Separated when I was four. And I went to live with my grandparents who are unfortunately deceased now. I'm going to make this as brief as possible.

RITA. Take your time.

PETER. And—

RITA. We can go up to my place if you want. When you're done.

PETER. And-everything-worked-out-great-for-everybody-it-was-amazing.

RITA. No, go on.

PETER. Were you serious about that?

RITA. I'm off in about seven minutes. Your parents.

PETER. My parents. I'm four years old. I go to live with my grandparents. My grandfather had to go into a nursing home when I was nine, then my grandmother had to go when I was eleven; they were both sick, so I go to live with my mother who by this time is remarried to Hank.

RITA. Uh-huh.

PETER. Very unhappy person, ridicules me in front of the other two children they have created from their un-savory loins, so I go to live with my father, who is also remarried, *three* other children, Sophie, the new wife, hates me even more than Hank.

RITA. This is like Dickens.

PETER. The only nice thing Sophie ever did for me was make the same food twice when I had made the mistake of saying I liked it. Usually she would stop cooking whatever it was I said I liked.

RITA. What was it?

PETER. What I liked? Spaetzles?

RITA. Oh, God.

PETER. You've had spaetzles?

RITA. Oh, sure.

PETER. You like them?

RITA. I love them.

PETER. You do?

RITA. Uh-huh. Anyway.

PETER. You love spaetzles. Anyway, everyone is unhappy now.

RITA. Uh-huh.

PETER. Sophie really can't stand the sight of me, because I remind her that my father was married to someone else and . . .

RITA. Right.

PETER. Any my father does not seem too fond of me, either. I don't know if he ever was, but so one night I say I'm going to go to the movies and instead I go to Europe.

RITA. What movie?

PETER. *The Wild Bunch,* I think, why?

RITA. Did you call them first?

PETER. Not until I got there.

RITA. Europe?

PETER. And I called collect.

RITA. That is . . .

PETER. Yeah.

RITA. Good for you.

PETER. Yeah. So. Why'd you ask which movie?

RITA. That is fabulous.

PETER. That's the story.

RITA. How did you eat? I mean . . .

PETER. Oh, I had about three thousand dollars saved up from my paper route. But that's a whole other kettle of . . .

RITA. Spaetzles.

PETER. Yeah. So . . .

RITA. You lived in Amsterdam?

PETER. You're a spy, aren't you?

(TOM *enters, behind the bar.*)

TOM. Hey, kiddo.

RITA. Hi. Tom, this is Peter.

TOM. Hi.

PETER. Good to meet you.

RITA. *(To* PETER.*)* You want to go?

PETER. Now? Naaaaaaaa. *(To us.)* I love the little sign when you buy your ticket to the roller coaster: "Ride at your own risk." As if the management is not at all concerned with your safety, the entire contraption is about to collapse, and to top it off, there are supernatural powers out there just waiting to pull you off the tracks and out into, you know, your worst, cruelest nightmare—the wild blue. They want you to believe that anything can happen. *(Beat.)* And they're right.

(Outside. They walk.)

PETER. Uh-huh.

RITA. So.

PETER. So they disowned you?

RITA. No. I never told them.

PETER. Oh.

RITA. It was like . . . I mean, they didn't need to know what I was involved with. I don't tell them everything.

PETER. I've never known a Communist.

RITA. Socialist.

PETER. Socialist.

RITA. But . . . I mean, I was only in the Party for about two months.

PETER. What happened?

RITA. Oh, I just . . . I felt like they were basically not interested in anything except being right.

PETER. Right.

RITA. And they didn't support the Soviet Union, not that they should—

PETER. Uh-huh.

RITA.—and they didn't support Mao, and they didn't support the United States. It's like where are you going to live?

PETER. Right.

RITA. But . . . I started by doing leaflets for them and then posters. I still did that after I left. What?

PETER. Nothing.

RITA. It was such a strange time. . . . You're a good listener.

PETER. So now you're . . .

RITA. Oh, I guess I'm a Democrat.

PETER. Me too.

RITA. But . . . they're such Republicans.

PETER. Your parents?

RITA. No, the Democrats. Beneath the skin.

PETER. Oh, uh-huh?

RITA. But . . . I don't know. I guess it's like the U.S.
It isn't perfect.

PETER. Right. *(Pause.)* Where do they live?

RITA. My parents? Englewood Cliffs. It's right across
the bridge. It's nice, actually.

PETER. What do they do?

RITA. My dad's a dentist.

PETER. Oh, really?

RITA. Uh-huh.

PETER. Wow.

RITA. Why?

PETER. No, I just think that's . . . interesting.

RITA. It is?

PETER. I think so. I don't know.

RITA. My mother's a mother.

PETER. Do you have brothers and sisters? *(She shakes
her head.)* They must dote on you.

RITA. What's Amsterdam like? D'you speak Dutch?

PETER. Ja.

RITA. Say something in Dutch.

PETER. Uh . . . *Je hebt erg witte tanden.*

RITA. What's that?

PETER. You have very white teeth.

RITA. Oh. Thank you.

PETER. Now you say, *Om je better mee op te eten.*

RITA. What is it?

PETER. *Om je better mee op te eten.*

RITA. *Om je metter—*

PETER. Better . . .

RITA. Better . . .

PETER. . . . *mee op te eten.*

RITA. . . . *mee op te eten.*

PETER. *Om je better mee op te eten.*

RITA. *Om je better mee op te eten.*

PETER. Great. You've got a good ear.

RITA. Oh. Good ear, clean teeth.

PETER. You do.

RITA. What did I say?

PETER. I can't tell you.

RITA. *(Overlapping.)* I knew you were gonna say that, I knew it!

PETER. No, it's untranslatable.

RITA. I'm sure it is. No, come on.

PETER. I'll tell you someday. . . .

RITA. So what did you do there?

PETER. In Amsterdam? I will, I promise.

RITA. How old were you when you went?

PETER. Sixteen.

RITA. Oh, wow.

PETER. I catered for the first couple of years and made sandwiches during the day; then I tutored rich little cutie-pies on their English and went to school at night. Finally I came back when my dad died.

(Pause.)

RITA. Do you see your mom or your family at all? *(He shakes his head.)* Never?

PETER. Nope.

RITA. Do you call them? *(He shakes his head.)* You miss them?

(Headshake. Pause.)

(RITA's apartment.)

PETER. This is great.

RITA. You want a Molson?

PETER. You drink Molson—

RITA. Uh-huh.

PETER.—in your own home?

RITA. I've been known to.

PETER. That's really . . .

RITA. A coincidence.

PETER. A coincidence. So why can't you sleep? I want to solve this.

RITA. I really wasn't exaggerating. It's been since I was fourteen.

PETER. That's a lot of journal keeping. . . . Have you seen doctors?

RITA. I've seen all the doctors.

PETER. Uh-huh.

RITA. Of every known . . .

PETER. Right.

RITA. *(Overlapping.)* Persuasion. I've ingested count-less . . .

(She hands him a Molson.)

PETER. Thanks.

RITA. Pills, liquids, I've seen an acupuncturist.

PETER. You did? What did it feel like?

RITA. Little needles in your back.

PETER. It hurt?

RITA. Sometimes.

PETER. They always lie.

RITA. I know.

PETER. You're really beautiful. *(She laughs.)* You are.

RITA. Thank you. That's . . . No, thank you.

(They kiss. She laughs.)

PETER. This is not supposed to be the funny part.

RITA. No, I know, I'm sorry. . . . I'm, I guess I'm nervous.

PETER. Why are you nervous? Don't be nervous.

RITA. All right.

(He approaches to kiss her.)

PETER. Don't laugh. . . . All right, you can laugh. *(They kiss.)* Am I going too fast? *(She shakes her head.)* Is this tacky of me? *(Headshake.)* Oh good. *(They kiss.)* This is definitely the highlight of my weekend. *(She smiles.)* So maybe we should just, you know, watch some TV, have happy memories of this and anticipate the future—*(She is shaking her head.)*—We shouldn't? *(They kiss.)* I would really, really like to see you with all of your clothes off and stuff like that.

RITA. I would really, really like to see you with all of your clothes off and . . .

PETER. Stuff like that? *(To us.)* When you're first getting to know someone and in that blissful, psychotic first flush of love, it seems like every aspect of their personality, their whole demeanor, the simple, lovely twist of their earlobes and their marvelous phone voice and their soft, dark wet whatever is somehow imbued with an extra push of color, an intensity heretofore . . . you know. *Unknown.*

(RITA's apartment. Later.)

PETER. Christ!

RITA. What?

PETER. Happiness! . . . Are you?

RITA. Uh-huh.

PETER. You are? It's like a drug.

RITA. It is a drug.

PETER. Sex?

RITA. To snare us into mating.

PETER. I must be peaking then.

RITA. No, the body manufactures it.

PETER. Uh-huh.

RITA. Like epinephrine or something.

PETER. Maybe that's where they got the word "crack."

RITA. Shut up. I prefer hole. Frankly.

PETER. Hole?

RITA. And dick.

PETER. Slit.

RITA. Ugh.

PETER. This is sick.

RITA. Tool, I like.

PETER. Uh-huh.

RITA. It's practical.

PETER. Wait a minute, did I detect an earlier note of cynicism in your comment about mating?

RITA. Oh. No.

PETER. You don't like kids?

RITA. No, I love them.

PETER. But you don't want to have them?

RITA. No, I don't, but . . .

PETER. Why not?

RITA. I just don't.

PETER. Your career?

RITA. What career? No, I think kids are great, I just don't think it's fair to raise them in the world. The way it is now.

PETER. Where else are you going to raise them? We're here.

RITA. I know, but . . .

PETER. It's like what you were saying about the socialists. (RITA *hesitates.*) Say.

RITA. People . . . Like *The White Hotel,* people do die

in lime pits, in the real world, not just in books. Women
go blind from watching their children being murdered.

PETER. Not in this country, they don't. Do they?

RITA. What—I mean, your grandparents getting sick
and dying and you being passed from one . . .

PETER. I survived. You know?

RITA. I don't have a choice about already being here,
but I do have a choice about bringing more children into
a world where they have to live with the constant fear of
being blown up. I mean, I'll be like walking down the
street . . . or I'll be lying in bed late at night and I'll
look at the light in the room and suddenly see it all just
go up in a blinding flash, in flames, and I'm the only one
left alive. . . .

PETER. No wonder you can't sleep.

RITA. The world's a really terrible place. It's too precarious. (Pause.) You want kids, obviously. I wish I could
say I did.

PETER. It's okay.

RITA. What's your dirtiest fantasy?

PETER. Excuse me? No, I thought you just said what's
my dirtiest fantasy.

RITA. What?

PETER. No, I can't—

RITA. Yes, you can. Please?

PETER. I'm sorry, I can't. What's yours, though? I'd
be curious.

RITA. (Overlapping.) I asked you first. Come on.

PETER. Oh God.

RITA. Please.

PETER. Well, they change.

RITA. Sure. What's one?

PETER. One?

RITA. Uh-huh.

PETER. Well . . . One?

RITA. Uh-huh.

PETER. Might be that someone . . . you know . . .

RITA. Uh-huh.

PETER.—who might just happen to be around the
apartment—

RITA. Uh-huh.

PETER. *(Mimicking her.)* Uh-huh, uh-huh. Might . . . sort of just, you know, spontaneously start crawling across the floor—

RITA. Uh-huh.

PETER.—on their hands and knees and . . . more or less unzip me with their, uh . . . teeth.

RITA. I'd do that.

PETER. You would?

RITA. Uh-huh.

PETER. Right now? *(She nods to us.)* We saw each other every night for the next six weeks. And it wasn't just the knees and the teeth, despite what you think. I would stop by my apartment now and then to see if the view out onto the airshaft had improved any, but my clothes had all found their way over to Rita's and my books. And then . . .

*(*RITA*'s apartment. Six weeks later.* PETER *is serving dinner.)*

PETER. That was the Communist?

RITA. Socialist.

PETER. Socialist.

RITA. No. That was the one who liked to dress up, go out.

PETER. Oh, right. But you don't like to go dancing, do you?

RITA. Sometimes. I change.

PETER. Uh-huh.

RITA. People do.

PETER. So before that was the Communist?

RITA. Socialist.

PETER. *(Overlapping.)* Socialist. And before that . . . ?

RITA. Oh, it was just high school, you know. This looks great. No, wait, there was someone else, who was it?

PETER. Is that what's going to happen to me?

RITA. Oh no, John, I told you about John.

PETER. The one who wanted to run away with you? Is that what's going to happen to me?

RITA. You're gonna want to run away?

PETER. You're going to forget my name over dinner

with someone else equally enamored of you and just attribute it to your lousy memory? "Oh, yes, that's right, Peter. Peter—"

RITA. Probably.

PETER. "What did he look like?" And then you'll tell them my dirtiest fantasy and how you degraded yourself just for a home-cooked meal.

RITA. Mmmm. *(They are eating.)* I told my parents about you.

PETER. What did you tell them?

RITA. I said that you were very considerate.

PETER. In what way?

RITA. I said—Well, I mean, we talk very frankly about sex.

PETER. You and your parents?

RITA. And I said that you always brought protection. . . .

PETER. You did not.

RITA. And that you were very attentive to whether or not I had an orgasm.

PETER. This is such bullshit.

RITA. No, I said they should meet you, what do you think?

PETER. Protection.

RITA. They're nice.

PETER. I'm sure.

RITA. So are you free this weekend?

PETER. Sure.

RITA. Don't be nervous.

PETER. All right. Did you tell them about my family and everything?

RITA. My mother.

PETER. She knows the story?

RITA. Uh-huh.

PETER. All about me?

RITA. Uh-huh.

PETER. Will you marry me?

RITA. Uh-huh.

PETER. You will?

RITA. Uh-huh.

(Beat.)

PETER. I just wanted to see how it sounds.

RITA. It sounds great.

PETER. This is too fast. Isn't it?

RITA. Is it?

PETER. I don't think so.

RITA. Neither do I.

PETER. You'll marry me?

RITA. Uh-huh.

PETER. You will?

RITA. Uh-huh.

(The BOYLE *home. Doorbell.)*

RITA. Mom?

MRS. BOYLE. Nice to meet you.

RITA. Dad.

PETER. Dr. Boyle.

RITA. These are my parents. . . .

MRS. BOYLE. So I understand you're a manager in a publishing firm.

PETER. That's correct. Yes.

DR. BOYLE. That must be, uh . . . What kind of firm is it?

MRS. BOYLE. Publishing.

DR. BOYLE. What kind— Don't belittle me in front of new people.

MRS. BOYLE. Belittle?

RITA. Dad, please.

DR. BOYLE. What kind of publishing firm is it? I was asking.

PETER. It's, uh, scientific publishing. They publish, you know, scientific publishing—things—journals! I knew I knew that.

RITA. *(To* PETER.) You want a beer?

PETER. Sure.

MRS. BOYLE. In the morning, Rita?

RITA. Yes, Mother, we have been drinking nonstop for weeks, it's time you knew this about us.

MRS. BOYLE. I'll have one too, then.

RITA. You will?

DR. BOYLE. Me, too.

PETER. A bunch of lushes here, Rita, you didn't tell me.

DR. BOYLE. Oh, I can pull out four wisdom teeth on a fifth of Stoli.

PETER. You can?

MRS. BOYLE. He's teasing you.

DR. BOYLE. Scien— What kind of scientific?

PETER. Abstracting and indexing. It's a service.

DR. BOYLE. Like a database.

PETER. It is a database.

DR. BOYLE. It is a database. Covering . . . ?

PETER. All kinds of fields.

DR. BOYLE. All kinds.

PETER. Pretty much, you know, everything from energy to robotics to medical articles. I've memorized our marketing material.

DR. BOYLE. I've seen this.

(RITA *hands everyone his/her beer.*)

PETER. Thank you.

(*They clink bottles.*)

DR. BOYLE. I've seen this sort of thing.

PETER. Yeah.

DR. BOYLE. So you're the manager . . . ?

PETER. The manager of the fiche department.

DR. BOYLE. Microfiche.

PETER. Right.

MRS. BOYLE. The what is it?

DR. BOYLE. Microfiche.

PETER. It's like microfilm only smaller.

MRS. BOYLE. Uh-huh.

PETER. Little film.

DR. BOYLE. Why do you do that?

PETER. Microfiche?

DR. BOYLE. No, why does the company do microfiche?

PETER. Oh, I see. Because if you want to call up and—

DR. BOYLE. Oh, I—yes, yes, yes, yes, yes.

PETER. (*Overlapping.*)—ask for like—

DR. BOYLE. Right, a certain article.

PETER. Right. We can retrieve it for you. And we also film the abstract journals we actually publish so . . .

DR. BOYLE. To save space.

PETER. Right. Yes, in libraries, it saves space.

DR. BOYLE. All right. We approve.

RITA. Daddy.

MRS. BOYLE. Marshall.

DR. BOYLE. Maybe now she'll get some sleep.

MRS. BOYLE. Now how long have you two been going out?

RITA. Over a year now.

(PETER *looks at* RITA; *beat.*)

PETER. About that. Yeah.

MRS. BOYLE. Rita says you've been abroad.

PETER. Yes, I have.

MRS. BOYLE. Where?

PETER. Amsterdam, for the most part, but . . .

MRS. BOYLE. Marshall was in Korea.

PETER. Oh, was it nice? Oh, no, no, I see—

MRS. BOYLE. Nice!

DR. BOYLE. Some people might have been able to relax, I don't know, bullets flying.

PETER. *(Overlapping.)* Right. Right.

MRS. BOYLE. We're playing with you.

DR. BOYLE. Okay, here you go.

(DR. BOYLE *starts to untuck his shirttail.*)

RITA. Oh no, Daddy, please, God, please—

DR. BOYLE. *(Overlapping.)* This is the only scar you'll ever see in the shape of a saxophone.

MRS. BOYLE. It really is, people think he's kidding.

PETER. Really?

DR. BOYLE. If he's going to be in the family, he's got to see these things.

(*The* BOYLE *home. A month later.*)

PETER. *(To us, as he changes into his wedding garb.)* I stood in front of the full-length mirror in their upstairs guestroom, looking out over the yard at the little tent and the band and the food which had been catered; I felt a certain kinship with these people, the caterers.

(RITA *sneaks up, covers his eyes.*)

RITA. Don't look, it's bad luck.

PETER. All right, but— Wait, wait— You don't believe that, do you?

RITA. *(Overlapping.)* You looked.

PETER. I didn't look.

RITA. You're looking.

PETER. Wait, I won't look. I won't.

RITA. *(Overlapping.)* No, you've already cursed the first fourteen years of our marriage.

PETER. I love you.

RITA. What about when I'm a hundred years old with a mustache and yellow teeth?

PETER. I'll still love you.

RITA. And I'm sagging down to here and I'm bald?

PETER. I'll love you all the more.

RITA. Are you sure?

PETER. Yes, I promise.

RITA. And I won't ever want to make love and I can never remember anything?

PETER. You can never remember anything now.

RITA. That's true. Okay.

(She leaves; PETER's eyes remain closed.)

PETER. What about me?

(TAYLOR comes in with two beers; he is wearing sunglasses.)

TAYLOR. What about you? . . . You okay?

PETER. Great, Taylor.

TAYLOR. They're holding for the musicians.

PETER. Okay.

(TAYLOR helps PETER dress.)

TAYLOR. Now listen. There's nothing at all to worry about here.

PETER. I know that.

TAYLOR. This is a natural step in life's plan. Like sliding down a banister.

PETER. Right.

TAYLOR. That turns into a razor blade. No, I don't want you to think of this as anything more than one of the little skirmishes we all wage, each and every day of our lives, in the eternal struggle against mediocrity and decay. Straighten your tie.

PETER. I straightened my tie.

TAYLOR. Fix your face. You're not compromising yourself.

PETER. Thank you.

TAYLOR. Not at all. You see all those middle-aged guys down there in their checked pants and their wives in the flouncy dresses?

PETER. Mm-hm.

TAYLOR. They were all very hip once. But . . . There's the music. You okay?

PETER. Just go.

TAYLOR. Relax. I've got the ring.

PETER. Great. Go.

(TAYLOR *kisses* PETER *on the cheek, mouths "I love you."*)

(*The* BOYLE *home. Outside.*)

MINISTER. . . . to keep the solemn vows you are about to make. Live with tender consideration for each other. Conduct your lives in honesty and in truth. And your marriage will last. This should be remembered as you now declare your desire to be wed.

PETER. I, Peter, take thee, Rita, to be my wedded wife, to have and to hold from this day forward, for better or for worse, for richer or for poorer, in sickness and in health, to love and to cherish, till death us do part, according to God's holy ordinance; and thereto, I pledge thee my troth.

RITA. I, Rita, take thee, Peter, to be my wedded husband, to have and to hold from this day forward, for better or for worse, for richer or for poorer, in sickness and in health, to love and to cherish, till death us do part, according to God's holy ordinance; and thereto, I pledge thee my troth.

MINISTER. For as much as Rita and Peter have consented together in holy matrimony and have witnessed the same before God and this company, pledging their faith and declaring the same, I pronounce, by the authority committed unto me as a Minister of God, that they are Husband and Wife, according to the ordinance of God and the law of this State, in the Name of the Father, and of the Son, and of the Holy Spirit. . . . (PE-

TER *and* RITA *kiss.)* I think a little applause would be in order.

PETER. *(To us.)* And there was some polite applause as if we'd made a good putt or something, and we all made a beeline for the champagne with the strawberries in it.

(The BOYLE *home; outside. Later.)*

RITA. Peter, you remember my Aunt Dorothy and Uncle Fred.

PETER. Yes, good to see you.

UNCLE FRED. Peter and Rita, that's very euphonious.

PETER. Yes.

AUNT DOROTHY. Isn't it?

RITA. Sometimes we get Peter and Reeter.

AUNT DOROTHY. Oh.

RITA. Or Pita and Rita.

PETER. Excuse me, Rita, who's the guy in the green coat? Over by the food?

RITA. Oh . . . *(RITA sees the* OLD MAN.*)* Oh, yeah. I don't know.

MRS. BOYLE. Everybody shmush together, come on! Marshall! . . . *(People crowd together around* PETER *and* RITA.*)* Marshall!

DR. BOYLE. What?

MRS. BOYLE. Get in the picture, come on!

DR. BOYLE. Jesus Christ, I thought you were on fire.

MRS. BOYLE. Get in, everybody! All right. Say "bull-shit"! Smile!

("Bullshit." "Cheese." Flash.)

DR. BOYLE. Don't tell her—

MRS. BOYLE. Wait, I want to get another one. Don't move. Ohhhhh.

DR. BOYLE. *(Overlapping, continuous from earlier line.)*—you don't need a flashbulb in the middle of the day.

UNCLE FRED. My face hurts, hurry up!

MRS. BOYLE. All right, say "Bullshit."

(Again.)

AUNT DOROTHY. Oh, I had my face in a funny position.

UNCLE FRED. Whose fault is that?

AUNT DOROTHY. And don't say it's always that way.

PETER. Mom, who's the guy over by the bar?

MRS. BOYLE. Who?

PETER. See who I mean?

MRS. BOYLE. Oh . . .

(RITA and the OLD MAN toast each other with their champagne.)

RITA. Isn't he great?

MRS. BOYLE. No, I thought he was with your firm.

PETER. *(Shaking his head.)* Unh-uh.

(The OLD MAN starts toward them.)

MRS. BOYLE. Marsh? Right behind me, don't look now, he's very peculiar.

DR. BOYLE. Never seen him before in my life.

MRS. BOYLE. He's not with the club, is he?

(The OLD MAN comes up to them.)

OLD MAN. Congratulations. Both of you.

RITA. Thank you.

PETER. Thank you very much.

TAYLOR. *(Extending his hand.)* I'm Taylor McGowan.

OLD MAN. You make a lovely couple.

TAYLOR. Your name, I'm sorry?

OLD MAN. And what a wonderful day for it.

RITA. *(Mesmerized by him.)* Yes.

(TAYLOR shakes hands with the empty air.)

TAYLOR. Good to meet you.

OLD MAN. How precious the time is. . . . How little we realize 'til it's almost gone.

DR. BOYLE. You'll have to forgive us, but none of us seems to remember who you are.

RITA. It's all right, Daddy.

OLD MAN. I only wanted to wish the two young people well. And perhaps to kiss the bride. Before I'm on my way.

DR. BOYLE. Well—

RITA. I'd be flattered. Thank you.

TAYLOR. Some angle this guy's got.

RITA. My blessings to you.

(The OLD MAN takes RITA's face in his hands. There is a low rumble which grows in volume as they begin to

kiss. Wind rushes through the trees, leaves fall, no one moves except for RITA, *whose bridal bouquet slips to the ground. The* OLD MAN *and* RITA *separate and the wind and rumble die down.)*

RITA. And you.

(The OLD MAN *seems off balance;* DR. BOYLE *steadies him.)*

DR. BOYLE. Do you want to sit down?

AUNT DOROTHY. Get him a chair, Fred.

TAYLOR. Too much blood rushing to the wrong place, I guess.

(The OLD MAN *stares at* PETER *and* RITA.*)*

DR. BOYLE. Are you dizzy?

OLD MAN. Peter? . . .

(UNCLE FRED brings a chair.)

DR. BOYLE. Here you go now.

(He eases the OLD MAN *into the chair, takes his pulse.* PETER *remains fixated on the* OLD MAN. RITA *has withdrawn from the crowd; she examines her dress, her hands, the air around her, as if it were all new, miraculous.)*

MRS. BOYLE. I thought you said you didn't know him. *(*PETER *is mystified.)* Peter?

DR. BOYLE. Take it easy now.

OLD MAN.	DR. BOYLE.
(To PETER.*)*	You're okay now, just
Honey? Honey? . . . It's	breathe for me, nice and
me. What's happening?	easy.
. . . Why is . . . ? Why is	
everybody . . . ?	

OLD MAN. *(Staring at* DR. BOYLE.*)* Daddy, it's me.

AUNT DOROTHY. Ohhhh, he thinks Marshall's his father.

TAYLOR. Where do you live, can you tell us?

DR. BOYLE. Okay. He's doing fine. Everybody relax.

AUNT DOROTHY. Get him a glass of water, Fred.

DR. BOYLE. He's had too much to drink, I suspect. Am I right? A little too much champagne?

(The OLD MAN *begins to nod, strangely.)*

MRS. BOYLE. Should I call an ambulance? Marshall?

DR. BOYLE. No, no. He's going to be fine.

OLD MAN. I've had too much to drink.

DR. BOYLE. That's right. Somebody get him a cup of coffee.

(UNCLE FRED arrives with water.)

AUNT DOROTHY. Coffee, make it coffee.

MRS. BOYLE. Where do you live, can you tell us?

OLD MAN. Please . . .

MRS. BOYLE. Is there someone we can call?

OLD MAN. I'm sorry for any trouble I've caused.

(The OLD MAN starts to stand.)

DR. BOYLE. There's no trouble.

MRS. BOYLE. Don't let him, honey—

DR. BOYLE. *(Overlapping.)* We just want to see you don't hurt yourself.

UNCLE FRED. *(Returning with coffee.)* Here you go.

OLD MAN. No, thank you.

(The OLD MAN is backing away.)

UNCLE FRED. Don't burn yourself.

OLD MAN. No.

AUNT DOROTHY. He doesn't want it, Fred.

MRS. BOYLE. Don't just let him wander off is all I'm saying.

DR. BOYLE. All right, Marion—

MRS. BOYLE. He could fall and he could hurt himself, that's all—

DR. BOYLE. He's not going to sue us, trust me.

(DR. BOYLE and TAYLOR follow the OLD MAN off.)

MRS. BOYLE. And find out where he lives!

UNCLE FRED. He'll be fine.

AUNT DOROTHY. I'm sure he's a neighbor or someone's gardener.

MRS. BOYLE. Whose?

UNCLE FRED. *(Same time.)* That's right.

MRS. BOYLE. *(Starting to exit.)* I know everyone in a five-mile radius.

AUNT DOROTHY. Marion, stay here.

UNCLE FRED. Marion—

AUNT DOROTHY. Go with her.

MRS. BOYLE. He's not going to bite me, now stop it, Frederick, if you want to come, come.

(UNCLE FRED follows MRS. BOYLE off.)

PETER. *(To Rita.)* Are you all right? *(She nods.)* Are you sure?

AUNT DOROTHY. Oh, what a fuss. Forget all about it, pretend it never even happened.

PETER. We're okay, thanks.

AUNT DOROTHY. Don't you both look so wonderful, and you notice who he wanted to kiss, not me. Oh, you're going to have such a good time, where is it you're going again now? Marion told me.

(PETER waits for RITA to answer before:)

PETER. Jamaica.

AUNT DOROTHY. That's right. For how long?

PETER. Two weeks.

AUNT DOROTHY. Oh, they loved it there last year. . . . Your mom and dad . . . Well, I'm going to leave you two alone. Do you want another glass of champagne while I'm at the bar?

PETER. No, thanks.

AUNT DOROTHY. No . . . ?

(AUNT DOROTHY moves off.)

PETER. That was so weird, wasn't it? Calling me honey? He just seemed so vulnerable. I swear I've never seen him before. . . . You're okay? *(RITA nods.)* You sure? You seem . . . kind of . . . Okay.

(The others begin to filter back on.)

TAYLOR. *(Overlapping.)* Unbelievable.

AUNT DOROTHY. What happened?

TAYLOR. Just took off down the street, kept going.

DR. BOYLE. *(Overlapping.)* Everything's fine now, it's all under control.

TAYLOR. *(To PETER.)* Guess he thought you were both kind of cute, huh . . . ?

MRS. BOYLE. Oh, my poor babies, to spoil your whole wedding.

AUNT DOROTHY. Have some champagne, Marion.

MRS. BOYLE. No, my God, I'll throw up all those strawberries. *(To RITA.)* Your father thinks that's the Evans' gardener, but I don't think it is, do you? . . .

DR. BOYLE. *(Overlapping.)* Enough, Marion.

MRS. BOYLE. That's not the Evans' gardener, is it? . . . Rita?

(All eyes on RITA; *she turns to look over her shoulder before turning back and smiling.)*

RITA. Must have been my kiss is all.

AUNT DOROTHY. That's right.

DR. BOYLE. *(Overlapping.)*   UNCLE FRED.
That's right.   There you go.

RITA. Drives the men wild.

UNCLE FRED. Hear, hear!

TAYLOR. This is a party,   DR. BOYLE. *(To* MRS.
come on!   BOYLE.*)* Come on, give
                                  me a kiss.

MINISTER. A toast!

AUNT DOROTHY. Here's to   TAYLOR. *(Singing.)*
the lucky couple!   "Celebrate, celebrate!
                                 Dance to the music!"

UNCLE FRED. Hear, hear!   MINISTER. To the lucky
                                 couple!

(Someone starts to sing "For they're a jolly good couple!" *Everyone joins in, then singing fades.)*

PETER. *(To us, as he strips down to bathing trunks.)* And there was a toast to us and to love and to Jamaica and to our plane flight and to airline safety and to the old drunk whoever he was. Whoever he was. I was completely trashed by the time the limo pulled up to take us to the airport. Dr. Boyle told us to sign anything we wanted onto the hotel bill, his treat, and off we went. . . . The whole way down on the plane and straight through that first night in the hotel, Rita slept like a baby. I couldn't. For some reason. I kept hearing that poor old guy calling me "Honey." "Honey, it's me." Who's "me"? And I'd wanted to protect him. *(Pause.)* In the morning we headed down to the pool, husband and wife.

(Jamaica. Poolside. The WAITER *stands beside* PETER *and* RITA, *both in chaise longues.* PETER *holds a drink in a coconut shell, decorated with a paper umbrella.)*

PETER. *(To* RITA.*)* Don't you want to try one?

RITA. *(To the* WAITER.*)* Just a seltzer water.

PETER. Okay. *(To the* WAITER.*)* I'll take another,

thanks. *(The* WAITER *retreats. Beat.* PETER *notices something on* RITA's *wrist.)* What's that?

RITA. You like?

PETER. Well . . . sure, where'd you get it?

RITA. Just now.

PETER. In the shop? Here? It's not gold, is it?

RITA. Fourteen-karat.

PETER. You're kidding. How much was it?

RITA. Fifteen hundred or so.

PETER. Dollars?

RITA. Why? He said to charge anything.

PETER. You charged fifteen hundred dollars on your dad's bill?

RITA. I like it.

PETER. Well . . . You do? It's sort of like a . . . it's like a charm bracelet, isn't it?

RITA. It is a charm bracelet.

PETER. Like old women wear? I'm sorry. Look, if you like it, I think it's great. And he did say . . . You're right, he's your dad.

RITA. Relax, we're on vacation.

PETER. I know.

RITA. And you're my puppy puppy.

PETER. Your puppy puppy?

RITA. And the world is a wonderful place to live, admit it! . . . Do my back?

(He takes the sunscreen, looks at it before applying it.)

PETER. Twenty-five? . . . I keep thinking about that crazy old schmuck from the wedding.

RITA. Mmmm, that feels good, darling!

PETER. Who do you suppose he was?

RITA. Hm?

PETER. The old guy.

RITA. Oh, I don't know. . . . My fairy godfather come to sprinkle the fairy dust on us.

PETER. Aren't you curious?

RITA. Nope. Come for a swim.

PETER. You just put the stuff on.

RITA. I know. Come on, I'll race you!

(She runs off.)

PETER. *(To us.)* Our first full day being married and

she seemed like a different Rita. I told myself, It's the excitement. And, come on, it's the rest of your life, you want it to be wonderful. It's natural to ask, "Is this the right person for me? Am I the right person for her? . . . Who the hell is she, anyway?"

(RITA returns, dripping wet.)

RITA. Oh, I love it here, don't you? *(Singing as she dries herself.)* "Yellow bird, so high in banana tree . . ."

PETER. Are you sorry you married me? . . . Rita, you were supposed to laugh.

RITA. Oh, shut up.

PETER. Okay.

RITA. I want to go jet-skiing and I want to go scuba-diving and I want to go up into the mountains and see the monkeys, okay? And maybe go to a soccer game? *(She plants a noisy kiss on him.)* With you on my arm.

(Beat.)

PETER. Do you ever think how we're each a whole, separate being beside one another. Each with a heart pumping inside and a soul and all our memories. How I can never, no matter how close we ever become, share your past, be with you as a nine-year-old, as a baby.

RITA. Don't worry about it, all right?

PETER. I wasn't.

RITA. Just take things as they come and enjoy them. That's what life's for.

PETER. You're right. You're absolutely right.

(Pause. RITA catches PETER staring at her.)

RITA. Feast away!

PETER. All right, I wasn't going to bring this up, but . . . Now just hear me out first; I know what you're going to say, but . . . Okay. You know how you never get any time to work on your portfolio and—Well, now that we have just the one rent, what if—just for a while, not forever—you quit tending bar and let me support you.

RITA. Sure.

PETER. What? You'd consider it?

RITA. Why not?

PETER. Really?

RITA. Let you bring home the bacon for a while. Right?

PETER. Right.

RITA. If it'd make you happy.

PETER. Baby, I'm sorry, I'm freaking out. Are you sorry you married me?

RITA. No. *(Remembering.)* Oh. Ha-ha-ha.

PETER. I'm serious this time.

RITA. Don't be a silly.

PETER. Okay. Okay. *(To us.) Not* okay. The days went by. We went to the soccer game, we windsurfed, or windfell, we ate, we snorkeled, we walked on the beach, always under a ton of sunscreen. And Rita was tireless. Fearless. And sleeping, not that there was anything wrong with that. No, no. Nothing was wrong—exactly. But nothing felt . . . nothing *felt.* *(Pause.)* About a week into the vacation . . .

(The pool. The WAITER *stands beside them.)*

WAITER. Something from the bar?

RITA. Another seltzer, please, and clean this up, would you, it's drawing flies.

PETER. Oh, I'll have a Long Island Ice Tea this time, thanks. *(The* WAITER *moves off.)* Doesn't it ever bother you sometimes, though? The black/white thing? I mean, it's so obviously a class issue here, not that it isn't in New York. But you'd think they'd all just rise up and kill us all poolside.

RITA. Why is that?

PETER. Because. We have the money and they don't.

RITA. We worked for it, didn't we?

PETER. Well, your father worked for it, in this case. But, I mean, you talk about the world being so precarious, everything ending in a blinding flash; it would seem a little less likely if things were a little more egalitarian, wouldn't it? If there were a slightly more equal distribution of the wealth, that's all.

RITA. You want to give 'em your money, go ahead.

PETER. No, I . . . Why would you—?

RITA. Peter, you're doing it again.

PETER. I know.

RITA. You take a perfect situation and you pee all over it. Be happy.

PETER. Okay, I was just referring to the people we saw

living in abandoned cars and refrigerators out by the airport.

RITA. That was terrible. But you don't have to look at it, do you?

PETER. Oh, good attitude. . . . Look, I'm just trying to make conversation, Rita, you're the Commie in the woodpile, not me.

(Beat.)

RITA. Whatcha reading?

PETER. The case histories? Freud.

RITA. Oh. Sounds interesting. Can I read it when you're through?

(PETER stares at her. The WAITER returns.)

WAITER. I'm sorry, sir, the bartender say he don't know what that is.

PETER. A Long Island Ice Tea? *(To RITA.)* What goes into one? . . . Rita? An Ice Tea? How do you make it?

RITA. I'm sorry, darling, I've forgotten.

PETER. What, do you have it all written down behind the bar or something?

RITA. I'm on vacation.

PETER. So you can't remember a drink recipe for something I'd like to order?

RITA. *(Overlapping.)* Yes. That's right. On the money. Bingo! It's a real busman's holiday with you around, you know? You could fuck up a wet dream!

(She walks off. Beat.)

PETER. *(To the WAITER.)* Nothing right now, thanks. *(To us.)* It's one thing to forget a drink recipe or a book you read a long time ago, maybe, *maybe,* but your *ideals*? It was as if she had switched channels, switched . . . *something.* *(Pause.)* Our last night we walked out on the beach in a light mist . . . like cloth being pulled across your skin.

(The beach. They walk.)

RITA. Oh, it's so beautiful, isn't it? It's great to be alive. And young. There will never be a more perfect night. Or a better chance for two people to love each other. If they don't try so hard. *(Beat.)* I remembered the recipe for Long Island Ice Tea. White rum, vodka—

PETER. You don't have to prove anything to me, Rita. *(Pause.)* You know . . . I was thinking about you growing up. What— Like, what was it like having a surgeon for a father?

RITA. Oh . . . well, it was nice. I always thought, "He helps people."

PETER. What about your brothers and sisters? How did they feel about it?

RITA. You'd have to ask them.

PETER. *(To us.)* Nobody's memory is that bad! Or was she toying with me? That wasn't like her at all. Unless something was terribly, terribly wrong.

RITA. Peter? Make love to me.

PETER. Here?

RITA. No one'll see. I want to have your baby. . . . I want your baby inside me.

PETER. You don't know how that makes me feel.

RITA. Yes I do.

PETER. You don't want babies, don't you remember? You've read Freud's case histories and your father's a dentist, not a surgeon. You don't have brothers and sisters.

RITA. Why are you telling me all this . . . ?

PETER. What, you were teasing me?

RITA. Of course I was teasing you. Did you think I didn't know those things? . . . Sweetie?

PETER. You never call me that or "Puppy puppy," you never say "Don't be a silly" or "Bring home the bacon" or pull the skin off your chicken. You're not drinking, you're not using salt, Rita, you're suddenly—

RITA. I want to have your baby. I'm taking better care of myself. Now, please, darling, relax. You're having some kind of a—

PETER. No. No! You're a Communist, Rita, or Socialist, Democrat, whatever you are, you don't defend the social order in Jamaica or anywhere, you have . . . You're just not . . . You're not . . . *you*. It's like you don't even need me anymore.

RITA. You need to take a hot bath and look at the moon and breathe life in.

PETER. Rita is afraid of life, she doesn't drink it in.

RITA. I'm going to insist that you see someone as soon as we get back to New York.

PETER. *Je hebt erg witte tanden.*

RITA. Thanks.

PETER. What did I say?

RITA. You said my teeth are white, you know what you said.

PETER. *(Embracing her.)* Yes! Thank you. My baby. What do you say?

RITA. What do you mean?

PETER. What's your line? What do you say? Your line, you memorized it.

RITA. I'm sorry, Peter—

PETER. *(Overlapping.)* In Dutch! Rita, what do you say?

RITA. I say good night.

(She turns, starts to walk off; he grabs her.)

PETER. No, please! Rita!

RITA. *(Overlapping.)* Hey! Watch it, pal!

PETER. I want you to be you, Rita, I want you!

RITA. I am me. This is all I am. I'm sorry I can't be whatever you want me to be. This is me. And maybe what you saw wasn't here at all.

(She walks off. Pause. PETER *looks at us. The sound of surf breaking. Lights fade.)*

ACT II

(The BOYLE *home.)*

MRS. BOYLE. Peter!

DR. BOYLE. There they are.

MRS. BOYLE. Don't you both look wonderful.

DR. BOYLE. Not much of a tan here.

PETER. Well, we decided not to age on this trip.

MRS. BOYLE. Well, you both look wonderful.

DR. BOYLE. Rested.

PETER. That's right.

MRS. BOYLE. *(To* RITA.*)* Did you sleep? *(*RITA *nods.)* Ohhhh.

PETER. Like a baby. Every night straight through.

DR. BOYLE. Well, you're having a good effect on her.

RITA. It's so good to see you both.

MRS. BOYLE. What'll you drink? Beer?

RITA. Nothing for me, thank you, Mom.

DR. BOYLE. Peter?

PETER. Sure, thanks. Rita's quit drinking.

MRS. BOYLE. Ohhh. Really?

DR. BOYLE. Wonderful.

MRS. BOYLE. So now tell us everything.

RITA. It was terrific.

PETER. It was just great and we can't thank you enough.

MRS. BOYLE. How was the weather?

RITA. Perfect.

PETER. Oh, yeah. Really.

DR. BOYLE. Did you get any golf in there?

RITA. That was the one thing we didn't quite get to, I'm afraid.

MRS. BOYLE. *(To* PETER. *)* He's teasing her.

DR. BOYLE. We took Rita for golf lessons every year for I don't know how many years—

MRS. BOYLE. Three.

DR. BOYLE. Or four.

MRS. BOYLE. Three.

DR. BOYLE. Three. Okay.

RITA. Well—

DR. BOYLE. *(Overlapping.)* She never got with it.

RITA. Maybe I'll try it again. I'm serious, I might like to.

(Beat.)

MRS. BOYLE. Did you go snorkeling?

RITA. Oh, sure.

PETER. You name it, we tried it. Rita even wanted to go up on one of those kites—that they haul from behind the boats?

MRS. BOYLE. Oh, you're kidding. No!

RITA. Peter was upset by all the poverty, wanted to give them all our money.

(DR. and MRS. BOYLE turn and stare at PETER.)

PETER. Oh, show them the bracelet you bought, Rita.

(RITA shakes her head.)

RITA. I didn't bring it.

PETER. Ohhh, too bad.

MRS. BOYLE. I want to see.

PETER. It's gold. It's incredible. All these big things hanging down from it, just weigh about a ton. . . .

MRS. BOYLE. Sounds expen—

DR. BOYLE. *(Overlapping.)* But you know, that's the reality— Excuse me— You can't escape it, wherever you go. *(Pause.)* Poverty.

MRS. BOYLE. No.

RITA. That's what I told him.

DR. BOYLE. It's reality.

(Pause.)

MRS. BOYLE. Oh, speaking of which, that man from the wedding, Rita— Your father told me not to bring it up, but—was not the Evans' gardener. I called up over there after you left for the airport.

DR. BOYLE. All right, enough.

PETER. Who do you think he was, though?

RITA. I told you, I thought he was my fairy godfather.

DR. BOYLE. That's right.

(Pause.)

PETER. Strange.

MRS. BOYLE. *(To* RITA.*)* Well . . . Why don't we let the men talk about whatever it is men talk about and you can help me set the table?

RITA. Great. Fun.

MRS. BOYLE. And I can show you the sketch I did of your father in class. We'll be ready to eat in about fifteen minutes, gents.

PETER. Terrific.

*(*RITA *follows* MRS. BOYLE *off.)*

DR. BOYLE. When do you start work?

PETER. Tomorrow.

DR. BOYLE. You folks gonna have enough room in that apartment of Rita's?

PETER. Oh sure.

DR. BOYLE. Another beer there?

*(*PETER *shakes his head. Beat.)*

PETER. Does Rita . . . ? She seem okay to you?

DR. BOYLE. Why, something the matter?

PETER. No. No.

DR. BOYLE. Tell me, for godsake.

PETER. No. She seems changed a little bit.

DR. BOYLE. Well, you're married now. And you're dealing with a slippery entity there.

PETER. Uh-huh.

DR. BOYLE. She's always had the highest expectations of everybody. Especially herself. But . . . I don't know, in some way she's always been . . . uncertain. Drove her mother and me crazy for a while.

PETER. Yeah, she told me a little bit. Her politics and stuff.

DR. BOYLE. Politics?

PETER. Oh . . . n—

DR. BOYLE. *(Overlapping.)* What politics?

PETER. No, no, I was mixing it up with something else. . . .

DR. BOYLE. You'll get used to her. She's young. You're both young.

PETER. She gets, you know, really forgetful sometimes.

DR. BOYLE. I know.

PETER. Forgets whole . . .

DR. BOYLE. Years. I'm aware.

PETER. She's given up salt, too.

DR. BOYLE. Oh, she has. I've got to do that.

PETER. And she pulls the skin off her chicken.

DR. BOYLE. Oh. Well, she's way ahead of me. Watching out for her old age already . . .

(Pause.)

PETER. She's thinking of maybe quitting her job at the bar, too, so. . . .

DR. BOYLE. She is.

PETER. Yeah. So I can support us.

DR. BOYLE. Outstanding. You must be making her very happy. Congratulations. . . .

PETER. Thanks.

(PETER's office.)

TAYLOR. Hey!

PETER. Hey!

TAYLOR. No tan.

PETER. No tan.

TAYLOR. We missed you.

PETER. Thanks.

TAYLOR. Welcome back. Listen, Kollegger wants to know what happened to April.

PETER. Oh. The N.I.H. never sent the documents.

TAYLOR. Oh. What do I tell him?

PETER. Tell him the N.I.H. never sent the documents.

TAYLOR. *(Overlapping.)*—never sent the documents. I like the angle.

(TAYLOR starts to leave.)

PETER. Listen, Tay?

TAYLOR. Yeah.

PETER. If you could switch souls with somebody . . . ? Like go inside their body and they go inside yours . . . ? You know? Switch?

TAYLOR. . . . Yeeaaaaah?

PETER. Do you think it would be possible, if you didn't know someone, to impersonate them, by just being inside them and . . . looking like them?

TAYLOR. Where are they?

PETER. Inside you.

TAYLOR. And you're inside them?

PETER. Right.

TAYLOR. Why would you go inside another person's body if you didn't know them?

PETER. It's conjecture.

TAYLOR. I think I know that, Peter. But wouldn't you do better to pick someone you knew, a particular person you envied—

PETER. Right.

TAYLOR.—or admired so that you could do or be or have the things this other person did or bee'd or had?

PETER. Maybe. Yes.

TAYLOR. Are you Rita now? Is that what you're telling me? You two have merged?

PETER. All right, here's another question. Have you ever . . . This is sort of a bizarre question. Have you ever been having sex with somebody . . . ?

TAYLOR. Nope.

PETER. And they're doing everything, you know, right more or less.

TAYLOR. Oh, right, sex, I remember, go ahead.

PETER. And you just get the feeling that . . . something is wrong? I mean, they pretty much stop doing some of the things they used to do—

TAYLOR. Ohhhh.

PETER.—and only do certain other things now, more . . .

TAYLOR. Right.

PETER. . . . traditional sorts of things.

TAYLOR. Blow jobs, you mean.

PETER. No, I'm not talking about anything specific.

TAYLOR. No one likes to do that.

PETER. Well, that happens not to be strictly the case, but . . .

TAYLOR. No woman has ever enjoyed doing that, I'm just telling you. It's common knowledge.

PETER. You haven't had sex, but you know all about it.

TAYLOR. Hey, you asked me.

PETER. Yes, I know I did.

TAYLOR. I'm just trying to help.

PETER. Thank you. A lot.

TAYLOR. Welcome back.

PETER. Great talking to ya. *(To us.)* That night everything was miraculously restored. . . .

*(*RITA *and* PETER*'s apartment.)*

RITA. Hi.

PETER. Hi.

RITA. How was work?

PETER. Okay.

RITA. It was? . . . Making you a surprise.

PETER. What?

RITA. Guess.

PETER. I can't. What's this?

RITA. Dewar's.

PETER. What, you're back on the sauce? What's the surprise? *(She sniffs the air; he does too.)* Spaetzles? *(*RITA *smiles.)* You're kidding.

RITA. I'm sure they won't be anywhere near as good as Sophie's, but then I'm not such a cruel mama, either. You want a Molson?

PETER. Sure.

(She goes off; he picks up a book.)

RITA. *(From off.)* So, I don't know, I made some calls about taking my portfolio around today, but the whole thing terrifies me. . . . *(She returns with his Molson.)* And I started reading that, finally.

PETER. *The White Hotel*?

RITA. Cheers.

PETER. Cheers.

RITA. You didn't call the doctor, did you?

PETER. No, I will.

RITA. No, I don't want you to. . . . I know things were hard in Jamaica. Maybe it's taken me this time to get used to being married, but . . . I love you, Peter.

(They kiss. He pulls away, holding on to her.)

PETER. You read her journal, didn't you? You figured out how to fix your hair from the pictures in the albums and what to wear, what she drinks . . . Where is she? Please. I won't be angry. You can go back wherever you came from and I won't tell a soul, you don't have to tell me who you are. Just tell me where Rita is and we'll pretend this never took place. *(Pause.)* Okay. Play it your way. But I'm on to you.

(PETER walks out.)

(The Tin Market. The OLD MAN is seated as PETER enters.)

TOM. Hey, Pete, you're back. How was your honeymoon?

PETER. Good, thanks.

TOM. How's Reet?

PETER. Great.

TOM. Where is she?

PETER. Oh, not feeling too well, actually. Let me have a double vodka on the rocks. . . .

TOM. Got your postcard.

PETER. Yeah?

(PETER sees the OLD MAN.)

TOM. There you go. It's on the house. *(PETER does not respond.)* Don't mention it. *(To the OLD MAN.)* Dewar's?

(The OLD MAN nods.)

PETER. Is he a regular?

TOM. Oh, yeah, last couple of weeks or so, I guess. Why? You know him?

(PETER downs his drink as TOM takes the OLD MAN his. PETER crosses to the OLD MAN's table.)

PETER. Have we . . . Have we met? *(The OLD MAN nods.)* Mind if I sit? *(He does.)* You were at my wedding, weren't you? *(The OLD MAN nods. Beat.)* Do I know you? *(The OLD MAN nods.)* What's my stepmother's name . . . ?

OLD MAN. *(Unable to remember.)* Uhhh . . .

PETER. What's the movie I said I was going to see the night I left for Europe . . . ?

OLD MAN. *The Wild Bunch*!

PETER. *Je hebt erg witte tanden.*

OLD MAN. Not anymore.

(He shows PETER *his teeth.)*

PETER. What shape's your father's shrapnel scar?

OLD MAN. He thinks it's shaped like a saxophone, but it's not.

PETER. I knew it wasn't you! I *knew* it. Oh, I knew it! Oh my God, Rita.

(They embrace.)

OLD MAN. Baby.

PETER. Oh . . . *(Beat.* PETER *pulls back.)* . . . God . . . Maybe we shouldn't . . . Maybe . . . How much do we owe you here, Tom?

TOM. No, man, it's on the house.

PETER. Oh, okay, great. Great. *(To the* OLD MAN.) Okay? *(To* TOM.) I'm just gonna walk the old guy down to the subway.

TOM. Okay.

PETER. Good to see you, Tom.

TOM. You, too. Tell Rita I hope she feels better.

PETER. I will. I will. *(To the* OLD MAN.) Come on, let's get out of here.

(Outside. They walk.)

PETER. How are you?

OLD MAN. I've missed you.

PETER. Where have you been?

OLD MAN. Brooklyn. In Borough Park. I stayed with his family. Julius Becker. He had his wallet on him. I didn't know what else to do, where to go; I couldn't call my mother or go to the police. Who would believe me, right?

PETER. Let's head back toward the apartment. Okay?

OLD MAN. They could throw me into an institution or an old folks' home; I didn't even have our keys. I had to pretend to be him until you figured it out. And I knew you would.

PETER. I think this is like one of those dreams where you tell yourself, Just hang on, and we're all gonna wake up. We'll walk in and she'll be there and it's gonna be okay, Rita.

OLD MAN. I just keep thinking there's something I'm forgetting. . . . When he leaned in to kiss me I saw this look in his eye, you know? And something . . . I've got to slow down, I'm sorry.

PETER. That's okay.

(They slow their pace.)

OLD MAN. I get short of breath.

PETER. Better?

OLD MAN. What was I saying?

PETER. You get short of breath.

OLD MAN. Before that. Peter, I'm not senile.

PETER. I know, I know.

OLD MAN. I was holding your hand and then I wasn't. I was turned all around. You were over there and I was over there. I thought it was a mirror, that's why I reached out—to steady myself, and instead I saw his hand . . . this hand . . . on me. . . . And then everybody was staring at me and my dad was saying I'd had too much to drink and I don't know, I thought I had salmonella.

PETER. Really? That's great.

OLD MAN. I thought if I went along with it, then you'd all come running out after me and say, "It's a joke, come on, Rita, you're going on your honeymoon." And we'd laugh. . . . I just kept walking, past all the cars parked for the wedding. I was afraid to look down at my shadow to see if it was true—my reflection in the windows. . . . I found this card in his wallet. *(He shows* PETER *the card.)* "In case of emergency, please notify Mr. and Mrs. Jerome Blier." His daughter and her husband. They came and picked me up. . . . *(Beat.)* So how was our honeymoon? *(*PETER *does not laugh.)* Oh, come on!

PETER. I'm fine.

OLD MAN. Does he know you know?

PETER. *He?* Yeah. He does.

OLD MAN. She. Whatever. He does?

PETER. Yes, I think so.

(They have stopped walking. They look up at the apartment.)

OLD MAN. Is he there now?

PETER. *(Nodding.)* I think maybe you should wait outside in the hall in case he tries to bolt. All right?

OLD MAN. Peter?

PETER. What? . . . I know, come on.

(The apartment. PETER *enters. The* OLD MAN *stands outside the open door.)*

PETER. Rita?

*(*DR. BOYLE *emerges from the bedroom with a suitcase; the* OLD MAN *recedes out of sight.)*

DR. BOYLE. Peter.

PETER. What's the matter? Where's Rita?

DR. BOYLE: I'm sorry about all this, Peter.

PETER. Did something happen?

DR. BOYLE. You know I am. You know I like you.

PETER. What do you mean you're sorry?

DR. BOYLE. Rita's gone back to New Jersey with her mother, Peter.

PETER. Why?

DR. BOYLE. I think it would be best if you didn't come out to the house or call for a while until she calms down.

PETER. I went for a walk. Calms down?

DR. BOYLE. We brought both cars so I could pick up some of her things. And I'll be out of your way momentarily.

PETER. Wait a minute, Dr. Boyle, I'm . . .

DR. BOYLE. I'm sorry for whatever personal turmoil you're going through, Peter.

PETER. Turmoil? What did she tell you?

DR. BOYLE. If you want me to refer you to somebody . . . Rita says you're suffering from delusions, Peter. And I should tell you she's talking about filing for a divorce or an annulment, whichever would be—

PETER. What? Wait.

DR. BOYLE. *(Overlapping, continuous.)*— most appropriate under the circumstances. I'm awfully sorry.

PETER. What circumstances? What sort of delusions did she say I was suffering from?

DR. BOYLE. Rita . . .

PETER. Go on. I want to hear this.

DR. BOYLE. She was hysterical, Peter, when she called us.

PETER. What did she say?

DR. BOYLE. Rita says you're convinced that she's someone else.

PETER. Someone—? What, and you believe that? What does that mean? Dr. Boyle, I went for a walk. We had a— Okay, we had a fight. I went out. You and Mrs. Boyle never have fights? We had a difference of opinion.

DR. BOYLE. I practically had to carry her to the car. Are you telling me that nothing else has happened between the two of you? Nothing at all?

PETER. Seriously, Marshall, think about what you're saying. Rita . . . You're—

DR. BOYLE. *(Overlapping.)* If you'd seen that girl's face—I'm sorry, I'm just—I'm going to have to defer to my daughter's wishes.

PETER. I can't believe this. You're just going to take her word?

DR. BOYLE. It's a little difficult to believe . . . knowing Rita as I do, son, that this—

PETER. You don't know her.

DR. BOYLE. *(Overlapping, continuous.)* —is all about a squabble, a tiff as you say.

PETER. *(Overlapping.)* You don't know anything about her, that's the absurd part. You don't know your own flesh and blood.

DR. BOYLE. Well, I'm sure you're right.

(DR. BOYLE starts to leave; PETER halts him.)

PETER. Rita was a Communist, did you know that? That she was in a Communist—Socialist party? And, all right, here's something else you don't know: We didn't go out for a year. We didn't go out for anything like a year; we went out for two months—at that point, six weeks. We haven't known each other six months now! You wouldn't know if she was lying to you, because you don't know her; you only see what you want to see. And she's lying to you now, Dr. Boyle, she may know certain facts—

DR. BOYLE. Let go of my sleeve, please.

PETER. *(Under, continuous.)* —but that's from reading Rita's journals! She doesn't —Watch her! Watch the way she sits! Her eyes!

DR. BOYLE. See a doctor, boy, all—

PETER. *(Overlapping.)* Rita —Watch the way she listens to everything we say, the way she *chews* for godsake, it isn't her! Open your eyes!

DR. BOYLE. I'd like to leave now, Peter. *(Beat.)* Thank you.

(He goes out.)

PETER. This isn't happening.

(The OLD MAN *returns.)*

OLD MAN. He didn't see me.

PETER. Look . . . I like you very much. I'm not equipped for this. I'm sorry. I still like you.

OLD MAN. *Like* me?

PETER. I'm not . . . I don't feel the same way about you, I'm sorry. I'm not attracted to you.

OLD MAN. What, are you nuts? I don't think that's the issue, Peter, have a seat, come on, you're—

PETER. If I thought that you were really here, Rita . . . What's the name of the guy you went out with in high school? Wait. You told me once—Rita did—but I've forgotten. And if I can't remember, then you can't. The one who wanted to run away.

OLD MAN. John.

PETER. Oh Rita. *(Beat.)* It could have been in my unconscious. You know that. You've read Freud. Haven't you?

OLD MAN. You're not imagining me. Or we're both insane. . . .

PETER. All right, *think.* We've got to try to figure out how. . . . This just does not happen.

OLD MAN. Tell me about it.

PETER. All right . . . let me see his wallet, please. May I? *(The* OLD MAN *hands over the wallet.)* Thank you. Becker! Is he Dutch, do you know?

OLD MAN. Is it a Dutch name?

PETER. You're the one who says you live there, Rita, Jesus!

OLD MAN. Well, they don't speak Dutch. I mean, I can't exactly ask. I'm trying to keep a low profile in case they find out I'm really a girl, okay?

(PETER has rifled through the wallet's contents, found the card.)

PETER. How do you say the daughter's name?

OLD MAN. Blier. Leah and Jerry. Why?

(PETER picks up the phone, starts to dial.)

PETER. How old?

OLD MAN. Old, I don't know, you know. Forty? . . . What are you doing?

(Phone rings. LEAH enters, carrying receiver.)

LEAH. Hello?

PETER. Hello, Mrs. Jerome Blier?

LEAH. Yes?

PETER. Hi, my name is Larry . . . White from the Delancey Street Human Resource and Crisis Intervention Center. Is your father a Mr. Julius Becker?

LEAH. Is something wrong?

PETER. No, no, he's right here, Mrs. Blier.

LEAH. He is?

PETER. Yes, he's fine, he's in good hands.

LEAH. *(Overlapping.)* What happened, please? Where—?

PETER. *(Overlapping.)* Nothing's happened, Mrs. Blier. He apparently walked up to a couple of young gentlemen and, uh, asked them if they knew what city he was in and they were kind enough to call us here at the hotline.

LEAH. I see.

PETER. But your father's here now and he seems to be fine.

LEAH. Where are you, let me write it down. My husband's—

PETER. *(Overlapping.)* I'd like to ask you a few questions first if that's all right.

LEAH. My husband's gone to move the car. I'm sorry.

PETER. Where was your father born, Mrs. Blier?

LEAH. Oh, in Amsterdam. Nobody seems to know the exact year.

PETER. And is he on any medications?

LEAH. He's done this before, you know.

PETER. He has.

LEAH. Two weeks ago he disappeared. We had to go and pick him up in New Jersey.

PETER. Was there some reason? Did he know someone there?

LEAH. Not that I'm aware of, no.

PETER. Are you sure?

LEAH. No.

PETER. Is your father suffering from any mental or neurologic disorders, Mrs. Blier?

LEAH. He's been . . . He hasn't been himself since my mother died last fall.

PETER. I see.

LEAH. Then he had to move in with us. . . . I'm sorry, is he there now?

PETER. Yes.

LEAH. Could I speak to him, please?

PETER. Well, I'd like to finish filling out my form—

LEAH. *(Overlapping.)* I won't be a moment. . . . Please.

PETER. All right. Hang on. *(To the* OLD MAN.*)* Mr. Becker, it's your daughter.

(The OLD MAN *shakes his head vigorously.)*

OLD MAN. *(Loud, for* LEAH*'s benefit.)* Who?

PETER. She'd like to talk to you. Your daughter!

(The OLD MAN *takes the receiver.)*

LEAH. Daddy? . . . Daddy?

OLD MAN. Yes?

LEAH. It's Leah. Are you all right?

OLD MAN. I'm fine.

LEAH. Where are you?

OLD MAN. I'm here.

LEAH. Where did you go?

OLD MAN. I didn't go anywhere.

LEAH. Now you stay there.

OLD MAN. I'm not going anywhere.

LEAH. And you do what the man says.

OLD MAN. Oh, stop worrying about it.

LEAH. All right. I love you.

OLD MAN. Don't worry about it.

LEAH. All right, let me talk to the . . .

OLD MAN. *(Under, to* PETER.*)* Here, you talk to her.

(The OLD MAN *hands* PETER *the phone.)*

PETER. *(Into the receiver.)* Mrs. Blier?

LEAH. Yes?

PETER. Is there anything about your father's condition, is there any reason why he might—

LEAH. I can't put him in a home . . . !

PETER. No one's suggesting that you put your father in a home, Mrs. Blier, not at all.

LEAH. I'm sorry. I didn't mean to burden you with any of this.

PETER. You're not burdening anyone.

LEAH. We found out he has lung cancer three months ago. And cirrhosis he's had for years. I can't put him away. He doesn't even have a year to live. You know? . . . If you knew the man he used to be. He ran his own stationery store for forty-seven years. *(Beat.)* Let me have your address, please.

PETER. I'm going to have to call you back, Mrs. Blier.

LEAH. Well, wait, my husband's just gone to park the car.

PETER. *(Overlapping.)* No, I'm sorry, I'm—I will, I'll call you back.

(He hangs up.)

LEAH. Hello?

(LEAH disappears.)

OLD MAN. What? What's the matter? . . . What did she say?

PETER. Nothing.

OLD MAN. Am I sick?

PETER. No.

OLD MAN. This is me, Peter, remember?

(Pause.)

PETER. You have lung cancer. And cirrhosis. She said she thought you had a year to live.

(Pause.)

OLD MAN. Well . . . Am I Dutch, anyway? . . . Okay, first thing, we need a plan. What does he think happened to me? Where does he think I am? Maybe he doesn't think. Maybe it wasn't intentional. Is that possible?

PETER. It was intentional.

OLD MAN. Maybe it's some form of hypnosis. *(Pause.)* All right, here's what we know: He wouldn't have called my parents if he was going to disappear. Obviously he wants to be me. Why? . . . Well, who wouldn't? He doesn't know I've found you, so I probably shouldn't go outside in case he's spying on us and Leah will definitely go to the police anyway, so . . . My dad isn't going to leave me alone with you for a while, I know that. Mom's the one who's going to want us back together; she's crazy about you, and she isn't going to want me around the house, and she certainly won't believe what I'm telling her, she never does, so . . . I say that our best bet is try and get her to bring him here. Don't you?

PETER. He'll scream.

OLD MAN. Let him. The last time somebody broke into one of these apartments, they used a blowtorch and nobody even called—I mean, I had a fire in the kitchen once and went screaming out into the hall. Nobody even opened their doors. . . . We'll think of something. *(Pause.)* Okay? . . .

(Pause.)

PETER. *(To us.)* The next six days were the worst, the strangest of my life. I called in sick. We moved back and forth from room to room. We played cards, I cooked, we watched TV. It was as if we'd been married forever, suddenly, without the sex. At night I could feel the loneliness coming off of both of us like heat. The third day I called her parents; no answer. I tried again later—the same. The next day, same. After dark we went out to the house; not a sign. We used the spare key to get in; a few suitcases missing, according to Rita, that was all. The next night, still nothing. I called Rita's Aunt Dorothy in Cincinnati. She had no idea where they were and wanted to know why I didn't know. I told her Rita and I had split up. She was sorry to hear it. Rita and I, meanwhile, kept up the pleasantries, the old married couple we'd become.

(The apartment. PETER *stares at the TV.)*

OLD MAN. Something to eat? . . . Maybe I should teach myself to cook now that I've got the time. What do you think?

PETER. Great.

OLD MAN. Who's winning? *(PETER shrugs.)* Who's playing? *(PETER shrugs again.)* Well . . .

PETER. Rita?

OLD MAN. What?

PETER. What if they never come back? . . . What if they're gone forever?

OLD MAN. Well . . .

PETER. I miss your face.

OLD MAN. Don't think about it.

PETER. How soft it was.

(Pause.)

OLD MAN. I miss it, too.

PETER. Your hair was so great.

OLD MAN. Oh, come on.

PETER. And your little white feet.

OLD MAN. What, you don't like these? *(Pause.)* You know . . . if you think how we're born and we go through all the struggle of growing up and learning the multiplication tables and the name for everything, the rules, how not to get run over, braid your hair, pig-Latin. Figuring out how to sneak out of the house late at night. Just all the ins and outs, the *effort*, and learning to accept all the flaws in everybody and everything. And then getting a job, probably something you don't even like doing for not enough money, like bartending, and that's if you're lucky. That's if you're not born in Calcutta or Ecuador or the U.S. without money. Then there's your marriage and raising your own kids if . . . you know. And they're going through the same struggle all over again, only worse, because somebody's trying to sell them crack in the first grade by now. And all this time you're paying taxes and your hair starts to fall out and you're wearing six pairs of glasses which you can never find and you can't recognize yourself in the mirror and your parents die and your friends, again, if you're lucky, and it's not you first. And if you live long enough, you finally get to watch everybody die: all your loved ones, your wife, your husband and your kids, maybe, and you're totally alone. And as a final reward for all this . . . you disappear. *(Pause.)* No one knows where. *(Pause.)* So we might as well have a good time while we're here, don't you think?

PETER. I don't want you to die, Rita.

OLD MAN. I don't want me to die, either. And I'm going to. So are you. Hopefully later and not sooner. But we got to have this. I mean, what a trip! Meeting you and being in love. Falling. It was bitchin' for a while. And okay, so this isn't such a turn-on, I admit. But . . .

PETER. I adore you.

OLD MAN. What? My hearing. No, I'm serious.

PETER. I said *I adore you!*

OLD MAN. That's what I thought.

PETER. For better or for worse.

OLD MAN. Huh?

PETER. I said: You would have hated Jamaica. Trust me.

(The OLD MAN *rises, crosses to* PETER. PETER *stands. They face one another for a moment. The* OLD MAN *hands* PETER *the phone.)*

OLD MAN. Try again.

*(*PETER *dials. Phone rings.* MRS. BOYLE *enters with receiver.)*

MRS. BOYLE. Hello?

PETER. Oh, Marion, it's Peter.

MRS. BOYLE. I thought it might be you.

PETER. Where've you been? I've been worried. How's Rita?

MRS. BOYLE. They've just run down to the store; I may have to get off. She's terrible, Peter. We took her to London. She was so shook up, Marshall thought she needed a rest. I don't know, I was tempted to call you from over there, but I didn't, I'm sorry.

PETER. Is she okay?

MRS. BOYLE. What happened between the two of you, Peter? If you don't want to tell me you don't have to.

PETER. No, I do, I just am not sure I know. I said—I guess I must have said something about her not being the same person. And then I lost my temper with Dr. Boyle; I said some things I didn't mean. I was just so surprised to see him here. You know? Did he tell you?

MRS. BOYLE. No, Peter.

PETER. But I would do anything to get Rita back. *(Looking at the* OLD MAN.*)* I love her with all my heart and soul. . . .

MRS. BOYLE. Well, she says that you're unstable and she's sorry she ever met you. I don't know, you don't seem so unstable to me.

PETER. No.

MRS. BOYLE. Maybe I'm being naive.

PETER. No, you're not.

MRS. BOYLE. That's what all unstable people say, Peter . . . I'm teasing you.

PETER. If I could just see her . . .

MRS. BOYLE. You can't come here, Peter. If either of them knew I was talking to you, they'd have me shot at sunrise.

PETER. How's she been? Is she okay?

MRS. BOYLE. Oh, I don't know what her problem is.

PETER. If she wants me to see a psychiatrist . . .

MRS. BOYLE. Well . . .

(The OLD MAN *scribbles something on a pad and hands it to* PETER, *who reads as he talks.)*

PETER. Marion, what if . . . it's just a thought, but what if you told her I was going away on business for a couple of weeks—

MRS. BOYLE. Are you?

PETER. No, wait.

MRS. BOYLE. Oh.

PETER. And you said she could stop by to pick up the rest of her things from storage in the basement, you know, all her old letters and journals from her childhood and all that stuff she's left here, and then when you came by with her I'd be here. And we could talk.

MRS. BOYLE. Oh, I don't know, Peter.

PETER. I have to see her. Even if she won't even speak to me. . . . Please.

(Pause.)

MRS. BOYLE. When would you want us?

PETER. Anytime.

MRS. BOYLE. I'm not promising anything.

PETER. I understand. . . .

MRS. BOYLE. Monday?

PETER. Monday's great.

MRS. BOYLE. All right, I'll try. That's all I can do.

PETER. I understand. Thank you.

MRS. BOYLE. What time?

PETER. Anytime.

MRS. BOYLE. Noon, say?

PETER. Noon's great. Fine.

MRS. BOYLE. High noon.

PETER. High noon.

MRS. BOYLE. All right.

PETER. Thank you very much. . . .

MRS. BOYLE. Peter?

PETER. Yes?

MRS. BOYLE. What you said before about Rita not being the same person?

PETER. Uh-huh . . . ?

MRS. BOYLE. They never are, Peter. They're never Rita. They're never Dr. Marshall Boyle, not the way that you think they should be. They're always someone else. They're always changing.

PETER. Uh-huh.

MRS. BOYLE. That's life. That's marriage. They're always growing and shifting and so are you.

PETER. Right.

MRS. BOYLE. She may not be the picture of the woman you thought she was, but that's an image, Peter. That's just a picture. Words.

PETER. I know.

MRS. BOYLE. I'm sure you're not always the prize either.

PETER. No.

MRS. BOYLE. Nobody is. But I know she loves you and misses you.

PETER. I miss her too.

MRS. BOYLE. All right. We'll see you Monday then.

PETER. Thank you, Mom.

MRS. BOYLE. All right.

PETER. Bye.

MRS. BOYLE. Bye now.

(They both hang up. MRS. BOYLE *disappears.)*

PETER. She'll try.

(Long pause. PETER slowly kneels and kisses the OLD MAN tenderly on the mouth.)

(The apartment. Darkness. RITA and MRS. BOYLE enter, switching on the lights.)

MRS. BOYLE. I don't want you to be angry with me.

RITA. I'm not. Relax.

MRS. BOYLE. *(Looking around.)* He keeps it clean.

(PETER enters. RITA does not see him at first.)

RITA. Yeah. He likes things in their proper— *(She sees PETER.)* —places.

MRS. BOYLE. Now I want you to talk, Rita, I want you both to talk, that's all. Peter has something he wants to tell you. If after you've heard him out you don't want to stay, then I'll be downstairs in the car. You can do that much, since you took the trouble to marry him. You might actually thank me someday.

PETER. Mom, are you sure I can't get you something to drink?

MRS. BOYLE. No, thank you, Peter. *(To RITA.)* This was my idea, by the way.

(MRS. BOYLE goes out. Pause.)

PETER. How've you been?

RITA. I'm sorry.

PETER. Why? You're here now.

RITA. I wanted to come, I just . . .

PETER. You did? Really? Well . . . It's been real lonely here without you, Rita. *(PETER has maneuvered into a position between RITA and the exit. The OLD MAN appears behind RITA; he carries a kitchen knife and a length of rope. She does not see him immediately.)* You went to London, your mom says. *(RITA turns, sees the OLD MAN as PETER grabs RITA from behind.)* Okay. Tie his feet. *(RITA and the OLD MAN are holding each other's gaze, unable to move.)* Rita! Come on!

RITA. You don't have to do this.

PETER. Tie him!

(PETER takes the rope as RITA and the OLD MAN continue to stare at one another.)

RITA. This is not necessary, kids.

PETER. Give me the knife. *(PETER still holds on to*

RITA *from behind.)* Give it to me! *(*PETER *takes the knife in one hand, holds* RITA*'s arm behind her back with the other.)* Now kiss him. *(The* OLD MAN *kisses* RITA *on the mouth. They separate.* PETER *releases* RITA *and wields the knife, particularly wary of the* OLD MAN.*)* Rita?

OLD MAN. No. It didn't work.

PETER. *(To* RITA.*)* Is it you?

*(*RITA *is shaking her head.)*

OLD MAN. No!

PETER. Rita?

RITA. I don't know how it happened. I don't know what I did.

PETER. *(To* RITA.*)* I'll kill you, I swear to God.

OLD MAN. Peter.

PETER. *(Threatening her with the knife.)* How did you do this? How the hell did you do this?

OLD MAN. Put the knife down, please.

PETER. *(To the* OLD MAN.*)* I'll take care of this, Rita! It's a trick, don't you know that much?

OLD MAN. *(Overlapping.)* He doesn't know. Give it to me. *(The* OLD MAN *is holding out his hand.)* Please. Peter.

*(*PETER *is looking from one to the other, paralyzed with doubt.)*

PETER. Are you here? Rita?

OLD MAN. I'm right here.

PETER. Talk to me if you're here.

OLD MAN. Give me the knife.

PETER. I can't. I'm sorry.

OLD MAN. Then just put it down. *(Slowly* PETER *lowers the knife.)* Thank you.

(Beat.)

RITA. *(To the* OLD MAN.*)* Where'd you go?

PETER. Watch him.

RITA. I couldn't imagine what happened to you.

OLD MAN. Twelve twenty-two Ocean Avenue.

RITA. How is Leah?

OLD MAN. I think she misses you. . . . She keeps putting on professional wrestling on the TV and I just sorta sit there, trying to look interested.

RITA. Interested? It's a joke. We laugh at it together.

OLD MAN. She keeps making soup and offering me another cup and another cup.

RITA. Oh, it's full of fat, she doesn't know how else to make it. . . . Your mother . . . she isn't serious about the peanut butter and mayonnaise?

OLD MAN. Oh, she made you one? A sandwich?

PETER. Stop this.

OLD MAN. I haven't had one of those since grade school, I forgot all about— Did you try it?

PETER. Rita!

OLD MAN. Oh, they're really good. . . .

(Beat.)

RITA. I wanted it, that's all. That's all I know. I'm not hiding anything from you; I don't know any more than that. I started out to take a walk. To just try and get as far away from me as I possibly could, I didn't care. I took the first bus I saw at Port Authority: "Englewood Cliffs." It sounded romantic enough.

OLD MAN. Englewood?

RITA. Yeah. I got off the first street corner; dogs came up to play. And what's this? A *wedding*. Young people starting a life. I had some champagne, nobody bothered me. What did it matter what I did? I wished to God I were that young bridegroom starting out. Or the bride, for that matter. Look at the shine in those eyes.

OLD MAN. You're kidding. I was freaked from the moment I woke up.

RITA. Yeah?

OLD MAN. I was terrified.

RITA. No, I thought to myself, If I could shine like the light of that girl over there, I'd never take another drink, I'd let my liver hang on another decade, stay out of the sun, eat right. This time I would floss.

OLD MAN. I remember now. Oh God. Oh God. It was your eyes I saw flashing back. And I thought, Look at that guy. If I could get inside that somehow.

RITA. Yes.

OLD MAN. If I could just know what it's like for one second of one day to have lived all that time, and be so alive, so sure of something, anything. Oh, please God, let me know what it is to have so little to lose.

RITA. If I could just get inside. I'll kiss the bride.

OLD MAN. So much past.

RITA. I'll be the bride.

OLD MAN/ RITA. So much life inside.

OLD MAN. My whole life would be behind me.

RITA. My whole life again from the other side of the mirror. All ahead of me again.

OLD MAN. With nothing to lose.

OLD MAN/ RITA. *(Simultaneously.) At last.*

RITA. All you've got to do is—

OLD MAN/ RITA. *(Simultaneously.)*—want it. *Bad enough.*

(Without touching, the OLD MAN *and* RITA *switch souls; a wind passes through the room—a low rumble— as they say:)*

RITA. The soft arms.

OLD MAN. The strong arms.

RITA. The white teeth—

OLD MAN. The back.

RITA. The sweet smell on her breath.

OLD MAN. That smell.

RITA. Not like something rotting, coming up from your insides, but soft—

OLD MAN. Like a father—

RITA. Like a baby. And white.

OLD MAN. A man.

RITA. Clean.

OLD MAN. An old man.

(RITA is now standing; the OLD MAN *is now seated.)*

RITA. My God.

OLD MAN. Like an old suit . . .

PETER. Rita?

OLD MAN. Don't you see? My wife and daughter had a bond. I loved them both so much I wanted to eat them alive.

RITA. I saw their photographs. Your mom. You just wanted them back, the way they were.

OLD MAN. And women cry, you think. It feels good.

RITA. Yes, it does.

OLD MAN. Women make a life inside their body and that life comes out and holds on to them—

RITA. Yes.

OLD MAN. Clings to them, calls them up from school and says, "I'm sick, Ma, come pick me up." That baby is theirs for life. Where are they now? My wife. My mother.

RITA. They're right here.

OLD MAN. To be able to look back from their side of the bed with their eyes. At last. *(To* PETER.*)* And you, my boy. I tried to be patient, I tried to be interested. I called every hotel in Kingston, "What the hell is a Long Island Ice Tea?" You're a sweet kid, no hard feelings, but you're not my type. . . .

PETER. Please.

OLD MAN. I don't know. . . . The idea of living forever . . . It's not so good. *(Beat.)* And those parents of yours you can keep.

RITA. Thank you.

(The OLD MAN *walks to the door, turns back.)*

OLD MAN. Do yourselves a favor: Floss.

(He goes out.)

PETER. Rita? . . . Oh, Rita . . . Oh my beautiful . . .

RITA. My body. My body.

(He unties her feet.)

PETER. There they are. Look at those. Yes! Your hair.

RITA. I'm here. I'm not afraid.

PETER. I know.

RITA. I'm not afraid.

PETER. Oh, I love you. . . . Give me a smile. *(She does.)* Je hebt erg witte tanden. Je hebt erg witte tanden.

RITA. Ohhhhhh, I don't remember what I'm supposed to say, Peter, I know I memorized it.

PETER. *Om je better mee op to eten.*

RITA. You promised you'd tell me. What does it mean?

PETER. The better to eat you with. Oh, Rita. Never to be squandered . . . the miracle of another human being.

RITA. You're the miracle.

PETER. No, you are.

RITA. You.

PETER. You.

(They clasp one another. Music plays. PETER *lifts* RITA

and carries her, finally, across the threshold as the Vo-
calist sings: "How my lovesong gently cries/ For the ten-
derness within your eyes./ My Love is a prelude that never
dies:/My prelude to a kiss." Lights fade.)

Appendix: Contemporary Obie-Winning Plays

Following is a list of Obie-winning plays of the 1980s and into the 1990s. In keeping with our conviction that art is not competitive, the Obie committee doesn't make nominations from which a single "winner" is selected. And in keeping with our belief that creativity can't be channeled, we don't confine our awards to rigidly defined categories. We have chosen, rather, to honor artistic achievement whenever and wherever it emerges, which means that in some years we award several playwriting Obies, in some years none, and that Obie recipients range from more or less traditional playwrights to performance artists to monologists to ensemble-created scripts. The only guideline given the Obie committee, in short, is to search for the best work done Off-Broadway.

1979–1980
Lee Breuer .... *A Prelude to Death in Venice*
Christopher Durang .... *Sister Mary Ignatius Explains It All for You*
Romulus Linney .... *Tennessee*
Roland Muldoon .... *Full Confessions of a Socialist*
Jeff Weiss .... *That's How the Rent Gets Paid*

1980–1981
Charles Fuller .... *Zooman and the Sign*
Amlin Gray .... *How I Got That Story*
David Henry Hwang .... *FOB*
Len Jenkin .... *Limbo Tales*
Emily Mann .... *Still Life*

1981–1982
Robert Auletta ....*Stops; Virgins*
Caryl Churchill ....*Cloud 9*
Martha Clarke............. *Metamorphosis in Miniature*
Harvey Fierstein ....*Torch Song Trilogy*
Tadeusz Kantor ....*Wielopole, Wielopole*
Squat Theater .... *Mr. Dead and Mrs. Free*

1982–1983
Caryl Churchill .... *Top Girls*
Tina Howe .... *Museum; The Art of Dining;*
   Painting Churches
David Mamet..*Edmond*

1983–1984
Samuel Beckett ....*Ohio Impromptu; What Where;*
   Catastrophe; Rockabye
Lee Breuer and Bob Telson .... *Gospel at Colonus*
Maria Irene Fornes.......... *The Danube; Sarita; Mud*
Vaclav Havel .... *A Private View*
Len Jenkin ....*Five of Us*
Franz Xaver Kroetz ....*Through the Leaves;*
   Mensch Meier
Sam Shepard .... *Fool for Love*
Ted Tally .... *Terra Nova*

1984–1985
Christopher Durang .. *The Marriage of Bette and Boo*
Rosalyn Drexler......................*Transients Welcome*
Maria Irene Fornes................. *The Conduct of Life*
William Hoffman .... *As Is*

1985–1986
Eric Bogosian ....*Drinking in America*
Martha Clarke.......................... *Vienna: Lusthaus*
John Jesurun.....................................*Deep Sleep*
Tadeusz Kantor .... *Let the Artist Die*
Lee Nagrin ....*Bird/Bear*
Wallace Shawn .... *Aunt Dan and Lemon*

Permissions

ALL THE WORLD'S A STAGE

☐ **FOUR PLAYS BY TENNESSEE WILLIAMS: SUMMER AND SMOKE, ORPHEUS DESCENDING, SUDDENLY LAST SUMMER and PERIOD OF ADJUSTMENT.** Love, hate, comedy, tragedy, joy, sorrow, passion, violence—all come alive in these four magnificent plays.   (525124—$5.95)

☐ **THREE BY TENNESSEE WILLIAMS: SWEET BIRD OF YOUTH, THE ROSE TATTOO and THE NIGHT OF THE IGUANA**, three of the Pulitzer prize-winning author's most brilliant plays.   (521498—$5.95)

☐ **CHEKHOV: THE MAJOR PLAYS by Anton Chekhov.** New translation by Ann Dunnigan. Foreword by Robert Brustein.   (522702—$3.95)

☐ **IBSEN: FOUR MAJOR PLAYS, Volume I, by Henrik Ibsen.** *The Master Builder, A Doll's House, Hedda Gabler,* and *The Wild Duck.* New translation with Foreword by Rolf Fjelde.   (524063—$3.95)

☐ **ISBEN: FOUR MAJOR PLAYS, Volume II, by Henrik Ibsen.** *Ghosts, An Enemy of the People, The Lady from the Sea,* and *John Gabriel·Borkman.* New·translation by Rolf Fjelde.   (525159—$3.50)

Prices slightly higher in Canada.

Buy them at your local bookstore or use this convenient coupon for ordering.

PENGUIN USA
P.O. Box 999 – Dept. #17109
Bergenfield, New Jersey 07621

Please send me the books I have checked above.
I am enclosing $_____ (please add $2.00 to cover postage and handling).
Send check or money order (no cash or C.O.D.'s) or charge by Mastercard or VISA (with a $15.00 minimum). Prices and numbers are subject to change without notice.

Card #_____ Exp. Date _____
Signature_____
Name_____
Address_____
City _____ State _____ Zip Code _____

For faster service when ordering by credit card call **1-800-253-6476**

Allow a minimum of 4-6 weeks for delivery. This offer is subject to change without notice.